W9-DGU-036

BOARDING PARTY!

"Stand by to snug and board!" Dalton called.

Grapples flew and lines were hauled. Dalton caught a shroudstay, drew his sword, and swung himself upward. Then he was over the rail facing a mass of cutlass-wielding pirates.

There were others around him, and for minutes that seemed endless the little group held the rail, a tight crescent of defense. It was cut and slash, parry and thrust. But it was soon apparent that while the pirates were poor sailors, they were fierce fighters. There seemed to be no stopping them as they pressed down upon the little ring of boarders as a howling mob, hampered only by the fallen men underfoot and the slicks of spilled blood on the deck. . . .

Other Zebra and Pinnacle books by Dan Parkinson

A Man Called Wolf
Summer Land
The Fox and the Faith
Gunpowder Wind (with David Hicks)
The Westering
The Way to Wyoming
Shadow of the Hawk
Jubilation Gap
Thunderland
The Sundown Breed
Brother Wolf
Calamity Trail
Blood Arrow
Gunpowder Glory
The Slanted Colt

Dan Parkinson
THE FOX
AND THE
Fury

PINNACLE BOOKS
WINDSOR PUBLISHING CORP.

PINNACLE BOOKS

are published by

Windsor Publishing Corp.
475 Park Avenue South
New York, NY 10016

Copyright © 1989 by Dan Parkinson

All rights reserved. No part of this book may be reproduced
in any form or by any means without the prior written
consent of the Publisher, excepting brief quotes used in
reviews.

First printing: December, 1989

Printed in the United States of America

To

Glenn Heath,
for waterline × 1.4 and other wisdoms

Heidi Hannusch,
for the touch of her native tongue

Spec. 2C Ronald Hull, USCG

Kipp Soldwedel and his magic brush

Jack Coggins

Tre Tryckare

and others,

many thanks.

I

For two years and more the hostilities had mounted—grievances by the colonies, conflicts of policy, and disparity of interest that intensified with each season until no questions remained save one: Could the upstart colonies survive a war for independence, a war which must be won at sea against the greatest navy in the world?

Only a dozen years had passed since Great Britain had consolidated her worldwide empire in the Treaty of Paris. Now the British flag flew over Gibraltar, Minorca, Bengal and the Circars Coast, Madras and the Bahamas, and over the Floridas to the south and all the great waterways to the north of the rambunctious thirteen colonies. France had been evicted from North America, and Spain had been driven back to the Mississippi. Throughout the Atlantic hemisphere the Union Jack held sway. Could the Continental Congress of the Colonies play David to such a Goliath?

Where men gathered to discuss such matters, few reckoned that they could. Yet some, upon reflection, did wonder. Pitt was no longer in power, and England's government had fallen into the hands of a king whose mind was narrow, whose understanding of anything beyond his own comforts was limited, and whose single ambition was to rule. In the House of Commons there were grave doubts whether the Royal Navy was equal to the task of policing the trade restraints of 1775 while still protecting Great Britain itself and all its new holdings. Even the ministries of Lord North had concern over the practicality of it all, though the king's mandate was clear. To rule was to rule by force, and thus did George III see it.

Civil war in the colonies was in the wind in those early months of 1775. Then, abruptly, it was no longer speculation. At Machias in Maine, colonists armed with pitchforks and axes, aboard the tiny trading sloop *Unity*, boarded and took the armed schooner *Margaretta*, and their war cries were echoed at Lexington and Concord.

Response was immediate. Two hundred and seventy ships had George the King, and more than half were ships of the line and well-gunned frigates. Dominate the seas and the colonies would wither.

Still, where men gathered to discuss such matters, in Massachusetts and Connecticut, in Virginia and the Carolinas, in New Hampshire and Rhode Island and Providence Plantation, there were those among them who knew that fully a third of the king's vessels were American-built, and while the Congress in Philadelphia debated the "building of a squadron of frigates," and the fitting out of merchantmen with weaponry, there were those who saw opportunity beyond the simple winning of independent trade.

Her hull was assembled in yards below Wilmington, and those who designed her had the finest of craftsmen at hire and the resources of a continent at their doorstep. No man could surely see the future, and so it was agreed that she should be so constructed that she could serve either as merchant vessel or as warrior. They envisioned speed and strength, and drew rigging plans with an eye to all possible sail and a hull that could support it. Deep and trim they shaped her sturdy keel, with space for the ballast that would be required to hold press of sail aloft in strong winds. Sixteen gunports they ribbed in below her channel wales, with framing fore and aft that would support press of cargo if more guns were not needed.

Yet even as the sleek hull was fined and tarred for launch down sliding ways, events were shaping her. The carrying of cargoes presented a less and less inviting picture to those whose investment lay in the building of her. Instead, they spoke of a more precarious, but immensely more profitable, use for such a vessel. Though the ports of the colonies swarmed with shipping, and able mariners were to be found in any grog shop or hostel, there was no real navy. Benedict Arnold's motley little flotilla on Lake Champlain had, it was true, wrecked the plan of General Sir Guy Carleton to invade from the lakes, but the battle at Valcour the past October had cost eleven of the sixteen vessels in Arnold's command. A pitiful few ships were being built as rapidly as possible, for deployment on orders of the Continental Congress. But it was clear that if ships were to stand against the British fleet, they would have to be private ships. The investors listened with interest to tales of Dale's privateers to the south, and of Haraden with his fourteen-gun *Tyrannicide*. In just months, it was said, Haraden had taken five English ships, including a ship of the line and the fast brig *St. John*. Six months out of the Salem ways, and already the builders of *Tyrannicide* were wealthy men, Haraden himself was wealthy . . . even a fourteen-year-old cabin boy, they said, had shared to the extent of seven hundred dollars, a ton of sugar, and twenty pounds each of ginger and allspice.

They looked again at the riding hull of their

creation and knew what she would be: a privateer.

But the ways below Wilmington were a poor location for the fitting out of a predator. So the hull was taken, by stealth and darkness, down the coast and into Chesapeake, where they found a secret place to finish her. And the questions of equipage were resolved. Her ballast would be shot lockers, her midships would hold an armory, and her two masts would be rigged to carry the press of as much canvas as could be bent onto her spars.

And as they amassed their yard crews there, in the wilderness, armies of men with axes, adzes, saws, chisels, hammers, augers, and grindstones—a full company of shipwrights, sailmakers, riggers and careeners—the talk was of how she should be called. By jackmast rigging she was a snow, and by gunspace an eighteen—seventy-two feet of gundeck and twenty-four feet abeam.

In legs and teeth she would be a cruiser and in mission a privateer. They scratched their heads and toyed with words that each might feel would properly belong on her escutcheons, and it was a transient sailmaker with eyeglasses on his nose who brought them to agreement. "Royals and studding-sails," he said, shaking his head in wonder. "Spinnaker and a ringtail for the driver. If she doesn't capsize herself on her first tack, she'll be a very fury on the sea."

And so it was decided, and her escutcheons were shaped.

Her name was *Fury*.

II

"One can see now what scuttled her," Patrick Dalton nodded as he paced the precarious platform slung from the tipped hull of the ship lying half on its side in Caradine Cut. "She wasn't rammed so much as she was sideswiped. Those chain stays there, see how they're bent? They took the brunt of the collision, and the strain on them warped the lowermain wale upward."

As Dalton's fingers traced the edges of parted timbers, Claude Mallory, following behind him, leaned closer to peer through the foot-wide crack into dark bilges within.

"Don't get your nose too close," Dalton warned him. "These timbers are not set in their warp. If those chain plates should part, they'd snap together like turtles' teeth."

On the raft below Billy Caster raised his head from the foolscap pad where he was writing notes, numbers, and cyphers. Then he went back to his work. The captain must be speaking in idiom, he decided. Or else he referred to Irish turtles. The only turtles young Mister Caster had seen were American turtles, and none of them had possessed teeth.

"That would be a likely way to repair her, then," Claude Mallory said. "A few stout swats on a chisel

11

and those plates could be parted."

"Aye," Dalton nodded. "She is salvageable, it seems."

"Aye," Mallory's sun-dark face parted in a grin. "The one as abandoned her must have been a fool. Or a fugitive, mayhap."

"More likely the latter." Patrick Dalton eased himself down to sit on the edge of the scaffold, his muddy boots swinging ten feet above Billy Caster's head. A solid week of back-breaking toil—first turning the derelict on high tide and then careening her over on a mud bank in a wilderness stream, with a dozen good oak trees on the near bank serving as anchors for the haul—had left him numb with fatigue. The seven of them had done the work of seventy, it seemed, just to reach this stage.

"Cap'n Dalton?" Billy Caster's adolescent voice came from below. "Do you suppose whoever left her here might have run aground on purpose, so he could come back and claim her?"

"We're not likely to know that, Mister Caster, unless the former owners return. But my guess is they didn't know how much damage they had, and took her to be lost."

"She hasn't been here long, Cap'n." Ignoring Dalton's warning, Claude Mallory had his entire head stuck through the gaping jaws of the ship's sprung planking. "These strakes are fresh as day inside. And I can see some line and tackle down there."

"If one of those stays should snap," Dalton pointed out, "your head will get a closer look."

"Oh. Aye, Captain." He withdrew from the gash and sat beside his captain on the scaffold. Late-afternoon sun sifted through the autumn foliage on the far bank of Carradine Cut, speckling the great dark hull from which they hung. The vessel paced off at more than ninety feet hull length, a ketch-rigged cargo cruiser with the plain lines and comfortable width of a scow. Its great main mast, more than two feet in diameter at the base, was set far back, just forward of center, leaving the entire foredeck clear for the loading of cargo.

She carried no name. Her escutcheons had been removed, and as much belowdeck as was not underwater had been carried away. Even her sails had been removed.

Cadman Wise had found her, more than a week before, by the purest chance. Avoiding a Hessian patrol on the Daltry Road, he had taken to the woods. Then, as befit an experienced able seaman late of His Majesty's White Fleet, he had become hopelessly lost in the forest. Wandering aimlessly, he had come upon a slough which, as he followed it, broadened to a sizable stream. Then, here in the wilderness east of Chesapeake Bay, he had found this ship, stripped and abandoned.

A day had passed and another begun before the disoriented tar found his way back to the Daltry Road and came finally to the little cove where Patrick Dalton's fugitive crew awaited capture, the war's end, or good fortune, whichever came first.

They were a sour and disheveled lot, these survivors of the fighting schooner *Faith*. Of the nine of them, only young Billy Caster did not have high charges against him.

In a span of months Patrick Dalton had gone from proud first officer of the armed brig *Herret*, and acclaimed one of the finest young officers in the King's Navy, to a harried fugitive with warrants out against him charging treason, desertion, sabotage, mayhem, and probably piracy. The charge of treason had come of his acquaintance with The Fitzgerald after that doughty old warrior had been identified as a leader of the current rebellion in Ireland. The remaining charges Dalton had accumulated in his

13

efforts to escape the consequences of the first. The taking of the schooner *Faith* in New York Harbor might have been forgiven by the Admiralty since the vessel was not committed for Crown registry. But the sinking of approximately seven times its own weight in Royal Navy shipping by the fugitive schooner with Dalton at the helm could hardly be overlooked, not to mention the burning and sinking of a forty-four-gun first-rate frigate in open battle on the high seas.

No, those escapades would haunt Patrick Dalton as long as the Union Jack flew over American waters . . . or any waters where he happened to be. Audacity was all well and good, but His Majesty's fleet officers did not take kindly to humiliation.

The rest who had been aboard *Faith* were fugitives, too.

Six of them were escapees from the stockade at Long Island Yards. Charley Duncan had been serving time for thievery, Claude Mallory for mayhem upon the person of a paymaster, Victory Locke and Purdy Fisk for dismantling a tavern, Ishmael Bean for dismantling the same tavern's proprietor, and Cadman Wise for relieving himself upon the boots of a senior officer.

Michael Romart, an American colonial, was wanted by the king's courts for sabotage and by the colonial courts in Delaware for fornication.

Billy Caster was with them by choice. After serving as Patrick Dalton's clerk aboard *Herret* and as crew aboard the *Faith* in her escape from the White Fleet, the homeless youngster had come to worship Dalton. Billy's home was wherever his captain was.

Tales would be told one day of the flight of the schooner *Faith*, and even stranger tales of her final duel at sea. But few beside these nine would know the truth of it. All of them had been aboard her when she fled, and all but Billy had been there when she turned

14

and fought. And not one among them had not grown to love her.

Patrick Dalton shrugged his tired shoulders now and shaded his eyes to look downstream to the bend where Carradine Cut widened and disappeared toward the bay. "They should be back soon," he said. "It shouldn't take so long to look at a bay and see what traffic is upon it."

"Have you ever been on the Chesapeake, sir?" Mallory rubbed at the growth of brown stubble on his chin. "Mister Romart says there is a sight of it. Bigger than Long Island Sound by half, and a very maze of channels, cuts, and hidey-holes. Mister Romart, he does know these parts, sir."

"I am sure he does," Dalton agreed. "And he and Mister Duncan can take care of themselves. But they have our only boat, and we'll need it soon if we're to find tools and supplies."

"I've been making a list of what we shall need, sir," Billy Caster said from below. "It comes to quite a lot of material, just to get a ship this size afloat. Then there'll be a suit of sails, and ship's stores and provisions, and . . ."

From the woods behind them, muffled with distance, came the sound of gunfire, at least three distinct shots.

"Rifles," Billy judged. "Those were rifles, sir. Muskets sound thumpier."

"Maybe the jolly lads have found us some dinner," Mallory said wistfully. "A brace of grouse would do for me."

"One doesn't volley grouse with long rifles." Billy folded his papers and pushed the raft away from the ship's exposed belly. "A shot per bird is sufficient. Most likely they have become lost in the forest. Shall I go and bring them in, sir?"

"I expect you had better, Mister Caster." Dalton picked himself up and stretched tired shoulders in

15

the fading sunlight. "We'll use the second raft."

With a shake of his head the boy poled his raft to the stern of the careened ship and grounded it ashore. He hurried through the makeshift campsite there and vanished into the woods.

Dalton and Mallory clambered up the ship's hull and let themselves down the pitched deck with knotted lines. The starboard gunwales were submerged, and a second small raft was lashed to the mainmast's after pinrail.

"If it were the lads," Mallory said, "I hope their volleying hasn't brought someone to look in on us."

"When has there been a day that we haven't heard gunfire somewhere on this bay?" Dalton reassured him.

"Aye, but usually it's cannon, sir."

"That's because there is a war going on, Mister Mallory, and a great deal of it seems to have been conducted nearby in recent weeks. How is our supply of tea?"

"Ample, sir. We've no shortage of tea, thanks to Mister Duncan finding that bale of it last week." Mallory lifted the lid from a water cask and peered into it. "Also, we still have water. Would you like for me to brew some tea, Cap'n?"

In their camp Dalton stirred the fire and added wood while Mallory set about assembling tea. With the sun gone, evening chill had begun to set in, and he pulled on his threadbare blue coat and went to sit in the one chair the site offered. It was an odd chair, built of split rooftree timbers and shingles, but he had retrieved it from the wreck of *Faith* when there was little else to retrieve. It had memories for him, that chair. It reminded him of Constance Ramsey.

There had been twenty-three of them then, a motley, mismatched mixture of felons, fugitives, and free spirits thrown together aboard a small, sleek schooner with one purpose in common . . . to escape.

Some of them had been sailors of the king, some of them American rebels. And one had been a pixie with auburn hair and a fierce temper who had tormented him ruthlessly . . . then comforted him when he needed it most.

She had been a Faith, as much one of them as any man aboard and better than some, and at the end of it, when the *Prizemaster*'s hulking frigate lay aflame on the water behind him, waiting for its magazines to explode, he had turned his mind to her and had known hope.

Such a journey they had known, and along the way the brothers Grimm, a pair of habitual rapists and the finest seamen a man could want to command, had built a chair of rooftree stuff in honor of the lady.

Constance was gone, and where Dalton was going, he doubted he would ever see her again. When the battles on the Delaware had run their course, John Ramsey would bring his household back to Wilmington and there she would reside. But Patrick Dalton could not return to Wilmington. Nowhere in this bloody land was there room for an Irish fugitive from the King's justice, so he must try for other lands where the Union Jack did not fly. It was in his mind, as it had been from the first, to somehow find a vessel to take him to New Spain. From there, well—no one knew the future.

As Mallory worked over the fire, Dalton hunched himself down in Constance Ramsey's chair and stretched long legs before him. His mood was becoming bleaker by the minute. Yet as he looked again at the great shadow of the careened vessel lying at the bank of Carradine Cut, something brightened within him. He had wanted a vessel. This, though an abandoned wreck at the moment, might yet be a vessel if a man put his mind to it. She might float proud and sturdy upon the waters, and take the wind in tall sails, and raise her nose to the open sea while

17

whiskers of spray grew at her bow.

Her song would never be *Faith*'s song, but even this poor old tub might sing for the proper hand at her tiller. How had she come here, abandoned in a wilderness, alone and deserted on a mud bank? Where had they gone, those who left her? What had hit her hard enough to separate the strakes all along her port midships?

"Mystery," he said aloud.

Mallory, bringing tea from the fire, arched a brow. "Sir?"

"I said '*Mystery*,' Mister Mallory. Yon derelict was left without a name, so I have named her. Her name is *Mystery*."

"Ah." The sailor set his burden on an upended keg and pulled off his hat. "*Mystery*. A likely name, Cap'n. A right likely name indeed."

Carrying his tea, Dalton walked across the darkening clearing to where the taut careening hawser, a tarred rope four inches thick, was secured by splice and clamp to a great iron anchor ring from which lesser ropes fanned out to the bases of oak trees. The hawser, head-high at this point, stretched upward toward the creek, where it was secured to the top of the vessel's mainmast. It was this device which held the ship on its side. Redoubled stays from mainmast to the ship's port stanchions reinforced the mast, holding the great weight of the vessel's port hull high above water.

They had careened her hard over, using the onboard windlass as a winch, sweating to keel her over an inch at a time until her wound was fully exposed and dry. The hulk lay so far over on her starboard side now that when the tide was in, her deck was nearly vertical.

Dalton examined the splice on the anchor ring and found it holding solidly. The ship would stay where she was until they found the means to repair her.

18

"When Mister Duncan and Mister Romart return with our boat," he told Mallory, "I will row up to Eagle's Head and discuss this with Mister Ramsey. Possibly he will want to finance her repair."

There was no answer, and suddenly Dalton became aware of scuffling sounds and clink of metal behind him. He turned.

In the gloom he saw a large whaleboat nosing ashore under the ship's stern, and men leaping from it, charging up the bank. Two men had Claude Mallory pinioned, and as Dalton turned, he saw a third raise a club and bring it down on the sailor's head. Mallory crumpled.

Dalton's only weapon was his sword, and it stood at the base of a tree with his blankets, beyond the fire. He started to run for it and something hit him in the abdomen, doubling him over. Then rough hands had his arms, twisting, hauling him upright.

Four men held him helpless there as others prowled the campsite. In a moment lanterns were lit and he could see them better. They were rough men, a dozen or more, dressed in the motley garb of the American backwoods. Bay scavengers, he realized, jackals who roamed the backwaters, looting what they could.

One of them came forward then and thrust a heavy pistol into his face, its barrel rim crushing his lips against his teeth.

"Ye ain't alone here," the man growled. "Where's the res' of yer crew?"

Ducking his head aside, Dalton spat blood and struggled against the arms that held him.

"Oho!" One of them rasped, "'E's got fight in 'im, 'e does." Someone grabbed his hair and yanked his head back cruelly. The one with the pistol raised his free hand and swatted Dalton across the face, heavy knuckles bruising his cheek. The world reeled about him, and the man hit him again. "Answer me!" he roared. "I said where's yer crew?"

Dalton sagged, half conscious. "Gone," he whispered.

"Is that yer ship, then?" The man glanced back at the careened hulk dark in the gloom. "What be the matter wi' it?"

With the last of his fading strength Patrick Dalton raised his head, choking at the blood and spittle that filled his mouth. These men were outlaws, he knew, and he was alone among them. He had no chance. Hot anger rose in his throat, and he focused hard eyes on his tormentor. "It leaks," he rasped, then spat full in the man's face.

In the instant of shock that followed, he wrenched one arm free of his captors' hold, swung full around, and lashed out at a grinning face, feeling bones break as he connected. He kicked another in the stomach and whirled, trying to get loose of the tangle of them. Then they had him again and bore him down, fists pummeling him, boots brutal in his ribs and back.

"Brain the bastard!" someone shouted, and the leader's voice was a roar above it. "No! String him to the tree yonder. No man spits on Clive Hensey! String him an' let him dangle awhile. He'll talk civil when we starts cuttin' parts off him, he will."

Dalton awoke to pain and vertigo. Long moments passed before he became oriented enough to see the upside-down scene about him. He was trussed with rope, hanging by his ankles from a tree limb, his head three feet off the ground. A dim lantern on a stump revealed sprawled figures about the campsite, including a tied and unconscious Mister Mallory on the creek bank. He tried to move and pain shot through him, forcing a groan from clenched teeth. His nose and mouth were gorged with drying blood, and he could hardly breathe.

At the sound someone arose and walked over to him, looking down at his shadowed face. "Awake, be ye? Feel like talkin' a bit now?" It was the leader, Clive Hensey. The man knelt and peered into his face, then shoved a thumb into his eye. Dalton flinched away, and the movement sent flames of agony racing through his body.

"Aye," Hensey said judiciously. "Ye're awake. Now tell me, civil-like, what's wrong with the ship yonder? Can it be fixed up?"

Finding a thread of voice, Dalton shook his aching head. "You can go straight to hell."

"Oh, my," Hensey straightened. "'E is hostile, ain't 'e?" Pivoting, the man delivered a vicious kick which set Dalton to swinging like a pendulum. The upside-down world spun . . . light and shadow, twig and stump, glimpse of a buckled shoe beneath a bush . . . even as pain and vertigo tried to engulf him, Dalton came fully awake. "I'll talk," he croaked. "Enough. I'll talk."

Rough hands stopped his swinging, and Hensey knelt again, looking pleased.

"The ship has a sprung seam on the port wale," Dalton gasped. "It might be repaired."

"Where's the port wale, then?" the man taunted. "An' don' gi' me yer damn sailor talk. Talk plain."

"It's on the hull. On the high side as she's tipped. There's a platform there. See for yourself."

Hensey turned and studied the hulking mountain of the careened ship. "On th' other side?"

"Yes." Dalton's voice was hardly more than a whisper. "On the other side."

"We'll take a look, then." Hensey kicked him again, brusing his ribs, and strode off across the camp, arousing his men. "Come on, lads! Off yer butts an' get more lanterns a'goin'. Be mornin' soon, an' time to move. Up! Up!"

When they were all awake, he told two of them to stand guard and hustled the rest into the whaleboat. "We're goin' aroun' to see the bottom o' this tub," he said. "If we can float 'er, she's worth a bundle."

As he swung in the breeze, Dalton caught whirling glimpses of the whaleboat putting off, backing into the stream, disappearing behind the careened hulk of *Mystery*. Good name, that, he thought. A right good name.

He dangled and turned, and the buckled shoe was no longer where it had been, behind the bush. His back was to the clearing when he heard a thud and faint strangling noises, but they came as no surprise. The lads were back from their hunting trip.

In silence Billy Caster and Victory Locke cut him down and removed his bonds, and the agony of renewed circulation almost paralyzed him. Then, with their help, he managed to get to his feet. He leaned on their shoulders, gasping.

"What now, Captain?" Billy whispered.

"Can you find my sword?"

"Aye, sir," Purdy Fisk came forward with the bucklered blade. "One o' these scum was wearin' it. Here it is."

"Has someone seen to Mister Mallory?"

"Aye, sir." They kept it to whispers. "Mister Bean and Mister Wise are looking at him. He seems to be alive."

"Very well, Mister Caster." With an effort Dalton balanced himself on leaden feet and hobbled across to the hawser harness. He drew his sword and tested its edge. Then he began cutting.

Moments passed as he sliced at the big rope, cutting above the anchor ring. A strand parted, and another. Seventy yards away, beyond the careened hulk of *Mystery*, there were voices and the glow of lanterns. Dalton shifted his grip on the sword and sliced again.

Billy Caster and Victory Locke stood aside and stared at him, their eyes widening as they realized what he was doing.

22

The hawser vibrated and thrummed as another strand parted, then suddenly it separated with a crack like a rifle shot, and Dalton was thrown backward. With a cacophony of creaks, groans, and gurgles, the ship at the bank yielded to the free weight of its keel and rolled upright in the water, sending tidal waves racing across the cut. One startled cry mingled with the sound of crunching timbers beneath it, then there was only the splashing of ripple-waves as tons of wooden keel nested into the mud bottom of low tide.

"My Lord in heaven," Victory Locke whispered.

"Squish!" Billy Caster allowed.

Dalton sat spread-legged on the ground, trying with shaking hands to sheath his sword. "I think I'd like my chair," he said. "And a mug of tea. When there is enough light, we can begin careening her again. It shouldn't take so long this time, now that we know what we're about."

III

"They've taken Philadelphia, you know." John Singleton Ramsey shifted his bulk on the plank bench and sipped light grog from his tankard. "Your General Howe landed field troops at Head of the Elk and threw them across at George Washington's defenses. They broke through last Tuesday and Howe holds the city, though Washington has him besieged there. The Howes will have to take the Delaware now, I suppose, to provision their forces. And there are still two squadrons off the Chesapeake. Rather leaves us caught in the middle, doesn't it?"

"With some valuable stores in hiding, I assume." Patrick Dalton raised an eyebrow . . . and regretted it immediately. Various parts of his face were still too sore to ignore, as were other parts of his anatomy.

"Possibly. Trade can be quite precarious in wartime, you know." He raised the lamp to peer more closely at the tall Irishman. It was gloomy in the shuttered smokehouse where they met, but far safer than exposing Dalton to the open compound of Ramsey's Virginia estate, with redcoats and Hessians swarming over the countryside. "Do you know, Patrick, you look like the very devil with your eye and jaw all swollen like that. We'll have my surgeon take a look at you before you go. He's well paid and can be trusted."

"I am mending nicely," Dalton shook his head. "If a man . . . as you said . . . possibly had valuable cargo hidden somewhere, I expect it might be worth some investment to get it safely away toward a port of purchase?"

"It might," Ramsey conceded. "But the risks of losing it all would be awesome . . . providing there were such a cargo."

"Losing it? Or would the risk of having it found and identified be greater, Mister Ramsey?"

"Why do I begin to suspect you know what I might have that needs transporting, Patrick?"

"I don't know what you have, John. But I have come to know you, and to think highly of your, ah, mercenary instincts. There is bound to be something in your possession that might turn a handsome profit at the proper port. And I have the vessel to take it there for you."

"In return for supplies and outfitting? I'm surprised you don't demand a share as well."

Dalton's dark face went stern. "I am not interested in dealing in contraband, sir. Despite all that has occurred, I do consider myself a loyal subject of His Majesty."

"Oh, piffle. Everyone knows His Majesty is a rank tyrant. Not to mention an unbearable nincompoop into the bargain. You do have the strangest principles, Patrick. Here you are, with warrants against you that could hang you seven times over, yet you balk at a bit of honest smuggling? War or no war, lad, business is business."

"I have a list of the things I shall need, sir. With these items I could have a ship under sail inside two weeks, provided my men have her hull patched and her bilges pumped by the time I return."

"Your list is rather long, Patrick. Complete outfitting and provisioning for a ship, right up to a suit of sails and heavy arms. You are asking a great deal of money.''

''But nothing like the value of your cargo, I am sure, sir.''

''You don't even know what my cargo might be.''

''Nor do I care to. But I know you would not deal in mundane commodities. The guns, by the way, would be solely for the purpose of defending your valuable cargo.''

''And how would I know that once outfitted you might not simply run for New Spain, cargo and all?''

''My honor, sir.''

''You are Irish, sir.''

''And you are a smuggler, sir.''

''Well, at least you do not invoke my daughter to make your point. I rather thought you might.''

''What have you heard of Miss Constance, sir? I hope she is well.''

''Quite well, thank you. I sent her and the servants off to Baltimore. Most of the Continental Congress has gone there, you know, and one usually can rely upon politicians to know the best places for their personal safety. Constance should be quite secure at Baltimore until this unpleasantness hereabouts runs its course.''

''If she stays there.''

''And why should she not? I have promised her that all will be well here, that I am perfectly safe. . . .'' He clamped his mouth shut, then hastened to take another sip of three-water grog.

''And?'' Dalton prompted, puzzled.

''Well, sir, I also had to promise her that I would see to your safety in her absence . . .''

''A bit difficult to do.''

''Yes.''

''And?''

''Well, I also promised her that I would keep you . . . well . . . in tow, so to speak. That I would see to it that you don't go running off somewhere without her."

"Ah. I see."

Ramsey shrugged. "My daughter can be difficult at times."

"Yes. I know. In that case, then, I suppose there is no point in discussing further my venture, sir?"

"I didn't say that, Patrick. Actually, I rather like the idea myself. Quite risky, of course."

"A man with a good ship and enough sail should be able to slip past a squadron or two of warships in an estuary as large as Chesapeake, sir."

"I wasn't really thinking of the risk of warships, Patrick, although that risk is considerable. And then there are the privateers, and all the outright pirates that frequent these waters, and the risks of weather in this season . . . but I was thinking mostly of the risk posed by my daughter, should she get wind of this. Heaven only knows what it might enter her lovely head to do."

"Mister Ramsey, she's only a girl, after all. Quite a lovely young woman, of course, as you said, but still only a . . ."

"Oh, come now, Patrick. Be honest with me. Would you rather face the wrath of warships or of Constance?"

Dalton frowned, then nodded. "Warships, sir. Any day."

"Me too. However. A week, you said."

"I said two weeks. From delivery of the provisions."

"Too long. Black Dick Howe's fleet is at this moment approaching Delaware Bay. I have moved my stores here to Eagle's Head, but I expect there will be Hessians putting about here within two weeks. The Delaware's defenses will not last long. After that the Howes will move to consolidate on land. It's either ship now or dump some valuable materials in the bay, I'm afraid."

"Mister Ramsey?"

"Yes?"

"Did you somehow know that I might be here today with a proposal to carry your cargo?"

"Actually, Patrick, I had expected you yesterday. One of my factors employs several Indians . . . quite civilized aborigines, really . . . and they have had a look at your derelict vessel. . . ."

A rap at the door was followed by a dark head peering in. "Soldiers comin', Mister Ramsey. Up on the road."

"Thank you, Colly. Very well, Patrick. Get your vessel afloat and stand by for cargo. Put a man at the mouth of your cut to wag a lantern when he sees three and three, and we'll see how many barges we can slip past the damned King's Navy."

"Barges? I would have expected wagons."

"There aren't enough wagons in this county right now to haul the load I have, Patrick. But don't worry about that. Just see to your ship, and I shall attend the rest."

Without further pause, Ramsey stood and slipped out of the smokehouse, carrying the lamp with him, and Dalton was left alone in the darkness. He waited until the sounds of footsteps had faded, then eased the door open, looked out into the evening, and slipped out and around the secluded block building into forest behind. At a cove a mile away Billy Caster waited for him with a stolen dinghy, and there were hours of rowing ahead before it would be safe to hoist the little boat's lateen sail and make for the hidden cut where *Mystery* again lay on her side, having her hull repaired.

Making his way through darkening woods, Dalton had much on his mind. Constance was safe, and that was a relief. But he shared her father's concern about her. Constance Ramsey had a whim of iron, and her small, interestingly contoured person housed a

29

temper that could be truly volcanic on occasion.

He worried, too, about Charley Duncan and Michael Romart. Nearly ten days had passed since he'd sent the pair of them out in a launch to scout down Chesapeake Bay and study its traffic. He had no way of knowing whether they were captured, dead, or lost, though it was not likely that Romart would be lost. The American knew these lands.

And now he worried about another thing: not enough wagons, Ramsey had said. Not enough wagons for what? What was the merchant planning to load aboard *Mystery* that couldn't be delivered by a few heavy wagons? Dalton had the gnawing suspicion that his view of proper cargo limits and Ramsey's might be very different things. Scruples be damned, he almost wished he had asked for a manifest.

For Charley Duncan and Michael Romart, things had not gone at all well. Romart had been somewhat aghast at the captain's charge that they scout out Chesapeake Bay. "Sir, a man could spend a good bit of his life scouting Chesapeake," he had offered. But Dalton had sent them anyway. "All I want is a general traffic report," he told the skeptical colonial, "not a survey."

So they had set out, in the battered launch that but for rafts and a dinghy was the only vessel the onetime crew of *Faith* now had at its command.

As late first officer of *Faith*—following the death of one-legged old Clarence Kilreagh before a frigate's guns—Duncan was officer in charge of the venture. But as the only one of the pair even vaguely familiar with American waters and American ways, Romart was the expert. When it came to the handling of the vessel's stubby lug sails or its oars, both of them were crew, though the Irishman did feel a certain proprietary interest in the entire boat. It was he who had "found" it when the presence of British forces on the Delaware had made it discreet that felons, fugitives, and free spirits retire to the wilderness waters beyond.

Duncan had obtained the boat in some mysterious fashion on the second day that a flotilla from Admiral Lord Howe's fleet had anchored in the Delaware, and had brought it upriver to Squire Ramsey's private cove, then had stood by with the rest, beaming smugly, while Patrick Dalton inspected it. The smugness had diminished rapidly.

Not once had Dalton asked him where he found the boat. The captain had simply inspected it, measured it and delivered a running commentary in the process:

"A sturdy ship's boat, Mister Duncan. A fortunate find. Most unusual that people would leave such craft lying about unclaimed . . . and devoid of escutcheons, as well. And the raw wood where the escutcheons might have been still as fresh as though no spray had ever touched it. Quite recently mislaid, I'd judge, since that bit of caulking there by the sternpost shows no more than a few hours of immersion. One would suspect that as recently as yesterday this launch hung in its davits on some fine British vessel . . . possibly the *Doughty* herself."

It was at that point that Mister Duncan's smile extinguished itself. "I never said where I found it, sir," he pointed out. "You didn't ask."

"Would I ask such a thing of you, Mister Duncan?" Dalton's lean face was without expression, his dark eyes unreadable. "A gentleman doesn't question good fortune, particularly of the man who once got a good price in thieves' market for the helm of the vice admiral's flagship. Though, of course, one wonders how such things are accomplished."

"Very carefully, sir, I assure you," Duncan admitted. "But, sir, the *Doughty*? How might a gentleman come to think of that particular ship?"

"The launch is British," Dalton shrugged. "Its timbers say as much. Also, it is twenty-four feet long and six across the beam. Our British shipwrights are creatures of formula and habit, Mister Duncan. Less inventive than their American cousins, I'm afraid. The formula for a proper ship's launch for a British vessel is 2.6 times the square root of the length of the ship . . . and of course the beam is one-quarter of that figure. Therefore this launch might recently have been the property of a man-of-war ninety feet in length, which might conveniently mount twenty-six guns, and the only twenty-six-gun vessel anywhere about right now is the brig *Doughty*. I shouldn't be at all surprised if the deck officers and bosuns of that vessel are scratching their heads right now, trying to remember where they mislaid their number two launch."

Origins aside, it was a dainty launch—five oars to the side, single-banked, with well-greased tholepins to secure them, two sturdy masts that could be stubbed in, and spars ready trimmed for a pair of lugsails. All the boat needed, in Duncan's opinion, was a gun and a name—launches and such usually carried the name of their ship, but since the former *Faiths* were without a ship at the moment, Duncan had felt uneasy about the launch not being named *something* . . . and had said so.

And at that point the disciplined non-expression on Dalton's face had lost its edge. "Very well," he said, "then we shall name her something."

Something had made the voyage from the hidden cove below Wilmington, across Delaware Bay and under the noses of His Majesty's little squadron off Lewes Point and downcoast toward The Horns almost without incident. Almost. In the dawn off Metompkin a brace of punts out for sport had

32

identified *Something* as either a British vessel or waterfowl and had riddled their foresail with bird-shot. But the encounter had been brief. Billy Caster and Victory Locke had volleyed the punts with American rifles, while the rest lay to the oars and outran them.

Their only casualty had been Ishmael Bean's tar hat, which might yet—Bean had decided—be floating somewhere in the Atlantic. It had been a good hat.

But the incident had left Charley Duncan thinking about punt guns—those monstrous fowlers so freely used by colonial baymen. He dreamed of somehow acquiring a pair of the murderous little weapons to mount bow and stern on *Something* to serve as chasers. Considering relative size of the vessels, he felt such guns could serve *Something* just as that pair of long eights he had once spirited off a colonial snow in Rhode Island had once served the schooner *Faith*.

Thus the scouting of bay traffic which Dalton sent him and Mister Romart to accomplish was complicated by incursions into many a cove, hidden inlet, and forest-shrouded river in search of those havens from which puntmen might operate—and where punt guns might somehow be had. On one such incursion they ran afoul of Indians.

The two were at oars, pulling up a secluded tributary, when *Something* balked at her sweeps and became sluggish in the water, and a gurgling sound came from her stern. Charley Duncan, rowing at second bank, shipped his oars and went back to have a look. Kneeling beside the lashed tiller, he bent over the rail to peer into the turgid water, then turned to Romart. "Best lay to for a moment," he said. "Something has fouled our rudder."

Romart shipped oars, glancing uneasily at the patches of sky visible among the towering trees. There should have been more birds there, he thought. "Can you see what it is?"

Duncan's voice, from below the stern where he was working with something, was muted. ". . . fishes . . . with feathers . . ." was all the Colonial heard. Then Duncan came upright again, holding high a mass of fouled twine from which feathers were suspended here and there, and two or three flopping fish. "A gilling string," he said.

"A what?"

"Gilling string. Someone has been taking fish here."

"I know what it is," Romart said. "But why did you call it that? It's a trotline."

"I know a gilling string when I see one."

"Well, I never heard of a gilling string, but I've seen plenty of trotlines, and that's what that is. Those feathers on it, that's an Indian trick. Makes it easier to see under the water."

"Well, it's ruined, whatever you call it . . . Indian? You mean there are Indians here?"

"Last I heard." Romart had his rifle up now and was checking its prime. "When you've cleared the foul, I think we should leave. But you might as well keep those fish for supper."

Duncan loosed a few fish from the tangle and tossed them into the bilges, then finished cutting away the mess of twine fouling the rudder. He added another fish to their collection and leaned far over to run his fingers down the sternpost. "Sweep us off a stroke, Mister. I think it's clear now."

Romart didn't respond, and Duncan hoisted himself and looked around. The colonial sat frozen where he had been, his hands before him, palm outward. And on the bank, only yards away, a half-dozen swarthy visages glared at them down the shafts of arrows drawn to the head in stout bows.

Just upstream, a long canoe glided toward them, carrying more warriors.

Duncan put on his most disarming smile. "How do," he told the nearest savage. "I've just been salvaging your fishes."

The following minutes had been uncertain for both Duncan and Romart. But once it was established that the Indians had decided not to kill and scalp them but only to negotiate a suitable recompense for their ruined fish trap, they were amiable enough.

The negotations took up all of that day and most of the following one, lasting more or less to the point that all the edible provisions aboard *Something* had been consumed.

Two of the Indians, a pair of brothers named Squahamac and Pitacoke, spoke a form of English that, though unintelligible to the colonial, was easily fathomed by the tar. "Your problem, Mister Romart," Duncan explained, "is that you've never visited London. Many's the time I've heard the blessed same dialect among the good folk of Heathrow and St. Ives. Why, were it not for bein' red and half naked, Michael, these gentlemen would be right at home in Picadilly."

Pitacoke gnawed at a fish and frowned at Duncan. "Oi aye nough' o' Picadilly," he corrected solemnly. "Squahamak an' mesel', we pu' up a' Nanticoke."

"Nanticoke?" Duncan raised a sandy brow. "An' where's 'at, then?"

"Downwater," Pitacoke said, pointing. "Ha' a league. Ol' Nahamish yon." He indicated a sturdy savage of middle years who seemed to be more or less in charge, "Blee'in' tommy as is, he be th' head man o' these parts. Nanticoke, too. It's 'im'll put th' wage on ye."

"What's that he's going to put on us?" Romart demanded.

"Th' wage," Pitacoke said slowly. "Th' due. Th' se'lemen'. Th' wot's fair, manner o' spea'in. Blimey, ha' ye nough' 'eard Henglish, swagger?"

"He says Nahamish over there is the gentleman who'll decide what we owe," Duncan explained to the colonial.

In his good time, Nahamish decided what they owed, and Squahamac and Pitacoke translated to Duncan, who translated to Romart. Nahamish spoke solemnly and at some length, then turned to Squahamac.

"E'll caw i' quits f' a brice o' tawlin cobbers," Squahamac explained.

"He says he'll settle for a pair of twine spools," Duncan explained.

"But we don't have any twine," Romart pointed out.

"E' 'lows we go' 'n," Duncan translated for Squahamac.

Squahamac explained it in Indian for Nahamish. Nahamish shook his head, then again spoke at length in his own language.

"E's bleedin' well on ye go' na tawlin," Squahamac told Duncan. "Bu' 'e 'lows ye'll righ' sma' filch a bi' an' a tot o' us be wi' ye' abou' 't."

Duncan shook his head and turned to Romart. "The chief knows we don't have twine. He wants us to go and steal some for him, and some of these lads will go with us to help."

"Does he know where some is to steal, then?" Romart was becoming exasperated.

Duncan turned to Squahamac. "'s 'e go' a clue w'ere 't . . ."

"Oi stoo' 'im righ' enou'," Squahamac interrupted. "Be tawlin an' plenty o'er t' w'ere th' bleedin' blokes go' th' new ship a'jobbin'."

"New ship? Where . . . ah, w'ereabut is't then?"

"Ovawater," Squahamac shrugged. "An' a ha', two league."

Duncan was thoughtful as he turned again to the glowering colonial. "'E . . . uh, *he* says someone is

36

building a ship across the bay. Says there'd be a-plenty of twine there."

"There aren't any shipyards around here," Romart said.

"'E 'lows th' be na . . .'"

"'Eard 'im m'sel', righ' enou'," Squahamac cut him off, impatiently. "Be 'un, too. Blokes go' 't hid, 'sall."

In last light of evening *Something* slid out of the Choptank estuary and made for the west bank of Chesapeake. With all the oars manned, a grumbling Michael Romart on first bank, and muscular savages manning the other four sets while Charley Duncan called stroke and Squahamac navigated, the launch made far better time than she had with only two aboard.

In the dusk they entered another estuary, and by full dark they were several miles into the shrouding forest. Past the screening spit and towering forest of its mouth, it was a surprisingly wide and deep waterway, and Duncan's hopes soared. A perfect hideaway for baymen and thieves, he decided. And a likely place to find the people whose little boats sported punt guns.

Then new revelations crowded such thoughts to the back of his mind. *Something* rounded a bend in the wilderness stream and ahead was lantern light. Sounds of voices carried across the water, and the unmistakeable creaks and rattlings of tackle being secured. With muffled oars they crept closer, and the two white men stared in wonder. "Mother an' saints," Duncan breathed. "It's a bloody shipyard, an' look what they're puttin' the touches to."

"It's a ship," Romart decided.

"Ship, nothin'," Duncan corrected him. "That yonder is a fine new snow with her tackle aright and guns in place and her suitin' out bein' tested. She's even got her colors up. Yonder's a slick privateer vessel, Michael, with long legs and tearin' teeth. Mother Mary, what a prize for some lucky Crown vessel."

"Or what a demise for some unlucky one," Romart said. "How many guns do you count there, Mister Duncan?"

"Sixteen . . . maybe eighteen . . ."

"Cypher th' bleedin' belchers an' ye go' 'oliday," Squahamac ordered the pair. "'T's tawlin Nahamish charged ye filch."

"A blinkin' great jaunty snow sits here in the howlin' wilderness," Duncan shook his head, "a spit-an'-polish new jackmast snow with to'gallants and royals and spreaders for studdin's'ls, spanker rigged for a ringtail an' a gundeck with sixteen bright muzzles a'sproutin' . . . *all that* an' the friggin' aborigine wants twine."

"Then let's get his twine and be gone," Romart growled. "Folk in these parts like their privacy, Mister Duncan. When they hide a thing it's because they mean for it to stay hid, and don't likely welcome people coming around to look at it."

"Oh, very well," Duncan said. "If you and your red Cockneys will put me ashore over there, I imagine I can locate some twine."

"Tell *them*," Romart shook his head. "I don't speak the language. And if you plan to go ashore yonder, we'd better trade coats and hats, Mister Duncan. And for heaven's sake, comb out that pigtail! You look like a British sailor."

"I *am* a British sailor," Duncan reminded him. But the advice was sound. Still, as he worked loose his braided pigtail and shrugged into the colonial's coat, his eyes held on the lantern-lit ship rocking at anchor just upstream. He wished Captain Dalton could be here to have a look at her. No man loved better the grace and vitality of a jaunty man-of-war than did Patrick Dalton, nor did any seaman he had ever known have such a way with vessels. Who else could have taken a little commercial schooner and made of her a fighting ship as Dalton had done with *Faith*? A fighting ship that was a match in battle for a first-rate frigate. No man among the fugitive crew would ever recall *Faith* without a bit of moisture gathering in his eyes. And no man of them would be content again until they once more set sails to the wind and flew free aboard a trim vessel with Patrick Dalton's hand at the helm.

They were hauling the lifts over there, securing the topgallant and royal yards high above the topmasts, and hauling sheets to turn them this way and that, a test of rigging before the sails were bound in place. Jibsail and staysail already were in place, as was the driver on its rising boom, and soon the snow would be in full suit. Boats worked between her and the shoreline, boarding tackle and supplies and, he supposed, kegs of powder for her magazine. Torchlight from a longside skiff lighted an escutcheon and he could read her name: *Fury*.

A trim, proud vessel. He wondered whether her letter of marque as a privateer would be from the Virginia Burgesses or the rebels' Continental Congress. The striped colors she flew could be either. But it didn't matter Soon she would be afield and hunting, and she had an eager look about her. More than one good British vessel might feel the sting of the *Fury* in times ahead, he thought.

"Mind wot yer 'bou'," Pitacoke growled at him. "'Ere's th' bloody shore."

"I think he said for you to pay attention," Romart offered. "The bank's just ahead."

"I heard what he said," Duncan sighed.

Wearing Romart's floppy hat and butternut coat, Charley Duncan went ashore and made his way through dark forest to the sizeable clearing where several dozen men were at work, hauling things from

39

a wagon dock down to the water's edge. He wandered around for a time, saw no twine, and finally approached a bearded man with a musket under his arm and a lantern in his hand. He seemed to be someone in authority.

"Pardon," Duncan said. "I'm supposed to pick up some twine, but I don't know where it is."

"Twine?" the man glanced at him, raising his lantern. "Who are you, then?"

"I just got in," Duncan shrugged. "They said bring twine, but they didn't say where to find it."

The man peered at him for a moment, then lowered his lantern, said something unkind about teamsters, and swung his musket in a general point. "Sailmaker's shed yonder. Where else would it be?"

In the shed he found twine and selected two twenty-pound spools. Bedamned redskins should be able to catch every fish in Chesapeake with that, he allowed. He did a quick inventory of the shed's contents then, for good measure, and wandered off to the next structure—a chandler's hut—and inventoried that as well, his mouth watering at the wealth of fittings, fixtures, and forage that was stowed there.

First things first, though. He hoisted his twine and started back the way he had come, then stopped. Where there had been one or two armed men near the clearing's perimeter, now there were a dozen, and they seemed thoroughly alert. Something was afoot.

A man wandered past carrying a keg, and Duncan said, "What's happenin' there? Trouble?"

"Nobody tells us anything," the man panted. "Just another alert, I reckon."

"I just got in," Duncan said. "What are the alerts about?"

"Who knows?" The man set down his keg and sat on it, willing to take a moment to rest. "Some've been out here three months or better, outfittin' that vessel there, an' they say there's alerts every time a fish

40

splashes in the bay or a pigeon flies over and drops its ballast. There was," he counted on his fingers, "the time the Georgie fleet went by goin' up-bay. And the time they went by again, goin' down-bay. And the time some punters spotted Georgie tars in a launch. And then there was the time a pair of sloops got into a shootin' match down by St. Mary's. They wouldn't let us go down and watch that. Just made us keep on workin' and called another alert. And the time Clive Hensey and his bunch was pokin' around in the woods yonder, though they never came anywhere near to here, so they say. And lately it's been about that Spanish pirate that somebody thought he saw skulkin' around off the Horns. Captain was afraid they might come up here an' find *Fury* and try to take her. Their ship's a wreck, damn near."

"Stays busy here, doesn't it?" Duncan offered.

"Always somethin'. Just yesterday somebody come in and said there was Hessians wanderin' around in the woods below the Annapolis Road."

"My," Duncan said.

Someone with a lantern came near and paused. "You men," he ordered, "Look lively there or you'll feel a boot on yer backsides."

"Nice chattin' with you," the carrier said, and lifted his keg again. "Just don't get too near the perimeter when there's an alert. Those people don't hesitate to shoot."

"I'll keep that in mind," Duncan assured him.

He looked around, wondering if there might be a better way out, and his eyes widened as they lit upon a boxy object bobbing just beyond the sloping bank. A punt . . . with punt guns fore and aft. "Well, well," he muttered. "Mercy me."

As efficient and officious as any supervisor on the yard, Charley Duncan approached a line of carriers coming up from the bank and handed his twine to the first of them. "You men come with me," he

41

ordered. At the sheds he set them to bringing out various items that had interested him, and to rigging a hauling skid to transport his goods down to the punt. The little craft was stacked high with commodities in an hour, and had barely eight inches of freeboard.

With two men helping him at oars, he set out for the anchored *Fury*. Coming alongside at a chute he told his helpers, "Go aboard there and tell them to rig a deck winch a'port amidships."

When the men were gone he pushed off, then rowed around *Fury*'s stern and into the darkness beyond, heading for the place he had left *Something* and her mixed crew.

With the heavily loaded punt in tow, it was true toil to get the launch back across the bay. Dawn was on the water when they nosed into the Indians' estuary, hauled well past the screen of forest and made fast below Nahamish's camp.

Romart had been fussing the entire way about Duncan's laden punt. "Set out for twine and you bring back half a fitting yard," he grumbled. And, "What are we going to do with all that truck, anyway? How can we scout Chesapeake Bay with a ton of stolen property in tow?" And, "I do expect Captain Dalton intends for us to return eventually, Mister Duncan. Most likely he expects us sometime this year."

Duncan mostly ignored it, finding conversation with Pitacoke and Squahamac more productive.

Dutifully Duncan delivered the two spools of twine to Nahamish, then returned to *Something* with two Indians trailing after him. When he stepped into the launch the braves did likewise, seating themselves at second and third oar banks.

"Now what are we doing?" Romart wondered. "Mister Duncan, I distinctly heard Captain Dalton tell us to scout the bay and then return."

42

"And that's what we are doing," Duncan assured him.

"Then why are they in this boat?"

"Oh, them? Why, I signed them on as crew. They felt there was little future in gill fishing when there's a war going on all around, you see."

"Billy 'ell 'swell," Squahamac told Romart seriously. "T'boot, 'sna true taw now an' oursel's cob th' lip, y'see."

Duncan nodded. "He says besides all that, old Nahamish is a hard man to work for, and these two haven't been very well accepted since they learned to speak good English."

Felix Croney reached Wilmington after five days of miserable travel overland, long days of bumpy coaches on dusty roads with uncountable and interminable stops at roadblocks and checkpoints and twice at blown bridges. Everywhere south of Staten Island, it seemed, the rebels roamed unfettered and took delight in the stopping of traffic and the interrogation of travelers.

Croney had not been concerned with the dangers of capture or betrayal. It was unlikely that anyone outside the fleet stronghold at Long Island—and various officers and men on king's vessels—would know him on sight, and the documentation he carried made him a simple bondsman en route from the Hudson ports to the tobacco plantations of Virginia. A small man, gray-seeming and seldom noticed unless he wore his uniform, he might be harassed by the obstreperous colonials, but none likely would detain him long. He didn't even bother to use a false name. Few enough would recognize his real one.

And this far from fleet headquarters, none would have heard of the chief guard officer of the Long

Island yards. Those who might know him and wish him harm were mostly either on their way to England now to face the king's justice, or locked away in prison hulks to rot and die.

With the arrest warrants for the Fitzgerald's associates in the colonies had come a new commission for Croney. He was warrant officer, charged with the finding and bringing to justice of those accused of the treason in Ireland, and he had used the resources of his guard captaincy to execute his orders. Only one of those so named had escaped custody—the Irishman Patrick Dalton.

Only one! Of all the names on the warrants, delivered months hence by fleet packet from London, only one remained. But that one, above all, Croney had sworn to himself he would find. Partially it was because Dalton had become almost a legend in recent months. Fleeing the king's justice the rascal had either caused or at the very least been party to the destruction of two sail of the line in New York Harbor, the damaging of a pair of armed brigs, the loss of a sloop of war in Long Island Sound, the escape of a dozen n'er-do-wells and outright felons from stockade, the disappearance of a coastal packet off Cape Cod, the sinking of at least two gunboats, and the destruction of several docks and the sinking of a 44-gun frigate in the open sea off Delaware Bay. It was said that he had also had a hand in the sending to yards of a rebel cutter and some sort of an invasion of Little Bay in Rhode Island, though none of those details were clear.

All that, though, and the scoundrel yet had champions among the Admiralty—even among the peerage. Admiral Lord Howe himself had ridiculed the charge of treason by way of association, though it was proved beyond a doubt that Dalton had known the Fitzgerald in past years.

Still, there could be no dismissing the damages he

44

had done since his escape from Long Island, and Felix Croney was not a man to make personal judgments where fugitives were concerned. Patrick Dalton was wanted. Patrick Dalton must be found.

At an inn in Wilmington, after capping his bruising journey with a wet passage across the river aboard a smelly dinghy whose owner overcharged unmercifully, Croney found a dark corner and made himself unobtrusive. Wilmington was the last place Dalton had been seen ashore, by reports . . . either Wilmington or South Point, just down the river.

After five days of uncomfortable travel, Felix Croney simply sat and listened. And, as he knew it would, intelligence came. The fugitive Dalton had been seen in the company of a local gentleman, the squire John Singleton Ramsey. But Ramsey was no longer in residence, and his great house was boarded up—as were many with the advent of the fleet into Delaware Bay. Where, then, had Ramsey gone? Two more days of listening gave a clue. The merchant had a second residence, a plantation house at Eagle's Head in the Chesapeake region.

Like a ferret, relentless, Felix Croney paid his fare at the inn and continued his search. Somewhere the fox Dalton must go to ground. And Croney meant to be there when he did, with a platoon of armed marines or Hessian guards to take the man into custody.

Two squadrons had remained on Chesapeake after departure of the transports from Head of Elk, and for a time a great silence reigned on the big bay, punctuated by the thunder of great guns now and then when one of the Union Jack vessels strayed a bit from its companions and was set upon by the myriad armed vessels that the Continentals seemed to have hidden in every alcove and creek. Punts and cutters, swarms of madmen aboard dinghies and canoes, even rafts took their shots at the British vessels. Little enough harm was done, but the harassment was such that the cruisers were ready to leave when their orders came. With a final sweep of known lairs and a few broadsides into the forests for good measure, the squadrons terminated their rearguard action and sailed out and northward. Part of the group would join the blockade on the Delaware, the remainder would repair northward to escort transports from New York to Newport.

Regally, the warships departed Chesapeake in line-ahead formation, found dark water, and wheeled as smartly as so many sail of the line into a crisp line abreast—a thumbing of the nose at those they knew watched from the secret places of the wilderness bay.

When the last sail had disappeared from view, the cautious traffic upon the bay resumed itself—fishing boats in tiny fleets, coasters and barges here and there on furtive runs from point to point, and not a few laden cargo vessels with loaded guns, heading for secret places where other vessels were being outfitted for the business of war. The first mail packet in almost a month crossed from Lancaster Court House to Metompkin, and at half a dozen little estates on the Delmarva Peninsula, refugees and travelers prepared to continue interrupted journeys southward, some making for the Virginia mainland, others going toward the Carolinas.

One such party was that of Jean-Luc Toussaint, Chevalier du Canille, late of Marseilles and recently fled from the embattled city of Philadelphia. Trapped on the peninsula, Toussaint and his little group had taken refuge with friends of the American trader Ian McCall to await safe passage to the Carolinas.

Weeks had passed, but now the word came that the British had departed Chesapeake and a packet would come soon from Williamsburg to carry them some fifty miles by water to a place where coaches would be waiting to take them to Richmond for passage southward.

The Chevalier set his servants to packing and gathered the women about him—his wife Eunice and their daughters Eugenie and Lucette. "My doves," he said, "the English have gone elsewhere for a time and we may continue our journey. In a day or two, three at the most, a pleasant sailing craft will come for us to take us to Virginia. I warrant you that we shall all celebrate the Christ mass at Saint-Germain and be back in Marseilles to welcome the new year."

IV

It was an uneasy alliance which bound together Conte Don Geraldo Lostrato y Baldar de Vas and the pirate Enrico Pinto. But it was an alliance of mutual necessity. Through right of entitlement from the Court of Charles III, Lostrato had invested his favors due from the king—and a good bit of his inheritance as well—in the obtaining of a letter of marque from the Governor General of New Spain and was thus entitled to indulge in the taking of certain ships at sea as a legitimate privateer. Pinto, on the other hand—a coarse and burtal sort but a respected mariner and strategist—was a wanted man. Charges against him rested, awaiting his capture, in four Crown colonies as well as in various British and French ministries. Piracy, looting, and the murders of crew and passengers of three vessels were among the charges. No letter of marque would ever be issued in his name, but he could supply the ships and men that Lostrato needed.

The rebellion in England's North American colonies had brought them together. For a time they both had done fairly well, separately, on proceeds from prizes in the thriving trade lanes between Bermuda and Havana and the northern coastal ports. But then, suddenly, times changed. The rich hunting grounds became battlegrounds, and abruptly the seas sprouted men-of-war with heavy arms and no patience for Spanish raiders, legitimate or otherwise.

Lostrato had lost his forty-gun *Isabella* almost at the first clash of arms in the Bermuda lanes. A British frigate pursued him directly into the port at Havana and blew *Isabella* to kindling where she lay at anchor. The frigate's commander had carried a warrant claiming that *Isabella* had boarded a merchantman in Florida coastal waters.

For Pinto it had been the same, except that his nemesis was an American privateer, the brig *Newport Lady*. His own *Escobar* lay now at the bottom of the sea off the Carolina coastline. At the little harbor of Beaufort he and a boatload of brigands had gone to ground, bound their wounds, then boarded and appropriated a cutter and set out to try again.

With the cutter he had taken an ancient but seaworthy brigantine, the transport *Columbine*, and mounted the cutter's guns aboard her, then he had been chased into hiding at New Orleans by a pair of brigs flying the Union Jack. At New Orleans he had found Lostrato looking for a ship and a solution to his own problems.

Pinto seethed at Lostrato's demands regarding the maintenance and discipline of his ship. The haughty aristocrat did not attempt to assume command, but he did insist that Pinto wear the plumage and regalia of a Spanish captain, and that the ship be kept in spotless condition. Compliance with these demands had cost Pinto two good cutthroats. He had killed them himself.

Uneasy as the alliance was, though, their first venture had been a success. They had taken a cargo merchant in the Florida straits and sold the goods at New Orleans for a fair profit. Then they had gone out again . . . right into the teeth of a pair of Virginia cutters with more guns and more sail than seemed possible for such diminutive vessels. In the running battle that ensued, *Columbine* had been badly wounded—holed twice at waterline, a spar shattered and a sternbrace shot away. Only a squall had saved her. The heavy weather had been to the advantage of the larger vessel, and she had lost her pursuers.

Yet now, as they prowled the Virginia coastline, they were in poor condition. Sullen hands too long unpaid made shift to lay fothering over *Columbine*'s holed hull and to patch the broken sternbrace with cable and clamps, their ill tempers held in check only by *El Capitan* Pinto's murderous discipline.

And between *Capitan* and *Patron*, things were little better. Pinto's brigand nature told him to make southward on the autumn winds, to find a haven on a lawless coast or, with good fortune, to return to the safety of New Spain. But Lostrato did not agree.

"We came to take prizes, *Capitan*," he told the big pirate coldly, his hand on the buckler of his rapier. "We have some damage, but we are in the waters now where prizes may be found. We shall wait here for a time and see what comes our way."

Pinto stared moodily at the broken shoreline just a few miles off, little islands scattered before a barrier spit beyond which were the reaches of Chesapeake. Lostrato was a swordsman, they said, schooled in the academies of Leon. Many times, Pinto had been tempted to learn for himself what that meant, but it had never quite come to that. Now he rounded on the smaller man, holding his temper barely in check. "On my ship I say what *shall* occur, Don Geraldo. *Only* I say that. I listen when you suggest what we *should* do, but you do not say to me, we *shall!*"

Lostrato did not budge an inch, though his fingers tightened on his buckler and his impeccable little beard quivered slightly as his lips tightened. "Need I remind you, Captain, of whose letter of marque it is that allows us haven in Spanish ports? Or that without it there would be *no* port in the civilized world open to you? What use the taking of prizes if you have nowhere to sell them? I say again, we *shall* remain in these waters for a time."

"And if I choose otherwise?"

"Should you choose otherwise, then you and this rattling barge may go your way, but without me. I can easily find another pirate to do my bidding. Put me off your ship—*if you can*—and see how long you then survive."

"When I put you off my ship it will be as food for the fishes, *Don* Geraldo. And it will be my own saber that divides you for their pleasure."

"It will be my pleasure for you to try . . . one day," Lostrato purred. "However," with a shrug of disdain he turned his back, "this accomplishes nothing for either of us now. We will proceed as I say, Captain, for one reason on which we can agree: the storms of winter are not far off, and I for one do not propose to return to New Orleans empty-handed."

"But why here?" Pinto growled. "British forces have only recently been on the Chesapeake. No commerce is coming out of that by now. What is there here to take?"

"A more suitable ship, Captain." With a sneer, Lostrato flung out his arm to point at the great inlet hidden beyond the barrier. "Do you think I enter upon ventures without informing myself first? In that bay and its tributaries, the American rebels are outfitting vessels to fight the ships of England. Ships with press of sail and many guns. This . . ." he wrinkled his nose in contempt, indicating the *Columbine*, "this is a scow. Look what two armed cutters did to us! I want one of those vessels. With such a ship we can take what the shipping lanes offer us, and stay out of reach of men-of-war."

"Perhaps there are ships in there," Pinto shrugged.

"What good does it do us, then, to beat back and forth out here, if what might come to us is such a ship? Do you think we can take a warship at sea?"

"Maybe not at sea," Lostrato said. "But in there! If we know when such a ship is entering the bay, and can fall upon it suddenly . . . then the contemptible skills of your crew might serve us well. Hardly one among them is a man I would choose for seamanship, but they do know how to board and kill."

Pinto grumbled for a time, still pondering upon what a pleasure it would be to kill this pompous jay. Still, there was sense in what he said, and a pleasure might be deferred for a time . . . if they could do what he suggested. "And how do we know when such a ship comes from its hiding place?" he asked. "We could spend a winter searching Chesapeake, even if we were not hunted down ourselves in the process."

Lostrato's sneer became almost a smirk. "His Catholic Majesty has many observers among the American colonies, Captain. I have corresponded with some of them long since, and I have sent the proper signals."

"You sent signals? From my ship? When?"

"While you were gorging yourself on that slop your cook considers breakfast, Captain." He pointed a casual thumb at the deck officer standing by the helm. "*Teniente* Torero was right there with me all the time, though I think he didn't know what I was doing." He grinned at Pinto's furious frown. "Ah? So maybe you will have the *Teniente* keelhauled, Captain? What a waste that would be. Of all our riffraff, he probably is the only one who really knows the way to sail a decent ship."

Mystery would never be a jaunty lady, Patrick Dalton admitted to himself. Serviceable and seaworthy, yes, but *Mystery* remained just what she was—a cargo ketch. With the careening completed, they had cut away the damaged stays on her port channel, letting the warped wales snap back into place. And snap they had, almost closing the long slit in the hull below. What remained was a narrow split that they repaired with coppers from her beam and tar from a keg floating in her flooded hold. By the time she stood aright once more, rocking on mud at low tide, the first of John Singleton Ramsey's craftsmen had arrived—a sailmaker named Titus Wilton who brought with him two assistants and a wagonload of sailcloth and canvas. A stubby little man of middle years, he arrived at the little clearing with a frown on his face and an irritated gruffness in his manner. Climbing from his wagon, he stalked directly to the bank of the cut, peered over his glasses at the standing rigging of the ketch, hauled out a pad of foolscap and a clay pencil, and began making notes.

"Indecent," he declared. "Unseemly and unprofessional."

Among those of Dalton's crew who had watched wide-eyed at his arrival and brusque entrance, Purdy Fisk stepped close and removed his hat. "What might that be, sir?"

"Eh?" the sailmaker turned and tilted his head, peering at Fisk through his narrow lenses.

"I wondered, sir, what it is that displeased you. And . . ."

"The circumstances, young man! This outfitting of sailing vessels in ridiculous hidey-holes out in the wilderness. No proper facilities anymore. Certainly no niceties or conveniences. It seems lately that half the vessels to be suited out are either in hiding or in bad repute. Or . . ." he glanced around in disapproval, ". . . possibly both. This is even more unseemly than the last place where I was commissioned."

"And also we wondered who you are," Fisk finished. "So that we might tell Captain Dalton who's among us, you see."

"Captain Dalton?"

"Our captain, sir. He's due here directly. If you'd state your business, sir . . ."

"My business?" the stubby man turned and pointed. "If you will cast your eyes yonder where my louts are offloading valuable sailcloth from that wagon in their usual fashion . . . you there! Quincy! Mind what you're about! Those bales are to be set out in the order in which they are numbered! . . . then you will most likely deduce directly that I am a sailmaker and that yardage is intended to become sails for this ungainly craft that you people have here. And we expect to be fed and provided proper bedding during that process. And my name is Titus Wilton." With a curt nod he went back to his note-taking.

Fisk shrugged, put on his hat, and went back to the others. "They intend to suit us in sails," he explained. "And he wants to be fed."

"He'll eat when it's ready, just like everybody else," Victory Locke snorted. "I never asked to be cook for this crew, and I'll add no random meals to my labors."

"Rest easy, Mister Locke," Claude Mallory said. "None of the rest of us are any happier about you being the cook than you are." Wrinkling his face in exaggerated sympathy he turned away, then leaned close to Cadman Wise to mutter, "Mister Locke cooks just the way he handles American rifles. Much more dangerous to his mates than to the enemy in either case."

"I heard that," Locke growled.

Aboard the ketch, Ishmael Bean raised his head above the midships gunwale to shout, "Can someone find the time to raft across here? I need a hand with

55

these bedamned pumps!"

The sailmaker completed his inventory of spars and rigging, then stalked back across the clearing to order the setting of a tent at a place of his choosing. "Uncivilized conditions," he muttered. "The wages of poor planning. They should build their ships first in proper yards, *then* have their war."

He watched the quick erection of his tent and the placement of his sewing and cutting tables, then glanced at the sun. The day was yet young. He unlocked one of his tool chests and brought out tapes and measures, then turned to where some of the ex-*Faiths* were working a windlass attached to an oak tree, laying out cable to be taken aboard for hoists. "Which of you is an able topman?"

"We all are, sir," Purdy Fisk said. "There aren't enough of us right now to specialize, you see."

"I shall need a topman to drop tapes from those spars so that my assistants can take the leech measures. Also, I shall need an inventory of what boltrope, buntline and leechline stock, grommets and cringles you have on hand."

"We don't know that yet, sir," Fisk apologized. "Everything below her knees is flooded. Mister Bean is just now repairing the pumps."

"Well, see to it."

"Yes, sir."

"And where is that captain of yours? I am not accustomed to commencing a task until my commission is validated. He is supposed to do that, you know."

"No, sir, I didn't know. But he should be back soon. He and Mister Caster have gone to Queenstown. To recruit hands."

The village of Queenstown, a tiny tobacco, grain, and fishing port separated from its archrival and twin of Dover by thirty miles of peninsula, had undergone change in the year or two since the conflicts had begun in earnest. Most of those changes had come about in the short weeks since the advance of the British squadron up Cheseapeake to disembark troops for the taking of Philadelphia, and the subsequent withdrawal down Chesapeake to reform for the Delaware campaign.

Only months before, Queenstown's resident population had been no more than two hundred people . . . not counting slaves. Now its population was nearly a thousand, not counting either former residents or slaves. No one knew for sure how many skirmishes had occurred on Chesapeake during the Head of Elk campaign, but there were wrecked or damaged vessels in dozens of hidden coves all up and down its length, and many hundreds of beached seamen sitting idle in places like Queenstown. Ables and ordinaries, topmen and taffmen, deck hands and bilgers, pirates and petty officers, they haunted every inn, grog shop, and hovel. Patriots and tories, merchant seamen and not a few British tars either deserted or misplaced among them, they drank what they could get, ate what came their way, brawled and philosophized at whim, and waited for a chance at a berth on any sort of vessel.

It was a likely place to recruit for a fugitive crew, and John Singleton Ramsey had spoken highly of it for that purpose . . . if not in any other respect.

In two days at Queenstown, Patrick Dalton had lost his hat, clubbed three men insensible—two with the pommel of his sword and one with a cooper's mallet—and had signed on eleven hands to ready and sail the ketch *Mystery*. Billy Caster trailed after his officer, keeping records and accounts, entering names and qualifications in the log, and defending Dalton's back with a cocked and primed rifle each time the proceedings became uncivilized.

To *Mystery*'s roster now had been added the names and marks of Tobias Quinn, able seaman late of the

New Haven privateer *Thunder*, unemployed now because *Thunder* lay at the bottom of Cold Pass; the brothers Toliver and Talmadge Fanshaw, originally of Liverpool, late HMRN able seamen deserted for unspecified reasons; Joseph Tower, carpenter, late of the Virginia commission brig *Burgess*, more recently an escapee from the Commonwealth stockade at Williamsburg where he had faced charges of mayhem; chief gunners Ethan Crosby and Floyd Pugh, both late of His Majesty's 74-gunner *Royal Lineage*, deserters following a dispute with a bosun's mate; the brothers Donald and Gerald O'Riley, ordinary seamen late of the sugar galley *Clemency* until it was taken at sea by Spanish pirates, and their shipmate Sam Sidney, a topman who had escaped with them; a huge, bull-shouldered ex-master at arms named only Hoop, late HMRN petty officer aboard the frigate *Prowler*, beached now because twenty or thirty of his shipmates had thrown him overboard off Albemarle Sound; and a monkeylike, able bosun of some fifty years, John Tidy, late HMRN petty officer who had jumped ship at Head of Elk and was in no great rush to return either to England or to English service.

A motley press, Dalton realized as they stood at ragged attention outside the Cock and Bale for his inspection. Able men and good lads, each in his way, no berserkers or connivers among them, though each and severally they did reek of potential havoc. But he had been careful in his selections. In addition to experience and skills, each of them also either was a fugitive or, at the very least, had no scruples about associating with the breed.

An ironic smile tugged at his cheek as he thought of what a strange qualification the latter would seem to any of those he had served with aboard His Majesty's vessels *Athene* and *Herrett*. But then, much had changed in that short time since Dalton had brought home what was left of *Herrett*, brought the limping wreck safely to fleet anchorage in New York

Bay after Captain Furney had been shot away with his helm in battle with a pair of privateers—a battle in which *Herrett* was betrayed and abandoned by the Crown warrant *Courtesan*.

Much had changed. Two days ashore and Dalton had found himself accused of treason against the king. The charge was groundless, but that mattered not. Treason in wartime . . . and he was Irish. He would never have lived to see a board of inquiry.

So, abruptly, Patrick Dalton, loyal young officer in His Majesty's Royal Navy, was a fugitive. His escape from New York aboard the stolen schooner *Faith* had sealed his fate. The charges now would be more than treason. *Faith*, simply trying to get away, had destroyed or damaged some seven times her own weight in King's vessels, not to mention the mayhem done to colonial vessels and one colonial port.

Dalton was a wanted man—by His Majesty's Admiralty and by the colonial authorities alike. He and all his *Faiths* with him. Fugitives. So those he signed on to be his crew must be fugitives as well. It was harshly ironic.

He turned to the boy at his heel. "What is your impression of this lot, Mister Caster?"

"Despicable, sir," Billy said honestly. "They should fit right in . . . eventually."

"Aye," Dalton nodded. "So they should."

Mismatched and misbegotten, they watched him with furtive eyes as he strode along their line, getting the taste of them and letting them take his measure as they would. Four among them—two a set of brothers—who wore the pigtail queue of British tars. Two others—a hulking giant of a man and a wiry little graybeard—with the remnants of king's uniforms for clothing. A Connecticut privateersman and a Virginia carpenter, a pair of red-Irish brothers from South Carolina who had sailed as merchant marine, and a Massachusetts youngster who had been their shipmate. He looked them over one by one, then

59

stood before them to say, "Each of you has made his mark and been attested. From this moment until released each of you is a *Mystery*."

The Englishmen glanced one at another, and the Americans looked various degrees of puzzled. The carpenter, Tower, a wiry young man with large hands, hesitated a moment, then asked, "We're a what, sir?"

"*Mystery*. It is the name of the vessel on which you will serve, at my command. I am Patrick Dalton. My clerk here is Mister Caster. These things you are to remember: *Mystery* shall be carrying cargo of unspecified nature, possibly without license and certainly without proper authority; second, you will have noticed that we here have various origins, and I shall expect you to remember that *Mystery* will attempt to remain aloof from both the present hostilities and the politics pertaining to them. We are neither British nor colonial, and neither man-of-war nor privateer. Nor are we a proper merchantman . . ."

"Beg pardon, sir," a hand went up in the rank. One of the red-Irish Colonials. "If we're not any of those things, then what are we, sir?"

Dalton pursed his lips, then answered, "We are a sailing vessel which shall try to make its way as unobtrusively as possible from one point to another, with cargo to earn its keep."

"Aye, sir."

"Point the third: I do not abide laxity aboard my ship." Behind him Billy Caster coughed. Dalton ignored him. "Are there any questions before we go aboard, then?"

The same hand went up again. "Sir, are we maybe smugglers, then?"

It was a fair question. "Quite possibly," he told them. "Our factor has not been very specific about our cargo. Does that possibility offend any of you?"

There was whispered conversation among them, and Dalton waited until it died down.

"Well?" he demanded.

The privateersman from Connecticut, Quinn, glanced at the others and then shook his head. "Smugglin's an honorable profession, sir, as all of us see it."

"Very well, then. Are there any other questions?"

One of the tars, a Fanshaw brother, raised a hesitant hand. "Ah, sir, you said we was about to go aboard. Aboard what, sir? There isn't a vessel anywhere about that we can see."

"*Mystery* is about twenty miles from here," Dalton explained. "We shall ride partway aboard a hay wagon, then walk the rest of it."

"Sir . . ." Billy Caster whispered behind him. "Sir, ask about rifles."

"Quite right, Mister Caster. You men, we have in our possession several of these American rifles, such as this lad is carrying. Do any of you know how to operate such weapons?"

Five hands went up, all American. But though not a tar among them knew how to use a rifle, several of them looked at the sleek contraption with curious interest. Once before, Billy Caster had developed a rifle company of British sailors. It looked as though he might have the opportunity again.

Dalton looked them over once more, then pointed to the aging ex-bosun. "You, Mister Tidy. March them off, and smartly. Mister Caster will show you the way."

They went single file, Dalton following, along the little road that was Queenstown's street, and many a curious eye watched them out of sight. The wagon waited beyond a bend, screened by forest. It had two mules and a white-haired old black man as driver— Ramsey's own servant, Colly.

The road was no more than a path beyond Queenstown, barely wide enough for a wagon, but Colly knew his business. They had proceeded two or three miles when he rounded a bend and reined in.

Ahead of them, lined across the road, were Hessian grenadiers. Dalton counted five of them, one wearing the abbreviated braid of a low-rate noncom—possibly a corporal.

Dalton swung down from the wagon and strode forward. The corporal barked at him and he turned and strode back to the wagon. "Does anyone here speak any of the German tongues?"

John Tidy stepped down. "Just a bit, sir. Can I help?"

"You can come and talk to this man and see what he wants."

"Aye, sir." Tidy went forward and entered into halting discussion with the Hessian. After a time he turned to Dalton. "This is Corporal Heinrich Wesselmann," he said. "These are some of his men. They have become separated from their unit and would like to know which direction is Philadelphia."

"Then tell them, Mister Tidy. And ask them to stand aside and let us pass."

"Aye, sir." Again Tidy conversed with the young soldier, pointing back toward the northwest. Finally the corporal barked at his men and they pulled back to stand beside the road.

"Thank you, Mister Tidy," Dalton said. "We can continue our journey now."

They climbed onto the wagon and Colly snapped the reins. After a moment or two Dalton looked back. The Hessians were not going away toward Philadelphia. They were following along behind the wagon, half a cable back.

"Mister Tidy, I understood you to say that those soldiers were trying to get to Philadelphia."

"Oh, no, sir," Tidy looked chagrined. "They only asked where it is, sir. They don't want to go there. That's where their unit is. The Fourth Grenadiers. They're lost and they want to stay lost. These five, they came to America to farm."

V

Titus Wilton had his bolts cut and his measures taken and had completed staysail, spritsail, jibsail, and spanker for the ketch. He and his mates were stitching courses when Victory Locke, setting stays in the vessel's sheered foretop, raised his head as movement caught his eye, then called below, "Ho the camp!"

Ishmael Bean, nearest at hand on shore, cupped his hands and tipped back his head. "What is it, Mister Locke?"

"Small craft on the channel!" Locke pointed. "Dead astern a mile or less!"

Claude Mallory and Purdy Fisk, dripping with sweat and odorous cleanings, scrambled up from the vessel's wide hold to peer past the stern rail. In the near distance the channel curved out of sight and they could see nothing as yet, but they cleaned their hands and hurried to the port shrouds to take up the rifles standing there.

On the near bank Bean and Cadman Wise picked up rifles of their own. Wise checked his prime and said, "Keep a watch here, Mister Bean. I'll slip off a way and see who it might be." A moment later he was gone among the brush.

Titus Wilton looked over his glasses with the air of

one abused and aggrieved. "Most certainly hostiles," he told his mates. "For our part, I believe we shall ignore them no matter who they are. We are here to outfit a vessel with sails, nothing more. Palm and needle, lads. Palm and needle . . . Quincy! Mind how you lap the cording at those clews! I'll not have a Wilton sail snapping unbound corners! Omer, go over there and tell those people on board that we need beeswax. Hurry along, now."

He stitched for a few moments more, then lifted his head to shout at the only crewman who seemed to be in the near vicinity, "You, there!"

Distracted, trying to watch the channel through a break in the forest screen, Ishmael Bean turned half toward him. "Sir?"

"Why is the blasted foremast on that vessel twice the size of the after?"

"Sir?"

"The foremast! Why is it . . ."

"*Mystery*'s a ketch, sir. She doesn't have a foremast. That tall one's the main. The short one's the mizzen."

"The main, then! Do you realize we'll have ninety-four feet of leech by the time we've done a course, a topsail, and a topgallant?"

"No, sir," Bean shrugged and turned away. "I certainly never did realize that."

"Barbarian," Wilton muttered. He adjusted the buckle on his "palm" and went back to his sewing.

Omer returned from the bank of the cut empty-handed. "They say they don't have the time right now to go in search of beeswax, Mister Wilton. They prefer to keep a watch on the channel until they find out who might be coming along."

"Barbarians," Wilton muttered again. The war was an annoyance and a nuisance to him. More than that, it had become a downright inconvenience.

Behind him, in the brush, he heard voices and the

64

thump and crunch of many feet on littered forest floor.

"Somebody else coming," Omer said as Ishmael Bean caught the sounds and turned to peer past them, upstream. Distinctly the sounds grew and blended with swishing and crackling of brush as men pushed through it.

"Unless their business has to do with sails," Wilton said, "they also are none of our concern."

"Getting a bit crowded out here, though," Quincy allowed.

"Mind what you're about," Wilton growled. "Palm and needle, palm and needle."

"Fresh meat," Patrick Dalton recited, pushing through thick underbrush. "Salt meat of any sort that men can palate, *pommes de terre*, milled oats, dried peas . . ."

"Moment, sir," Billy Caster interrupted, scribbling furiously as he followed his officer. ". . . Oats, dried peas . . . go ahead, sir."

"Vinegar," Dalton continued. "Juice of lemons, tea, loaf sugar and honey, allspice, shelled corn if it's to be had, onions, ah . . . let's add to the list a keg or two—make it three—of Jamaican rum and a bit of brandy."

"Brandy, sir?"

"Squire Ramsey isn't likely to stint on the cargo he expects us to haul. It's only proper that I not stint on the provisioning for the vessel that's to haul it. Shouldn't we be there by now?"

"Just ahead, sir."

Dalton turned to his ragged line of recruits. "Stand back from us a bit, lads, until we are recognized at our yards. I'd not care for any of you to be shot for strangers."

Almost before he had started on, Billy came out in

a deadfall clearing and stopped. "Mast sighted," he said. "Just there past those trees, sir."

Dalton stepped into the clear and squinted in the sunlight. A cable length away tall masts—top and gallant of one, top of a shorter one beyond—reared above the trees. The men had been busy aloft in his absence. Backstays were taut and trim, the high shrouds clear of debris; and the main topmast cap, with its crosstrees and spreaders, had been rebraced. Everywhere that he could see, cable and line was clean and showed no patching. The hold of the ketch apparently had yielded adequate cable to replace what was needed. Both masts were sheered of spars, their braces run out and lifts dangling from the hounds.

"The sailmaker must have arrived," Dalton noted. Leaving Billy to hold the new men there, he crossed the deadfall and the thicket beyond and stepped out in the camp clearing, inspecting as he did. Near at hand stood a tent with a wagon just beyond, and a pair of hobbled horses grazed at a distance. Just past the tent men sat cross-legged on great spreads of new canvas, sewing sails, and beyond them Mister Bean was shading his eyes, squinting at him. Dalton raised his arm in salute. "Ahoy the camp," he called. "Captain and ship's company reporting!"

Bean returned his salute and hurried toward him. "Glad you've made it back, sir. We've a watch on the channel. Small craft spotted from the tops. Mister Wise has gone to have a look, and now it sounds like people are chopping trees yonder."

Dalton glanced toward *Mystery*, noting the men aboard, armed with rifles. "Very good, Mister Bean. I'll hold your rifle while you walk off yonder and bring in Mister Caster and our new crewmen. Oh, and Mister Bean . . ."

"Sir?"

"Has there been word yet from Mister Duncan and

66

Mister Romart?"

"Nothin' yet, sir."

"Very well, Mister Bean. Carry on."

Bean handed him the rifle and entered the woods at a trot. Dalton cast an eye over the camp again, appraisingly, then returned the distant salutes of Victory Locke in the tops and Claude Mallory and Purdy Fisk on the deck of *Mystery*. The ketch floated nicely now, standing tall in the wilderness stream, dark striping on its wales indicating how much of its hull had been raised from the water. They had done a thorough job of pumping and sealing, he judged. The gunwales of the wide-bellied vessel were nearly four feet higher than they had been at uprighting.

From here at least, a'starboard of her, there was little evidence that the ketch had ever suffered damage, and he wondered again how she had come to be in this hidden place, derelict and abandoned. But then, there might be many such in this region. Chesapeake and its environs was a huge area of land and water, and a hundred casual encounters might have occurred during the passage of men-of-war and troopships to the landing below Philadelphia and back to sea.

The sailmakers had barely glanced at him, then returned to their labors, and he started toward them, then stopped and cocked his head. Distant and muted, but clear, he heard the ring of axes. Somewhere far off, toward the open bay, someone was chopping trees.

The sailmakers had canvas spread over what seemed to be at least an acre of ground, and were working as a team, a pair of sturdy young men steadily bending and seaming at the edges of great strips, binding on the cordage that would frame a large course—apparently the mainsail—while a stubby older man with a tricorn hat and glasses sat cross-legged on canvas where two cuttings adjoined, scooting himself backward a foot at a time as his busy hands gathered, paired, lapped, and stitched the strips to make one broad sail. Dalton felt a touch of real approval. He had watched sailmakers at work before, in the lofts at Dublin and at Serrey, and he saw the skill at hand here.

At his approach, the older man glanced around irritatedly, noting the field boots that he wore, and said, "Mind where you step! This is sailcloth, not a mudrug."

He stopped. Behind him he heard the voices and tread of the men entering the clearing, and the trot of Billy Caster coming to join him. The boy hurried to where he stood, started to say something, then stopped with his mouth open and squatted to peer at the cross-legged sailmaker, hunkering to see his face below his hat. When the man glanced up, Billy gasped and stood at smart attention. "Sir," he stammered. "Ah, sir, I didn't know . . . ah, is that really you, sir?"

The sailmaker stopped his stitching and looked up, over the tops of his spectacles. "I don't recall ever hearing a more ridiculous question," he growled. "Of course I am me. Who else would I be?"

Billy was still almost speechless. "But . . . but Doctor Franklin . . . I'd never heard that you made sail."

Dalton and the sailmaker both stared at the youth. "You know this man, Mister Caster?"

"Why yes, sir . . . I mean, well, no, I don't *know* him, but *everybody* knows Doctor Franklin, sir. I mean, in America, at least."

The sailmaker shook his head and got to his feet. "You must be the captain of yonder vessel that Squire Ramsey said I was to suit."

"Patrick Dalton," Dalton said.

"Aye. My name is Wilton. Titus Wilton. Firm of Wilton and Chesterfield, recently and—one hopes—

soon again of Philadelphia. Finest sailmakers this side of the . . ."

"You . . . you aren't Doctor Franklin?" Billy erupted, astonished.

"Absolutely not! It's only my misfortune that a gentleman who seemingly cannot concentrate on his chosen trade for getting involved in politics happens, some have said to my discredit, to resemble me. I've taken a cane to more than one on that account, young man."

"But . . ."

"That will do, Mister Caster," Dalton said. "Wilton, is it? My compliments, then, Mister Wilton. You are skilled at your craft, beyond question. How do we stand for sails at this moment?"

"Fore-and-afts are completed, one of each, and we've begun on the courses. Though why in the devil's name that mast is so tall, I'll never know. Do you realize, sir, that we'll be binding close upon a hundred feet of leech to the side just to suit out that one mast, much less the least one behind it?"

"Aft of it," Dalton said distractedly, his attention on several of his new recruits, who had parted company from the rest and now were standing about almost at his heels, gazing at Wilton. He turned to them. "You men are supposed to go with Mister Bean. He'll begin sorting you out, and I shall be along in a moment." Even as he said it he realized that the five of them were all colonials. The rest of the contingent had started toward the bank of the inlet, then paused, wondering why these had detoured.

"Aye, sir," one of the matched pair of Carolina red Irishmen said. "We just stopped to have a look at Doctor Franklin, sir."

From the distant tops Victory Locke's hail came. "Small craft coming up, sir!"

Dalton turned, shading his eyes, and a moment later a strange procession hove into view on the

69

channel. For a moment he hardly recognized the launch *Something*, with its heaped cargo and its pair of mounted chasers stem and stern. Two of those at oars were Charley Duncan and Michael Romart. The other two were naked Indians. In tow behind the launch was a small boat also heaped with cargo—a punt. And in the punt was Cadman Wise.

At sight of him Duncan stood and snapped a happy salute. Romart started to do the same, then hesitated and leaned to squint for a moment, then pointed and began talking excitedly to Duncan.

Dalton decided that Billy Caster was right. Everyone in the colonies apparently *did* know Doctor Franklin.

Romart's excited oratory stopped abruptly when he looked around again, and seemed to freeze in place for an instant before diving for his rifle and bringing it up. Dalton turned, then whirled back and raised his arms. "Hold your fire, Mister Romart! All hands stand down!"

Behind him five Hessian soldiers had come from the brush into the clearing. At sight of the distant Mister Romart with his rifle, four of them had snapped their muskets to their shoulders.

"Achtung!" the corporal roared at them in echo of Dalton's command. The word was followed by a fast flow of German imperative, and the soldiers grounded their muskets. Romart also had lowered his rifle, and everyone present except Indians and sailmakers came to abrupt attention when the monkeylike recruit John Tidy hauled a bosun's whistle from his blouse and shrilled a no-nonsense "To quarters."

Dalton sighed and shook his head. There was going to be a great deal of explaining required here, and after that a considerable amount of shaping up. "Thank you, Mister Tidy," he said. "Mister Bean, for the moment you have charge of the recruits. Please assemble them yonder by the bales. Mister Mallory,

70

please ask Mister Duncan to come ashore and stand by to report. Mister Tidy, if you please, step over there and see if you can determine what those Germans are doing here and why they have followed us this far. Mister Caster, be so good as to stop staring at Doctor Franklin and . . .''

"Wilton,'' the sailmaker snorted. "My name is Wilton, not Franklin!''

". . . at Mister Wilton, and see what logs and inventories are ready for my attention. Oh, and please ask Mister Locke to finish what he's doing in the tops yonder and come down. We shall want supper for . . .'' he counted rapidly, ". . . for thirty at two bells of the dogwatch.'' He turned to the sailmaker. "You will be needing your commission signed by me, I expect.''

"I certainly will.''

"Very well. Bring it around after supper and I shall inspect it. Did Squire Ramsey specify other than sails?''

"He specified a full suit of sails for your vessel and provisioning of your sail locker.''

"Amend that, please, on my authority. I shall want eighteen serviceable hammocks by close of dog-watch.''

"Hammocks?''

"Yes, sir. For men to sleep upon. Mister Duncan will see to the placement of them . . . ah. Here he is now.'' Charley Duncan was hurrying across the clearing, his shoes sloshing and his stockings and breeches wet to the hips. "Mister Duncan, did you and Mister Romart have a pleasant voyage in our launch?''

"Aye, sir. We . . .''

"You have returned with more vessels than you set out with.''

"Aye, sir. We . . .''

"And a pair of Indians.''

71

"Aye, sir. They . . ."

"Would it please you to make your report now, Mister Duncan?"

"Aye, sir. I believe it would. We ran afoul of a gilling string, so we had to retrieve some twine for the Indians and we found where some people are outfitting a snow, sir, and . . ."

"Yonder, Mister Duncan. I believe I should sit in my chair while we unravel this."

"Aye, sir." He hurried off, following his limping captain, and Billy Caster turned to the sailmaker. "Pardon, Doctor . . . ah, Mister Wilton. Close of dogwatch means eight of the clock this evening. That would be eight bells, but we don't have a bell yet. Not unless Mister Duncan has acquired one somewhere."

It was a tired and aching Patrick Dalton who sat by lantern light near four bells of the evening watch—first watch, they had taught him in His Majesty's Navy, though to the Irish mind *evening watch* was the better term—rubbing tired eyes as he read again through the stack of papers that Billy Caster had handed him "in rough." Later, he knew, the boy would rescribe everything "in fine" as fit his meticulous notion of how his captain wanted—or at least *should* want—his command to perform. He probably would be awake now, working on a stump with a lantern at his elbow, had Dalton not sent him packing off to sleep when the first hammocks were strung.

In *Mystery*'s now-dry interior they had found a fair amount of provision and stowage, most of it still usable. The ordinary contents of sail lockers and chain lockers, of galley and bins and ship's hold of a working colonial merchantman. No cargo was aboard except for a salt-water–soaked bale of tobacco wedged against a stanchion. But there was cable and line, a pair of windlasses and a working capstan, and a ton or more of various tools and fittings meant for repair of a sailing vessel between ports. Some of the stores had been fouled by immersion, but soaking in salt or brack did no harm to barrels of salt meat and casks of water.

And the mystery of *Mystery* was no longer quite such a mystery. A scrap of jotting from the stern cabin told what had happened to her. She had run afoul of British troopships and taken a ball along her portchannel. Its impact had dislodged her chainplate below the main shrouds and warped her wales to open her hull. What had become of her crew was fairly obvious. They had decided she was sinking and had abandoned ship, taking everything they could.

From there, only God knew what her course had been. But some kind tide or errant wind had shunted her into this hidden channel, where there was mud beneath her keel by the time she filled and settled.

He set the lists aside and looked again at the revised crew list that Billy had made for him. Counting the nine remaining fugitives from *Faith*— himself and Billy included—and his new recruits from the Queenstown docks, *Mystery*'s complement now numbered twenty. Ample for the sailing of a ninety-four-foot ketch along the trade lanes. Ninety-four feet of length—deck and hold—yet the ketch was no larger a vessel than the schooner *Faith* had been. Only where *Faith* had been all legs, *Mystery* was all hull. She existed for the delivery of goods . . . and now, maybe, to give a mix of fugitives some distance from the centers of the war.

Twenty seamen. Himself as captain, Charley Duncan as first, ten other ables, an experienced bosun in John Tidy, a master at arms, a pair of gunners, a carpenter, and two ordinaries who had sailed before. He had done with worse.

And then there were the two Indians that Mister Duncan had found and, as first officer, had promised berths aboard. What could he do with two aborigines

73

aboard a sailing vessel? He could barely understand the English they spoke, though Mister Duncan seemed not to have such problems about it. Duncan had made a deal of explaining his own youthful visits to Picadilly Circus and such haunts, but Dalton still found it difficult to decipher such phrases as "'wa'd 'e soy?" and "Gi' 'm blee'n 'ell 'ey di'." It did, though, *almost* sound like English.

Possibly they could serve as ordinaries. It would be up to Mister Duncan to train them—and to shepherd their bows and arrows into the small arms locker.

Twenty-two, then.

And then there were the Hessians. Through Mister Tidy, Corporal Heinrich Wesselmann had petitioned him for passage . . . to any point of his choosing where there wasn't a war being fought at the moment and where five young farmers might begin to seek a place where there was soil to be tilled.

The thought came unbidden, a random question as to whether Mister Hoop as master at arms might make temporary marines of a hand of Hessians for the duration of their voyage to wherever John Singleton Ramsey had a mind for them to go.

There was much to think out, much to plan, and much to do. And all of it revolved around the need to—as honorably as possible—dodge the war here in the colonies and wait for a chance to clear his name.

He would like to have a clear name. There were things he might discuss with Constance Ramsey . . . if his honor and his name were ever again intact so that he could.

Patrick Dalton fell asleep in the shingle chair, and when the air turned chill, Billy Caster crept from his hammock to cover his captain with a quilt and to blow out the lamp beside him.

VI

General Sir William Howe's occupation of Philadelphia was complete. Cornwallis held the American strongholds on the right flank, von Knyphausen's Germans had broken the colonial center at Chad's Ford, and Washington was in retreat with nearly 10,000 colonial regulars. Philadelphia was in Crown hands. The ships of Admiral Lord Richard Howe had returned to the Delaware to clear that waterway, the final preparation for the planned campaign of his brother William up the Hudson River. It was imperative now that the New England rebels be isolated from their southern allies, and in the north Burgoyne waited on Lake Champlain. Though weakened by Benedict Arnold's makeshift "navy" at Valcour Island, Burgoyne yet held the northern ways and the Howes prepared their assault northward as Cornwallis pursued Washington and Sullivan toward New Jersey.

Lord Richard Howe's attempts at reconciliation had failed, and now Lord North's ultimatum was in effect: crush the rebels—hold the south and concentrate on the north. So from Chesapeake and Delaware Bay the theater of war pressed northward, a jaw to close against the jaw of Burgoyne along the Hudson.

And now began the mopping-up of operations

south of Philadelphia—shore patrols to sweep the tidewater lands, cruisers to hold the Delaware, and squadrons to prowl offshore.

For the privateer Lostrato and the pirate Pinto, maintaining uneasy truce aboard the battered Spanish prize *Columbine*, it was a fleeing colonial merchantman that brought about decision. Prowling offshore south of Chesapeake, they awaited signal from Lostrato's agent ashore, a scavenger named Clive Hensey. Hensey was to have scouted Chesapeake for prey and got word to Lostrato when he found it, for which Hensey would have shared in the prize. But no word came. Days passed, and *Columbine* crept again and again to within sight of Cape Henry. Twice Pinto saw sails emerging from the great bay, running to sea, each time clear and beyond his reach, but the Cape Henry shoreline showed them no flags by day nor lights by night.

Hensey should have told them of those vessels before they cleared. Both could have been prizes, had *Columbine* been upwind and had the weather gauge on them when they emerged.

"Something has happened to your agent," he told Lostrato finally. "It is time we proceed my way."

And Lostrato had no argument, because it was clear that Hensey had failed.

So Pinto took command and did not hesitate to grin his satisfaction at the sullen aristocrat whom he had come to hate. Once again *Columbine* beat northward to the waters off Cape Henry, and maneuvered there through a morning until sails were sighted coming down with the wind and Pinto made the vessel to be a Colonial sloop, heavy-laden and lightly armed. A good enough beginning. *Columbine* tacked outward, cutting off the sloop's route southward, and the sloop responded. Too small to brave the vagaries of the far sea in this uncertain season, the little merchantman chose the only escape open to it. It made for the mouth of Chesapeake, trusting its slim hull and fore-and-aft sails to escape the predator up the bay.

"We will take that one," Pinto decided. "You, Torero! Take the helm. Hands to sheets! Come about, Torero. Through the wind. Raise that jibsail! Raise flying jib! Hands to the fore, reef that course! May you all be damned, this is a brigantine, not a mud scow! Trim those staysails!" With Torero at the helm he strode along the deck, sword in hand, laying about with the flat of it to enforce his commands. "Sheet home main staysail! Haul that line, there is slack! Cleat in, curse you! Now, sheet home that maintop staysail! Trim your spritsail to the wind!"

He raised welts and drew blood, but in moments the sullen *Columbine* was trimmed to a tight tack, heading into Chesapeake on a course almost parallel to that of the fleeing sloop.

"It will be a slow and tedious chase," Lostrato said dryly. "You have more press of sail, Pinto, but not better sail for this wind."

"Let it be as long as is needed," the pirate growled. "He has nowhere to go. And if he scurries like the mouse, then I will be the cat that plays with him. Who knows?" He rubbed his whiskers thoughtfully, "Maybe the squeal of the mouse will bring more mice out of their holes."

"And if there are warships up there ahead?"

"If there were warships there, our mouse would never have chosen this path. He likes the British no better than he likes us, Don Geraldo."

Ian McCall was one of those who could not return to Philadelphia—or to any city or port now where the flag of England flew. Like the delegates to the fateful Congress the year before, like Generals Washington, Sullivan, and Wayne, like Patrick

Henry and John Boyle and Nathan Hale, like the silversmith Paul Revere and the lumberman Jeremiah O'Brien and the tactician Artemas Ward, like these and nearly three thousand others, Ian McCall was a wanted man with only a revolution standing between himself and Crown justice.

The king's ministers had a list of names, and those on the list faced death if taken. The trade road from Philadelphia to Baltimore had been jammed with refugees from the moment it was learned that troop ships were approaching Head of Elk, and many of the evacuating parties had organized guard companies for escort. McCall, already proscribed for his activities in the launching of colonial privateers, had arranged such a company and shared its safety with such associates and their families who also fled the imminence of invasion. The households of George Burton, John Singleton Ramsey, Henry Thomely, and a dozen others of the merchant community that stretched from Philadelphia to Wilmington and South Point had joined him—wives and children, servants and retainers, all of those the merchant gentlemen wanted to see safe . . . to Baltimore at least, or if necessary to Elizabeth Town or Martinsburg or places beyond. None knew what battle lines the Patriot forces might hold, or where the British muskets might appear.

McCall had seen his party safely to Baltimore and arranged for further passage if it was necessary. But now the squadrons had withdrawn from Chesapeake to bolster the fleets on the Delaware and at New York, and Ian McCall had paced the grounds of Tarleton House as long as he could stand. He feared for his investments and his properties in Philadelphia, and he feared for those projects scattered here and there about the tidewater lands—principally the three hidden shipyards where craft were being readied that could win back for him the fortunes he had lost, and

78

more besides. He itched to go and see how they fared, and on a gray day he saddled a fine mount and set out to make a tour.

At Annapolis, he found abandoned yards and a message awaiting him. There had been a skirmish with German mercenaries, and his crew there had moved the two cutters down to Cole's Bend, where there was less chance of their being found and taken. Above Marlboro, work was nearing completion on the brig *Porphyry*, her guns in place, her rigging tested and her fresh sails even then being bent on. But there was concern. Each day brought fresh sightings of troops in the forest and along the roads, and *Porphyry* had no commander to take her out to sea. McCall made a decision. The brig was ready to go to work, but the word from Cole's Bend was that the snow *Fury* would require a few more weeks of preparation to make her right.

What crew was ready at Marlboro he put aboard *Porphyry* in the charge of a veteran bosun, while he sent men to Cole's Bend to bring back *Fury*'s assigned commander and such men as he required. Solon Hays was a good man and a capable commander. Rather than the snow, he could command the brig, and would be glad to have his waiting ended. There would be another who could take command of *Fury* when the snow was ready to embark.

McCall waited there long enough to see the transfers made, and shook hands with Hays at the dock where *Porphyry*'s launch awaited him. "For God and country, Solon," he said. "Go among them where you find them and see what sort of dent you can make in His Majesty's damned trident. Have your sport and enjoy your ship . . . and be mindful of the choice prizes. I count on you to make this war profitable for both of us."

From Marlboro, McCall slipped across to the fields outside Queenstown and made his way from there by back roads to John Singleton Ramsey's estate at Eagle's Head. Twice he saw patrols, and learned from a planter that Admiral Lord Richard Howe's fleet was anchored off Chester, preparing to mount campaigns against the American defenses on the Delaware below Philadelphia. The colonials had blocked the river at Billingsport with pilings and had a redoubt on the Jersey shore overlooking the blockade.

Battles were in the offing, the man reckoned, for no man on the Delaware now favored making it easy for Black Dick to supply his brother's army at Philadelphia.

McCall did not welcome the news. The only thing a redoubt and a row of steel-tipped stakes could buy was a bit of time, and when Billingsport fell, so would Fort Mercer above it. Mercer, he knew had only fourteen guns. He himself had supplied them.

At Eagle's Head he made his signal, then waited near the smokehouse until Ramsey came along.

The squire verified all that he had heard, and added more.

The lads holding the Delaware would put up a brave fight, Ramsey assured him, but it was only a delay. Their only real hope was to give General Washington the time he needed to clear a route of retreat from Philadelphia toward the Hudson.

And while Ramsey talked, McCall gazed at the merchant with a slight, quizzical smile playing at his lips. "I swear, John," he said finally, "Did I not know you so well I'd almost believe you have become partisan in this affair. It strikes me that you speak as a patriot might."

"No such thing," Ramsey growled. "I am a businessman, Ian. It doesn't serve my interests to take sides. Oh, I am aware that Admiral Howe considers me at least a liberal, if not an outright Whig . . . and that there may be a few among the Continental lot that whisper that I am a conservative, if not an outright Tory. I go my own way and try not to be involved. You know that."

"Aye," McCall grinned. "And send your daughter to Baltimore with the escaping Congress and rebels like myself. Does it never bother you, John, to be such an old fraud?"

"Not in the slightest. How is my daughter? I trust she is behaving herself."

"With difficulty, yes. The lass is much like her father, it seems to me. Hardheaded as the day is long."

"Well do I know that," Ramsey admitted. "Whim of iron, she has."

"And the young man she is so taken with? Your pet fugitive?"

"He's well hidden and thoroughly occupied for the moment. I am financing him in a venture."

McCall pursed his lips. "I can think of only one sort of venture to suit a fugitive British seaman in this land at the moment. Bit of smuggling, perchance, John?"

Ramsey looked pained. "At the moment, he is simply reclaiming a derelict vessel that looked to him as though it might be put to use."

"With your help."

"Well, it keeps him out of trouble for a time."

"And you will no doubt find a use for such a vessel."

"Possibly," Ramsey shrugged. "This isn't a time for hulls to lay idle, Ian. And I might have a bit of cargo here and there, you know."

"Aha!" McCall shook a knowing finger. "Just as I said. A bit of smuggling."

"If you call it that, it still is better than piracy, friend McCall. Oh, yes, I've heard about your own ventures in the secret places on Chesapeake. Men-of-war . . . for commercial purposes? I'd rather trade commodities delivered in the hold of a merchantman than iron shot delivered from the mouths of great guns. The taking of ships might be considered unseemly in some circles."

"Piracy is one thing," McCall wagged a finger at his host. "Privateering is quite another. Such ventures are of service to the federation. How else are we to sprout a navy to defend ourselves?"

"Acts of war," Ramsey looked down his nose. "Call it what you will."

McCall finished his grog and licked his lips appreciatively. "I call it the twin duties of a patriot," he shrugged. "To harass the King's fleet, and to make a profit while one is about it. And while we're on that subject, if the cargo I suspect you are about to ship from Chesapeake is what I truly believe it is, then my dear old friend, you are far more of a fraud in your guise of neutrality than ever even I suspected."

"In that case I won't ask what you suspect my cargo is, because I don't care to discuss it. And for your part, my rebel friend, I'd like to know that you are well clear of the roads in this neighborhood before darkness falls. The patrols come out at night of late. Please give my regards to those in Baltimore, and if Patrick Henry is there, you might tell him that the arrangements we discussed with the gentlemen to the south are satisfactory and are being made."

"I shall do that," McCall assured him. They shook hands then, and Ramsey signaled for Colly to have a look at the roads while he helped McCall tighten his saddle cinch and load his provisions.

When McCall was mounted he turned his horse toward the wilderness trail, waved, and started off, calling back, "I'll tell Constance that you are alive and well and give her your regards."

"Obliged," Ramsey called. "But for God's sake don't mention to her about Dalton or the . . ." But it was too late. McCall was gone.

Through the day a crisp breeze had blown cool and clean beneath a sunny sky. But now with evening it stilled, and mists of autumn rose in the valleys and on the waters around—mists that would be fog by nightfall. And in the stillness was the rumble of distant thunder. John Singleton Ramsey sighed as he walked back to the house. The sound was not thunder, he knew, for he had heard it often enough in recent months. It was the sound of guns on the Delaware—guns that had thundered on Chesapeake just weeks before as the White Fleet carried troops toward Head of Elk, and that now thundered on the Delaware to open the channel for the supplying of those same troops now occupying Philadelphia.

In the quiet of a lantern-lit study he read the reports brought in by messengers from Chestertown and Joppa. His barges were loaded and would be moving as soon as it was dark. By morning they would be assembled above the cut where Patrick Dalton was repairing his ketch.

He hoped the Irishman had his vessel ready to sail with the noon tide. The barges could not afford to wait. If they were discovered . . . he didn't want to think about that. But there was too much at stake to allow delay. Six barges carrying cargo for the ketch. Five of the six carried the guns that would be the teeth of a fortification on the Carolina coast—guns that would fire fifty-pound balls, eight inches in diameter, burning twenty pounds of powder with each shot. Guns that might hold a cotton and tobacco port against British men-of-war well enough and long enough to give the colonies trading power in their bid for alliance with France.

McCall was right, he thought . . . at least after a fashion. Right about him being a fraud. "Right now," he muttered to himself, "I am elbows-deep in

Patroit partisanship, supplying guns to be used against the king.''

As mists rose above the mirror-calm waters of Chesapeake, Purdy Fisk crouched on the trestletrees rigged high in the branches of a red oak and kept a watch on the bay. The clearing away of branches facing the water had been Michael Romart's idea, for a lookout point. The rigging of trestletrees from the cut limbs had been an embellishment added by Charley Duncan, who considered it beneath the dignity of any sailor to sit in a tree unless a proper ship's platform were rigged there.

Fisk had seen three sets of sails during his watch, the first two almost on the horizon, far down the bay—twenty miles, he reckoned, at least, for he had seen only tops or royals. The third suit of sails had appeared closer at hand, but still a good twelve miles downbay. His glass told him no details except that the vessel carried new sailcloth, gleaming in the last sunlight, and might be a brig.

They were all still out there, of course, all becalmed and waiting for a breeze. So they were of little concern. What held his attention now was movement nearer at hand, creeping large forms a few miles northwest, that seemed to be coming toward him. No masts could he see, and thus he had no definition of distance, but they were distinct dark shadows in the mist, and once he thought he heard the creaking of a capstan winch far away.

He watched for nearly an hour as evening shadows deepened toward night, and decided that whoever was out there definitely was coming toward him. A zephyr that touched the fog and drew tendrils from it brought him another sound as well. Distinctly, though far off, he heard the sound of oars in their mountings, then a splash, then again the creaking of a winch, and he knew how they were proceeding. Whatever they were, they had small boats operating ahead of them, carrying grapples to drop at cable length so that those aboard could winch themselves ahead that much at a time.

He eased himself around on the platform and looked down, starting to call an order. Then he hesitated. There was no one on the ground below. There should have been an Indian waiting there. Charley Duncan had given up on trying to teach the aborigines a fast lesson in splicing line and had set them as messengers for lookout. One of them was supposed to be right there at the base of the lookout tree.

"Bloody savage," Fisk growled. "Where in hell did he get off to?"

Directly below a shadow moved, and suddenly Fisk saw the Indian clearly. He would have sworn there was no one there.

The voice that came from below was harsh. "Mind 'oo 'ee cawl nimes, 'en. Wad' ee wan'?"

"Go tell Cap'n there's vessels broad on my starboard, might be the barges he's wantin'."

"Soy wa'?"

"Never mind. Just go get th' bleedin' captain!"

The shadow moved again and was gone, and Fisk muttered to himself, "I never been one to get persnickety about the company I keeps . . . but I may change my ways about that."

Minutes passed, then more minutes, and shadows came from the misty brush below. A familiar voice called, "Who is that up there?"

"It's me, Cap'n. Purdy Fisk. In the tops, as ye might say."

"Very well, Mister Fisk. What is your sighting?"

"Sails down bay, sir. Three ships becalmed, a good bit off. And small craft approachin' on cable winches off yonder a few miles."

"Whereaway, Mister Fisk, and how many?"

"Broad a'starboard, sir. Uh, I expect that would be north by northwest. Can't get a count, sir, but there may be four or five. Might be barges, sir."

"Very well, Mister Fisk. I shall send up a hooded lantern for you. The signal we want to see is three and three. If they make that signal, you may respond and guide them in."

"In, sir? Into the channel?"

"Just inside the mouth of it, Mister Fisk. If those are proper barges out there, we'd not have room upwater to step their cargo aboard to the hold. If these are our barges, we shall just have to come out to meet them."

"Aye, sir. Ah . . . sir, if there's wind by morning, those becalmed vessels will be moving. Two of them were inbound, sir, and *Mystery* has no guns."

"If those barges are ours, part of their cargo is to be deck guns and powder and shot. Stand your watch, Mister Fisk. I shall leave you a runner as before."

"Aye, Cap'n. Ah . . . maybe one of th' lads, sir? Those red savages don't . . ."

"Wa' yer mouf 'ere, Dingum," the shadow beside Dalton growled. "'Sna caw t'at!"

"Please speak civilly, Mister Fisk," Dalton said. "Pitacoke will do nicely here."

"Aye, sir."

Dusk faded to dark, the mists rose into the lower branches of the oak and obscured moonlight silvered a low skim of clouds overhead. Except for the utter calm and the rough bark at his back, Purdy Fisk might have believed that he did indeed crouch in the tops of a proper rig and that what was below him was a deck and not the soil of a wilderness forest. It comforted him to think that. The world, he found, made more sense from a mast top than from most other places. Once or twice he glanced down, but then he stopped doing that. He knew the Indian was there, and it didn't seem right somehow that the heathen should be able to become invisible at will.

At four bells he half dozed, then came awake with a start at the winking of a light in the mist not far away. The signal was repeated, three and three, and he leaned over the edge of the trestletrees to call, "On th' ground! You, redskin! Be ye there?"

The answer was so near at hand that he almost fell in turning. The Indian, Pitacoke, sat on a tree limb not an arm's length away, a shadow in the muted darkness.

"What are ye doin' up here, then?" Fisk demanded.

"Fog's u'," the Indian said. "Cawn' see f' na 'ere."

"Well, go down again, and tell 'em th' barges is here! Look lively, now!"

"Kee' y' shir' on, Dingum," Pitacoke assured him. "'moff." Silent as a cat's shadow he turned, lowered himself to a branch farther down, ran along it, and disappeared in the fog beneath.

Fisk uncovered his lantern, pointed it, and raised its shade, responding to the three-and-three. A moment later the signal came again, and he heard the sound of oars in the mist, followed by a splash, a muted shout, and the creak of a winch. The barges were coming.

VII

Those not on deck watch or camp guard had managed three hours' sleep when Charley Duncan and John Tidy rousted them out. It was time to break camp and prepare *Mystery* to be towed on the tide.

It was not a smooth operation, all things considered. Among sixteen members of the company who were qualified, able seamen, only one or two had a notion of how to break a camp in an orderly fashion, and of those remaining—five Hessians, two Indians, a Virginia carpenter, a pair of South Carolina ordinaries, and the hulking Mister Hoop— only Hoop had any real knowledge of what went where aboard a proper vessel.

And to make matters worse, Titus Wilton stamped and fumed as they loaded his precious canvas and tools aboard the ketch, and refused to board himself until Dalton suggested that he might have Mister Hoop carry him aboard across his shoulder.

"I am a sailmaker," he protested at the top of his lungs, glaring over his spectacles. "I work *on* ships, sir, not *aboard* them."

"You work on contract, sir," Dalton corrected him. "Your present contract is to provide a suit for *Mystery*, and that requires your presence where *Mystery* is located . . . which from this point forward

89

is a variable location. Therefore you will have to work aboard."

"I didn't agree to a cruise!"

"Mister Hoop . . ."

"Never mind! Quincy! You two, see that my wagon gets safely home. Tell them that I have been forcibly detained aboard a merchant vessel and shall be back at the earliest opportunity." He stalked toward the waiting boat, muttering. A step behind, laden with gear and towering over him, was Mister Hoop.

By lanterns ashore and lanterns aboard, they transferred the woodland camp onto the crowded deck of *Mystery*, leaving her gaping hold free for cargo. Then when the ketch was aweigh in the channel and the rowers were at their oars aboard *Something*, Dalton poled out on one of the rafts, climbed to the mainshroud channel and was piped aboard by Mister Tidy. He returned the ragged salutes of the ship's company and stepped to the deck.

He cast a practiced eye over the pinrails and fiferail, and squinted upward into the standing rigging of the ship. Dim lantern light showed little of what was there, though he knew exactly. Yet as a display of propriety he asked, "What sail has been bent on, Mister Duncan?"

"All that's ready, sir," Duncan stood stiff and formal to respond. "Stays'l, jibs'l, sprits'l, and fore-and-afts on main and mizzenmasts. We're rigged jib an' jigger, sir."

"Very well, Mister Duncan. Mister Locke, how stands the helm?"

"Lash for tow, sir."

"Thank you, Mister Locke. Please stand by the helm. Mister Tidy, spotters to the maintops, if you please."

"Aye, sir. Mister Mallory and Mister Wise, aloft for tow watch."

They were shadows against the night as they swarmed up the mainshrouds, heading for the maintop and topmast spreaders. Aft, Victory Locke reached the helm and called, "Helm station, sir!"

"Stern sheets, Mister Tidy. Raise your mizzen gaff."

"Aye, sir. Hands a'deck, loft the spanker!"

Blocks rattled aloft and spar-rings rattled as the mizzen gaff crawled upward, carrying its sail with it. Its stirrup snugged home below the mizzen top, and Tidy called, "Peak aloft, outhaul, sheets home!" The sail spread below its gaff, snapped full out, and hung motionless in the dead calm of night.

"Hands afore, raise your jibs'l!"

Grommets sang as the batwing triangle ran up its stay and its sheetline was hauled amidships. Like the mizzen driver, it barely fluttered, then hung taut, a pale wing against the darkness.

Dalton surveyed the deck, approving. All the maneuvers had been crisp and efficient. Of course, everything that had been done in the past few minutes had been done by experienced seamen—all except the bosum, John Tidy, former *Faiths* and accustomed to working as a team. It was how he had instructed it be done, to give the rest a look at how things were supposed to work aboard his vessel. He would have little enough opportunity to shape up a crew from this motley lot, and every chance for them to learn by observation was important.

"Set your rowers to rowing, Mister Duncan," he said. "I should like us to be shipping cargo aboard by first light. Come with me, Mister Caster." He started toward the stern. "You may begin your log as of six bells of the midwatch. Mister Hoop! Please station your Hessians . . . ah, your *marines* . . . at the starboard gunnels amidships. They can help with the loading."

"Aye, sir!" A moment later, Hoop had the five

grenadiers backed against the main fiferail, roaring at them in a voice that might carry for miles. Dalton turned. *"Mister Hoop!"*

"Aye, sir?"

"They don't speak English, Mister Hoop. They won't understand, no matter how loudly you shout at them. Simply show them, Mister Hoop."

"Aye, sir."

The interlude had given him another thought. "Mister Duncan?"

From amidships, "Aye, sir?"

"Where are your Indians, Mister Duncan?"

"I don't know, sir. Moment, please."

The ship shuddered and began to move sluggishly as rowers in the launch ahead bent to their oars.

"Astern!"

"Yes, Mister Duncan?"

"Found the Indians, sir. They went aloft with Mistery Mallory and Mister Wise."

"Then get them back down here, if you please! Give them something to occupy their time."

"Aye, sir."

Dalton strode past Victory Locke, standing alertly by the lashed helm, and ran his fingers along the crisp foot of the inert mizzen sail just above his head. A hundred thoughts tumbled through his mind, sorting themselves into working order. "Mister Caster, enter those who have been assigned duties as of now, then work out a watch schedule to begin effect when our cargo is aboard."

"Aye, Captain."

"Also, have your roster of ship's company ready for a general muster on my call, and have an oilskin prepared to receive ship's credentials and cargo manifests."

"Aye, sir."

"How fares the day, Mister Caster?"

Billy raised his head, looking around. It had

become a game with them, this constant teaching by the captain of the nuances of seamanship. "Tide's up and ebbing, sir. Wind calm. Mist to the maintop and an overcast aloft. At the glass, sir, six bells of the midwatch."

"And how shall it turn, Mister Caster?"

"Light wind by morning watch, sir. North coming northeast by midday, five to seven knots."

"And what makes you think that, Mister Caster?"

"Because that's what it has done the past two mornings, sir, and there's no change in temperature that I can tell."

"Good reasoning, Mister Caster, but I wager the wind will rise to ten."

"How so, sir?"

"Look aloft again. Do you see where the moon has risen above those trees a'port? There seems to be a circle around it, do you see? Well, it's held that a circle around the moon means a change in the weather. Some even say there are ice crystals forming up there, to cause that sight as a prism throws a rainbow. Watch for such things, Billy, for it is by such signs that a sailor can read in sea and sky not just what is, but what may yet be."

Mystery was making better time now, her inertia overcome by the rowers in the launch. She crept along in the dark, forest-walled channel with ripples whispering against her hull.

"Do you know yet what our cargo will be, sir?"

"No, except that I warrant it will be something to make me wonder whether it was wise to deal with Squire Ramsey in the first place. The man has it in his nature to be a scoundrel, and it's only his better instincts that hold him in check."

"Aye, sir. And possibly Miss Constance."

"Yes, possibly Miss Constance as well." He watched the shadowy banks creep past, felt the soft tug-tug-tug of the vessel's motion, a gentle rhythm in time with the gurgle of the rowers' oars ahead. Seven bells of the midwatch, he calculated. Half past three in the morning. It would be five of the clock before they reached the mouth of the cut, beyond which were the opening waters of Chesapeake. "Find a hammock now, Mister Caster, and get a bit of sleep. We shall be busy with first light."

Hammocks had been slung in the forecastle and along the port gunwales, several of them occupied now by men not otherwise needed. Billy yawned and went off to find an unoccupied bed.

Charley Duncan came aft with his pair of errant Indians and sat them atop the little deck house just a'fore of the mizzenmast. "St'y 'ere, 'en," he commanded them, then walked to the stern rail to approach the captain. "I believe those aborigines will make topmen, sir. They climb like very monkeys."

Dalton considered it. The tops were a good starting point for young sailors, though certain skills were involved beyond native ability to climb and not fall. "Can you teach them to reef, Mister Duncan? And the difference between buntlines and leech lines?"

"Aye, sir, I think so. We had a bit of instruction when I went up to get them, and I believe they learn fast."

"Can you teach them to speak English so the rest of us can understand them?" A topman would likely draw lookout, and Dalton wasn't ready for signals from aloft that sounded as though the caller's tongue had been sewn to his teeth.

"Might take a bit of doin', sir," Duncan grinned, his teeth a brightness in the murk. "But I'll work on it. They seem good lads, sir, for all of bein' heathen savages."

"Very well, Mister Duncan. Tell them to find hammocks now, and get a bit of sleep . . . and make it clear that they are to do nothing which might soil the hammocks."

"Aye, sir. I believe Indians put themselves to sleep very much as white men do, though." He went forward to the deck house, sent his charges off to bed, and returned, followed by the bosun. "Will you want Mister Locke relieved to begin breakfast, sir?"

"I think not." Dalton had found his shingle chair near the coaming, stacked atop a heap of camp provisions. Now he righted it, set it on deck near the helm, and retrieved a quilt from the tarp-covered bedding stack by the after rail. He wrapped the quilt around his shoulders and sat. "I believe we should assign Mister O'Riley as ship's cook."

By the helm, Victory Lock glanced around, his expression pained even in the dim light of the running lamp.

"Mister Riley is an ordinary," Dalton added. "We've a full complement now, and I'd rather not waste a good able seaman on galley duty."

Locke squared his shoulders and seemed content.

"Which Mister Riley, sir?" Duncan asked. "You brought us two of them."

"It doesn't matter. Neither is any more a cook than Mister Locke. Just pick one of them and ask him to prepare breakfast. I assume the stores are in the galley."

"Aye, sir. Not sorted, but they're dumped there. I reckon he can make something out of the mess."

"Ask him to brew some tea while he is sorting, if you please."

"Aye, sir."

"Mister Tidy, please bring in your rowers for their rest and put fresh hands aboard that launch. We've a way yet to go. And when we reach the mouth of the cut, send the punt out to fetch Mister Fisk. I shall want his report directly he is aboard."

"Aye, sir. Ah, sir, if you please . . ."

"Yes?"

"Those square heads over there . . ."

"Hessians, Mister Tidy."

"Yes, sir. Those Hessians over there by the starboard rail, Mister Hoop is having some difficulty keeping them keen on standing watch there, what with the fog and nothing to see. If you've no use for them at the moment, I could have them help Mister O'Riley get things in order in the galley, sir."

"Very good, Mister Tidy. But when we sight our cargo barges, I shall need the marines at station."

"Aye, sir."

"On deck!" The call was from aloft.

Dalton squinted, peering upward into the darkness. "Yes, Mister Mallory?"

"Light ahead, sir. Above the mist."

"Very well, Mister Mallory. Keep a sharp eye for Mister Fisk. Report to Mister Tidy when we have him broad a'port."

"Aye, sir."

The launch with its punt guns swung around and came alongside, and its sweating crew clambered aboard to be replaced by other hands; then it took the lead again, the hawser went taut, and *Mystery* continued her creeping journey down the widening cut.

Patrick Dalton, wrapped in a quilt, sat in his shingle chair waiting for his tea and worrying about what John Singleton Ramsey had waiting to go into *Mystery*'s hold.

At eight bells of the midwatch Purdy Fisk's lantern was dead ahead, and by first bell of the morning watch it was broad on the port and coming abeam. The rowers belayed their efforts, and *Mystery* rested dead still as Michael Romart and Talmadge Fanshaw set off in the punt to retrieve their one-man shore party.

Safely aboard again, Fisk set his lantern on the deck house and sought out the captain. "Six barges, sir. Just off there where the . . . well, where you'd see the brushy spit was you up in that tree. I expect tops can see the place. Gentleman in charge is a trader name of Gwinn, delivers goods for Squire Ramsey. One of the barges is stores and tack for *Mystery*, sir. They brought four six-pounders for us, sir, two long and two short. And a swivel gun. The other barges is cargo."

"Sixes." Dalton considered it. He had hoped for something a bit more authoritative. "Well, sixes are far better than remaining naked as we are now. Thank you, Mister Fisk. Did the gentleman say what the cargo is?"

"Yes, sir. Guns, he said. Batteries. That's all he felt obliged to tell me, sir, but he urged you rig preventer tackle on the lower masts, off-side from your shipping gear, and set tonnage blocks on the spars for four tons. That's what he said, sir."

"Four tons!"

"Aye, sir. So he said."

Charley Duncan, standing to one side, whistled long and low and raised his eyes to peer at the darkness aloft, where sheered spars above the bent-on canvas awaited square sails yet to be sewn. Could spars and stays on a vessel that size support four tons? Batteries, Fisk had said. Guns . . . but what sort of gun weighed four tons?

As if answering his silent question, Dalton said, "Forty-eight pounders."

"Sir?"

"They must be forty-eight pounders, at that weight. And five barges? That would be one per barge. Five forty-eight-pound cannons . . . twenty tons of founded and strapped iron, to somehow be secured aboard a wallowing ketch? Madness." He dearly wished now that he had inquired of Ramsey just what it was he was supposed to deliver.

"Aye, sir," Duncan nodded, his eyes glittering in

the muted lantern's light. "Madness it be."

"We shall need a tree," Dalton muttered. "Stanchions along the starboard gunnels and a straight tree to step there to brace the mainmast. Mister Duncan, what spar stock is aboard?"

"Mister Caster has the inventory, sir. Shall I . . ."

From the shadows Billy Caster's adolescent voice piped, "We have spare course spars for both masts, sir, and a tops'l spar for the main. And a bit of rough stock that can be worked. We've the block and tackle gear we salvaged from the holds, that's been cleaned and stowed, and six tiers of cable. Is that enough?"

"Four tons of hoist," Dalton muttered, as though he had not heard. "Of course, we've a double capstan. Mister Tidy, please take a lantern below and inspect the lower head of our capstan. I shall need to know the condition of the rack and placement of the pawls. Possibly if we had a windlass on the foredeck . . ."

"We have no heavy windlass, sir."

"Those are barges out there. Every barge of my acquaintance mounts at least one windlass."

"Those people might object to our dismantling their barges, sir."

"Quite possibly. Mister Hoop, come aft, please!"

When the burly master-at-arms had joined them, Dalton said, "Mister Hoop, please have your marines stand by with their muskets loaded and primed. Mister Locke, I shall need a rifleman in each top as well. We may have to become persuasive."

"Aye, sir." Hoop glanced at John Tidy, on his way to the hold coaming.

"I'll be glad to translate for you, Mister Hoop," the bosun said. "As soon as I inspect the capstan."

"Mister Caster . . ."

"Aye, sir."

"Please find our carpenter, ah . . ."

"Mister Tower, sir."

"Yes. Please find Mister Tower. He should be in

98

one of the hammocks. We have a ship to rig for taking aboard of cargo.''

"Aye, sir.''

"Mister Duncan, please find Mister Romart. Break out axes and a saw, and go ashore and find us a tree. A nice hickory or even a pine tree might suffice, just so it is straight. It should be sixty-five feet long and not less than five inches across at its narrow end.''

"Aye, sir. Just the two of us, sir?''

"You may take a pair of lads with you. Take . . . ah . . . Mister O'Riley and . . .''

"Which Mister O'Riley, sir?''

"Whichever one isn't fixing breakfast.''

"Aye, sir. I might suggest Pitacoke and Squahamac as well, sir. They do know these woods.''

"Very well, Mister Duncan. Take them.''

"Misters Fisk and Caster, you may take the launch and two oarsmen. Go out to where the barges are waiting. Present my compliments to Mister Gwinn there and ask him to bring his documents and call on me aboard, if it pleases him, so that we may plan the transfer of his cargo. Oh, and Mister Caster, see if you can have a look at the barges while you are collecting him. See what size windlass they carry, and how they are mounted, please.''

"Aye, sir. Windlasses.''

"Mister Wise . . . where is Mister Wise?''

"He's in the tops with Mister Mallory, sir.''

"Mister Bean, then. Where . . . ah, there you are, Mister Bean. Please take a party into the holds and break out the reserve spars and cable. You can hoist those items to the deck while we are rigging the masts.''

"Aye, sir.''

Dalton licked his lips and thought dire thoughts about John Singleton Ramsey. Five forty-eight-pounders! A treasure in armament . . . and a terrible burden to wish upon a barely armed and awkward ketch in wartime. So far as he knew, no ship of the King's navy mounted forty-eight-pounders. The largest he had ever seen were forty-twos, and those were rare—great guns reserved for the very largest ships of the line. Guns of such size were what shore batteries were made of.

In the fog-shrouded hours of predawn Elliott Gwinn, exporter, chandler, tobacco farmer, and sometime smuggler, was brought up the cut to view a sight that made his mouth drop open. In the confines of the channel, screened by forest and the holding mists, a wide-bodied ketch lay in midstream. Lines from bow and stern anchored the vessel to sturdy trees on both banks, lanterns were set or hung at every vantage, and the ship swarmed with men from channels to tops. Spars jutted from rail ports on the port beam, big timbers thrusting up and outward while winches snugged cable from their ends up to the mast tops. On deck a fresh-trimmed tree trunk stood leaning against the mainmast while men studded in its butt against the starboard gunwale and others aloft bound its top to the high mast. Spar rigging aloft had been doubled, the hoists coupled with cable rigged to block and tackle, and hawsers from the cable tiers hung serpentine from starboard yardarms, secured there by blocks as massive as shroud deadeyes. And aft, at the mizzen, spars were being secured to make a tripod of the shorter mast— two new legs butted down against the starboard sills.

What had been a sailing ketch now resembled nothing more than a floating crane.

"Remarkable," Gwinn said. "I argued with Squire Ramsey that there would be no means to hoist our cargo aboard his vessel. He assured me that Captain Dalton would find a way."

Fresh breezes whispered through the treetops and made the mists roil and dance, and Billy Caster peered upward, trying to fare the winds as Captain

Dalton had taught him. At first he could make nothing of them. The forests acted as windbreak and, though they sang and whispered, they said nothing of direction. Yet there was a chill edge to the night air now, that said the weather might come northerly. Ten knots by morning, the captain had estimated, and Billy knew that he was right. He pulled his collar about his cheeks and felt a tension build in him. He had seen the barges and what they held, and he guessed they would be a good many hours in shipping their cargo.

And there were ships on the bay. Mister Fisk had seen three suits of sails at evening, becalmed then but not becalmed now. The brig, the nearest of them, was bound outward toward the sea. But the other pair were inbound and would be coming on—slowly, tacking against an unfriendly wind, but coming nonetheless.

Something edged into the deck shadow of the ketch, and the roiling mists were alive with the sounds of hammer and grip, block and tackle, shouts and pipes. He heard the familiar "Launch alongside, sir," and called, "Cargo party alongside! Permission to come aboard with Mister Gwinn!" Then he turned to their passenger. "I expect Captain Dalton will want to invite you to breakfast, sir. Follow me, please."

VIII

Solon Hays had waited for three years for command of a cruiser. Since the earliest engagements between colonial adventurers and Crown vessels, indeed since the taking of the *Margaretta* on the coast of Maine, he had known there would be no turning back. Since the advent of the king's party in London, the grievances had mounted in the colonies—grievances seldom redressed and often suppressed.

Solon's skills at seamanship and in battle had come the hard way. Impressed by a Crown man-of-war short-handed from the scurvy, he had served nearly three years before the mast by the time his ship was taken by a French first-rate and Solon found himself beached at Cap François. To get home to Virginia, he signed aboard a Dutch merchantman found for Malaga, made his way from there to Cadiz, and paid a forger to enhance his papers. What had been afterguard duty on His Majesty's line vessel *Castor*—now taken and gone—became midship training aboard that same vessel, and with that as a base he talked his way into a junior berth on another Dutchman, bound for Dublin. From there he had finally returned to the colonies as a junior lieutenant.

Three things had the years given to Solon Hays—a grasp of the craft of seamanship, a keen appreciation of the taking of prizes at sea, and a burning desire to do harm to the ships of the king.

For two years he had supported himself with brief cruises along the coast, carrying and then escorting trade among the colonies, while he petitioned again and again for command of a privateer. Good fortune in the person of Ian McCall finally had answered his petitions.

Now, freshly in command of the newly outfitted brig *Porphyry*, Solon Hayes wasted no time putting the spit and polish to his ship and his crew. Even becalmed and enfogged on the gray-mirror waters of Chesapeake, he put his rigging crews and gun crews through drills as long as there was light to see. Tricing tackle was hauled taut and the brig's gunports gaped. Then, as pipes wailed and topmen and sheetmen drilled on the sails, teams of gunners practiced smart "run in-run out" drill with their cannons. Nine men to a gun, they went through the rituals of running, loading, running out, and firing, gunnery captains drilling them mercilessly on the precise and rapid handling of quoining the barrels up and down, training for windage with train tackle, and the handling of handspikes, rammers, sponges, and worms. Hays wandered his decks, observing, and when the crews were near exhaustion he belayed the drills and had the guns secured for sea and equipment inspected.

In th daylight hours before the fogs had grown, his topmast lookouts had seen sails hull-down to the south. The nearer vessel appeared to be a small trading sloop. The further one was larger, but not recognizable. He wanted to be ready for whatever came to hand.

By four bells of the morning watch there was a pretty breeze, but the fog had deepened and was into the tops. Hays put out a single stern stream anchor and waited for visibility.

*   *   *

Aboard the sloop *Arbitrary*, sweat-soaked and exhausted hands strained at the capstan bars while their master, Hibley Speakes, paced from midships to stern, alternately cursing and blessing the mists and the darkness. For a time, the calm had worked in his favor. Pursued by a hostile vessel into the great estuary, *Arbitrary* had fled upwind through a long half-day, creeping on tack-and-reach against a fitful wind that thankfully gave no more aid to his pursuer than it did to him. Then had come the calm, then the fog, and Speakes was using it for all it was worth.

Through the long hours, *Arbitrary*'s single launch had worked back and forth from the sloop's stem to a cable-length ahead, carrying out and dropping first one kedge anchor and then the other while the rest of the ship's company plied the capstan on alternate cables, hauling *Abitrary* along a dark, blind course guided only by the errant point of a bobbing float marking the direction of the tide. With the stilling of the tide, though, prior to the beginning of ebb, there was nothing at all to point the way. Still the kedging continued, and Speakes prayed that they were proceeding in a straight line. The predator behind—he hoped it was still astern and not now abeam or even ahead—might be a king's vessel or a pirate, but it certainly was not a friend. Further, with the coming of wind he knew he could neither outrun nor outgun the larger vessel. His only hope was to get away before the weather changed, to lose himself in the fog.

The Crown schooner *Swift*, attached to Admiral Howe's fleet as a message carrier, was anchored on the windward of Tangier Island completing rudder repairs when her spotter on the island's south point signaled sails inbound, and Commander Curtis Hedgely climbed to the maintop to glass them. A pursuit, it developed, but an exceedingly slow one—a little trading sloop pursued by a somewhat larger vessel with the lofted quarterdeck of an old-fashioned brigantine. Neither vessel flew colors, but there was no doubt that the larger was making to close on the smaller as they beat upwind off Pocomoke Sound.

Hedgely concluded that the brigantine—if that was what it was—might be a Crown vessel of some status, and thought for a time of running up his high laterals to assist. Coming out from Tangier with the ebbing wind on his starboard beam, it would be no great trick to intercept the sloop and either claim it as a Crown prize himself, or at least hold it for the following vessel. He was wary, though, for want of a fair report on his rebuilt rudder, so he waited, only watching occasionally through long afternoon hours as the two vessels beat slowly nearer. There was plenty of time. Even past his vantage, the little sloop would be no match in crosswind speed for the schooner.

The sun was far down in the west when his first reported the rudder ready for stressing, and Hedgely went down to the deck to supervise. It was a makeshift job at best. The rudder had been almost carried away by a stray ball that gouged *Swift*'s sternpost just at the water when a swarm of armed galleys from the Delaware had appeared at the entrance to Cape Charles Pass to harass the outbound troopships coming from Head of Elk. Sail alone had carried *Swift* away from the fray, and for long days they had struggled to salvage what they could of the smashed rudder and repair it with raw stock from the hold. It was neither a pretty nor a trustworthy bit of patching.

On deck, Hedgely inspected the tackle secured to the inboard gunwales on each side of the tiller, heaving lines run through blocks from which cable ran to the tiller's bar. Ten men to a line, they would heave the tiller from side to side as violently as possible. If it would withstand that, it would take them home for proper repairs.

Hedgely checked the securing of the lines, then backed away. "Proceed, Mister Jones," he told his first.

Then began a rhythmic tug of war that shook *Swift*'s trim stern and set up froth at her beams. "Heave a'port!" and the schooner skidded to the right, trembling all the way to her jaunty jib. "Heave a'starb'd!" and she reversed her skid, shoved by her protesting rudder.

"Heave a'port!" Abruptly there was a groan of strapping, and the tiller bar lurched lose, men going to their knees as their line slacked. "Belay and stand down!" Jones shouted.

With his first at his heel, Hedgely hurried to the stern rail and looked over. His carpenter and four helpers stood off the stern in the ship's jolly boat, already moving in to see what had given way. After a minute's inspection the carpenter looked up. "Heel strap gave way, sir. Not nearly as bad as I feared."

"How long will it take to secure it?"

"Hour, sir. Maybe two. All the other strapping is firm."

"Very well," Hedgely sighed. "Do it right this time."

"Aye, sir."

An hour had passed before Hedgely again had opportunity to go into the tops with his glass. A brief freshening of the breeze had stepped up the chase out on the bay. The sloop was abreast the island now, tacking hard away, trying every trick its master knew to escape its pursuer. Hedgely glassed it, musing. Just a little coastal provisioner, barely armed and not heavily loaded. What would make such a small fish worth the hours of slow pursuit the larger vessel had devoted?

He turned his glass onto the pursuer. Certainly a

brigantine—an old style seldom seen in these times, yet well armed. He saw the guns at its midship rails, and raised his glass to scan its rigging. There should have been colors there, at least the bunting of proper pursuit or the courtesy of identification. For a time he watched as the ship neared, realizing that with his masts sheer and the island intervening he was almost invisible to those aboard. It came on, making all use of its tack, then came about sluggishly and reset for the course the sloop had taken. Hedgely swung his glass to its deck and could see the men there, and he scanned back toward the stern . . . then stopped and held as a flash of bright color caught his eye. The man in command was there by his helm, and the brilliant colors of his coat were colors Hedgely had seen before, in the Mediterranean Sea.

Spanish! The brigantine was a Spaniard! "Mister Jones!"

"Aye, sir?"

"How much longer until repair?"

"Few more minutes, sir. Just binding on."

"Look lively, then. And please call in our lookouts."

Within twenty minutes the schooner was prepared to sail. But it was too late. With a few last, fitful gusts, the errant breeze died to noting. The waters of the bay settled to a mirror sheen in the last light of evening, a mirror reflecting the now-distant limp sails of the Spanish vessel in mid-bay toward Lancaster Point and the tiny, hull-down speck of sail that was the sloop beyond.

As the light faded, mists arose upon the water and hid them both from view.

At a hidden shipyard in a cove off the west bank of Chesapeake, colonial guards stood perimeter in the darkness as men worked by lantern light to secure towing lines to the snow *Fury*. Riders had come in the midnight hours to warn them. At least two companies of the embattled British units holding Philadelphia had slipped through the cordon of Continental troops and moved southward. Somehow they had bypassed Baltimore and the deployments there, and were now somewhere on the Alexandria road. They had field pieces with them.

Ian McCall's yard supervisor had made his decision. *Fury* must be removed from jeopardy. Redcoats with field pieces could stand off and cut her to pieces if they found her.

There was the makings of a crew among those at the yards—men with sailing experience enough to take a ship into the bay or even out to sea if necessary. But with Solon Hays's transfer to the brig *Porphyry*, there was not one among them who had commanded. Therefore it fell to an old bosun, a retired sailor who bossed a rigging crew.

"We have no other choice, Mister Carlyle," the supervisor told him. "You have seen command by others and you know the drills. Take her out and see if you can slip down to Lancaster town or Gloucester. There are patriots there. Get her hidden, Mister Carlyle, and send a messenger you can trust when she is secure. I shall advise Mister McCall of the move."

By the time there was breeze in the fogged dark hours of morning, *Fury* stood with her stem to the bay awaiting the chance to slip away.

Above and across the bay from *Fury*'s hidey-hole, *Mystery* stood off the mouth of her sanctuary, her starboard rails looming over the decks of lashed barges, the entire assemblage an island of lantern light and feverish activity in a dark world of roiling fogs.

The preventer spars jutting outward from the

ketch's port scuttles to reinforce the straining masts and lower yards now did double duty as outriggers from which dangled every anchor available to her. Their weight, manipulated by block and tackle from the winches, was a counterbalance for the tons of cargo that must be hoisted over the starboard rails.

The supply barge had been offloaded first, yielding to *Mystery* a full complement of ship's stores and needed fittings as well as additional sailcloth, tackle, and ship's guns—two long-sixes cradle-mounted to serve as bow-and-stern chasers, a pair of fusty little short sixes on carriages to lash a'beam and a swivel gun which Dalton ordered mounted ahead of the companionway and deck house. Shot lockers and magazine were supplied, stores secured, and then the supply barge—much to the amazement of Mister Gwinn—was dismantled and its windlass secured at the base of *Mystery*'s jib to add its power to that of the capstan winch.

Cable keened, spars creaked with the strain, and structural timbers groaned as first one and then another huge gun was hoisted from its bedding aboard the barges, dallied alongside *Mystery*'s fore-rails, and swung ponderously inboard to be lowered into the gaping hold. Nearly twelve feet long and bearing foundry marks from New Hampshire, where they had been cast, the five great guns were unmounted—simply huge, elaborate iron tubes thickened at the breech and belled at the muzzle, strapped for reinforcement and with projecting cascabels at rear and trunnions at the sides. The bore of each one was eight inches in diameter.

In the hold, the first gun was lowered directly amidships to rest between stanchions on the heavy keelson timber. Joseph Tower, the carpenter, assembled cradles along its sides with braces studded to the inner hull framing where it lapped the ship's curving ribs. The second nested to the right of it and just above, the third to the left, and the fourth cradled atop these two.

"It's all we can take, Captain," Charley Duncan declared. "We've waterline almost at the chain plates now, and no place to rest that fifth one. Either side of the stack and we'll be sailing at a tilt."

Gwinn the bargemaster grinned at Dalton, an evil, delighted grin. "Your factor is obligated for all five of those guns," he said. "Not just four. You've already added the price of a barge to his bill. Sail without the fifth cannon and there will be no contract."

Dalton paced across the deck, deep in thought. The mists that hid them were alive now with the light of dawn, and *Mystery*'s loosed canvas fluttered in the makings of a fair breeze. Soon he would need someone in the tops to spy the morning. And soon, if the mists would dispell, it would be time to begin a journey. He had his stores and supplies now, he had his cargo—though it rankled him that Ramsey had put such aboard his ship—and he had his destination: the colonial port of Charleston, far to the south beyond the treacherous coastal bend where Hatteras Cape had lured so many worthy ships to their doom. The guns were assigned to an individual named Marion, to be delivered to him by prearranged signals upon arrival at Charleston. It reeked of smuggling, and it smacked of treason, and he would have to close his mind to the possibility—even the probability—that these guns would be used against king's subjects. A fugitive from the king's justice might still be a loyal subject, but he had few options in times like these.

"On deck, then," he told Duncan. "Hands to the hold to shift ballast a'port. Shift enough to put the main wales a'port into the water. Then we shall hoist the fifth gun and rest it a'deck right there." He pointed. "Have Mister Tower set cradling here, right alongside the helm. We can secure its cascabel to a ring on the deckhouse stanchion, and lash its nose at the stern rail."

"Aye, sir." Duncan turned away, muttering, "Bloody nuisance that is going to be, having a battery gun to stumble over on the afterdeck." But he hurried to get them busy in the hold. At least with the cargo shipped they could make sail and get out of this infernal wilderness.

Mister Tower came up from the hold, carrying his tools and panting from his efforts below, and Duncan explained what would be wanted astern.

"What sort of cradle can hold that monster on deck?" the carpenter objected. "I've not seen the like."

"I don't know," Duncan shrugged, then brightened. "You've built carriages, haven't you?"

"I have, but what sort of trucks could I put under a carriage with that weight upon it? And God Almighty, Mister Duncan, imagine what would happen if it should break loose in a rough sea."

"Then don't use trucks," Duncan decided. "Just stud the carriage underside to the deck. Carriages might break loose on trucks, but cannons don't part company from their carriages."

Shaking his head, Tower went off to look to his rough stock and plan a carriage for a shore battery on the deck of a ship.

As his saw and hammer began their songs, *Mystery* chuckled and trembled to the shifting of ballast below. With the loading of the great guns aboard they had put most of their original ballast over the side—bits of stone, large scraps of metal, foundry tailings, and the like, several long tons of weighty garbage. As ballast, it was replaced by the two hundred iron balls which were part of the gunnery cargo—eight-inch balls to be delivered with the guns at Charleston. The balls weighed near fifty pounds apiece and were easily shifted, though the securing of them required sturdy bins which Tower had built alongside the stack of guns below.

The mists were definitely alight and lanterns no longer required by the time *Mystery* sat a'tilt, leaning to the left and ready for final cargo. The sixth barge was hove to alongside, and once more the abused mainyard creaked and grumbled as four tons of iron rose regally from its delivery deck.

The huge gun crept upward and was slung carefully inboard, hands on deck and on the barge playing guidelines as it went. It was secured by tackle just aft the trunnions and hung in balance, horizontal. One wrong turn, a nudge or a missed tug and it could swing . . . and take out shroud lines. Carefully they swung it inboard, but this time not to be lowered into the forehold. Instead it was held four feet above the starboard deck while a cable from the mizzen was attached to its block. Then, slowly, heavy tackle at the mizzentop was brought into play from the capstan while the windlass was released inch by inch. Hanging thus, muzzle pointed astern, the gun crept rearward, four feet above the deck . . . it nosed past the mainmast, slowly entered the gallery between fife and mainshrouds, and continued its slow way, hovering over the starboard coaming of the small mid-hold where ship's stores and tackle had been secured.

Aloft a shriek sounded as a rigging eye slipped downward an inch, compressing the tapered mast by that much before preventer stays took the strain and held it. The great gun shuddered, and cable sang above it. Then the journey was resumed. Four tons of gun floated alongside the deckhouse and companionway, and the belled muzzle of it crept abaft the helm, its bulging dark body a foot from the spokepins, its trunnions edging toward the notches in the carriage cradle the carpenter had studded down there. Inch by inch the muzzle closed upon the stern

113

rail, looming almost over it.

"Down a foot!" Duncan called, and Tidy's bosun pipe bleated. Hard hands clenched the guidelines and muscles bulged as the gun settled toward its cradle. "Hold there!" Duncan knelt alongside the gun to judge its bearing on the aft rail. "Down just a bit!" Again the gun shuddered and settled, its muzzle now inches lower than the rail, aimed at the gaping scuttle port below it. "Run out!" Now hovering just above the cradle, the gun crept aft again, its bands scraping gouges in the helm housing. The belled muzzle thrust slowly beneath the rail and reappeared beyond, a foot or more past the stern timbers and barely clear of the sternpost.

Duncan and the carpenter knelt at the carriage notches, then exchanged nods. "Lower away!" Duncan called. The great gun sank, shivered once, and settled into its notches. Beyond, by the port gunwale, Billy Caster wiped a hand across his forehead and brushed away the sweat against his breeches. He glanced around, drawing a deep breath. Patrick Dalton stood beside him, but facing outward. Not once through the operation had he turned to watch, and Billy understood why. It was Mister Duncan's task to ship the big gun aboard, and the captain had let him do it without once showing concern . . . or even interest.

For a few seconds, as the gun's full weight settled onto the new cradle and Tower began the securing of the trunnions in their notches, *Mystery* grumbled and whispered with the settling of timbers below deck, tiny readjustments of fit as the great weight atop them was accommodated. Then the loading and securing was done, and Billy went to first one rail and then the other to look down at the hull timbers. *Mystery* rode level in the water—low, but level. The shifting of ballast had been enough to offset the starboard weight of the gun. Billy got out his tablet and made notes in it, noticing as he did how the forty-eight-pounder dwarfed the diminutive long-six on its carriage at the port after-rail. Beside the monster, the ship's gun looked like a toy.

Duncan turned a cocky grin on the amazed Mister Gwinn, then snapped a salute at the stolid back of his captain. "The gun is aboard, sir. All cargo is shipped."

Dalton turned then, finally, pursed his lips and nodded his approval at the securing of the cannon. "Very well, Mister Duncan, and pass along a 'well done' to Mister Tower and the lads at the hoists. Mister Gwinn, I'll have your signature on the bill of lading and the destination documents, if you please. Mister Caster?"

"Aye, sir." Billy got out the papers and held them with great ceremony while the bargemaster signed them.

Gwinn could not resist one last shot, though. He was still seething at the dismantling of his lead barge and the loss of his windlass. "You'll be lucky to get past Point Lookout with this load," he said, "much less to sea and around Hatteras."

"It is an odd thing about ketches," Dalton said. "They may be neither nimble nor jaunty, hardly more pleasing to the eye than sailing scows, but they do have sturdy knees, Mister Gwinn. Short of submerging entirely, a worthy ketch will float anything that's put aboard her . . . and given the time, she'll find her way to where she is supposed to go."

"Well, I wish you fair weather and a following wind, *Captain* Dalton. But, of course, one passing warship and you'll no longer have a destination to concern yourself about." He strode away along the deck and straddled the midships rail, then swung over and let himself down to his barge, glaring at the five Hessian "marines" who witnessed his departure.

Lines and blocks were released, and the barge cast off, towed now by the launch that had kedged it across when it was laden. Briefly the final barge was in sight, then it was lost in the swirling fog.

And Dalton took command of his deck. "Rig the launch for tow astern," he ordered. "Hands aloft to spy the weather. Mister Duncan, let's have a look at Mister Tower's carriage, if you please."

Duncan reappeared from the fore, and they knelt together while Dalton inspected the manner in which the great cannon's cradle was studded to the deck. Deep in thought, he pursed his lips, and Duncan said, "It's secure, sir. It isn't going anywhere."

"Secure, yes," Dalton nodded. "Secure enough for cargo. I am curious, though . . . wouldn't it be far more secure if Mister Tower were to rig timbers from the deck braces here . . . and here . . . say down to the mainmast buttress? You see, this decking here could be drilled out, and a sturdy brace fashioned that could take considerable stress—as much stress, I believe, as the ship itself can withstand."

"Aye, sir." Duncan scratched his head. "That could be done, right enough. But . . ."

"Then I believe that is what we should do, Mister Duncan. Please see to it at the earliest convenience, once we are away."

"Aye, sir."

Dalton stood and strode off along the deck, and Duncan tipped his head in confusion. Why should the captain want this gun braced into the ship's very structure? There was no possible need for such measures . . .

Not unless he had in mind to try and fire the bloody thing.

116

IX

Somewhere on this morning the sun was shining bright. Somewhere the fair breeze that tormented these mists played clean and free across waters unshrouded. But not, on this morning, on Chesapeake.

Patrick Dalton had fared the morning truly. By eight bells and the beginning of the forenoon watch there was a ten-knot breeze and Dalton put *Mystery* to mid-channel—or as near as could be by sounding line and topwatch—and set her stem southward by the compass. His charts told him the bay was ten miles wide here, and eyes in the sheered tops saw only hint of distant shores each way. Still, he was blind on deck and he put Cadman Wise out on the jibboom to sling the sounding line and report any first evidence of shoaling.

The wind had flattened the top of the mist and created troughs that sometimes bottomed below the mast tops, giving the lookouts aloft occasional view of a bright world between mists—blue-white clouds above and gray-white mists below where the shadows of *Mystery*'s masts rode ghostly, extending far off the starboard beam. The chatter between them up there was illuminating but not very informative, for each trough in the mists was bounded by higher rollers of

117

fog angling away fore and aft, hiding whatever might lie ahead.

By log and line, *Mystery* was holding at four knots, wallowing along with the wind at her tail and only laterals spread to catch it. For an hour Dalton took the helm himself, judging by hand, ear, and feel of the deck the workings of the little ship, learning its balance, guessing at its moods. To the curious glances and whispered comments of some of the recruits, Billy Caster noted, "It's how the captain fares a vessel. He wants the song of it in his ear, the feel of it in his hand, and the whims of its rigging in sight. Captain Dalton is a seaman and a commander —but first he is a sailor."

By three bells of the forenoon, Dalton knew what *Mystery* could tell him on this day. She was no dancer, no racer, but she was a sturdy craft and willing to answer to her sails if they were properly set. Wide of beam and stubby of stem, her grace was in her steadiness. She was a ketch, and would do what a ketch could do.

Hard-helmed, she would be sullen in heavy seas but not likely to skitter about or skew broadside as many a jaunty racer might. With square sails on her high yards she would fight her rudder in a fair wind and would give a weary helmsman cause to curse her. A stubborn, steady, methodical vessel, she would not respond lightly to whim—her own or anyone else's. Yet there was a sureness that would be comforting as long as she was set on course from point to point.

"Every inch a merchantman," Dalton told those about him. "Designed to deliver, built to deliver, and tempered to deliver. I suppose there is little more that one might ask."

Yet in his voice they heard—those who had sailed with him aboard the trim schooner *Faith* and the one, Billy, who had served him previously on fighting ships—a measure of regret. The warrior

118

consigned to the running of errands, the rider of hunt-bred steeds who now must put his saddle on a placid ox, the task at hand was acceptable but it must be done with a sigh.

"As well that the captain was not with us when we saw the snow," Charley Duncan admitted to Michael Romart. "'Twould make his heart bleed were he to vision such a vessel when all he has at his command is this."

"The man has commanded warships, then?" John Tidy asked.

"Not commanded, but he was second aboard a fighting brig and brought the wreck of it home when few men could have managed," Duncan told him. "And the schooner we had . . . that *Faith* . . . ah, such a lady she was. Yet when the need was there we fitted her out to fight and . . ."

Romart touched his shoulder. "There's been enough said about that, Mister Duncan. You know how the captain feels about carrying stories."

But the bosun raised a brow. "Aye? There was a tale I heard—and others as well—about a little schooner that played bloody hell with the fleet at New York and then, some say, went back out to take on a frigate. It's only a story, but it's fact that the 44-gunner *Courtesan* hasn't been seen since that day, and many a man has wondered these past times on what's become of her."

Duncan shook his head. "Mister Romart's right. Enough has been said of that. If the captain wants more told about it, he can tell it." He went forward to let himself into the great hold, clambering over the piles of kegs and stores beneath which rested four of the cargo batteries and their attendant rounds. Aft of these, planks had been removed from the rear bulkhead, and Joseph Tower worked by lantern light, studding in heavy cleats where the mainmast was stepped to the keelson. Duncan crawled to him

119

and peered past. "How are you coming with this, Mister Tower?"

"Well enough, considering I've never seen the like of it," the carpenter growled. "First it's a deck carriage for a short battery, now it's a stanchion from carriage to keel . . . and that isn't as easy as it sounds, either! Stanchions might angle up or down, Mister Duncan, but they do not angle from side to side. Anybody knows that. What I'm doing is cleating a'starboard so there'll be something to butt the stanchion against when I set it."

"I see." Duncan shook his head in the gloom. "How long do you need to be in this hold, Mister Tower?"

"Just a bit. I'm about done here. I'll peg these planks up again, then I'll craft the rest of it from aft . . . though that Irishman yonder is going to howl when I run a stanchion through his galley."

"What Irishman?"

"Mister O'Riley. He says he's cook, and has got right possessive about his galley since breakfast."

"Which Mister O'Riley is it?"

"I don't know. The one that's cook. I can't tell 'em apart."

"Well, I'm sure the captain will sort it all out. As soon as you've done here, Mister Tower, please come on deck and plank over this main hold. It will make a place for the sailmaker to work."

"Dr. Franklin?"

"He isn't Dr. Franklin, Mister Tower. His name is Wilton."

"He looks like Dr. Franklin."

"He says that isn't his fault, though."

In the sternsheets Patrick Dalton handed over the helm to Victory Locke and called Billy Caster to him. "You have begun the ship's log, Mister Caster?"

"Aye, sir. As instructed, though the first day's entry is mostly a reference to cargo."

"Very well. Please note that we were under way by eight bells of the midwatch on this day, bound for Charleston on the South Carolina coast, and that the sailmaker is to be assigned mates as he requires to expedite the completion of sails for the yards. Also, when Mister Duncan emerges yonder, my compliments and ask him to assemble hands amidships excepting the two at tops, Mister Locke at helm and Mister Tower."

"Aye, sir."

"And, Mister Caster, for the sake of protocol, present to Mister Duncan my request that hands at muster be ranked by qualification according to naval custom. First muster is important, for the making of custom, and it is best to condone no laxity aboard ship."

"Aye, sir."

"Have you stowed gear in the cabins?"

"Aye, sir, but not sorted. I had thought the starboard cabin for yourself, sir, since it has a cabinet in it, and the port for Mister Duncan as first officer. But with the stanchion Mister Tower will be installing beneath this gun," he indicated the great bulk of the 48-pounder, "well, it will reduce the space in the starboard cabin, sir . . . as well as in the galley. Mister O'Riley has already complained about that, sir."

"Which Mister O'Riley?"

"Mister Gerald O'Riley, sir. It was him wound up being cook. It was his boiled oats that we had for breakfast, sir. But with the changes below, sir, probably you should take the portside closet and have Mister Duncan in the . . ."

"Very well, Mister Caster. Place both my gear and Mister Duncan's aport, and put yourself and Dr. . . . ah, Mister Wilton in the starboard space. You will want a table for the keeping of reports. Mister Wilton is a guest aboard until he gets our sails bent on.

121

Where is Mister Wilton now?"

"He's forward, sir, complaining of not having adequate space to work."

"He shall have space shortly, Mister Caster. Atop the great hold."

"Aye, sir. Shall I tell him that?"

"Please do, Mister Caster. It might keep him from colic."

Billy went off to do his rounds, and Dalton squinted abeam, annoyed at the blind fog that seemed to encase them like a burial shroud. He guessed that it might clear by noon, but in changing weather there was no way to know for certain. He turned to the helm. "Mister Locke, I shall be below for just a bit. Hold her as she goes, and . . ."

"On deck!"

He raised his head, seeing the misted tops aloft and the lookouts there.

"Report, Mister Bean!"

"Sail, sir! Just a glimpse and then it was gone !"

"Whereaway, Mister Bean?"

"Abaft, sir! Broad of the starboard beam!"

"How far?"

"Couldn't make out, sir! Two or three miles . . . maybe half a league."

"Keep a sharp watch there, Mister Bean! Maintop, who are you?"

"Mallory, sir!"

"Watch the fore, Mister Mallory! Look sharp!"

"Aye, sir!"

He turned again to Victory Locke at the helm. "I shall be below, Mister Locke. Hold as she goes."

"Aye, sir."

In the tiny port closet at the bottom of the companionway, just aft the galley, Dalton dipped water from a bowl and washed his face, rubbing tired eyes. Then he found and unfolded the battered blue coat that had once borne the buttons and cuffs of a

122

Royal Navy lieutenant. It was just a coat now, though its white facings might, to the careful eye, have betrayed its origins. He dusted it and hung it aside, then searched for a fresh shirt. There was none to be found, so he stripped off his soiled one and brushed it as well, then put it on again. With a fresh stock at his neck and his waistcoat buttoned, the shirt was fairly hidden.

With a bit of lampblack and wax he dressed his boots, buffed them, then stood and buckled on his sword. Finally he put on his coat, sleeked back his dark hair, set on his head the uncomfortable tricorn hat John Ramsey had pressed on him, and returned to the deck. Over the usual sounds of sail and rigging came the staccato racket of hammers in the fore. Through the mist he could see the carpenter and others battening the hold hatch with planks. "Report, Mister Locke?"

"Steady on, sir. As she goes. No more sightings, though Mister Mallory took a bit of a look from the main royal's hound and he says it's clearing aloft."

Dalton frowned, turned and tipped back his head, cupping his hands at his mouth. "Mister Mallory!"

"Aye, sir?"

"You were assigned the maintop, Mister Mallory, not the high hounds!"

"Aye, sir. Just thought I'd have a look up there."

"Such hazards are seldom necessary, Mister Mallory. Nevertheless how much clearing have we?"

"The mists are moving to the south, sir. Horizon clear astern."

"Any sightings, Mister Mallory?"

"No, sir."

Dalton turned, still peering upward. "Mister Bean!"

"Aye, sir?"

"Further sightings, Mister Bean?"

"Nothing, sir. Just fog here."

"Carry on, tops."

"Aye, sir."

Charley Duncan came aft, followed by the final echoes of the battening. "Sailmaker can commence, Captain. Plenty of space for him now."

"Thank you, Mister Duncan. Please ask him to come aft for a moment, if you will. Then you may muster hands for ship's discipline."

"Aye, sir." He turned, then turned back. "Mister Wise is still sounding on the jib, sir, but he hasn't found bottom in a bell."

"Bring him in, then. But have a sounding at each turn of the glass, if you will."

"Aye, sir."

Disheveled and grumpy, Titus Wilton came aft to glare up at Dalton over his spectacles.

"I realize this entire situation has inconvenienced you, sir," Dalton began, "but . . ."

"Inconvenienced, he says," Wilton muttered.

"But I believe we can expedite your business aboard now. As you see, we are committed to sail and . . ."

"*He's* committed to sail, he says," Wilton grumped.

". . . and it is rather urgent that we get some canvas on those yards up there as smartly as possible. This ketch was not designed for sailing on her fore-and-afts. Therefore, at your pleasure . . ."

"*My pleasure*, he says," Wilton hissed.

Dalton frowned down at the thorny little man. "Repetition of my attempts at communication merely prolongs this business, Mister Wilton. It is obvious that you understand my words, so pray pay attention to their meanings for a moment. I am no happier about requiring your services aboard than you are, I assure you, and the sooner we can bend some sail onto those yards the sooner both of us will be content. We have provided an ample space for your work, there on the . . ."

"Ample space? Four paces by four paces? Sir, I am accustomed to working where I can spread my materials. There isn't ample space on this entire scow to . . ."

"Ketch."

"On this entire ketch to spread bolts properly. And without assistance . . ."

"Canvas folds," Dalton assured him. "Most sailmakers are well aware of that. And as to mates, you may have your pick of men not on duty, as many as you need whenever you need them."

"To teach my trade to a bunch of tars and scrubs?"

"To make sails for *Mystery*, Mister Wilton. The sooner that is completed, the sooner I can put you ashore. We are short four square sails. How long do you estimate that task will take you?"

"Under these conditions? A month at the very least."

"Do you relish the spending of a month on top of yonder hatch, sir?"

"Two or three days, then."

"If you could do it in half that, I believe I could put you ashore at a bay port. After that, we might be committed to sea for some period of time."

"What men can I have?"

"If you see a man idle and can fit him with a tailor's palm, he is yours until needed for duty."

Wilton sighed. "Have them set out my bolts and tools, then." He turned away, muttering, "Abominable . . . unendurable . . . may double my bill . . ." and the mutters trailed away toward the fore.

Duncan came aft and the crew began assembling itself amidships, John Tidy's whistle prompting them.

"We should have some proper sail bent on soon, Mister Duncan," Dalton said quietly. "I believe Mister Wilton's enthusiasm has been renewed."

Tidy got them ranked in some sort of order, able seamen aft of the mainmast shrouds—former *Faiths* first, the seniority won by having served with Dalton in the past, other ables flanking the companion hatch on the port—specialists and ordinaries a'star-board, crowding around the big gun that lay there. In this rank were Mister Hoop and his Hessian charges, the brothers O'Riley, gunners Ethan Crosby and Floyd Pugh, and the Indians Pitacoke and Squahamac. Aloft were the lookouts Claude Mallory and Ishmael Bean, both former *Faiths*, and Victory Locke stood the helm. From below decks came the clatter and thud of the carpenter's reinforcing project. Even as they assembled, a drill poked upward through the deck planks almost at the toe of Squahamac, then disappeared and reappeared again six inches aport.

When they were in satisfactory order, Dalton took the roster from Billy Caster and studied it momentarily, glancing up now and again to place a face with a name. Finally he handed it back. "You," he said, "Each and every one of you, hear me now. Some of you have sailed with me before, some have not. Each man here has reasons to be aboard this vessel as part of this company . . . most of us," he added dryly, "because it is preferable to being somewhere else at the moment. At any rate, each man of you has made his mark and been attested as crew of the sailing ketch *Mystery*. This vessel. Mister Caster, my clerk, has read to each of you the articles of service for this voyage and each of you . . . Mister Caster, you *did* include these Indians, did you not?"

"Aye, sir. They've had their articles. Mister Duncan helped."

"Blee'n ri', 'e di'," Pitacoke assured the captain. "Bally bi' o' shi' i'wa, 'swell."

Tidy's whistle shrilled and Charley Duncan hissed at the Indian, "Belay that! Silence in ranks!"

Squahamac looked at him. "W'a'ey?"

Duncan turned an embarrassed glance on Dalton, then rephrased it. "Kee' y' blee'in lip shu' 'n 'ear th' bloke."

126

"Blee'in ri'," Squahamac agreed cheerfully. Then to the captain, "Spea' y' mind, cawb."

Dalton turned partly away to get his face straightened, then continued, "We are bound for the port of Charleston, in the South Carolina colony beyond . . ."

"State, sir," one of the O'Rileys offered.

"What?"

"State. Sorry, sir. But it's a state now, not a colony. We're from there."

"Silence!" Duncan roared, almost drowning Mister Tidy's whistle.

"State of South Carolina," Dalton amended. "You have all seen the cargo we carry. Among other items, it consists of five battery guns. Now, there being at present a state of insurgency . . ."

In the rearmost row, a hand went up. Dalton paused. "Mister Romart?"

"Sorry, sir. But it's considered a state of war. Only the British call it an insurgency."

At the helm, Victory Locke could not contain himself. "The captain *is* British, you dolt! Most of us are. Besides . . ." his voice trailed off and his face went red. "Beggin' your pardon, sir. It won't happen again."

Dalton sighed. "A proper point, though, and one I was about to address." He squared his shoulders and addressed the assembly. "Once and for all, understand this. *Mystery* is not partisan in reference to the present state of . . . hostilities. We are not colonial, nor are we Crown. Our purpose is to deliver cargo for a private patron to his private consignees, nothing more nor less. It is my intention to do so as unobtrusively as possible, and as expeditiously as possible . . ."

"W'a lip's 'e twiddin'?" Pitacoke wondered aloud. "S'na Henglish, is't?"

". . . as possible, hopefully without confrontation of any kind. Most of you men have seen service on men-of-war. Know you especially that *Mystery* is not

127

in any sense a warship. We are a merchantman . . . and a rather small, clumsy one at that. Therefore we shall do all in our power to avoid confrontation with anyone, for any reason. We carry some small armament, of course, but only for purposes of self-defense in a case of last resort.''

A hand went up. "Sir?''

"Yes, Mister Crosby?''

"Can't help but notice that this,'' he indicated the great gun on its cradle, "is being studded in right stoutly for a bit of cargo.'' As though in response, the drill appeared again from below and a plank saw followed it, beginning to cut a hole in the deck. "In case of last resort, me an' my mate would fancy testin' the monster out, so to speak.''

A look of horror appeared on the pocked face of Cadman Wise. "You're balmy, mate. Touch that thing off . . . Lord, this cockleshell would pleat like a squeezebox.''

"Belay that!''

"Thank you, Mister Duncan. I do not care to discuss contingency at the present moment. Now . . . all hear this. I am commander of this vessel and will be addressed aboard as Captain. Mister Duncan is your first officer. Mister Tidy and Mister Wise are bosuns, watch-and-watch. Mates will be appointed only if necessary. Mister Tower . . .'' The saw completed its work, and a rectangular hole appeared in the deck, at the rear of the great gun's cradle. A face appeared in the hole and said, "Sir?''

"Proceed, Mister Tower.''

"Aye, sir.'' The face disappeared, and a heavy timber sprouted where it had been, butting up against the gun carriage.

"Mister Tower is ship's carpenter, obviously. Mister Gerald O'Riley is ship's cook. Mister Hoop is master-at-arms. Mister . . . ah, *Corporal* Wesselmann is . . .''

"Jawohl, mein Herr?''

Dalton waved him down. "Mister Tidy, please translate this for the Hessians as soon as we are completed. The five German gentlemen there are to be considered as marines, and under the supervision of Mister Hoop for shipboard duties."

"On deck!" The urgent voice rang from aloft.

"Yes, Mister Mallory?"

"Sail sighted, sir! Two cables distance, starboard beam!"

"Assembly dismissed," Dalton grunted to Duncan. "All hands to stations. Mistery Mallory, what colors do they show?"

"None, sir. 'Course, neither do we."

"What are they doing?"

"Nothing, sir. Just running abreast and looking back at us."

"Mist is dropping off, Cap'n!" Bean called from the mizzentop. "It's the same sail I saw a bit ago, but now they're right out there beside us. It's a snow, sir, but ill trimmed, seems to me."

A snow! The deadliest modification on British cruiser designs ever originated by the colonies . . . two cables abeam! All along the deck's length, men scampered to stations, ready to handle what sail the ketch had, or to fight with what they could wield, or both. Dalton whirled on Locke. "I'll take the helm, Mister Locke. Find a pair of lads to help you break out rifles. Mister Hoop: Marines amidships, starboard rail! Gunners a'starboard, prime and fuse!"

Men ahead of him were swarming both main-shrouds. He noticed that one in the lead was Charley Duncan, and approved. His first was going to where the enemy could be seen . . . if enemy it was. Fogs still held the deck in blind captivity and he could see nothing even a cable off, much less two.

"On deck!"

"Report, tops!"

"She's running up signal, sir!"

"Colors, tops?"

"Not colors, sir. But she signals!"

"Can you make them, tops?"

"Moment, sir!" Then, "Aye, sir. She declares as a neutral. Also she is passing us, sir. She bears three points forward of our beam and gaining."

"It was not surprising. To avoid passing the creeping ketch, a snow would have to reef down to jib and jigger in any wind at all. "Mister Caster, signals please. Run up our merchant's colors and wish the snow safe passage."

"Aye, sir."

"By the grace of Mary," Duncan's voice came from aloft, "it is that same snow, sir. The one we saw being fitted. But she's limping, sir. Sails are poorly trimmed and she scuds a bit."

Then, as though a huge, cold hand had pressed downward and away, the mists cleared in a trough of visibility, and Dalton could see the stranger. He stared, sucking cold air between his teeth. She was a beauty . . . a dancing lady of a trim cruiser, full suited and fresh, mounting at least sixteen guns— though her sails did indeed luff and her guns were not on train. What sort of hand was at her helm, what sort of command directing her, that she should flounder so in such conditions?

Though coming two points on the beam and receding toward the waiting fogs, still he could see the faces aboard her and read her escutcheons.

Her name was *Fury*.

"On deck!"

It was Duncan, his voice distant. Dalton peered upward. Duncan had gone on top toward the hounds, clinging to the high topgallant mast.

"Sail ahead, sir!" he called. "Small craft of a single mast broad on port, larger vessel dead ahead maybe three miles. May be a pursuit, sir."

X

Freshening winds had ploughed the mists of morning into long, roving furrows angling across the broad waters of Chesapeake, and the furrows became rolling moles of mist scudding off toward the south. Dalton kept the snow in sight until it disappeared into a fog bank, then he eased *Mystery* to starboard and angled toward the distant west shore. For a laden ketch with inadequate sail and only a few six-pounders to defend herself, the mid-channel waters were too busy for his taste. After a time the fog mole drifting ahead of them broke into swirling mists under a hazed sun, and the snow was again in sight . . . miles ahead now and close inshore near the west wilderness. A fine ship poorly handled and furtive, she seemed to be trying to hide herself against the shoreline as she went.

Dalton called Michael Romart to the stern and pointed. "What is the nature of those waters there where the snow has gone?"

Romart squinted. "Shoals and shallows, mostly. There are fishing banks along there, as I remember. Tidal channels, but they are shifting and treacherous. Silt from the rivers moves them around."

Not a proper route for a vessel bound outward, then, Dalton thought. Either the snow was seeking a hidey-hole, or there was something out in the bay that she wanted very much to avoid. The other sails that Duncan had spotted from the tops? Possibly. Visibility still was patchy and sporadic at any distance.

He decided to play a hunch. The snow had offered no hostility, though they had passed close abreast. He eased more to starboard and hailed Duncan down from the hounds. "Take the deck, Mister Duncan," he told him. "Put a man forward on the spreaders to sound for you, and try to follow where that snow has gone. I believe they know more than we do about what's ahead. There may be shoals, but there should be channels as well. Steer by dark water and line, and I will assist from the tops."

At the mainmast shrouds he stepped to pinrail and gunwale and swung outboard to climb the ratlines. In the maintop Claude Mallory greeted him with a steadying hand and reported, "Still high and dense ahead, sir, but it's shifting. Last sight of those sails, the little one was beating for the far shore and the big one seemed to be making about to pursue."

"We shall do our best to avoid them, whoever they are," Dalton said. He swung onto the topmast shrouds and headed for the crosstrees above. "Stand by to relay calls, if you please, Mister Mallory."

"Aye, sir."

Standing on the crosstrees where the topmast ended and the topgallant began, Dalton clung to the abbreviated high shrouds and peered out across the misted distance ahead. Here, seventy feet above *Mystery*'s deck, the slight roll of the ship was pronounced. The mast swung lazily back and forth, ten feet each way, and the effect was a giddy sensation that Dalton had often enjoyed when, as a boy, he had worked the tops on midshipman cruises. Now, though, he found it distracting. Combined with the luminous mists rising tenuous ahead, the motion made it even harder to see distances. The mists played tricks with the eyes, and the fogs played tricks with the mind, and he chided himself as he retrieved his glass from a coattail pocket, remembering with little pleasure a dark morning when he had directed course of a vessel from this height, guiding it through a tight channel while he let a pursuer edge alongside to take the fire of a cutter lying in wait. A fool's maneuver, he thought now. Desperation and far too much rum. Yet apparently heaven had not been ready to receive him just then, himself or most of the others aboard that ill-fated vessel. It had worked.

He peered through his glass, seeing the fogbank as the flying mane of a white racer, with perceptions of distance beyond. The snow was off there, astern now as *Mystery* angled toward its course, its tops standing clear of the bewildering mists. The snow would be deep keeled, he thought. It was built for press of canvas, and might draw two-and-a-half to three fathoms. Even laden as she was, the ketch could go where the snow could go, if they could find the channels. Much would depend upon the man out on the jib, perched above the spreaders to work his sounding line. Shreds of mist clung close atop the water and made spotting from the tops unlikely.

For a time he studied the deck below, hazed by drifting mist. Cadman Wise was out on the jib, just at its doubling where the spreaders sparred out, holding the sprit's shroud lines. Fluting shadows of the batwing sails above him touched the mists alongside as he swung and dropped his sounding line, then reeled it in, coiling it from elbow to thumb. On the foredeck behind him, men stood or worked, some still shifting kegs and crates into better positions, two or more securing the hastily set lines of the long-six set there as a bow chaser, others watching the planked-over arena where Titus Wilton sat cross-legged, grumbling and making sail. An unpleasant sort, Dalton admitted, but the little man's hands fairly flew as he stitched bolts together to form a maincourse.

A pair of the deck hands were doing the sailmaker's bidding, hauling up bolts for him, shifting canvas as he sewed, securing leach hardware as he directed.

Directly beneath, past the squatting figure of Mister Mallory at the mast top, men stood by the main fiferail in front of the mast, and others at the pinrails at each side. The short-sixes were secured at the waist, and the two gunners were scrubbing one of them while Mister Hoop and the Hessians ran lines on the other. Five muskets were stacked in a neat pyramid before the deckhouse.

His eye roving aft, he considered the wiry John Tidy pacing restlessly here and there, keeping an eye on everything; Billy Caster and Michael Romart bent over a chart, with two Indians looking over their shoulders. He wondered if it had occurred to anyone to use the Indians to spot landmarks ashore. Who would be more familiar with such?

Joseph Tower emerged from the companionway with one of the brothers O'Riley at his heels, shaking a menacing fist. The carpenter ignored him, set down his armload of materials, and knelt at the breech of the huge cannon resting alongside the deckhouse. For a moment he peered under it, then he went to work, building another brace.

Purdy Fisk was at the helm now, with one of the new men—one of the Fanshaws—standing beside him. Just behind them Charley Duncan stood, looking up at Dalton, awaiting orders or report.

All in all, he thought, a reasonably well-manned vessel. Not a pretty ship. She never would be. She was only a ketch. But for a ketch, not too bad.

Hazed sunlight warmed his head, and he took up his glass again, scanned ahead, then held. The mists were diminishing, tendrils rising and dancing on the winds, and the errant breeze cleared a view for him. For a moment he could see miles ahead, even see the east shore of the bay low on the horizon, and there were sails. For a second it seemed to him that the bay was alive with them, as though a flotilla had gone astray in the fog. He gripped his glass and scanned more slowly.

Two miles dead ahead, the snow crept along the shore on ill-set sails, for all the world a great winged creature now injured and trying to hide. Beyond and farther out, several miles away, a largish vessel beat slowly northeastward, its bow aimed at a tiny spot of sail far out across the bay, nearly at the far shore. Even at this distance he could see the quiltwork patching of the larger vessel's sail, the glint of guns on its deck, and he studied its rigging, wondering. It was years since he had seen a brigantine, but there was one out there, and it had done battle, and it was in pursuit of a vessel.

And another sail stood beyond the course of the brigantine—crisp, bright canvas of a warship recently reworked, a full brig aimed southward but just now making to come about. It was running up colors, and they were not the colors of the king. A privateer, then, and it had sighted a target. The brigantine? Probably, he thought. The clearing out there had only just come this far up, and he doubted the brig had seen either the snow or himself . . . at least not yet.

As mists closed across the distance again, he had just a glimpse of still other sails—one far distant and hull-down, just rounding off a little island, the other a small craft that seemed to stand at the east shore, just putting out.

The bay was huge, but abruptly he realized that it was crowded. "Mister Mallory," he called down, "tell deck to hold as close inshore as sounding will allow, and tell some more of the lads off to assist

135

Mister Wilton. We are about to have need of some proper sails."

The message was relayed, and a response came from below. Mallory lifted his face. "Sir? Mister Duncan says beggin' your pardon, sir, but would you mind telling a body what in hell it is you've seen out there? With respect, sir, he said that."

"Sails, Mister Mallory. Tell deck that there are people on this bay at this moment doing various things. There is a limping snow, a privateer brig, an armed relic that looks like a battered brigantine, and at least three other vessels in glassing distance. Tell deck to please have all guns loaded and fuse at hand, and to stand by to bend on sails the very moment Mister Wilton completes them. I shall be down directly."

"Aye, sir."

Again the view was misted, though not so much as before. The snow was still in sight ahead, and for a moment he could see more clearly the little ship hard down across the bay. A single-master. A trading sloop, he thought, and even now coming about for a long tack toward this side of the bay. He judged the wind, guessed at the sloop's capabilities and traced in his mind the direction of its tack. It would reach the shoals of the west shore ahead of *Mystery*. Its course would coincide with the snow's. They were on course to meet a few miles ahead, not in itself a matter of concern to him. The snow had shown no hostility, and a trading sloop was unlikely to be interested in *Mystery* beyond simple curiosity.

But he had seen the course of the brigantine as well and had no doubt that it was in pursuit. Where the sloop went, the brigantine would go, and it had an ominous look to it. It bore the marks of predator.

For a time it had been clear, and Hibley Speakes

136

had glassed the predator on his tail nervously as he made about for another tack across the bay this time toward the west. At first he had been sure he could outrun the larger ship, using the sloop's big fore-and-aft sails to advantage as he tacked against the northering wind. But he had not gained perceptibly, even with the kedging he had done during the foggy calm. And now he saw why. The pursuer was a brigantine, old and battered but still fully suited, and had a fine amount of fore-and-aft rigging of its own. Further, with each of his long runs back and forth across the bay on tack and reach, he had had to go full distance to get as far northward as possible. But the brigantine had made slightly shorter sweeps than his, sacrificing northerly advance for increased proximity. And he understood that, too, now that he had a view of her. The brigantine carried at least twelve guns, and he guessed that some or all were ranging pieces. The brigantine did not have to fully overhaul him. It would be enough just to stand off his beam in broadside reach. Once the pursuer had that position, there would be no options left. Speakes could either surrender his vessel or be shot out of the water, and his little defense guns would mean nothing at all.

His greatest hope finally had been to reach a certain cut on the east shore—a place he knew where the draft across silted shoals might just allow his sloop at this tide and where the pirate behind him might not be able to follow. He had made it to the cut, and from a hundred yards off had seen the wrecked ship blocking its entrance, a souvenir of the recent British excursion. Now he fled once more across the bay, this time westerly, and had one chance remaining. Ghostly in the morning fog he had glimpsed another vessel somewhere ahead, coming down the bay. Whether friend or enemy he did not know, but he had heard the rumors of McCall's

137

privateers in these waters, and he prayed now that somewhere out there might be one of them, an armed vessel with the strength and the will to protect a peaceful trader. The mists had closed again, but he had a direction and he held it as his mate ran up his trader colors and flew the buntings that said "enemy in pursuit" and "assistance requested."

"A commodity sloop," Don Geraldo sneered as he lowered his glass. "You have wasted a day for nothing, Pinto. It is not worth overhauling."

"Maybe," Enrico Pinto shrugged heavy shoulders, straining the elegant fabric of his sweat-stained *Capitano* coat. He stepped to the starboard after-rail and spat, deliberately upwind of the aristocrat, then turned his attention to the fore again. "Maybe the little sloop is all there is here for us. Or maybe that is only what you think because you do not listen to my man there at the mast top."

"The man calls his reports in a bastard tongue. A gentleman does not learn such tongues, *mi capitan*."

"Does a gentleman ever learn anything, señor? Often of late I have wondered."

"What does your lookout say to you, then?"

Pinto turned, hard eyes insolent upon the aristocrat. "He tells me what I need to know. It is what lookouts are for. Tell me, Don Geraldo, have you never baited a hook to catch a fish? Or is that another thing that *gentlemen* never learn to do?"

"I have fished. Of course I have fished."

"Ah. With your own soft hands, possibly? If you have, then you know that to catch the big fish one baits with the little one."

"And what big fish do you think there is to catch here?"

"We shall know soon, I think. There are more sails on this bay today than just ours and the trader's there.

138

Even you know that. And now the bait has seen the big fish, I think."

"Why do you think that?"

"Why else would he run up his colors and signal for help?"

"He has run up his colors? What are they?"

"Private. Colonial."

"Not English?"

"No."

Lostrato swung to face the larger man. "In that case, idiot, why do we still pursue? My warrant does not give me leave to take colonial shipping in these waters."

"We take whatever we want, señor. I thought we had agreed to that."

"If we can do so privately, yes. But you said there are other vessels. We will be witnessed. What you are doing is . . ."

"Piracy? Of course it is. But you don't know what I am doing, señor. Therefore please do not interfere with my doing it."

"You plan to take the sloop and try to draw a more valuable prize with it. I see that."

"You do not see, señor. I have no intention of 'taking' the sloop. I think we will have no need of it."

An hour passed then, Lostrato pacing the deck in sullen silence as the pirate Pinto directed his ship. An hour and part of another, and abruptly there was a break in the thinning mist and a shoreline lay just ahead with two vessels standing out from it. Lostrato hissed his surprise. The smaller one was the sloop they had followed, just putting about in the shallows there. But not a cable-length down from it was a warship. He raised his glass. Brig-sized, it glittered with fresh trim, and its luffing sails were golden in the sudden light. Gunports lined in rails, and bunting flew above its stays—bunting that was being hauled down rapidly even as he watched. There had been a message, an exchange between the two, and now the little one was coming about instead of sidling behind the big one for protection.

"Port guns ready," Pinto ordered his lieutenant. And to the helm, "Steady ahead, but prepare to come into the wind. Sheets to hand, prepare to come about to starboard, through the wind!"

"What are you doing?" Lostrato asked. "The warship is making a'port from us, not starboard."

"Shut up!" Pinto roared. "Ready to come about! Port guns out for broadside! Stand ready!"

Ahead of them the big ship—almost a brig but not quite a brig, a vessel rigged for more sail than a brig could carry—crept southward on ill-set sails while the sloop completed its turn, heeling over for a port tack, sliding at an angle toward *Columbine* and getting the wind in its sails as it drew off to the right.

"Come about!" Pinto roared. "Sight on the sloop! Fire as the guns bear!"

Lostrato watched wide-eyed. What was the man doing? Just yonder lay the kind of prize he had set out to find—a fine cruiser well-armed and poorly manned, ripe for the taking. A vessel that would put this wretched *Columbine* brigantine to shame. A vessel with which they could go forth and take prizes that would bring wealth, a vessel that might outrun or outfight the English ships that patrolled the commerce lanes. Yet Pinto was turning away from the real prize and going after the shabby little commodity sloop. In a rage of decision, the aristocrat drew his sword and thrust its point within an inch of the helmsman's throat. "Disregard those commands," he rasped. "I am taking charge of this vessel."

He never saw the heavy fist that came from behind to take him in the temple, didn't even feel the deck rising to meet his face. But after a time of pain and confusion, he was aware of the pirate Pinto standing over him, and felt the man's boot against his ribs.

"I should kill you now, señor," the heavy voice came through a fog of pain. "But it will wait for a time. You still have uses for me."

Then Pinto was beside his helm, and as Lostrato raised himself on shaking hands he saw the little sloop barely a cable off the port beam. He saw the faces of the men aboard, white, frightened faces staring across the closing waters at him. Then the view was gone, blanked out by sudden clouds much denser than ever the morning fog had been, and six of *Columbine*'s guns thundered in a ragged, point-blank broadside. Even in the echoes of the thunder he heard the crashing, rattling chaos where the little vessel had been. A scream, cut short, and the sound of gear and tackle falling across a ruined deck.

As the smoke drifted away he got to his knees, clinging to a rail. Out there the water was roiled and littered with the remains of the little trading vessel. Its stubby nose shuddered and swung upward to point at the sky as it went down by the stern. Among the litter afloat there was movement, a man struggling in the water. Then, somewhere near at hand, muskets barked and red-white gouts of spray erupted around the swimmer. He thrashed for a moment, then rolled over and sank from view.

Lostrato got to shaky feet and turned. Pinto was not looking at the flotsam where the sloop had been. He had his glass at his eye and was watching the creeping warship a half-mile away. He lowered his glass and grinned, a brutish grin that exposed black teeth.

"As I thought," Pinto said to no one except himself. "The ship has no fight to it. It has no proper crew and no master." For the first time he turned an evil glare on Lostrato. "I told you I would find a ship for us, señor patron. I have found a ship. For *me*. You with your warrant will be a passenger aboard my

141

ship, nothing more." He tipped his head downward, indicating where Lostrato's lost sword still lay on the deck. "You keep your blade. You hang it at your belt and any time you feel like it you draw it again. I will enjoy waiting for you to do that. I leave you alive this time. Next time I will kill you a little bit at a time."

He turned his back then, giving his orders. "Come full about and pursue."

Minutes later *Columbine* stood abeam of the luffing privateer, her starboard guns trained on the vessel while one of Pinto's cutthroats—one who spoke English—hailed those aboard and instructed them to strike all colors and prepare to be boarded. *"Mi capitan,"* the man shouted, "is a merciful man. He takes your ship but you will be put ashore safely if you do not resist."

Across the shoaling waters sails were furled and the transport flag came down. The snow stood dead in the water.

"Boarding party," Pinto said. "Clubs and cutlasses. Put those people into a launch and take them ashore. Kill them there. You, Torero, make ready to transfer main stores and long guns to that vessel. Place my gear in the captain's cabin and put Señor Lostrato aboard under guard. He may keep his sword, but if he draws it he is to be killed."

Within the hour the transfers had been made, and Pinto stood gloating on *Fury*'s deck. The shore party had returned, blood-spattered and grinning, four of *Columbine*'s twelve guns—the best of them—stood now at ports with the fourteen the snow had carried, and *Columbine* stood off with only Torero and a crew of five to man her, to follow where the *Fury* went and stay out of harm's way if they could.

"Make sail," Pinto instructed his crew chiefs. "It is time for us to go hunting."

XI

They had heard the thunder of the guns but could only guess at what it meant. Dalton had calculated, from his brief glimpse of the pursuit across Chesapeake, that things were about to become decidedly crowded on the west shore. So, back on deck, he had put *Mystery* over three points a'port, taking his bearings from the wind and hoping it held true.

An hour out, there had been a sighting from the maintop. Mallory spotted sail ahead, crossing their course, and Dalton estimated that it was the brigantine. They had gone on, coming just a bit to starboard to stay shy of the mid-channel, where other craft might be. *Mystery* held steady at four knots, barely throwing spray at her bow, and when the sound of guns rolled across to them they knew by its direction that whatever had occurred was behind them. It had not been the little sloop that fired. She could not have carried so many guns. Therefore it was the brigantine or the snow, and speculation ran back and forth the length of the ketch as they whispered southward in a brightening world. The forenoon watch came and passed to afternoon watch, and visibility was a steady half-mile. Gerald O'Riley turned out a meal of sorts, and they ate in shifts on deck while O'Riley fretted and cursed in the galley, trying to work around a tree trunk–like angle brace that was now a permanent fixture of his sanctum. Cormorants came to dive and sail around the ketch, and then seagulls floating in the pearly sky above.

"Coo, swagger," Pitacoke told Charley Duncan. "'Em wi' th' belchers'll ma' oor taw an' it opens."

"He said," Duncan relayed to Michael Romart, "If it clears soon those people shooting back there will surely see us."

"'Naws t'boot," Squahamac added.

"And others as well, he says."

"That won't be long," someone noted. "This stuff is burnin' away, like."

"Well, 'til we get some proper sail bent on, the best we can hope is that when the fog's gone there won't be anybody near enough to worry about."

Titus Wilton and a half-dozen willing hands worked steadily on the planked hold-top, stitching and plying, and most of a maincourse now lay piled alongside, volunteers cross-legged in a circle there setting grommets and binding in cringles to take the sheetlines that must work the big sail when it was hoist. Wilton and two men were at work on a topsail.

By the helm, Dalton paced restlessly. The business of sailing blind in close waters had never been to his liking, and the sounds of encounter nearby just made matters worse. With a full suit of sails and a holding wind, he could put Chesapeake behind him in two days. With the sail he had it would take three or more.

What *Mystery* would face on the open sea when she turned south toward Hatteras was something beyond prediction. There might be predators out there as well. There might be privateers, and there might be Crown vessels on blockade. Simply negotiating the tricky seas off Hatteras to reach the arch of coastline running down the southern face of the Atlantic would be a treacherous business in this season. But those concerns were yet ahead, and at least could be dealt with as a mariner deals with the sea. This recent business—the long weeks of hiding in the forest, the brash consigning of a cargo of great guns to a poorly armed and unescorted vessel manned by fugitives . . . he longed for the opportunity to take John Singleton Ramsey by his haughty lapels and shake him until his teeth rattled . . . and now this creeping game of hide-and-seek along a bay that held no friendly sail— all of it was taking a toll on his nerves.

Ramsey. The man had friends everywhere in these lands—likely enemies as well, but certainly *some* friends. He could have arranged a proper passage for his battery guns—a sturdy big cargo ship with an armed escort or two. Why had he not? There was only one likely answer to that, and Dalton knew it. The guns were contraband. Ramsey could not afford to have anyone know of them, at least not anyone who might be in a situation to speak about it. A wry smile played at his cheeks. That being the case, there could hardly have been a better lot of deliverers to stick with the task.

Virtually everyone aboard the creeping ketch was a fugitive of one kind or another. Escapees, felons, deserters, walk-aways from shore leave—from the captain with his charge of treason hanging over him right down to the five Hessian deserters who were his marines, there wasn't a person aboard who likely would be gossiping in some local pub. At least not anytime soon.

And that brought to mind a problem he had set aside earlier, in the press of business. "Mister Tidy, when the air clears, anyone with a glass will be able to see this gun lying here along our stern. See if you can't get it covered over with canvas, or something."

"Hammock nets, sir? We haven't rigged any yet, and along the rails they would screen this part of our . . . ah . . . cargo."

"Capital idea," Dalton nodded. "Please see to the

145

rigging of hammock nets along the aft rails. And you might set a few kegs and the like atop the breech, that should confuse anyone who might have a look at us."

"Aye, sir. Water kegs alongside, and we have some empty powder kegs now that we can stow on top."

"Please see to it, then, Mister Tidy." He turned to the rail, glass at his eye, and studied the drifting mists. Very soon they would be gone. Then they would see what they would see. Abruptly he lowered the glass and turned again. "*Empty* powder kegs, Mister . . . ?" But Tidy was gone forward, arranging for the rigging of hammock nets on the after-rails. One of the gunners, though, idled just beyond the deckhouse, and Dalton hailed him. "Mister Pugh, come here, please."

"Aye, sir."

When the young gunner was at hand he asked, "Mister Pugh, how much gunpowder have we dispensed?"

Pugh calculated briefly. "Sixty pounds, sir. Thereabouts. A load and a set-by."

"Sixty pounds? Thirty pounds a load?"

"Aye, sir. About that. Three pounds apiece in the six-pounders, you know, and a pound or so for the swivel. Ethan and me, we capped the vents proper so the loads will hold good until you have need of 'em, sir. If you have need of them, I mean."

"That is all very well, Mister Pugh. But where is the remaining seventeen pounds of powder?"

"Sir?"

"You have accounted for thirteen pounds of powder out of thirty. Where is the remaining seventeen pounds of the load?"

"Why, right here, sir. The command was, 'load guns.' We loaded 'em."

Dalton stared at the forty-eight pounder snugged along the deck, its muzzle to the wind.

"Actually it took a bit more, sir," Pugh admitted.

146

"Seventeen pounds loads a forty-two for most purposes, but since this is a forty-eight, we put in a few pounds more. Neither one of us has ever handled a forty-eight, sir, but we didn't want to chance an undercharge."

Dalton bit his lip. "Please be sure the vent is well capped, then, Mister Pugh. And let's have no lanterns or candles near that breech. Should that monster discharge itself, *Mystery* might jump right out from under the lot of us."

"On deck!"

"Report, Mister Mallory!"

"Th' fog's driftin' away, sir. I can see!"

At the mizzentop Ishmael Bean's voice was thin with surprise. "Great hairy goblins, so can I!"

"What do you see, tops?"

"Sails, sir! Lord a'marcy, look at 'em! Hard on the starboard beam, maybe a mile . . . and another three points abaft . . . two ahead, one just about dead on at two miles, the other a point or two to port . . . there's another one, a little one, just comin' out from the east shore . . . Jesus!"

And from the mizzen, "You'll see them in just a bit, sir. We're runnin' out of fog."

Dalton shouted, "Mister Duncan!" A second later Charley Duncan was before him.

"Mister Duncan, " Dalton pointed foreward. "I trust there is enough main course yonder to bend onto a spar. Please send it up now. We have need of it."

"Ay, sir. Mister Wilton . . ."

"If Mister Wilton is not through with it, send him up too. He can help catch the wind while he stitches."

"Aye, sir." Duncan turned a'fore and cupped his hands. "On the main! Topmen aloft to make sail!"

One of the marines leapt to a gunwale, bracing himself with a shroud, and pointed. *"Ich sehe ein*

147

segel . . . da drüben!"

Dalton swung his glass, and saw her, just visible, a mile a'beam on the starboard. The snow, the one named *Fury*—but even in the poor visibility there was something different about her. She had been limping, poorly handled and poorly trimmed. Now she limped no more.

"Zwie segeln," another marine pointed, then turned to Corporal Wesselmann, *"Wo gehen wir hin, Korporal?"*

Beyond the mainmast Squahamac leapt to the planked top of the great hold, scattering sailmaker's tools in his excitement. "Coo, swagger, loo'a th' passel o'm. Blimey!"

Pitacoke bounded past him and gained the gunwale alongside the clinging marine. His arrival almost sent the Hessian overboard as they both clung to the same shroud cable. "Gi'n a bi' o' lee 'ere, myte," the Indian snapped. "Le's ha' a bi'a loo', y'know."

"Ach du liber. Ist ein segel. Zwie segel."

Before they could come to fisticuffs on the starboard gunwale, John Tidy had them both by the scruffs and had them hauled back on deck and separated.

The Hessian glared at the Indian. *"Vernünstig mit Indianern zu verhandeln ist genau so schwer wie vernünstig mit Engländern zu verhandeln. Sie sind sich sehr ähnlich!"*

"Belay that!" Tidy roared. "Th' both of ye! We've enough on our hands without this!" Whether either of them understood or not, both did, and they backed away.

Duncan had paused on his way past. "What was that he said?"

Tidy shook his head. "He said being reasonable with Indians is like being reasonable with Englishmen, they're both the same."

Dalton glassed the dispersing mist. *Fury* was parelleling *Mystery*'s course, a mile away, going southward. Behind her and some distance, following, was the brigantine. Now he knew what had happened back there in the fogs. The brigantine had pursued the sloop and taken the snow. Even at this distance he could see far more activity on the snow's deck than had been there before, and an odd flash of bright colors in the stern. The ship was under new management now, and he saw no sign of shelling on its hull or in its rigging. Who, then, had fired at whom? There was no sign of the sloop.

Men swarmed the footropes of the maincourse spar now, dropping lines from tackle blocks to lift the new square sail into place while others on deck secured bowlines to the cringles along its leech sides and Titus Wilton danced and fumed. "It isn't ready for hoisting!" he protested. "There should be a second row of reef points, and the boltrope at the foot of it hasn't been properly bound. I don't release sails in such condition. It would never pass inspection!"

"I don't think the captain is suiting us up for inspection right now, Doctor Franklin," Michael Romart pointed out, trying to calm him. "I believe he is . . ."

"Wilton!" Wilton barked.

"What?"

"Wilton! My name is Wilton! I don't even know Doctor Franklin!"

"Yes, sir. Sorry, sir. But I think the captain is more interested right now in getting some sail on this vessel so that we can run from danger."

"What danger?"

"That danger," Romart pointed. A mile away the armed snow had seen them and was shifting its yards, trimming for a course to intercept. Behind it, the brigantine was already on a new course.

"On deck!"

149

"Yes, Mister Mallory?"

"They're both changing course, sir. They'll be coming this way."

"I see them, Mister Mallory. But not those ahead. What of them?"

"The one leading is a schooner, sir. Tacks like a dancer, she does. The one behind seems to be a brig."

"Colors?"

"Haven't seen their colors, sir."

"Keep a sharp eye there, Mister Mallory. We have the other pair in sight. Mister Tidy! How is that maincourse coming along?"

"Ready to take her up, Cap'n. Lift lines are secured."

"Look lively, then." Dalton turned again to glass the distance to starboard, noting despite his concern the graceful lines, the massive spread of yards and the jaunty movements of the snow. Duncan had told him of the snow they had seen, put in for fitting in a wilderness cove, and he knew this to be the same one. But since his first glimpse of it, the warship had come to life. He suspected it had been in transit, maybe from one hidden yard to another, when first he saw it. It had been poorly handled then, as though being shunted by men not familiar with the rigging and running of a fighting ship. But it was alive now, a deadly lady of the seas with curls of spray at its bow and its tall suit trimmed to meet the breeze.

"See the easy grace of her," he muttered. "A vessel worth noting and well worth watching."

Dalton had fought snows. He knew how deadly such a ship could be. Built and rigged along the lines of an English brig, the snow differed in only a few respects—but those differnces were awesome. Two-masted, like a brig, the snow had an added feature that was purely American in its invention. Directly behind the aftermast was a smaller, separate standing mast that was almost part of the aftermast, but not

150

quite. The big drive sail and its rising gaff were mounted on this auxiliary mast, barely two feet aft of the mainmast. Trysail mast, some called the auxiliary. To others it was a jackmast. Whatever the name, it allowed a sail to be set on the lower yard of the mainmast so that the snow could operate in all respects either as a square-rigged vessel or a fore-and-aft–rigged vessel.

And this one, this *Fury*, had been even further modified. High hounds raked the clouds aloft, with lifting spars above the topgallants. She could fly royals on both masts. And all the yards below them were blocked for the setting of studsails to widen her grip on the wind. She even had yards for adding a "ringtail" to the spanker, and could carry a spritsail under her jib if her master decided to.

"Who has her now?" he wondered, half-aloud, as he watched her heel a neat strake to increase her angle of approach. "Not her owners, apparently. She is a taken ship, but the man commanding does know how to use her."

There was something in the manner of her maneuvers that toyed with his memory—something notable in the rhythm of those handling her sails and her helm, a sort of quick-step synchronization that was just off the drill as he—and virtually every other midshipman aboard British and American vessels— had learned it. He pressed his memory and found it. The slight, puzzling difference was the difference between British schooling in the North Sea and off the home islands, and that other schooling that had evolved from the training of ship's crews in the Mediterranean and off the coast of Africa.

Spanish? He puzzled at it. What would Spanish be doing here? Spanish privateers were sometimes seen in the warm streams off the Indies, ships that sheltered in the Spanish ports at New Orleans and Antigua. But up here?

On purest hunch he thought, *pirates*. And as he toyed with the hunch it took shape. Spanish pirates on the prowl, far from their usual haunts. That would explain the battered brigantine. They had needed a better ship. They had come into Chesapeake and found one. And now they had a mind to see what sort of goods his ketch might carry.

The broad maincourse crept limp toward the waiting spar, then went taut at its crown as blocks snugged it in. Aloft, six topmen went to work securing it, bending it on to the spar. Dalton counted the seconds as they worked. This one sail would not get them away from harm. Even fully suited, *Mystery* could never outrun a dashing snow, not in any wind or any waters. But the new canvas would give them an extra knot or two, and would buy them that much time.

His eyes tearing at the strain, he tried again to count the guns aboard the snow. At least sixteen, he knew. Maybe more. And far bigger guns than *Mystery*'s short and long sixes. The snow would mount twelves and eighteens on its gundeck, possibly even a twenty-four or two. He glanced around at the keg-and-canvas-covered monster cradled alongside the helm. He could, if it came to that, show them something to amuse them. But only once.

And even as he thought it, something within him recoiled at the thought of touching off that monster against the proud snow. She was a beautiful ship. Even in the hands of Spanish pirates she showed her grace, and she deserved better than even the least that a ball from a battery gun, met head-on, would do to her.

"On deck! It's clearing ahead. Can you see them yet, sir?"

He turned his glass, his heart sinking. There were indeed two more ships out there, coming on, beating upwind to intercept, and now the sleek schooner in

152

the lead ran up its colors. The Union Jack unfurled from its stern halyard, flowing bright in the wind, and signal bunting ran up the mainmast, a signal that Dalton knew by heart. It was a command to come about and stand for boarding.

And far beyond, in the hazy distance, were more sails, also coming on.

Duncan came to join him by the helm. "What do you make of all this, Captain?"

"A free-for-all about to occur, is my best guess," Dalton shook his head. "Unless I miss my guess, the snow out there and the brigantine are Spanish pirates . . . privateers, possibly, but being in these waters makes them simply pirates. The schooner beating about ahead of us is a king's ship on patrol or pursuit. The far vessel coming on may be a brig, possibly a second Crown vessel, although we can't make its colors for a bit, I suppose. But it is either a Crown brig or an American privateer. In any respect there is enough hostile gunnery closing on that stretch of bay just ahead to sink everything you see out here . . . including us."

"The schooner commands a lay-by. Shall we respond? Mister Caster has the flags and signals dressed out."

Dalton turned his glass a'starboard. The snow and the brigantine were abreast now, three cables apart, but they too had seen the approaching sails and the schooner's signal. As he watched, signals went up on the snow, directed to the brigantine. The brigantine responded, and the snow altered its course by a point or two, lengthening the distance between them.

"Ah." Dalton read the signals. "The Spaniard has the snow, and has left just a short crew on the other. He intends to challenge the schooner yonder while his second comes to head us off. Do we have a full set of colors, Mister Duncan?"

Before Duncan could speak, Billy Caster came up

153

with the flag locker. "Everything's here, sir. I've inventoried. Squire Ramsey has fit us out to be any nationality it might please us to be. We even have a Dutch pennant. Would you like to be Dutch, sir?"

"Not at the moment, Mister Caster, but I believe it is time to play the bluffing game a bit. Have we a merchant company device there?"

"Aye, sir. At least I think that's what the blue one with the corner jack is."

"Very well. Mister Duncan, hands to the gaff halyard and maintop halyards. Please advise the schooner that we are loyal Indiamen on trade, and that the two vessels closing us abeam are pirates. Request assistance."

"When it's done and they inspect us they'll have us shot," Duncan pointed out.

"Very likely, Mister Duncan. Unless that far vessel yonder is an American, in which case there might just be confusion enough to get us out of this trap . . . if we had sail enough to scamper off while everyone is busy."

John Tidy's whistle pierced the air. "Main course bent on, sir. Permission to sheet home?"

"By all means, Mister Tidy. Sheet home at once."

Tackle sang and the bright new sail billowed below the maintop, then snapped full in the freshening wind as Titus Wilton's face drained of color. It snapped . . . and held. And *Mystery* climbed the chop of waters and took a modicum of spray in her teeth. A modest wake formed behind her, and the helmsman cursed as a newly stubborn helm fought his control. It was the curse of the ketch, with its sails spread far back to leave room for maximum cargo stowage, to be hard helmed.

From afore came the call, "We're making five knots now, sir. With a steady wind we may come to six."

"Hardly 'hull up and running,' is it, sir?" Duncan

154

noted with irony.

"We've been spoiled," Dalton shrugged. "*Faith* spoiled us. We've no reacehorse here, but only a plodding ox."

"On deck!"

"Yes, Mister Bean?"

"That one ship is still making to close on us, sir. He's seen our colors and demands that we strike."

Dalton studied the brigantine, wondering if his guesses were correct. "Mister Duncan, have a look at that fellow, please. What sort of guns would you say he has aboard?"

Duncan peered through the glass. "Can't be sure, sir. Sixes or nines, I make it. Maybe a single nine in the bow. If it is, he'll have the range of us soon enough."

Dalton stepped to the stern rail. The launch in tow pattered along in their wake, its proud new punt guns upthrust at bow and stern. "Mister Duncan, would you enjoy exercising those fowlers that you procured for our launch?"

"Yes, sir! Ah, aye, sir, I would."

"Then I have in mind to put you in command of a sortie, Mister Duncan. A nice diversion at this point probably would amuse just about everyone involved, I should think."

XII

As Lieutenant Domingo Torero, once of His Most
Catholic Majesty's service as an ordinary seaman and
now *segundo* to the freebooter Enrico Pinto, brought
Columbine within gun range of the scudding, half-
sailed ketch, he studied the little cargo hauler
through a glass and saw no particular threat there.
The ketch now had a main course taking wind—it
had been bent on since the first sighting—but still
it was three sails short of a suit. Further, it had been
towing a launch, and now the launch was gone. He
glassed the deck and the shrouds, counting. One man
was at the maintop, three others working the deck—
two of those appeared to be Indians—and a hatless
man in a blue coat at the helm.

There had been more aboard her, but that was no
puzzle. The remainder of the crew had taken the
launch and run away at his signal to strike colors. It
was obvious, because it was a thing he might have
done under such circumstances.

In the distance, down the bay, *El Capitan* Pinto
was putting the new prize through her paces, tacking
for advantage, trying to come into upwind range of
the *Ingles* schooner. Torero was left on his own to
deal with the sluggish ketch, and it pleased him to
note that the cargo ship sat deep in the water. It

carried something, certainly, and he would claim a prize share of its value if he took it alone without *El Capitan*'s assistance. Even Pinto could not argue such a point—not without a thorough mutiny on his hands.

Eight guns remained aboard *Columbine*, but beside himself there were only five men. But no matter. He should need only one shot to effect his capture. As he closed he had a pair of nine-pounders loaded and run out a'port, with a single gun crew to fire first one, and then, if necessary, the other.

Again he looked at the handful of men visible aboard the ketch. These had been left when the others made off in their launch. Did that mean these were abandoned for lack of space, or was one of these the master of the vessel and the others only those who had remained loyal to him when their fellows fled? Did any of those aboard know how to read his demand that they strike their colors? Did they know that it was necessary now for them to surrender?

As *Columbine* closed to within a cable length, coming in abaft the starboard beam of the ketch, he gave the order to his gun crew, and the first of the nine-pounders roared. Instantly a hole appeared in the vessel's new main course, and he saw the fear-whitened faces of those aboard turn toward him. One of those on the deck raced to the stern and began hauling down the flag there. A scuffle ensued between that man and the hatless one at the helm, then the flag was lowered all the way.

"Keep that gun trained on the mainmast," Torero ordered. "All hands pistols and cutlasses. We will come alongside and board when we grapple."

The brigantine eased alongside the ketch, and lines were thrown. At the rail Torero looked down to the stubby vessel's deck. Its forehold had been planked over, and various kegs and bales were piled here and there on deck, including a long, squat

158

covered pile beside the helm running from deck-house to stern rail. At Torero's signal his five hands crowded to the rail, ready to swing down to the lower deck. Then myriad scuffing, thumping sounds came from behind them, and they turned and found themselves staring into the muzzles of a line of muskets and rifles, with a dozen or more grinning seamen and scowling Hessian marines behind them.

A sandy-haired young man stepped from the rank and bowed flamboyantly. "If you all will please put down your weapons," he grinned, "then maybe we won't blow your friggin' heads off. Your ship has been taken."

Even as Torero and his five complied, more men were coming over his rail from the launch snugged tight against his starboard hull.

Herded into a tight cluster astern, guarded by threatening Hessians, Torero and his men watched helplessly as men swarmed the brigantine's shrouds to strip her of every scrap of usable sail. Others prowled belowdecks, and still others rigged hoists on her guns to swing them over to the ketch—and a young man barely more than a boy made notations as they came and went.

In the distance guns roared and smoke rolled across the water as the snow and the schooner found each other's range and opened fire. One quick pass and they parted, each circling for advantage. Far beyond them another ship beat its way slowly toward them, and Torero's heart sank. Alone, *El Capitan* could take or sink the English schooner, but it would take time. The snow was the more powerful vessel, but the schooner was fast and well armed, and it would be a stand-up fight at best. But the distant vessel, coming on, would turn the odds. And *El Capitan* would break and run. There would be no returning to rescue his lieutenant and these men.

It was a thing Torero understood because it was

what he would have done himself under the circumstances.

The hatless man he had seen at the ketch's helm came aboard *Columbine* and looked around, wrinkling his nose. "Pirates," he said. "The ship stinks of blood." He approached the prisoners. "Who here speaks English?"

"I, *señor*," Torero said. "A little."

"Very well, *señor*, then you can tell me who you people are and who that is aboard the snow . . . you can tell me everything I want to know."

"But *señor*, I . . ."

"Otherwise," the man said, "we will bind you all to your mast and burn this stinking ship under you."

Torero sighed. "Si, *señor*. I tell you what you want to know."

Even as he did so, the brigantine's foresails were being bent onto topsail and gallant spars aboard the ketch, and a stubby, middle-aged man on the ketch's foredeck was running armspreads on her big spanker, estimating its size.

When the pirate craft had been cleaned of sails, stores, guns, casks, and anything else that might be useful, *Mystery*'s crew returned to their own deck, cut loose the grapples, and raised their ill-assorted sails, leaving six Spaniards behind to make whatever shift they could of a derelict brigantine with nothing to catch the wind except sheeted spars.

"Never did get a chance to touch off the punt guns," Charley Duncan noted a bit sorrowfully. "They were so busy taking our ship, we didn't have call to shoot anybody with anything."

"Another time, Mister Duncan," Dalton assured him, gazing ahead where smoke again rolled on the water. "How says our log and line now?"

"Near eight knots, sir. Mister Wilton says he is shamed to have those rabble sails above him, but they are giving us advantage of the wind. Are we going to join the melee off there, sir? We've guns enough now to make an accounting ourselves, I believe.''

"Gi'm blee'n 'ell 'swot oi sie," one of the Indians seconded, squatting atop the covered great gun alongside the helm.

Dalton regarded the savage, trying to fathom the fathomless ebon eyes that looked back at him. There was, he decided, a limit to how much discipline could be impose on a mixed crew. The limit was obvious where Pitacoke and Squahamac were concerned. They had absolutely no concept of formality or civility. He shrugged and returned his attention to the fore. Not more than two miles ahead a pair of warships circled and sniped at each other while beyond them the high sails of a brig were turned sharply aslant, beating toward them. "On whose side, Mister Duncan?"

"Why, I imagine we could lend that schooner a bit of a hand," Duncan said. "After all, those are good English lads and that other lot is a bunch of stinkin' Spaniards.''

"And the one beyond?"

"Looks to be a brig, sir. But we could get there an' step in before he does.''

Dalton smiled grimly, knowing the excitement Duncan felt because he felt it himself. The guns were volleying, and it was in the blood of the warrior to wade in and take a hand.

"The brig is colonial," Dalton said. "That isn't two viewpoints being exchanged yonder, it's three.''

"How do you know the brig is colonial? It shows no colors.''

"Privateer," Dalton said. "Ramsey mentioned her. She belong to a Colonial, Ian McCall. I gather he has others as well. She's out for British prizes. Look there, Mister Duncan . . . the Spaniard pulls away. He has what he came here for, a good fast ship. Now

161

he will head to sea, rather than chance an encounter with two enemies in close waters."

The snow had indeed pulled away, turning southward with the wind at its tail, angling to pass the brig beyond gun range.

"Then that leaves us for them to squabble over," Duncan noted.

"Aye. If they get around to noticing us before we're gone." The schooner had come about and was starting after the snow, but the brig moved to cut it off, as Dalton had expected. The captain of that privateer would have no way of knowing who commanded the snow. But he knew the Union Jack when he saw it, and the schooner was prime game for him. Colors rose on his halyard, the colors of a privateer of Virginia—thirteen bars, alternately red and white. And as the brig's flag snugged at its gaff, a similar flag went up aboard the fleeing snow. The Spaniard had sealed the British schooner's fate with a simple lie. And assured his own escape from Chesapeake.

The schooner put over to run crosswind, westward, and the brig lay back and paralleled its course, blocking it. Within minutes both warships were a mile or more away, beyond the mid-channel, and *Mystery* plodded steadily ahead. In the distance the snow was making good time outbound . . . then it veered and slowed, luffing its sails. Dalton put his glass to his eye. The little packet vessel that had been trying to cross from east to west was there, and the snow stood directly above it, its tall shadow dimming the sunlight on the small craft's two sails. A boat was being lowered . . . in departing, the pirate had hesitated long enough to snatch some minor prize that chanced to offer itself. It was too far away to see what was happening there, even in the clear light of the quartering sun, which had dispelled the last of the day's fog.

At a steady eight knots, *Mystery* cruised down bay,

still many miles from the open sea but with no obstacles presently in sight. Echoes of thunder rolled across the bay, and they looked back. Back there two nimble sips danced and spat and circled each other, and Dalton's eyes held on the graceful sails of the schooner. Overmatched against a brig, still she was giving a fine account of herself, and his Irish heart flinched at the irony of fine seamen on fine ships—men who spoke the same language and might even share the same ancestors—so bent upon each other's destruction that nothing else mattered to them at all. But then, that was why such ships were built. And maybe that was why such men were born.

He glanced aside at Charley Duncan. The sandy-haired sailor's eyes glinted with suppressed excitement as he watched the sparring in the receding distance. And just beyond stood Michael Romart, the same hot, fierce intensity in his eyes as in Duncan's. An Englishman and an American, as alike in their ways as two peas in a pod, and of exactly the cut of those back there. Were these two on those vessels right now, he thought, one on each, they would be happily lashing away at each other just like those back there. They are too much alike not to.

And if I were on the deck of either, what would I be dong? Everything in my power to kill or capture the other ship, and never having a second thought about it.

Maybe it is in our blood, he suggested to himself. Maybe we are all crazy.

"On deck!"

He glanced up. "Yes, Mister Mallory?"

"Flotsam ahead, sir. Wreckage of a craft, and maybe somebody clinging to it."

Again he peered through his glass, then set it aside. "Bring us a point to starboard, helm. We'll have a look."

The man they pulled from the water amidst the wreckage of a small craft was dying, sliced across the belly by a cutlass or saber. They laid him on the deck and knew there was nothing to be done for him. But after a time he stirred, looked up at them, and spoke in French.

Dalton knelt beside him, but found his French wanting. "Can you speak English, sir?"

"Ah . . ." the voice was no more than a wheeze. "Ah, yes. A little, m'sieur. My . . . my daughters . . . the Spaniard has taken them. Please, m'sieur . . . please help them. They are so young . . . helpless . . . they count on me."

"Who are you, m'sieur?"

"I am Jean-Luc Toussaint, Chevalier du Canille . . . m'sieur." His eyes glazed over with pain, and for a moment they thought he had died. Then his breath caught again. "The Spaniard . . . I saw him. I saw him . . . oh, my Eunice! He . . . with his blade, he . . . she was a good wife, m'sieur. Always. He . . . ah, *mon dieu*, Eunice! I am coming, Eunice. Wait for me, I come. M'sieur, my girls . . . my Eugenie and Lucette . . . the Spaniard has them . . . in the name of God, m'sieur, please . . ."

Dalton knelt there for a moment longer, then stood. Nothing more could be done for the Frenchman. "Mister Tidy, please go and find Mister Wilton and have him sew a burial shroud. Mister Caster . . . oh, there you are. Please . . ."

Billy stared at him with stricken eyes. "Captain," he started, then had to start again, "The man, he called on you, sir. In God's name, he said."

"I heard him call on me, Mister Caster." He stood erect, chin high, staring into the distance where the snow's bright sails were now only a speck on the far waters. "But to do what?"

Billy shook his head. "I don't know, sir. I surely don't."

*   *   *

164

Pinto was pleased with his new ship. Like a playful bull he strode her decks, badgering and cuffing his sullen crewmen, working them without mercy as he put the vessel through its paces. Even with the loss of *Teniente* Torero and five hands, Pinto still had more than forty men—dregs of the barrios and stockades of half a dozen Spanish-held ports, cutthroats and thieves, mercenaries out of work, cutpurses and bludgeonists, assassins and outright berserkers, but every one a capable sailor and all thoroughly intimidated by the sheer violence and blood lust that their captain displayed on a regular basis. Forty men—three times the number necessary for the sailing of a ship, but all useful for the boarding and taking of prizes.

The exchange of fire with the English schooner had been little more to him than a testing of guns, a shaping up of crew stations aboard an unfamiliar vessel. Had there been no interference, he would have destroyed the schooner. But there had been other vessels, the brig beating up from the south, and that awkward ketch that somehow had bested Torero and *Columbine*. They took her sails! He had seen that even as he engaged the Englishman. A sitting target, the ketch had allowed Torero to come alongside . . . then had boarded the brigantine and taken its guns and its sails. He had seen the sheeted spars, had seen the old ship drifting naked and helpless, while the ketch ran up ill-fitted sails and came on as though nothing had happened.

Lostrato had blustered, but it was no great loss. With this new ship—this fine, charging bull of a fighting ship—he would take all the prizes he wanted. With *Fury* he could avoid the frigates and take his pick of anything sailing the merchant lanes.

The little packet boat he had caught crossing the bay, that had been a momentary thing, and profitable in its way. The Frenchman had carried a fat purse, and the woman had worn jewelry that would bring a price. He had killed them while his boarders cut down the two boatmen. The two young girls—flimsy French things and one of them only barely old enough to be of use to a man—he had secured in an after cabin with old Vasco at guard, to keep the crew away from them until he himself was through with them. It had struck him as a great joke to put Vasco to such a task. "I do you great honor, Vasco," he taunted. "I trust you to keep these little treasures safe for me." And then he had pointed at the crotch of Vasco's *pantalones* and laughed. "Your misfortune allows me to trust you above all others in such a matter as this." He had laughed again, and others around had laughed with him. It was a fine joke. All knew of Vasco's misfortune. A bit of canister shot from a British gun had carried away his interest in women.

As an afterthought he had called the aristocrat Lostrato to the companionway. "I think I will trust you, as well, Don Geraldo, because even with your sword at your side I have found you have no more *pelotas* than does this miserable Vasco. Therefore I want you to talk to the two French *doncellitas*. See if there is anyone who might be persuaded to ransom them from me."

The glare of pure hatred in the aristocrat's pale gaze was so like Vasco's that it set him to laughing all over again. *"Dos piratos bravos! Dos piratos sin testículos!"*

For an instant it seemed that Lostrato would draw his blade. But the aristocrat merely glared at him, then turned away, and Pinto went back to his deck still laughing.

Fury was indeed a fine vessel. Guns at every port, ranging guns at bow and stern, a ship well provisioned and fully equipped to take him anywhere he wanted to go. Massive sail . . . he had never seen so

166

small a ship rigged to take so much sail, and he kept his deckmen and topmen aswarm with the furling and unfurling, the reefing and sheeting, the running out and running in, the lifting, hoisting, testing, and lowering of first this sail and then that one.

Courses at fore and main, topsails, topgallants and royals . . . and three of the yards at each mast rigged for the press of wide-wing studdingsails. Even a second gaff and boom on the driver for what the Americans called a "ringtail." By the time Cape Henry was in sight, with the open sea beyond, Pinto knew the workings of the snow and had begun drills to teach them to his crew.

And in his cabin that night he celebrated in solitary splendor and drank golden rum until he passed out.

The Crown schooner *Swift* might have outrun the privateer *Porphyry*, but Commander Curtis Hedgely was not inclined to run. Even so, despite the brig's superior firepower, *Swift* might have outclassed the heavier vessel in pure ferocity . . . had the master of the colonial vessel been a lesser man than Solon Hays.

And so the two danced and nipped at each other for a time, each trying to go for the throat and the kill, each using every advantage to hammer away at the other until a mile of the mid-Chesapeake was clouded with rolling powder smoke and reverberated with their thunders, and two battered and proud vessels—one flying the Union Jack, one the stripes of Virginia—stood beam to beam and pounded away at each other across fifty yards of littered swells.

When it was done Hedgely himself hauled down his flag in submission, and Solon Hays stood at his rail to salute a valiant foe.

West shore patriots put out in punts and launches

167

to bring the battered ships to the retaken docks at Lancaster Court House, and the two masters shared a pint of grog at the tavern there while militiamen stood ready to deliver the Englishman and his remaining crew to the stockade at Buckingham.

"You'll not have many of the luxuries there, I'm afraid," Hays told the Briton. "The place is over-crowded with prisoners since the fighting around Phladelphia. But I'm told that you will be treated with some decency. It's better than the lockups at Fairfax, they say."

"Then I'm sure it will be more comfortable than what I could have offered you, I'm afraid," Hedgely shrugged. "The last privateer I took, off Delaware, I tried to intercede but there was nothing I could do. Master and men were put aboard the line ship *Cabot* for transport to England. I went aboard before they sailed. I am sorry that I did. Seventy-eight prisoners they had, all in a lower hold . . ."

"What ship was it, the privateer?"

"I saw where they put them, Captain. That hold measured twelve by twenty feet and was three feet high. Seventy-eight wretches in such a space, all the way to England. Do you really want to know who they were?"

Hays shook his head. "No. I think I would rather not, thank you."

"I thought not. There's times I think your lads do well to fight us to the death, Captain. There are worse things than death."

Hays regarded the Englishman. The young officer seemed hardly more than a boy, but his command of his vessel had been flawless. And his ferocity in battle had been intense. "You are quite a lad, Curtis Hedgely. What were you doing up Chesapeake and alone? Not seeking armed brigs and snows, were you?"

"I'd have thought twice had I known what I'd find

168

up there," Hedgely grinned a rueful grin. "Actually, I was in pursuit of Spanish pirates. I saw them from the shelter of an island."

"That brigantine? Spanish?"

"Aye. The brigantine. Though now they have a better ship. The American snow is no longer American, Captain. Those Spanish have it now."

"That explains that, then. I wondered. Well, they say the brigantine was found drifted ashore near Cross Pass. No one aboard, and all its sails and guns missing. A mystery, eh?"

"More than a mystery," Hedgely's grin widened. "A *Mystery*. Such was the name of the crawling ketch that helped itself to what it wanted of her."

"A ketch. Yes, I saw it, I think. I wondered if it might be the commission of an old friend of mine. There's been talk he has made a housepet of some wild Irish seaman. The same one who did the damage in New York, they say."

"Dalton?"

"If that's his name, yes."

"Wouldn't it be something," Hedgely muttered, "if Patrick Dalton is running loose again . . . and aboard a ketch."

It was some time after they had gone that the small, gray man in the near corner stood and put on his hat. He had heard enough for his purposes. A ketch. *Mystery*. And he had no doubt at all who would be in command.

At a dark place nearby Felix Croney waited, and when his service guard arrived he said, "Get a signal to fleet for me, please. Fugitive warrant and contraband, a ketch-rigged vessel, laden and outbound from Chesapeake. The name is *Mystery*."

XIII

"By the mark, four, sir, and steady as you please."
John Tidy stood at rigid attention to deliver his
report, the thin gray hair that whipped around his
face below the brim of his tar hat bright silver in the
morning sun. Then, the proper formality having
been observed, he relaxed visibly. "It's seven bells of
th' morning watch, sir. Will the captain an' all be
wanting their breakfast soon? Mister O'Riley would
like to scrub his pot."

Dalton glanced around from the papers on the
trestle table where he and Billy Caster were going
over inventories. "Have all hands been fed?"

"Aye, sir. All except yourself and Misters Caster
and Duncan, sir. But cook is fussin', sir. He says th'
rest of his slop will set up like foundry brick if
somebody doesn't eat it soon."

"Very well, Mister Tidy. Respects to the cook and
ask him to please send some slop up here. We shall
eat on deck."

"Aye, sir." Tidy disappeared down the companionway.

The trestle table with its ornate fittings had been a
cabin fixture aboard the brigantine, as had the four
chairs that encircled it now abaft the helm. Billy
Caster sat at one side, writing his previous day's log

171

"in fine" for the captain's perusal while Dalton and Duncan pored over long lists of items done in the boy's meticulous script.

"There are things here I had no idea we had taken aboard," Dalton said for the second or third time. "Such as this. It says: 'Four and a part of tallow soap.' What is that?"

"The soap is in the form of pot-slabs, sir," Billy explained. "One of the Fanshaw brothers found it in the aft hold, under some spilt hay. There were five slabs, but the Fanshaws took it to be ginger-sweet and ate part of one slab."

"I'm surprised those stinking Spanish had soap aboard their vessel," Duncan said. "I saw no indication that they even knew what soap might be for."

"They probably didn't know they had it, sir," Billy said. "That brigantine was an awful mess below-decks."

"The Fanshaws ate soap?" Dalton raised a brow. "What sort of condition are they in now, then?"

"Oh, they're fit, sir. They spent a good part of the night retching over the forerails, and then an hour or two asquat on the catheads, but they are chipper enough now. Only a bit pale, but that is passing, now they're proper purged."

"I should imagine. And this item: 'Linen, two bolts.' Is that good linen?"

"Aye, sir," Duncan told him. "Mister Romart found it in the sail locker. It should be worth a bit."

"And this? 'Assorted swords, cutlasses, belt axes, knives and daggers, total items one hundred and four.'"

"The buggers *are* Spanish, sir," Duncan shrugged.

Dalton thumbed further, then stopped. "Boots?"

Billy glanced across. "Aye, sir. Fourteen pairs of riding boots, assorted sizes, all new."

Dalton glanced down at his own battered boots,

then went back to his inventory. "Nine Spanish reales, gold. Did they leave gold coin just lying around, then?"

"Not exactly what you'd call lying around, sir," Duncan looked sheepish. "They were in that lieutenant's purse."

"We are not pirates, Mister Duncan."

"Oh, no, sir! But it wasn't like that, sir. I politely asked the gentleman's permission before I relieved him of the gold."

"And did he politely give it?"

"I can only assume so, sir. I don't speak Spanish."

Gerald O'Riley, red-faced from the heat of tub fires in the tiny galley, emerged on deck with wooden plates laden with what looked like solidifying glue. He set the plates before them, then went below again to bring up tea. "Slop," Duncan frowned.

"Food," Dalton corrected him, and dug into the pasty stuff. It was mainly boiled oats, but with bits and pieces of other substance scattered through it. He decided it was best not to know what was in it.

"On deck!"

Dalton looked up from his breakfast. "Yes, Mister . . . ah, Mister Duncan, who is that at the maintop?"

"One of the Fanshaws, sir. Toliver, I believe."

"We have a purged man in the tops?"

"Both of the Fanshaws are in the tops, sir. They volunteered. They didn't want to be near the smell of breakfast just now."

"I see. Yes, Mister Fanshaw?"

"Land a'port is narrowing, sir. There's water beyond, and a town just over there."

"Thank you, Mister Fanshaw. Stand your watch." To Duncan he said, "That will be The Horns. We shall be at sea this afternoon, and I will be grateful to leave these close waters."

"We certainly don't have just a lot of friends around here," Duncan agreed.

"On deck!"

"Aye, Mister Fanshaw?"

"Dispatch riders on that road over there, sir. Going down toward the end of the spit at a gallop."

"Thank you, Mister Fanshaw. How are you feeling?"

"Bubbly, sir."

Titus Wilton came from the fore, his tricorn hat snugged down almost to his ears. "Captain Dalton, do you know where we are?"

"Quite precisely, Mister Wilton. We are proceeding southward on Chesapeake Bay with Cape Charles in sight a'port and Cape Henry hard down ahead. Why?"

"You said you would put me ashore once this vessel had a full suit of sails."

"I said once you had completed the suiting-out of the vessel, Mister Wilton. You have not yet produced a main gallant or mizzen topsail for me."

"But you have a full suit of sails!"

"We are making do with what we took from those Spanish gentlemen, sir. It is hardly the same as having a sturdy new suit of our own."

"But we are running out of places to put me ashore!"

Dalton sighed, stood and stretched, getting the kinks of too many hours of inventorying out of his shoulders. "Did you have a particular place in mind where you wanted to go ashore, Mister Wilton?"

"I certainly did! Chestertown would have done nicely, or even St. Mary's."

"We passed those places miles back," Dalton pointed out.

"I know we did! Do you know the difficulty I will have trying to get home from out here?" He pointed an indignant finger. "What is that over there?"

"Cape Charles."

"I mean that place. That little town. Isn't that a town there?"

"It seems to be, though the charts don't say how it is called. But that portion of the cape is called The Horns. And I have no intention of stopping there."

"Why not?"

"Because there are dispatch riders on that road over there, and every chance that the messages they carry might concern this ship."

"Then what about Yorktown? It's off there ahead of us someplace. Or Hampton? If the damned British haven't shelled it to rubble, that is."

Dalton shook his head. "Mister Wilton, if you will use the remaining hours between here and Hampton in at least fashioning a mizzen topsail to replace that patched rag we presently have there, then I will do all possible to put you ashore at Hampton. It is the best I can do."

"On deck!"

"Yes, Mister Fanshaw?"

"Those people in that town over there are running signals up a staff, sir. And there are masts at a dock there."

"Can you read the signals, Mister Fanshaw?"

"No, sir. It would be a book code, sir."

"Can you read the masts, Mister Fanshaw?"

"Small vessel, sir. Two masts. Or maybe two with one mast each. Shall I keep a sharp eye, sir?"

"By all means, Mister Fanshaw. The very thing I was going to suggest." Dalton shrugged, turning his attention to deck level. "Bubbly, he feels." He pushed away the fist-sized iron shot he had been using as a paperweight and gathered the inventory lists. "Well, at least now we have fourteen guns instead of five—if one counts swivels as proper guns—and ample cable, chain, and rigging sheet for any conceivable purpose. One other thing, Mister Caster, what is this item here, just below the eighty-one grappling hooks?"

Billy squinted at the list. "Feathers, sir. Four bales."

"Feathers?"

"Aye, sir. Colored feathers. I've heard they are very much in demand in some of the European countries. They are used to decorate hats and things. Mister Sidney allows the Spaniards must have taken them off a Portuguese trader, sir."

"Feathers."

"Aye, sir."

"Ah, me." Turning, he almost collided with the sullen sailmaker. He had forgotten that the man was there. "Well, Mister Wilton?"

"Well what, Captain?"

"Can you give me a new mizzentop sail before we reach the vicinity of Hampton?"

"I intend to complain about my treatment when I get back to civlization, Captain." Wilton turned and strode off along the deck, brushing past Pitacoke and Squahamac, both of whom now sported clusters of brilliant feathers tied into their raven hair.

"Do we know who holds Hampton, sir?" Duncan asked.

"I haven't the vaguest notion, Mister Duncan. We shall just have to wait and see." He gazed out across the bright mozaic of wavelets to port. "A fine morning. Bright sky and brisk winds. Fair weather for the testing of a ship, wouldn't you say?"

Duncan grinned. He had learned before about Patrick Dalton's idea of "testing" a vessel. He had tried to explain it to John Tidy, of an evening at their campfire in the forest. "He has a way about him, the captain does," he'd said. "Hand him a fine blade and like as not he'll bend it to see where it breaks, then have it welded and retempered with reinforcement at that point. Give him a ship and a good wind and he'll put it through its paces right enough. Some repairs might be required when he's done, but by then he'll know every mood and whim of the vessel and from that hour on it will do his bidding and never let him down."

"Like the breaking of a horse?" Tidy had scowled at the thought. "I'd not say much for a man who would cripple a good horse in breaking it to the saddle."

"I'm not talking about horses," Duncan had returned the frown. "I'm talking about ships. Horses have nothing to do with it."

"Well, a moment ago you was talking about blades. Why would a man break a good sword?"

"He wouldn't."

"You just now said he would."

"I was only trying to make a comparison!"

"Well, I won't say much for a man who would snap a blade or cripple a horse, either one. And it seems to me that Captain Dalton is far too sensible a man to do either."

"He is."

"Then why do you say such things about him?"

Duncan had given up. But now he pursed his lips as he gazed forward, where Tidy was inspecting the set of lines at the fife rail. Hard-headed bosun, he thought, if the captain's of a mind to learn the song of this vessel, *then* you'll understand. But his own thoughts left him wondering. Dalton could, indeed, make a jaunty schooner sing. Duncan had seen him do that. The sleek ship had sung and danced, had darted and dazzled, had done things to make one gasp with wonder.

But *Mystery* was no schooner. *Mystery* was only a ketch. Duncan decided to keep his peace about the testing of ships. That, after all, was the captain's prerogative.

Dalton went foreward for a turn around the deck— and, Duncan suspected, to have a look at the new boots transferred from the pirate vessel. Few aboard the vessels of the time ever chose boots for their feet. Most preferred buckle shoes with high stockings. But boots were a part of the nature of their dark young

177

captain, just as was the moodiness that came upon him sometimes, the haunted loneliness of one whose memories are too much with him.

Easy enough for the rest of us, Duncan thought. Hardly a one among us hasn't seen the inside of a stockade for felonies fairly done. We're a bunch of thieves and wastrels, deserters and turncoats, scalawags of every kind and we've each man earned the charges against him. All except him. His only crime was in having once known a man who rebelled against the king. And for that he is a fugitive. For that, and for being Irish.

Easier for the rest of us, he decided. Not a one of us but can go back and start over, should we choose. Change a name, lie a bit and sign aboard a vessel as crew, and who's to know or care? But not so for Patrick Dalton. He carries the dark curse of the black Irish, and there'll be no easy ways for him. No changing of names, and what chance of ever *clearing* his name? And through it all, he remains loyal . . . for king and country.

"Pride," he said aloud.

"I'm sorry?" Billy Caster looked up from his work.

"The captain. It's pride that's his undoin'. Pure, stubborn pride."

"Oh."

"On deck!"

Duncan looked up, squinting against the bright sky. "Aye, Mister Fanshaw?"

"Those masts yonder, they're two small craft, sir. They're makin' sail, and there's people all about, looking at us."

Duncan picked up the glass. The village was abeam now, less than a mile to port, and there was a good bit of activity at its waterfront. The two small vessels were hardly bigger than launches, but they carried guns fore and aft, and had tall masts and large sails. "Harriers," he said. "British. They're making

178

ready to come out and have a look at us, I suppose. Hands to station! Mister Tidy, please pipe all hands!"

Patrick Dalton emerged from the stores hold, wearing a new pair of boots, and Billy Caster marked a correction on his inventory. Dalton stepped to the rail, gazed for a moment at the activity ashore, then strode aft. "Harriers, Mister Duncan. It would seem there are men-of-war not far away. What are the present reports?"

"We're holding at about eight knots, sir, reefed a third. Wind is twelve to fifteen, three points on the port beam. Sounding is 'by the mark, four,' and steady, though it may shoal before we round the cape."

"Very well, Mister Duncan. I shall take the deck now. Please lend a hand forward, and have Mister Hoop and his marines set all the short pieces a'port. Gunners stand by with fuse. If those people yonder come out to test us, a salute might be in order. Otherwise they shall waste a great deal of their time and ours. Helm, how does she handle with present sail?"

"Stiffly, sir," Cadman Wise said. "She's a hard-helmed vessel, and the high sails make her more so."

"Let me try the helm, Mister Wise. But stand by to assist. Hands aloft! Let's have full sail now, if you please! Hands a'deck, stand by the sheets! Mister Tidy, let's have a tight trim for present heading, then stand by the lines!"

"Aye, sir!" The whistle shrilled, and the deck amidships became a scurry of men. Beyond them on the main hold planking Titus Wilton found himself abruptly alone with a half-constructed mizzen topsail. "Here!" he shouted. "Come back here, you oafs!" Then, "Drat! You there! And you! Come here and give me a hand with this! Yes, you! Come here, immediately!"

Reefed canvas aloft fell full open and boomed as it caught the wind. On the deck, hard hands hauled at sheet lines as John Tidy orchestrated the drill, and the sails above stretched to taut, rounded drumheads, holding the wind, redirecting it to give frontal thrust to their spars and thus to the ship below. The spencer gaff on the mainmast was lowered and the new main course unfurled, a proud twelve-cloth canvas thirty-six feet wide and twenty-four high. Its clew blocks rattled and lines sang as panting hands hauled taut its sheets, setting their ties at the pinrails.

Mystery's leap, taking the wind in full for the first time, was grudging, but the croon of waters along her hull grew in pitch and became a strong, tenor hum, and bright waters curled beneath her stem.

Dalton tried the helm, a point this way and a point back, his shoulders bunching beneath his coat. The curse of the ketch, he thought again. To make space forward, deck and great cargo holds, they had designed her with masts far back. The main was squarely amidship and the mizzen far aft. Except for the batwings of fore staysail and jibsail thrumming above her foredeck, the ship had only its rudder to counter the turning thrust of wind slapping its backside.

"Hands afore!" he called. "Hoist the flying jib!"

A third triangle sail arose from the thrusting bowsprit, climbing the topgallant stay. Only the highest corner of the new sail was actually above the ship's stem. Its far clew, near the tip of the sprit, was more than thirty feet beyond the vessel's riding hull. As it was sheeted in the song of waters along the hull grew again in pitch, and *Mystery*'s nose came up a bit. Spray now showed at her stem, from the sheeting curls beneath. Dalton tried the helm again, found it just a trace more manageable.

"Ten knots, sir!"

"On deck! Those two vessels are coming out, sir! Making to intercept!"

180

Billy Caster had taken his lists below, and now he returned, shading his eyes to squint at the gliding shoreline. "Sir, do you suppose they don't know how we are armed?"

Dalton eased a point to port, feeling the stubborn rudder's vibration through the spokes of the helm. "Very possibly, Mister Caster. With all that's stacked on our deck, one might not notice the guns until one came close."

"Those dispatch riders, sir . . . do you think their message was about us?"

"It seems it might have been. But if all they have is harriers, we shouldn't be too much concerned."

"They can outrun us, sir."

"And a housecat can outrun an ox, but what is it to do about it when it catches it?"

"Aye, sir."

"As far as that goes, under sail in a fair wind our own launch could outrun us. But I think they won't come close . . . not if we suggest they stand off."

"Shall we suggest that, sir?" The boy's teeth glinted as a tight grin spread across his face. He knew why the ketch's guns were amassed at the port beam.

"If they press us, Mister Caster."

"On deck! The two are separating, sir. One's made southward, heading as we are. The other is still angling to intercept!"

"Blazes!" Dalton breathed. If one of the harriers was taking the alarm southward, then there was someone there to take it to. A warship? Even a squadron, perhaps? Delaware was not far away, and a good part of Admiral Lord Howe's fleet had concentrated there in recent weeks. "Tops!" he shouted. "Mister Fanshaw!"

"Aye, sir?" The response was from almost directly above, and Dalton glanced upward. "The other Mister Fanshaw, please! Mister Fanshaw on the main!"

"Aye, sir! Toliver, Cap'n wants you!"

"Aye, sir?"

"Have a look dead ahead, Mister Fanshaw!"

"Aye, sir!" There was a pause, then, "Shoreline hard down ahead, sir. Past the end of the spit a'port!"

"Sails, Mister Fanshaw?"

"Don't see any, sir! Just land off there! Bit of smoke . . . I think there's a town or something!"

"Thank you, Mister Fanshaw!"

"Aye, sir!"

Ahead, broad on the port beam, the nearer harrier was cutting a wide wake through the chop as it made to intercept. Within minutes they would be committed. Dalton frowned. His first months of service with the King's Navy had been aboard a little harrier jut like that one—a vicious, fast-darting little sailed boat with just enough firepower to be a nuisance to an enemy engaged with a man-of-war near shore. That and the carrying of messages were why the little craft were used. But he remembered fondly the dancing little *Lark*, and this one coming at him bore the king's colors just as that one had, and he wished it no real harm.

"Break out colors, Mister Caster," he said.

"Aye, sir. I have them right here. What colors would you like, sir?"

It didn't matter very much. At this point the harrier was not going to believe anything they claimed. A trace of grin tightened Dalton's lips. "Raise that Dutch ensign, Mister Caster. At least that might amuse him. Then run up 'come about and return to port.'"

The Dutch flag went up, and the buntings. Billy Caster picked up Dalton's glass. "They've seen our signal, sir. The gentleman at the tiller yonder just made a very crude sign in our direction. They are running out their guns fore and aft, sir."

"Oh, very well. Mister Duncan, please tell the lads at the port guns to salute the boat out there."

"Aye, sir. Hole or sweep?"

"Neither, Mister Duncan. Just fire for effect. I only want to get the man's attention."

"Aye, sir."

With deck hands training the guns, three short sixes and a stubby, ancient nine, the gunners knelt to their notches and lowered fuse, firing two and two. Spray scudded across the deck of the oncoming boat, and gouts erupted ahead and behind it. Abruptly the harrier heeled over, awkwardly, coming sharply to starboard, its stern skidding in the chop to swing around its stem. Then it settled there, aback to the wind, dead in the water.

"Mister Duncan!"

"Aye, sir?"

"I said to fire for effect, Mister Duncan."

"That's what the lads did, sir. They saluted them fore and aft, then gave them a bath and shot away their rudder to keep them out of mischief."

Sails thrumming, *Mystery* ran past the bobbing stern of the boat, three cables out, and a cloud formed at the tail of the little craft, powder smoke dispersing on the wind. Directly abeam of the ketch, water shot high as a ball clipped the top of a wave and skipped toward the ship, for all the world like a dark stone skipping over a pond. Again it threw water, and again, not ten yards out. Its thump against their hull as it grazed their keel, sinking, was plainly audible.

"I believe we got his attention, sir," Duncan called.

"On deck!"

"Aye, Mister Fanshaw?"

"Sir, that second boat is makin' for the far point, and goin' like a . . . pardon, sir. It's going fast. And making signal to somebody!"

"Keep a sharp eye ahead, Mister Fanshaw!"

"Aye, sir!"

"Mister Tidy, hands to sheets. Rig for wind dead

183

astern, please."

Some of them glanced around in wonder. The wind had come east of north, and would hardly serve them on a course south if the sails were set square port to starboard. But Tidy's whistle sounded and pins were released, sheet lines hauled and spars aloft creaked as the trim was reset. Sails fluttered and luffed, and *Mystery* slowed perceptibly.

"Mister Wise, if you please, give me a hand with this helm. Let us bring her smartly about a'starboard to put the wind on her tail."

"Aye, sir." They spun the wheel, using their combined strength to force the balky rudder, to heel the ship aside in a sudden, unprepared turn. Abruptly all their sails caught the wind, and *Mystery* lurched as though slapped from behind. Tortured stays sang and rigging howled, a sheet line abeam parting with a crack like a rifle shot. Belowdecks an ominous rumble grew as the feet of great masts absorbed the shock. Sudden thunder cracked over their heads, and Talmadge Fanshaw, at the mizzen-top, shrieked, "Sweet Jesus!"

Dalton gave the helm to Wise and stepped around the helm housing to look upward, others gathering to do the same. Aloft on the mizzen, above the trestletrees, a blown sail streamed in the wind, ripped from top to bottom so thoroughly that segments streamed out before it like dull pennants.

John Tidy edged close to Charley Duncan. "Is *that* what you was talking about that time?"

"The very same," Duncan grinned. "Now the captain knows what he can trust and what he can't aboard his ship."

Without looking around, Dalton said, "Mister Tidy, there is a rent line to be spliced yonder, and a blown sail to be taken down. But first have the lads retrim for proper course, please. We know enough about her, now."

"Aye, sir."

"Mister Romart, please go and tell Mister Wilton to not tarry with the new mizzen topsail. We no longer have temporary cloth in that position."

"Aye, sir."

When *Mystery* was again trimmed for an easy beam reach, and the west shore was clearly in sight, Dalton had Wise bring her over and they made again for the seaward end of Chesapeake.

Romart returned and said, "Mister Wilton says you'll have your bedamned . . . pardon, but it's what he said, sir . . . your bedamned sail by the turning of a glass, and he says he hopes the Captain has a love of festooning, sir."

"Festooning, Mister Romart?"

"Aye, sir. He set those Indians to work on it, and they've decorated it right fancy with colored feathers, sir."

"On deck!"

"Aye, Mister Main Fanshaw?"

"Sail, sir! Off beyond that point we're headin' for!"

"Can you read it, Mister Fanshaw?"

"Aye, Cap'n! Clear as day! It's a full-rigged man-of-war, sir! Ship of the line, an' it flies the Union Jack."

XIV

Fury rode at anchor within hailing distance of the rugged island barrier above Albemarle Sound, her deep keel almost resting on the bottom at the ebb of the tide. Through most of a night she had lain so, since first her lookouts saw the running lights of ships northbound in the deeper lanes offshore. With Captain Pinto in a drunken stupor below, with *Teniente* Torero no longer aboard and with the *Patron*, Don Geraldo Lostrato, disenfranchised and under a semblance of arrest by captain's order, there was no one else able—or willing—to decide what to do.

So the snow lay furled and lightless through the long dark hours while lookouts crouched aloft watching the ominous specks of light to the east where ships crept close-hauled against a perverse wind, and with first light their sails were still in sight, far northward now and still northbound. A squadron of Englishmen, sail of the line with frigates among them.

By luck or the grace of God the snow had not been seen, but it was a time to lie low and watch, and wait for *Capitan* Pinto to recover and take charge.

The receding ships were hull-down in the distance when one of the topmen called, *"Un navio esta abandonado los otros! Esta volviendo a la izquierda!''* Others went to see. Indeed, one of the distant sails had departed from the rest, edging off to port, toward land. For a time they watched intently, afraid that one might turn back, might come down on the wind, and find them. But it simply angled inshore, a bright speck in morning sunlight, and eventually was out of sight, rounding a bulge in the coastline. The rest continued their slow, tacking journey northward, inshore and out, beating against a wind still more north than east.

For a time, Lostrato was on deck, but he kept to himself, shunning the rabble that was Pinto's chosen crew. Easily, he could have commanded, but for their fear of Pinto. It would be nothing now, with so much open distance, to put on sail and cat the anchors and put the ship's nose to sea, then turn southward with a driving wind and put the Englishmen out of sight behind them. But he did nothing. Pinto had made his status clear, and a trace of grim smile formed on his hatchet face . . . almost a smirk of satisfaction. Idiots in the command of an idiot. Let him awaken to find his vessel thus, almost aground in treacherous shoals. And let these idiots answer to him when he did.

Lostrato had other things on his mind. He had talked with the French *muchachas* below, and had learned things of interest. Fortunes in ransom rested brightly in his mind, ransom that no barbarian pirate would know how to collect. Let Pinto strut and bluster about his strong vessel . . . it would be himself, Don Geraldo Lostrato, who would be in charge when the time of payment came. There would be matters of contact, of negotiation, arrangements of assured safety . . . matters that a gentleman knew how to handle. And Pinto had no one else to turn to when it came to that. It would be satisfying, the complex little series of humiliations he would thrust upon the pirate. And then, when it was done, he would kill him. With a vessel such as this, and his warrant for privateer ventures, he had no need of Pinto. Soon the bull would feel the blade, and would know then who was its master.

The sun climbed higher above the sea, and *Fury*'s rhythmic rocking at her anchor lines suddenly became errant. The chop of surf beneath her lost its synchronization, and an odd, hissing, rumbling sound just at the edge of hearing came up through her timbers.

Lostrato smirked openly then, and walked back to the companion hatch. Belowdeck he listened for a moment at the entry to Pinto's cabin, then stepped across to the other. "Ah, Vasco," he said quietly. "Good Vasco, listen to me. In that cabin you guard is a ransom greater than any prize you might share from ordinary piracy. You owe nothing to that drunken idiot Pinto. But stand by me and I promise you riches."

The man only stared at him, but his quick glance at the captain's closed cabin told Lostrato all he needed to know. He edged past the guard and lifted the bar on the prisoners' little cell. "I shall be inside, Vasco. Guard this entry well, and trust me. We go for a ransom in gold, Vasco, and I will be generous with you. Both of us have reason to hate our captain."

It was nearly an hour later when he heard Pinto's distant voice, roaring in anger. And the ship still lay gripped by the sands beneath her, shuddering as the surf flogged her and unable to move until the tide returned.

Mystery rounded off Hampton with hands aloft on her mizzen topmast, working to bend on a bright new sail made brilliant by the intricate weaving of colored feathers along its boltropes and at its reefing points. But in the bend of waters below The Horns the sail remained furled, and others were slacked ahead of it. The ketch stood tiny in broad waters while those aboard gazed wide-eyed at the thing that stood between them and the open sea. In the mouth of the bay, well inshore and coming on with good sail, was a full-rigged ship of the line, a trim and massive 74-gunner commanding the bay from Cape Charles on the north wing to Cape Henry on the south.

Mystery came dead in the water, and Patrick Dalton's heart sank. There had always been the chance of encountering a blockader here, and had it been a lesser vessel, there would have been the chance of evading it. In a channel ten miles wide at its mouth, even a crawling ketch might evade a brig or the like—possibly even a small frigate—with a favorable wind for weaving and dodging.

But not a seventy-four. There simply was no arguing with a seventy-four.

On a hushed deck, Dalton gave his final orders. "Mister Caster, run up colors, please. Merchant trader, private ownership, the nearest colors we have to the truth of us. And signal 'request permission to pass.' Mister Duncan, I've made an obligation with our sailmaker. Please put him aboard the launch, with yourself and any others who might face more than imprisonment upon capture. Also, take Mister Caster with you, and . . ."

"Please, Captain, I . . ."

"Belay that, Mister Caster. You will do exactly as I command. Mister Duncan, take as many as you can aboard the launch, and see if you can deliver Mister Wilton to Hampton. I believe that is Hampton, the village you see yonder. Go now, Mister Duncan, while there is yet time."

"Captain . . ."

"Do it, Mister Duncan. That is an order."

"Aye, sir."

*   *   *

At fifty-four years of age, Peter Selkirk was in his third year of command of His Majesty's Ship *Cornwall* and a veteran of nearly forty years' service to the Crown. Once comfortably ensconced as an academician, he had been recalled to active service at the request of Admiral Lord Howe prior to the deployment of the White Fleet in American waters. Thoughtful and studious, Selkirk's reputation in battle was of careful strategy, absolute attention to detail, and unrelenting ferocity once the enemy was engaged. Among his peers and juniors it was noted that "Hawser" Selkirk had the unusual ability to quote in detail the position of every vessel in every engagement he had ever experienced, as well as the armament of each, the credentials of their masters, and the tactics that each fleet officer on either side had favored. He also knew the names, strengths and weaknesses, personal leanings and temperaments— as well as the present situation—of every midshipman he had ever trained, including several who had taken the path of admiralty and thus become his superiors—at least in rank.

Selkirk was no stranger to dilemmas, and the one he faced now intrigued him. As *Cornwall* put Capes Charles and Henry on her beams and aligned her great stem toward Gloucester Point on the west shore, he read again the dispatches that had been put into his hand by the harrier's master an hour before. One was a copy of a warrant claim by one Felix Croney, a captain of the Harbor Guards, calling for the arrest of Patrick Dalton on a fugitive warrant and the seizure of his vessel for contraband. The second was a fresh message from the officer of Acomack Patrol, identifying a ketch-rigged vessel as Dalton's habitat.

Signals from shore had brought Selkirk inshore from his northward course, and these messages had been waiting. Quietly he fumed at the situation. A seventy-four-gun ship of the line, carrying two hundred and thirty men, diverted from its proper mission on a fool's errand . . . it was the price a proud empire paid for having fools in its political hierarchy, fools among its foreign guard and, quite possibly, a fool on its reigning throne.

Selkirk had heard the reports, months ago—the upheaval in Ireland and the subsequent Crown retaliation against a handful of chieftains there. And knowing more than a few of those involved on both sides, Selkirk was content that at least some of the "Dublin conspiracy" were deserving of charges of high treason. But some were not.

Now *Cornwall* stood in from the mouth of Chesapeake, and Peter Selkirk trained his glass on the oddly suited little ketch ahead. He saw the launch making its way southwestward toward the far shore and understood what was being done. He saw those who remained aboard the ketch, faces indistinct with distance yet, but all turned toward him as men who stared blankly at their fates and had nowhere to turn. He paused, studying the tall, dark-haired young man who stood beside the ketch's helm—a man who wore calf-high boots and stood his deck with the assurance of a born seaman.

"Stand us off one cable," he said. "Stand by to lower a launch."

Dalton watched *Something* depart. Once clear of *Mystery*, the launch raised sails on its stubby mast, heeled to the wind, and went scudding off toward the shore a few miles away—a trim launch with ugly little guns at each end and a press of desperate men between. Charley Duncan faced hanging if ever the British captured him, so Dalton had sent him away. With him went the sailmaker Titus Wilton and the rest of the Americans—Michael Romart, Tobias Quinn, Joseph Tower, the brothers O'Riley, Sam

Sidney, and Billy Caster, his pleading face looking back at the ketch and the captain to whom he had pledged his loyalty. And among them the five Hessian deserters, Korporal Heinrich Wesselmann, Klaus Doste, Jacob Tiehl, Wolfgang Mitter, and Rudolph Waltz—young men who wanted to lose themselves in the new world and become farmers. For them, capture would be instant death at the hands of their own officers.

Remaining aboard *Mystery* with Dalton were eleven Englishmen and a pair of Cockney Indians. With capture, the tars might feel the lash and the Indians might be impressed aboard some coastal vessel. But they would survive.

Dalton sighed, straightened his shoulders, and turned to gaze at the massive bulk of the approaching man-of-war. At the helm Victory Locke blinked moist eyes. "We gave 'em a good run, sir," he said.

Under high sunlight the great ship stood off at a cable's length, its shadow almost reaching the ketch. Davits swung outboard amidships and a boat was lowered. A blue-coated officer and nine striped-shirt tars were aboard, with a guard of four red-coated marines. Afloat, the boat cast off and started across toward *Mystery*.

"Yes, we did, Mister Locke," Dalton said. "A very good run, indeed."

Thirty yards out, the boat backed water and the officer got to his feet—a ruddy-faced young man, no older than Dalton himself. Using a flared hailing horn he called, "Ahoy the ketch!"

Dalton stepped to the rail and raised a hand in salute. "Ahoy the boat! This is the trader *Mystery*, on private haul!"

"My captain's compliments, sir, but he knows exactly who you are and he requests your presence aboard *Cornwall*, sir."

"Did he say, 'request,' sir?"

193

"Aye, sir, he did. If I might suggest, sir, if it were me, I'd consider that to be a very strong request."

"Come alongside, then. I suppose you intend to board me?"

"Captain didn't say to board, sir. He just sent me to fetch you aboard *Cornwall*."

Dalton turned away and saw that every man remaining aboard *Mystery* was on deck now, assembled in jostling order and facing him. He tried to think of something to say, then decided against it. Instead he saluted them, each and all. "It is your deck, Mister Tidy," he told the old bosun. "I wish you well."

The boat came alongside and he stepped down smartly, not wanting to look back at the men who had trusted him to get them safely away from harm.

The ruddy young officer saluted him. "Harrington, sir. Lieutenant amidships, His Majesty's Ship *Cornwall*. No, please, sir. Captain instructed me not to inquire your name. If you'd just make yourself comfortable right here, sir. Mister Forbes! Bring us about and return to the ship."

"Aye, sir."

At ten strokes of the oars they entered the shadow of the great ship, and Dalton felt a chill as one who might never again see the sun. Even so, when he was piped aboard the seventy-four, he felt the old thrill of awe. Could any man, no matter his condition, not feel thus when he sets foot on the deck of a fine ship? he wondered.

Trailed by the marines, Harrington conducted him aft, past a gauntlet of curious faces, up to the quarterdeck, and along that to the short ladder leading up to the poop. Here Harrington stopped. "Captain will want a word with you in private, sir," he said.

The man who stood alone at the carved rail facing away was thickset and thick-waisted in the manner of one who has been long at sea and always in command. His hair was iron gray beneath his hat, and he wore the double epaulettes of captaincy and seniority.

Dalton approached, stopped and saluted. "You requested me, sir?"

"Hello, Patrick." The other turned. "Still blessed with the troublesome luck of the Irish, I see."

A face from the past. A face that dominated his memories of classrooms, tactical lectures, and tours amidships. Hawser! Hawser of the grim discipline and iron will, Hawser who was called Hawser as much for his abrasive surface as for his unyielding taut strength . . . and who had never been called Hawser to his face by anyone his junior.

"You look as though you are seeing a ghost, Patrick. It hasn't been so long as that, you know. So close your mouth and respond properly before I change my estimate of you."

"Aye, sir!" Dalton squared his shoulders and saluted, seeing in the offhand response a thousand past responses of its kind, a hall of mirrors reflection from times long past.

"You've got yourself into something of a pickle, I understand," Selkirk said. "Oh, do stand at ease! You earned your marks fairly and this is no parade drill."

"Yes, sir. Ah . . . it's good to see you again, Captain Selkirk."

"Is it? Can't think how you'd relish the circumstances." The senior captain pointed. "And what, exactly, is that?"

"It's a ketch, sir. I . . . we found it derelict and did some repairs. Thought we might carry a cargo or two."

"And you have a cargo aboard, obviously. No, don't comment about that. If I decide to inquire, I shall see for myself."

"Yes, sir."

"Quite a story I've heard about you, Patrick. They say that you did significant mayhem to the fleet in New York harbor."

"I had little choice, sir. I've been charged . . ."

"Yes, I know about that. High treason, they say. Because you were once acquainted with the Fitzgerald. Bit of rubbish, of course. I knew the old devil personally for years, myself. But then, I'm not Irish."

"No, sir."

"But you were hardly quiet about going to ground, they say. What is your score to date in king's vessels, Patrick? Two brigs, I understand, both rather badly damaged, a gunboat . . ."

"Two, sir."

"Two?"

"Two gunboats. Sorry, sir, but there really was no choice."

"Of course not. What else?"

"Well, sir, there was a frigate."

"Oh? I heard no reports about a frigate."

"It was Jonathan Hart's *Courtesan*, sir. We . . . ah . . . we sank it."

"You sank a forty-four? With a civilian schooner? Marvelous. Wait until I tell them at fleet."

"That wasn't really a case of having no choice, I'm afraid, sir." Dalton sighed and stared at his feet. "I'm afraid I went hunting for *Courtesan*, sir. It was a personal matter."

"Well, you'll be glad to know that that one, at least, doesn't count against you with the Admiralty. Hart had gone outlaw, as they say. His warrant was rescinded, and of course his vessel was privately owned, so . . . but a *forty-four*, Patrick? With a *schooner*?"

"Yes, sir. I'm afraid so."

"I can hardly wait to tell them. Fancy that!"

"Sir, the lads aboard the ketch, they are good seamen, sir, and not really to blame for . . ."

196

"Did I ask you about them?"

"No, sir."

"Then mind your tongue. I have a question for you, young Dalton, and I want a direct and honest answer. Are you guilty of high treason against the Crown, as the warrants charge?"

"No, sir. I am not."

Selkirk pursed his lips, looking away across the bright, choppy waters of the bay. "No, I thought not. They say, as well, that you have been in league with rebels. How say you to that, Patrick?"

"Associated with Americans, yes. Matter of jointly escaping our problems, sir. But in league with, no. Nor would I, sir. Not intentionally or knowingly."

"The launch making for the shore yonder. Who is aboard that?"

"Members of my crew, sir. And a gentleman who makes sails by contract."

"I see. And I assume some of them are colonials?"

"Yes, sir. Some of them."

"On your honor, Patrick, you have done nothing to betray king or country?"

"Nothing I have initiated, sir."

"I shall accept that. Did my junior officer treat you courteously, Patrick?"

"Lieutenant Harrington? Yes, sir. In all respects, though he avoided learning my name."

"As I instructed he should," Selkirk nodded. "Harrington's a good lad. One of my own fledglings. Reminds me of you in some respects, though I hope he will do a far better job of staying out of trouble."

"Yes, sir."

Selkirk was gazing across at the ketch again. "I have seen emblazoned sails on capital ships from time to time, but never anything quite so . . . ah . . . gaudy as the portion of your mizzentop visible to me. What is that?"

"It's feathers, sir. I have a pair of Indians who have

197

been assisting my sailmaker. They fancy feathers."

"Feathers. I should like to see that sail unfurled, Patrick. Something to remember, you know."

"Yes, sir."

"I should like to see it coming and going. Do you understand me, Patrick?"

"Well, no, sir, not exactly. Of course I'd be glad to show you . . ."

Selkirk sighed. "Patrick, I have a handful of warrants here, broadcast apparently by one Felix Croney, who I suspect has begun to take his job too personally. Warrants aside, though, I have just paused to have a chat with a former student of mine who assures me he has nothing to do with any high treasons, and I am looking at a rather ugly cargo ketch with an emblazoned mizzen topsail that certainly does not appear in any descriptions I have seen of any vessels suspected of carrying contraband. Nor is it my assignment to inspect civilian cargo without probable cause. I have better things to do. Therefore I would consider it a favor if you would return to your vessel now and let me see what that sail looks like going away. God help you, Patrick, because I can't in any other way. But Guard Officer Croney doesn't issue my orders, and I've wasted enough time on a fool's errand here. I see no contraband, I see no vessels accurately described in my warrants and I have not seen you at all today. Go haul your cargo now and please try to stay out of the way of this damned war."

"Aye, sir."

"Oh, and Patrick . . ."

"Sir?"

"I've grown rather fond of old *Cornwall* here. I hope you've satisfied yourself with respect to the doing of mayhem on king's ships."

"Aye, sir."

The senior captain turned away, clutched his

hands behind him, and did not look around again. Feeling half stunned, Dalton strode to the quarter-deck where Harrington was waiting.

"Have a nice chat with the captain, sir?" the ruddy-cheeked Briton grinned. "Tough as a boot, he can be, but I never had a better teacher."

"Nor did I," Dalton assured him.

"Might I offer you a suggestion, sir?"

"Please do."

"When you get back to your ketch, you might want to drape a bit of something over your stern rail a'starboard. From behind, it looks for all the world like the muzzle of a battery gun there. Thing like that could get people to talking, sir."

With a brisk wind nearly abeam, *Something* breasted the choppy waves apace and made for the shore, holding right of the wide inlet that was the mouth of the James River. Most of those crowded onto her benches looked back again and again at the receding tableau, the squat, snoutish ketch limp-sailed and lonely-seeming, towered over by the great silhouette of the man-of-war.

But as the shoreline crept nearer, Corporal Heinrich Wesselmann pointed ahead. *"Segel! Zwei Segel!"*

Duncan extended his glass. A pair of sailing punts were just putting in at the fish docks below the village of Hampton. "Colonials," he said to no one in particular. "Whigs, I suppose."

"Of course they're colonials," Michael Romart reminded him. "Punters in the colonies usually are. Cap'n wouldn't have sent us ashore here if he thought the place was full of friggin' Englishmen, would he?"

"I *am* a friggin' . . . I *am* an Englishman," Duncan snorted. "Think about my problem, would you?"

"Well, nobody's likely to know unless you run

199

around telling them. Just because you have a striped shirt . . ."

"And how about those five?" Duncan jerked a thumb toward the clustered Hessians in the aftersheets. "I suppose they can pass for bleedin' colonials, too?"

"Something of a problem there," Romart agreed. "However, if we can get rid of their uniforms and persuade them to keep their mouths shut . . ."

"Achtung!" Wesselmann interrupted, pointing. The two punts had rounded on the fish dock and lowered their sails, and suddenly doors stood open at buildings beyond and redcoats swarmed across the common, converging on the docks.

"The town is taken!" Romart allowed. "There's friggin' Englishmen all over the place!"

"Makes it a different kind of problem, doesn't it?" Duncan shrugged.

In the bow, Titus Wilton turned and stared at the approaching docks. "Totally unacceptable," he decided. "Mister Duncan, I insist that we make about and go someplace else."

"Last I heard, there weren't landing parties down here," Joseph Tower said. "That must be a patrol down from the fall line. Maybe they're trying to surround Williamsburg."

"It's how they held Bedford," Sam Sidney pointed out. "At least, it's how they got hold of it before the minutemen drove 'em out."

"Where is Bedford?" Gerald O'Riley asked.

"It's in Massachusetts."

"Well, we can hardly go to Massachusetts."

"I didn't mean we should go there. I only . . ."

"There's another town down the way," Duncan said, peering through his glass. "I wonder what that is?"

"It's a little late to pass by quietly," Romart said. "They've seen us."

"Wo gehen wir hin, Korporal?" Klaus Doste asked Wesselmann.

"Tories must've led them in," Romart decided. "I don't think the people there have any great love for British troops."

Duncan turned. "Mister Quinn, bring us over a'port, beam reach. We'll try to get past before those boats come to cut us off."

"Aye, sir."

Something heeled smartly, taking spray over her port gunwale, and Duncan watched the sails going up again on the two punts. The boats were now full of redcoats. With a certain anticipation, Duncan looked from one to the other of his filched punt guns. "Misters O'Riley," he said, "between you could you get a fuse a'smolder? We might have need of it."

"If this is the best that can be offered," Titus Wilton snapped, "then why don't you just take me back to your ship!"

Billy Caster was looking at the Hessians, at their uniforms and their muskets, and thinking about the diversity of flags in *Mystery*'s signal locker . . . there, as Captain Dalton had said, for the purpose of amusing other vessels. "I wonder . . ." he muttered, and Korporal Heinrich Wesselmann peered at him and cocked his head.

"Ja," he said.

Rapid whispers in German were followed by a sudden grouping of the Hessians, who pushed aft, crowding through the others there, then turned with leveled muskets to face them, all but Rudolph Waltz, who faced aft with his weapon leveled at Tobias Quinn and Billy Caster.

"Seid ihr jetzt unsere gesangenen," Wesselmann ordered the bewildered sailors.

"What?"

"Ich bist . . ."

"I think he says we have to be their prisoners," Billy Caster offered.

"Well, I'm damned if I'll . . ."

"Please, Mister Romart. I think he is right. Please sit still and behave . . . ah . . . prisonerish."

"Ah," Duncan nodded. "Yes. We are all prisoners. But keep our nose eastward, please, Prisoner Quinn."

"Aye, sir."

The punts came out from their cove, angled to inspect, and Korporal Wesselmann waved and shouted in German, ending it with a crisp salute. For a minute or more the punts ran on, while soldiers at their wales peered across the narrowing distance. Then the punts turned away, making back the way they had come.

"Great hairy goblins," someone breathed. "It worked."

Billy Caster sighed his relief and turned to look once again at the distant lost ketch. His eyes widened. "Mister Duncan! Look at *Mystery*! She's making sail, sir. She's coming away!"

Wesselmann lowered his musket, and the others followed his lead. Formally, then, he turned the weapon and thrust it butt-first into the hands of Michael Romart. *"Ihr nehmt jetzt unsere musketten,"* he said, *"und vir sind euere gesangenen."*

XV

Enrico Pinto stormed and raged, the flat of his blade striping a dozen sullen backs as they hove *Fury* out of the shallows on a rising tide, then fought unfamiliar rigging to make way before the eastering wind could drive her aground again. As a result, it was midafternoon before he had occasion to think about his captives or why the ship had not been under any command during the night. When finally he did, he thought of both, and went to find Lostrato.

He found the confinement cabin still securely guarded, others there besides Vasco, and heard from them the promise of ransom that Lostrato had spread. "Stand aside and open the portal," he commanded.

Suspicious eyes in a half-dozen sullen faces peered at him, hesitating until he put hand to his sword hilt and repeated the command. Then they backed down and opened the little door. Pinto stepped through, his bulk seeming to fill the confined space beyond. He reached back to pull the door closed, but it had been swung all the way aside and six of his crew were there, defiance on their rough features.

From the gloom inside came Lostrato's silky voice. "Your men anticipate shares in the prizes here, *Capitan*. It has occurred to them that their shares may be worth more to them than your pleasure."

Pinto swung, peering into the murk, his eyes adjusting from the sunlight aloft. "They have been listening to a snake," he rumbled.

Two bunks occupied a third of the tiny space within, and two young women sat huddled close on the lower of these, their eyes huge and frightened in the poor light. Don Geraldo sat at ease on a cushioned keg opposite, the remains of a meal beside him on a rimmed shelf. Fantail shutters allowed a little light, and framed prisms in the decking above gave a bit more.

"They speak of ransom," Pinto rumbled. "How dare you tell the louts on my ship what prizes there might be, before you tell me?"

"I couldn't very well report to you, could I," Lostrato's voice was smooth and relaxed, as though he were enjoying a great joke. "You were besotted senseless well into the morning, then far too busy getting yourself out of the situation your own stupidity got you into, to hear any reports from me."

"Then tell me now!"

"Very well. These two little birds here . . . oh, don't worry, they speak no Spanish . . . are the daughters of a French gentleman, Jean-Luc Toussaint, Chevalier de Canille, of whom you likely have never heard, though it was you who killed him and his wife. But fortunately I know of him. The chevalier directs . . . directed . . . one of the wealthiest commercial estates in France, with connections in the Carolinas in the charge of a brother. The rebellion in the English colonies has virtually doubled the wealth of an already wealthy family, *Capitan,* and I believe if you had not killed the Frenchman and his wife, they alone would have been worth five times the value of this ship, in ready ransom payable at Charleston."

"So? Come to the point. What are *these* worth?"

"Not quite so much, unfortunately. Maybe only half that."

"Stop playing games! How much?"

"A matter for negotiation. But, at the very least, more gold per share than you likely have seen in your entire misbegotten life, Pinto."

"And what have you been telling *my* sailors?"

"Only that the goods must be deliverable, *undamaged*, to secure such a ransom." Lostrato stood, half-crouching in the low cabin, and his eyes glittered like snake's eyes. "In other words, *Capitan* Pinto, I think if you so much as touch either of these—or if you in any way interfere with my ability to negotiate a ransom—then poor Vasco will not be the only man aboard who has no *huevos* in his britches. I think your men would nail yours to a yardarm and let you dangle from them until you rot."

"Snake!" Pinto growled, red rage coursing through him, great muscles cording. "You think to make a mutiny!"

"No such thing," Lostrato smiled thinly. "Simply a bit of insurance—for our little prizes here, and for my own comfort until the day I decide to put my blade through your belly. Now get out of my way, *Capitan*, for I think I should enjoy a stroll on deck."

Pinto growled, but backed away. "What did you mean—before—when you said it was my fault that this ship went aground?"

"Totally your fault. You chose to get drunk, and forgot that aside from myself there was only one other man capable of handling this ship. And you left him back there in the bay, with a miserable little cargo ketch helping itself to his guns and sails."

"Torero was an idiot."

"Was he really? I don't think so. But I think if I were you, I would ask myself how a miserable ketch cost me a brigantine and a first officer, not to mention the trinkets that you left aboard *Columbine* in your haste to transfer to this ship. And I would ask myself what a ketch like that carries to make men defend it so, and what kind of men are they."

Faced with the inevitable logic of Lostrato's ransom idea, and backed by a small crowd of armed men who could grow mutinous at the slightest provocation, Pinto backed off, promising himself that he would one day kill this popinjay. He stepped away, turned, and went on deck, grumbling. *Fury* stood now on a good beam wind, almost out of sight of the coast, on a course that would take her in two or three days well into the merchant lanes. Yet Enrico Pinto looked back, dark brows like stormclouds over eyes that glinted with a cruel light. What, indeed, was aboard the crawling ketch? How had they taken Torero . . . and why had they been so desperate as to try?

"Bring us about," he ordered his helm. "Reverse this course, and trim for beam reach, wind a'starboard. Set us full and by, to bear northwest."

When the door was once again closed—the set-bolt on the outside of it thumping hollowly like an echo of the closing—Eugenie Toussaint covered her nose with one hand and fanned the air before her with the other, wishing away the rank odor that had pervaded the tight little space with the entry of that huge, squat man the others addressed as *Capitan*. He smelled far worse than the wiry, mustached Monsieur Lostrato who had spent so much time here with them, talking in his insinuating dry voice and his clipped, Spanish-accented French. At least the Lostrato one seemed to have washed himself sometime recently, and the perfumes he wore—while cloying—in some ways covered the harsh odors of boot oil and garlic that clung to him. But that *Capitan!* The man

206

smelled even worse than the limping, leering guard who had brought them food and water. And ugly! "That one has the face of a pig," she said.

"Eyes of a pig," Lucette agreed. "But his face . . . you see how he looked at us? God in heaven, to be at the mercy of such a one . . ."

"There is a striker on that shelf, Lucette. And tinder. Do see if you can get a candle lit, against the stink in here." And to keep yourself busy, she thought. To have something to think about besides what these people did to our poor mother . . . and maybe to our father as well . . . and to keep from thinking what they may do with us.

The perfumed one had asked so many questions, asking them over and over like an inquisitor. He had come before dark and asked questions for hours. Then, with morning, he had returned with more questions. About their names, the names of the relatives, about the *château* near Versailles and the time their *père* had taken them to the palace to introduce them to notables of the court. What notables had they met, Lostrato had asked. What were their stations in the king's court? How did they address your father? Which ones bowed and which saluted? And there were the questions about Uncle Claude and Uncle Pierre and their families, about the shipping they did, about what they had done in Canada and what they did now at Charles Town in Carolina. So many questions.

She had never been so frightened in her life . . . yet all the questions had seemed to have a theme, and she had clung to the thread of it desperately. What the Spaniard wanted to learn, it had occurred to her, was whether she and Lucette were valuable for ransom.

It was all she had. No weapon, no defense, nothing between herself and Lucette and those awful men . . . except a glimmer of an idea, suggested by the manner of the Spaniard's questions. Her heart beating like a

207

parade drum, she had responded, lying as little as possible for fear of being caught out, but still lying brazenly to the man, seeing Lucette's eyes go wide when she realized what was being said, willing Lucette to remain silent and give no hint of what she was doing.

And when it was done she had woven a fabric of half-truth, and she prayed that she could remember all the exaggerations—and that Lucette could as well. From modestly wealthy minor aristocracy, the family of the chevalier had burgeoned in this tiny, breathless cabin into a dynasty born of the wealth of the fur trade in Canada and now increasing its fortunes through the careful administration of the brothers Toussaint, one in Versailles dealing with high nobility and the financing of great enterprise, the others busily transplanting all of the recovered wealth of a Canadian empire into new ventures farther south, befriended by the highest and most powerful of the American colonial merchant traders, a veritable Parisian monopoly set in the flourishing trade of the lush Carolina colonies.

Between Lostrato's visits to the little cabin prison, the girls had drilled and reviewed, piece by piece, the fundamental fictions that Eugenie had created. Far better that than to think about what would happen to them if ever the Spanish did not value their welfare more than their femininity.

Eugenie, at eighteen years, knew enough of what could happen to them to cling desperately to any straw that might save them. And Lucette, just two years younger, sensed the dangers keenly. They were among barbarians, and their only safety lay in their wits.

Lucette had a candle aglow, its warm light adding just a little comfort to the tight little prison. But it did seem to freshen the air. The strips of daylight through the fantail shutters shifted, slowly moving across from one bulkhead to the opposite one, and the ship—which had been slanted in the direction of the shelf wall—changed its vibrations and its pace, then settled into a new pace, slanted now the other way. Shadows came and went across the little brightness that were the prism skylights of the cabin, and the sound of men's feet overhead was a constant, erratic echo.

The candle alight and nothing more to occupy her, Lucette sank into the chair by the shelf, her face lifted toward the skylights, tears welling again in her reddened eyes. Eugenie knew. One of those stamping shadows up there had killed their mother.

Past Hampton, Michael Romart said, there were no roads that led inland, except by going back through Hampton. There was a village of Norfolk past the James, he thought, but the only other road from Norfolk skirted the Great Dismal Swamp, winding down toward Albemarle Sound. Beyond there, none aboard *Something* had any idea what one might find.

Titus Wilton fussed and ranted, but Duncan was not about to turn the launch back up the bay—not with *Mystery* now under sail and heading out toward the sea just a few miles away, and certainly not with that massive seventy-four still standing in mid-channel beyond.

"Cape Henry is just off there," Duncan pointed. "Beyond is open sea. That's where *Mystery* is heading, and that's where we are heading. And I would appreciate hearing no more about it. Thank you."

At fifty degrees from the wind, *Something* shot smartly past Cape Henry Point and took the waves of a running sea as *Mystery* trudged more slowly along, closing course and following. When it was obvious that no one aboard the launch was going to be required to explain anything to anyone anytime soon, Corporal Heinrich Wesselmann leaned to retrieve his musket from the hands of Michael Romart.

"Mein muskette," he said. *"Danke."*

Aboard *Mystery*, a mile or two aft and coming up on tight tack to follow the course of the more beam-agile launch, ten English tars made shift to put on speed past the point while they glanced back again and again at the moody face of their young captain, wondering what he had done aboard the man-of-war that had bought each of them another reprieve from the lash, the stockade, or worse. Virtually unnoticed from the deck, two Indians swung on lines in the mizzen peak, pranced along yards, preened bright feathers, and made threatening gestures at the great warship still standing in the bay behind them. Both Pitacoke and Squahamac had painted their faces and upper arms with streaks of soot and carpenter's chalk in anticipation of a fight. Their disappointment that such had not occurred was deep and frustrating. Over the past seasons they had watched from forested banks as great sailing ships blazed away at each other on the waters of Chesapeake. The sheer magnitude of the mayhem that white men could commit upon one another had become a matter of awe for them . . . an almost reverent source of inspiration. They wanted to try their hands at it as well.

It became obvious now, though, that nobody intended to attack anybody at the moment, and as the distance between the vessels widened, they squatted on the topyard, one on each side of the mast, and turned to see what lay ahead. A sail on the mainmast ahead of them blocked their view of much of what was there, but as the ship swung to starboard a few points in the growing swells, Squahamac pointed. Far out on the sea there was a brightness. For a moment they watched it curiously, then realized it was stacked sails, and Pitacoke swung down from the yard to hang by an elbow from the footropes there. "Oy th' blee'in' deck!" he shouted.

For a moment there was no response as faces turned upward in surprise. Then the call came from below, "What are you two doing up there?"

Pitacoke ignored the triviality. "Syle!" he shouted.

Again there was the pause below, then a response. "Sail? Whereaway?"

The Indians conferred, Squahamac turning to look again at the distant bright speck. They spoke in rapid Accomac, attaining agreement, and Pitacoke cupped his free hand to hail those below, "'Sou' fron' o' us, myte. W'ere else?"

"Maintop lookouts aloft," Dalton ordered. "Have a look forward. Those two have seen something."

"Aye, sir."

Two swarmed shrouds on the main, and Dalton watched them, recalling others who had gone aloft on other masts, others who now would not climb again. Seeing Hawser Selkirk again has left me in a mood, he thought. Unbidden, memories came . . . that same Selkirk at the quarterrail of a frigate at anchor off Thames Docks, Selkirk stocky and solid against a lowering sun aswim in the smokes rising from London's warrens, Selkirk a silhouette, solid and implacable against vague backgrounds, saying, "One who will command is well counseled to make for himself a cardinal rule, young gentlemen. Allow no intimacy between master and men, between quarterdeck and forecastle, between sir and mister of any standing. Those who condone laxity aboard a man-of-war condemn themselves, gentlemen. A warship has but one purpose, and that is to fight, and any officer who knows more than the name of a man who might fall from the crosstrees at his feet, or be sundered by grape or severed by chain at his side, has

211

only himself to blame for the hells he must suffer then."

No laxity aboard ship. It had become a credo, not just for Dalton but for most of the midshipmen who had gone on to fill the ranks of officers of king's vessels. A credo, but at the same time an impossibility.

Patrick Dalton had known more than just the name of some who were cut down aboard *Athene* on those patrols in the Mediterranean. He had known more than just the name of many who fell when the brig *Herret* was sundered by bombards off the coast of the American colonies. The blood that had soaked his boots and splattered his face then had been the blood of men he had come to know.

And there was not a man among those lost when *Faith* ran the gauntlet of Long Island Sound and then put out to fight to the death against the frigate *Courtesan*, not a man of them whose memory did not linger with him in the quiet hours.

Selkirk had been right, right in every way. If only he had not asked the impossible.

"On deck!"

"Yes, Mister Fisk?"

"The sail's hull-down on horizon, sir, but coming this way."

"Can you read her, Mister Fisk?"

"Aye, sir, I think so. I believe it's that same snow, sir. The one we saw in the bay."

The launch *Something* was a sliver of sail in the near distance, past the chop of the shallows now and beginning to angle to the right on the smoother swells of blue water. Duncan was taking the boat on ahead, Dalton knew, for easier taking of tow when *Mystery* caught up. He would go well beyond the point with its tides and its currents, southward along the coast until he was well clear of inlets, then out to deeper water to await the ketch.

212

The snow had gone, had made its way clear, run out to sea, yet now it was coming back. Dalton wondered why. Those aboard, he knew, were pirates—ranging cutthroats out from some port of New Spain or the nether islands, out to take whatever came their way that they could claim as booty. And being pirates, they were no part of anyone's grand plan, not accountable to any command but their own and answering to no merchant or patron. Not, then, predictable by the nature of their enterprise.

To predict what such a band would do, one must look to what they sought.

What had they seen in Chesapeake that now might bring them back to reconnoiter? They had seen a harmless-seeming ketch coming under the guns of their confederates, and then they had seen the same ketch, the intended victim, stripping its attacker of sail and gun.

They might well wonder how that was done. Even more, they might wonder what made it worth the doing.

It was a strong likelihood that *Mystery* was what had drawn the snow back for another look.

"Mister Tidy, hands a'deck. Prepare to come southward past the shoals. Trim for port reach, if you please, at my command."

"Aye, sir."

"Sounder report when we pass 'by the mark, six.'"

"Aye, sir."

"Gunners aft, please." He glassed the launch, guessed it had not been seen. "Flags, send up a signal to Mister Duncan, please. Tell him to hold his course and a good lead, until I signal come about."

"Aye, sir."

Ethan Crosby and Floyd Pugh came aft at a trot. "Gunners reporting, sir."

"We may expect pursuit," Dalton told them. "Prepare to exercise our guns on command. Mister

213

Tidy will spell off gun crews as we come to course asea."

"Aye, sir."

At the turning of a glass, they passed the final shoals and made blue water. *Mystery* swung her stem southward, took the wind broad in all her canvas, and climbed the swells steadily, the diminishing coast of Virginia and North Carolina just visible to the west and the sliver of sail that was *Something* dead ahead and distant, holding course.

And now the stacked sail on the port beam was clearly visible from deck, and Dalton watched through his glass, muttering. Either his eyes were playing tricks, or the pirate in charge out there was playing games. The man had run a black flag to his masthead. Not in fifty years, Dalton thought, had anyone used a black flag except in signal sequence. But the man out there flew it as his colors.

And as the dark flag went up, the snow veered a'port sharply, setting a new course to intercept.

Was the black flag arrogance, audacity, or plain brutish posturing? It didn't matter. On an open sea with no help in sight and no friends anywhere, for a laden ketch that could no more outrun a dashing snow than a muskrat might outrun a wolf, it made no difference how the enemy proclaimed himself . . . only that he had proclaimed himself their nemesis.

XVI

With the Continental Army drawing the king's major forces north from Philadelphia, Baltimore was for a time a haven for those who required fortification against British attack. Most of the Continental Congress was there now, working feverishly to bind together a random alliance of separate colonies in the face of massed British wrath, trying to maintain communication with Generals Washington and Greene in the field, trying to supply General Lee in New Jersey, and trying to attract alliance from England's enemies. So far, only individual adventurers had responded. The young Marquis de Lafayette had answered the call, as had Baron Johann de Kalb, and some said that Baron Friedrich Wilhelm von Steuben would be made inspector general.

And with the delegates and their servants, others had come to Baltimore. From every trading center on the upper tidelands had come the families and associates of men who had the means and connections to secure sanctuary. Every inn, every shed, and every great house of Baltimore was full of people.

Ian McCall and his associates, in their various houses, quartered nearly a hundred displaced souls. Constance Ramsey, sent off at her father's insistence, was one of nearly thirty women, wives and daughters of tidewater merchants quartered in the two guest wings of Statler House off the grand square, And following his journey through the upper reaches of Chesapeake, McCall came to advise them all of the welfare and condition of their husbands and fathers.

"The squire is in excellent health," he told Constance, well aware that this quick-eyed, pixie-faced daughter of her father would detect any trace of deceit, no matter how well intentioned. "I can't say as much for his safety, of course, though he should be secure enough at Eagle Head, if he can just refrain from returning to Wilmington for the time being. There is an all-out campaign being waged on the Delaware."

"And Patrick? Ah . . . Captain Dalton? Did you see him, or did Father mention him?"

"I didn't see him, of course, Constance," McCall grinned. "A young man so thoroughly celebrated as your captain isn't likely to be receiving callers."

"But is he all right?"

"Your father assured me that he is well. The Squire even spoke of suitable employment for him, to while away his time. I am sure he is being well looked after." A rap at the door brought his gaze around, and he missed the sudden alarm in the girl's eyes. "Yes? Oh, Mistress Kimball. Do come in, dear lady. We were just discussing Miss Constance's father."

"Then I shan't interrupt, Mister McCall. A post has come for you, from Mister Dale in Carolina. I'll just leave it here by the door, sir."

"Thank you, Mistress Kimball. I'll attend to it at once."

When the door was closed, Constance blinked wide, innocent eyes at the famous man. "Is Father involved in anything beyond the usual press of business, Mister McCall?"

"He really didn't elaborate, Miss Constance. He

doesn't, you know. Not even to me. It may be one of the reasons for his continued . . . ah, success.'' He tightened his jaws. He has almost said, survival. But it wouldn't do to worry the girl. Most of those acquainted with Squire Ramsey had heard hints of what could occur when Miss Constance became upset. That rumor about her escapade of going after her father's stolen schooner . . . if only a trace of it could be believed, that should be warning enough. "I believe your father has a special shipment on its way to the southern ports somewhere, and I have my doubts whether it is documented goods, but when was that unusual for your father?''

He glanced at the little table by the door, a frown suggesting itself at his bushy brows. "If you will forgive me for a moment, Miss Constance . . .'' He stood, walked to the table, and broke the seal on the enveloped message there. As he read it, his frown deepened.

"Is there trouble, Mister McCall?'' Constance asked.

"Nothing more than is usual of late, Miss,'' he shrugged. "There is a gentleman in the Carolinas—a Mister Dale—who operates rather a nice fleet of privateers. A patriot, and one who will do rather well financially if the British can be held at bay long enough for our Continental Congress to assemble its resources . . . and some suitable allies for us. Our vessels—Mister Dale's and mine—have operated jointly on a few occasions, and we try to keep each other advised. He is advising me.''

"You seem upset at the advice, sir.''

"Yes, frankly I am.'' He took a deep breath and hissed it out through clenched teeth. "Some damnable fool has acquired a hand of battery guns and is sending them to a buyer at Charleston.''

For a moment Constance was silent, trying to show no expression. Then she asked, "But, sir, everyone is transporting guns these days. I understand fine guns are better than gold on the market, ever since the business at Concord."

"Yes, but not to be sent to Charleston. Not now at any rate. Dale says there is a Tory ring thereabouts that has got word of the shipment—that's how he learned of it, his men accosted one of the bast . . . beg pardon, miss, one of the Tory gentlemen, and obtained the information."

"Well, certainly they might object."

"More than object, miss. These particular royalists have a private squadron of armed interceptors who have played the very devil off Charleston and Savannah of late. This is no time for anyone—damned fool or whoever—to be trying to run valuable guns to the southern ports. They simply will never arrive."

"Doesn't one always take such chances . . . shipping valuable cargo?"

"Not a chance in this case, miss. A certainty. Either those guns will fall into Tory hands, or at the very best, be lost to those at Charleston who have great need of them. A shame. A very shame."

When McCall was gone, Constance paced the little drawing room in a sputtering rage. She knew beyond a doubt which damned fool had decided to ship battery guns to Charleston, and she knew with sure intuition who was in charge of taking them there. At that moment she would hardly have hesitated—had the chance presented itself—to strangle her father with his own studded galluses.

Through two bells of forenoon watch and into the early afternoon, *Mystery* held a steady eight knots south by east, gradually closing to within a mile of the bright coastline of Hatteras Peninsula. Though most aboard had sailed the offshore lanes here, few had ever seen this shore so closely. The best of mariner's charts gave little information regarding inshore waters here, except for dire warnings of treacherous currents, shifting bars, near-shore shoaling, and various other hazards. Even trading vessels making call on the few inland settlements beyond Albemarle and Pamlico Sounds made it a practice to stand offshore and conduct their commerce through shallow-draft ferry craft rather than risk going around or striking a submerged bar.

Even from a mile away, the wind-harried surf below the white sand beaches had an ominous look. A ship aground on such a shore could be battered to wreckage before it could be towed off. Still there was a striking beauty to the shore, bright beach stepping up to forests ablaze with the colors of autumn, tall pines standing above the profusions, giving their shade to palmettos and brilliant foliage below.

The stalking snow was closer by half now than when first the chase had started, its trim beam and press of canvas giving it an easy twelve knots to the ketch's eight, but Dalton rarely looked back. Instead he scanned the distances ahead and studied the shoreline with intense concentration. Somewhere ahead, by the charts, there was a cut where the long barrier of Hatteras Peninsula ended and the longer stretch of Hatteras Island began. On the charts the two land areas appeared as long, thin strips almost abutting end to end, but not quite. The cut was there, somewhere, a tidal pass where small craft could enter the bays beyond.

He didn't know whether the cut would be an opportunity. The charts gave no soundings, only a warning of hazardous waters. But the thought held that there might be a means of escape there. Judging by its stacked sails, Dalton knew the snow to be deep-keeled. How much deeper than the ketch? He could only guess, but probably a difference of at least five feet in draft, maybe eight or nine. With all the formulas and calculations that were standard among marine architects and shipbuilders, still there was no standardization among vessels themselves. A ship with the sails of the snow might draw fifteen feet—or it might draw only ten and compensate with ballast or an extended keel. Only by actual measurement could one be sure. His only hope was to find the cut before the snow could get *Mystery* under its guns, and that maybe the cut was deep enough for the ketch, and maybe it was not deep enough for the snow.

Maybe.

The shoreline crept closer, and he held his course, his eyes burning from concentration and use of the heavy glass. Beside him Billy Caster scribbled and jotted, referring again and again to the sketchy charts, trying to calculate speed and position. Often he looked up, shading his eyes to peer ahead, then returned to his calculations.

Dalton put down his glass to rest his eyes and paced half the length of the ship and back, breathing deeply, willing the tension from his shoulders, checking the set of sheets and pins, listening to the drum of sails aloft.

"By this Admiralty chart we should have found the cut before now," Billy told him. "We have made eight knots now for nearly five hours since leaving the bay. It isn't forty-five miles to Albemarle Sound."

"What does the trading company chart say?"

"It puts it a bit farther, though it is so poorly drawn that I can't be sure. Why aren't there proper charts of these waters, sir?"

Dalton shook his head. Charts were charts. Those done for the Admiralty were faultlessly executed, carefully lettered, and often illustrated in great detail. But they were done in England, often based on little more than haphazard reports and casual sightings, and they often disdained such trivia as the configuration of a foreign shore. The trader's map probably was more accurate, having been drawn by people who navigated these waters, but trader maps were far more concerned with the condition of shipping lanes and the location of ports than with such things as barrier breaks. It was as though the traders' cartographers simply assumed that everyone already knew about cuts and passes.

"We shall just have to keep looking," he said.

He raised his glass, then lowered it again. The treeline ahead seemed to be broken. "Have a look at this, please, Mister Caster. What do you see?"

Billy took the glass and steadied it, squinting. "Is that it, Captain?"

"It could be. How far ahead do you make it?"

"Three miles, sir. More or less."

Dalton cupped his hands. "In the maintop!"

"Aye, sir?"

"Do you see a pass in the shoreline ahead?"

A long pause, then, "No, sir. Not that I can make out."

"Odd," Dalton muttered. "Something we can see from the deck but the tops can't see?" He glanced back at the pursuing snow. It was less than three miles back now, farther offshore than *Mystery*, but angling implacably toward her, its big black flag streaming out a'starboard like a promise of death. "I think we had better arrange a closer look, Mister Caster. If you know the names of any saints, you might want to have a talk with them."

"Aye, sir. But I don't know any. My family was Presbyterian."

"Helm, bring us two points to starboard," Dalton said, and watched as *Mystery*'s distant sprit traced a short arc across the horizon sky. When he looked aft again, the snow had altered course just slightly, accommodating its advantage.

Ten minutes passed, and fifteen, and the man out

on the spreaders called, "By the mark, six!" a few minutes later he called again, "An' a half, five!" The shoreline now was less than a quarter mile off the beam, and just ahead Dalton could see clearly the wide break in the wall of tall pines, but still the tops reported nothing. With his glass he studied the breaking surf, the sandy beach beyond, and saw no break in it.

"On deck!"

"Report, tops!"

"There's a sort of clearing over there, sir. Looks like the woods have been cleared or burned and haven't grown over yet." Dalton drew a deep breath and let it hiss through his teeth. There was no cut there, no pass into the bays, only a trick of the forest—an illusion caused by a downing of trees. "Two points windward, helm," he said. "Mister Tidy, put someone amidships to hear the sounding and signal helm. I want to hold at 'by the mark, six.'"

"Aye, sir."

Two miles back and three points a'port the snow also corrected, continuing its closing stalk.

"On deck!"

"Report, tops!"

"Sir, I can't see the launch anymore! It was out there a bit ago, but now it's gone!"

Dalton scanned the fore horizon. The sliver of sail that had been ahead of them since leaving Chesapeake was no longer in sight. Through the nooning hours it had gained to five or six miles ahead, then had held its distance, just in sight of signals. It was doubtful whether the snow had ever even seen it. Yet now it was gone, vanished as though it had never been there, and Dalton had a sudden inspiration. "They've found the cut," he said. "They've gone in."

Billy Caster squinted in the distance, then went back to his charts. "That must be it, then," he said. "The trader chart is more accurate than the Admiralty

222

chart. It has a line of crosses abreast Roanoke Island that I suppose might indicate a passage. I took it for a reef or shoal."

"Well, let us hope it is a passage, and that it will admit us. Even then, it will be a close thing. That snow makes three miles to our two. It will be fairly on top of us by the time we arrive where the launch was last seen." He looked back now, using his glass to study the warship. It was a trim, jaunty craft, lean and deadly with its great mass of sails and its slender beam. The man commanding it knew how to use the wind to his advantage and how to calculate course . . . though there was a hesitancy in the trimming of sails that said his crew was sloppy in its work. What could a ship like that do with proper hands? A fine craft it was, just as Charlie Duncan had told him when he first saw it back there in its hidden cove. Intended as a privateer, obviously—a ship worth a fortune, fitted out for the taking of fortunes. And now in the hands of the lowest of seafarers. *Pirates.* That would explain also the sloppiness of its crew. They would be men chosen more for their murdering talents than for their sailing ones.

He thought of the dying Frenchman, of the plea he had made. His daughters . . . did they still live? It was a time now since they had been taken . . . long enough for those men—if they were the sort Dalton expected they were—to have . . . the thought was not worth thinking. It was likely those girls were dead by now, and that death had been a mercy for them.

The next half-hour seemed interminable. The bright shore of the peninsula crept by just a quarter mile away as the snow crept closer . . . less than two miles off, then barely more than a mile, big guns plain at every port, rolled out for firing, their muzzles shadowed by the triced-open hatches above them. A half-mile closer and the gun crews would be at their stations.

223

"On deck!"

"Report, tops!"

"Pass just ahead, sir! Not a mile!"

"Can you see our launch, tops?"

"Not a sign of it, sir. But there's fanbars out from the cut. Shoal water, sir!"

The voice was overlapped by another, from ahead, "An' a half, five . . . an' a quarter, five . . . by the mark, five . . . shoaling!"

"Mister Tidy!"

"Aye, sir?"

"Belay sounding at 'by the mark, three,' and have the sounder guide by dark water. You relay the signals yourself, please."

"Aye, sir."

"An' a half, four, still shoaling . . . an' a half, four . . . an' a half, four . . . an' three quarters, four, deepening . . . an' a half, four . . ."

"Helm, you heard my order to Mister Tidy?"

"Aye, sir."

"When the signals come, you keep a sharp eye on Mister Tidy yonder. Steer by his arms."

"Aye, sir."

"The snow is coming over, sir. Angling to fall in astern."

"Hands a'deck to the sheets! Prepare to trim to a new course at command!"

"By the mark, four . . . an' three quarters, three . . ."

"In the maintop!"

"Aye, sir?"

"The shoal ahead. Can you read it?"

"Aye, sir. It's a fanbar, comes out to dead ahead, then drops away."

"An' a half, three . . . an' a quarter, three . . ."

"Helm, come broad a'port. Hands a'deck, trim for beam reach!"

As smartly as ever a ketch might, *Mystery* heelèd and veered left, her sails angling to take a new wind.

Moments later the telltale broken swells and light tone of a sandbar slid past on the right.

"An' a half, five . . ."

"Helm, hard a'starboard. Hands a'deck, trim for starboard reach!"

Mystery heeled again, her stern coming through the wind, and spars aloft quartered around to take the new trim as they put the wind broad of the starboard beam.

"On deck! Clear ahead, sir, but there's shoaling at the cut. Sandbars, it looks."

Dalton looked aft again. *Mystery* had lost ground in making around the silt fan. The snow was coming up half a mile away—nine hundred yards at most—and twin clouds of smoke blossomed at its nose to drift lazily off toward shore. The sound of guns rolled across the intervening waters and bright spray sheeted astern of *Mystery*. A second later a gout of spray erupted short of her fleeing tail.

"Ranging guns," Dalton noted. "Eighteens? The snow is armed like a frigate." He gazed across sundappled waves at the larger ship, still coming on. "It isn't likely that he wouldn't know why we veered wide back there, more's the pity."

As if in response to his words, the snow heeled a'port to skirt around the fanbar, following the path *Mystery* had taken. Without taking his eyes off the pursuer, Dalton asked, "Mister Caster, what was the least sounding we discovered passing that bar?"

"By the mark, three, sir."

"Helm, how did we handle in coming about?"

"Stubborn, sir. This ketch has no liking for its rudder."

The snow would not be hard-helmed, he knew. With its foremast set almost at the step-timbers of its jib and its press of sail well forward on its hull—almost the opposite of the rear-driven ketch—its rudder would respond to a touch. What had been a hard turn for *Mystery* would be a quick turn for *Fury*.

"I wonder," Dalton mused, "if the arrogance of a man who would fly the color black might carry a touch of impatience in its blend."

"Sir?"

"A matter of curiosity, Mister Caster. I wonder whether that pirate back there will realize that his turns are much quicker than ours."

The snow had completed its passage of the sandbar, and now heeled sharply, coming to starboard to bring *Mystery* under its bow chasers again. It heeled, veered and shuddered visibly, stumbling leftward, and they could see men on its deck lose their footing and fall. High in the foreshrouds a tiny figure pitched forward, seemed to scramble in midair for an instant, then plummeted to the deck.

"I don't think he realized that, sir. He has grounded."

But the snow was still aweigh and moving. It had struck the bar a glancing blow only, then slid past. Dalton refined his estimate of the vessel's hull shape. Deep-keeled, drawing certainly more than twelve feet, maybe as much as fifteen. But not wide-bellied. "A hull like a schooner's hull," he noted. "He cleared at three fathoms, but not at two."

"On deck! Shoals ahead, sir. Bars in the pass."

Dalton glanced forward. John Tidy had heard the call, and the relay of arm signals from the stem had begun, spotter to midships to helm, guiding by dark water. It was a thing Dalton had done before, and in good light it was effective . . . although it was a bit like the threading of needles. "Cocked-hat sailing," such tactics had been called by the instructors of midshipmen. Such tactics were officially abhorred, but rare was the mariner who had not practiced such things when the occasion warranted.

"Tight water, sir!" called tops. "Narrow channels, and twisty."

226

Behind them the snow had corrected itself and was coming at them again, narrowing their lead. "Hands aloft," Dalton ordered. "Reef topsails and topgallant."

Billy Caster spun around, his eyes wide. "Reef sails, Captain? They'll overtake us . . ."

"They shall overtake us at any rate, Mister Caster. Our only chance is to go where they can't go, and it will come to nothing if we go aground in that pass."

As her high sails were reefed, *Mystery* slowed to six knots, then five, then four. Behind, across the water, they could hear now the closing sounds of the snow—the dull boom of her hull as waves broke about her, the drumming of massed sails, then a pair of roars as smoke clouds shrouded her stem. A large ball plowed water almost under the ketch's nose, another grazed her hull.

They were into the bars then, creeping along a narrow, twisting path that only the tops and the spotter out on the jib could clearly see. Another boom from behind, and a gaping hole appeared in the main course, the ball missing the mast by inches. Dalton looked across the closing space between vessels and guessed that surf and currents were making the snow dance just a bit, throwing its gunners off sight. At this distance, he knew, a fair gunner aiming at a mast probably would hit it.

Mystery shuddered as her keel grazed sand, then shuddered again, seeking to balk before she cleared a trough beneath and went on.

"On deck!"

"Report, tops!"

"We've done it, sir! We're past the bar."

"An' a half, three . . . by the mark, four . . . an' a quarter, four . . ."

"Hands aloft, we'll have full sail now, if you please!"

Again the ranging guns on *Fury* belched, but the

227

pair of shots went wide a'port as the snow's helm was put over. It had come to the sandbar. A trace of a smile touched Dalton's cheeks. "He'll sound there, then turn away. He has too much keel to pass." At six knots, *Mystery* came a'port and pointed her nose down the opening channel with the broad waters of Pamlico Sound ahead. "Mister Caster, up colors please. The red-and-white one, I think. Let's give that gentleman back there a glimpse of what colors look like when they aren't black."

"On deck! There's our launch, sir. Ahead a mile!"

"Stand down and retrim, Mister Tidy. Signal those people to come alongside, and we'll take them aboard."

"Have we lost the pirate ship, Captain?" Billy was at the charts again, studying the dogleg shape of Cape Hatteras, which was now a lee shore to port.

"Only if he decides to let us go, I'm afraid. We're in sanctuary here for a time, but eventually we shall have to come out. If he is interested enough, all he has to do is cruise down the coast and be waiting for us."

XVII

"Idiot!" Geraldo Lostrato paced the tiny compartment he had made for himself, venting his rage in muttered curses. "The moron! The imbecile! A fortune in our hands and he turns aside to pursue a commodity ketch! And runs up a black flag! The madman!" The sword at his buckler thumped his leg with each pace, emphasizing his anger. The sword itself was another example of the strutting arrogance of the *peone* pirate. It was a dare, like a slap in the face. It was Pinto's ultimate insult to him, that he insisted he keep his sword even when he had been under arrest. The man was goading him to fight him.

He would, he promised himself. Pinto would regret this sword. But first there was a ransom to negotiate, down the coast at the port of Charleston. A fortune to be had . . . yet Pinto, the mindless hulk, dallied along playing little games of piracy with a commodity ketch. What could such a vessel have of value? Tobacco? A few bales of indigo, perhaps? Nothing that could be worth the time Pinto already had expended. And yet, Lostrato reminded himself, it was he himself who had planted the idea that the ketch might be worth seeing. It had been a way to keep the brute occupied and keep his little mind off other things, and its success did reinforce Lostrato's certainty that he could control Pinto when necessary.

The ketch had barely escaped, by crossing into the bays and sounds beyond the barrier cape. Lostrato was surprised that it had made it through. The pass was a maze of shallows and shoals cut here and there by twisting tidal currents. Yet it had, and *Fury* could not follow, and now—finally—Pinto had turned southward again, toward the lower coast. Not rapidly, nor out in the sealanes, but at least they were going the right direction.

With Pinto occupying the main cabin aboard the ship, and the two girl prisoners the secondary, Lostrato had hung sailcloth across the companionway to make a space for himself. The space included the hatch to the French girls' quarters, so that he could guard it . . . and it was out of sight of Pinto when he came below. He had even added a tiny cot where Vasco could sleep, and they stood watch and watch on the captives. Since learning of their wealthy family and their relatives in Charleston, Lostrato had conversed only a little with the pair . . . just to implant the idea with them that he alone, of all aboard, was their friend and that they must trust him. The collection of ransom would be easier if they cooperated with him, and his mind turned over idea after idea about how that might best be done. What he sought more than anything was a plan that would entail his going ashore with the prisoners, just the three of them, to make the exchange—possibly while Pinto and some of his cutthroats held hostage some ships at dock or a warehouse. Such a transaction would be best. With such protection, Lostrato himself could make the exchange . . . then simply disappear. A thin smile formed at his lips as he pursued the thought.

Vasco entered with food from the galley, and Lostrato inspected it, twitching his thin nose. They had found the ship's stores well stocked, its galley clean and efficient. Now, in just this short time, Pinto's two cooks—a pair of waterfront cutthroats who had swamped cantinas at some island port—were reducing ship's fare to a noxious mess of greases and gruels hardly better than they had suffered aboard *Columbine*. He turned away stiffly. "Set it by the cabin door, Vasco. It will keep them alive at least."

"*Si, Don Geraldo.*"

The man set the plates on the deck, rapped at the portal, and stood away. After a moment the door opened a bit, and one of the girls grabbed the food, scampered back inside, and closed the door. In the dim lamplight Lostrato was not even sure which one it had been—it was only a glimpse of dull, tangled hair shadowing a begrimed face. He had thought of visiting them again today, spending a little time to see if there was more they could tell him that might help in making contact with their family. Now he changed his mind. Just such a short time before, they had seemed rather pretty little things. Even he had been tempted to dally with them a bit, despite his certainty that such would reduce their value. But not now. How quickly they had become hideous! He wondered if it was the food, or their fear . . . or simply something about the French that allowed even nubile charms to slip away and leave only ugliness. He hoped they were not ill. It would be difficult to collect a full ransom if they were not in good health. But he had no means of determining that. The drunken butcher who was Pinto's ship's surgeon would as likely kill them as cure them, and the saints only knew what he would do to them in the process of either.

Finally he strode to the curtain. There was a stink here that offended his nose, and he wanted fresh air.

"Guard them well, Vasco," he reminded the sullen eunuch. "Remember, you and I will share the riches their ransom brings. I will see to that. You have only to trust me, good Vasco, and keep the prisoners safe."

"*Si, Don Geraldo.*"

Lostrato pulled the sailcloth back, then let it drop into place. The hatch had banged open, and he heard the thudding steps of Pinto coming down the ladder to cabin deck. From the sounds of his progress Lostrato knew . . . the captain was drunk again, staggering with each step, lurching and bumping into the bulkheads of the narrow aisle that was the companionway.

Lostrato's hand rested on his sword. It would be so easy now . . . the oaf would not even know what was happening. He tensed, then relaxed. No, it would not be that way. When the time came—if it came—for Don Geraldo Lostrato to kill Enrico Pinto, he would do it in his own way. The captain was arrogant about his abilities with a sword, about how many men he had cut down. But Lostrato had seen him use a sword, and the memory of it curled his lip. Pinto was strong and ferocious, but his skills were those of waterfronts and back alleys. He had never faced a swordsman.

Pinto stumbled past the curtain and slammed his way into the main cabin, banging it closed behind him.

"Guard them well, Vasco," Lostrato said again, and let himself out. The stink in the confined place had really become abominable.

When Eugenie had retrieved the food and closed the portal, Lucette stirred in the far corner, eyes huge and frightened in the gloom. "Did any of them see you?"

"*Oui,* two of them, but only for an instant. It is the same two who are always there."

"Maybe you should have let them look more, Lucette."

"No, a glance is enough. Maybe they will re-

232

member and think I am worse than I can appear to be."

"I don't know how one could look worse," her younger sister shook her head, "than either of us. Oh, and this smell! It makes me want to gag. Please, put that food away somewhere. Just the sight of it . . ."

Eugenie set the foul-seeming food on the shelf and covered it, willing herself not to vomit, though it occurred to her that such would add to the smell in the little cabin and might not be such a bad idea. It had been the stink of the Spanish, the unwashed, cloying scent of them, that had given her the idea. Though she had carefully planted the fiction with Señor Lostrato that she and Lucette were worth much gold in ransom if they were unharmed, there had been the fear still. It was obvious that Lostrato was not in charge here, though he sulked and blustered. That other one, the huge, foul man with the greasy whiskers, he was in charge, and something about him said that he was not to be counted on, not to be expected to do even what was best for himself. He seemed erratic, unthinking, like the *frenetiques* one sometimes saw on the streets of Versailles or Paris—*les gens de la lune,* those beset by madness. Perhaps the Señor Lostrato could persuade him to not harm them. But for how long?

They had heard his bull voice roaring through the ship, had heard the sounds of his drunkenness beyond their door . . . and they had seen the leers of others aboard and heard their raucous laughter, their insinuating whispers among themselves. And Eugenie had told Lucette, "As bad as they appear, we must appear worse. And as bad as they smell, we must smell worse. It may be our only chance."

Part of it had been easy. Candlewax and soot to smudge their faces, the grease of boiled salt meat to dull and mat their hair, smoke to redden their eyes . . . they had worked on each other, perfecting the cronish disguises until they would have laughed were it not for their terror.

Then came the hardest part. The smell. "We must," Eugenie said, and finally Lucette agreed. They were both half sick when it was done. To some extent, their noses had become hardened to it now, but it still was sheer luxury to press their faces against the battened shutters of the cabin's aft bulkhead and breathe a little of the clean air that drifted through.

The terror of captivity, the revulsion, the grief for their parents . . . the worst of it for Eugenie was when Lucette dozed off from exhaustion and Eugenie heard her sobbing in her sleep. Heard, and wondered whether she too sobbed that way, and whether Lucette had heard.

How long had they been here? Eugenie was not sure. It was so dark in the tiny cabin, so gloomy, and she was not sure that she had counted the times when light came through the skylights and the shutters. A night had passed since the awful thundering of the guns, a night, she thought, and most of a day. Those guns! Their thunder had reverberated through the decks, rolling hollowly through the very timbers of the ship while the girls clung to each other, not knowing what was happening beyond. Who had they shot at? What had occurred? They had no idea, but they had seen the shifting beams of light as the ship turned to a new heading afterward.

The skylights gave a red-gold flush to the cabin now, and Eugenie thought it must be evening. Then, as the hue deepened, shadowed sometimes by the coming and going of rough men above, she knew that another day had passed, and she feared the coming of the darkness.

In her dark corner Lucette stirred. "Eugenie, someone will come to help us, *non?* Someone will rescue us from this?"

"*Mais oui, ma chere soeur,* someone will come. I

234

know it. We must believe in this."

"Who might come to help us, Eugenie?" Lucette sounded drowsy, and Eugenie was glad. To sleep was better now than to be awake, even though there were no good dreams to come with sleep. Still . . .

"Someone tall and handsome, Lucette. Someone strong and gentle. Close your eyes, my sister, and I will close mine. Maybe we will see him, if we try."

"He still stalks us, sir," Charley Duncan reported as signals came from the little shore party on the cape. "He stands offshore and paces us, just a few miles away, beyond that spit of land."

"A very determined pirate," Patrick Dalton nodded. "He has charts too, and he knows we must come out of these sounds."

"By the mark, four," came the chant from ahead. "An' a half, three. Shoaling again."

"We are losing our light, Mister Duncan, and these waters are as treacherous as a snake. I think we shall have to anchor here until dawn. Take the deck, please, and give the necessary commands."

"Me, sir?" Duncan gawked at him. Despite being nominal first officer for Dalton, Duncan's experience was as an able seaman, nothing more. He had never commanded anything larger than a launch.

"Of course, you, Mister Duncan. You know how it is done, and there is no time like the present for you to have a bit of practice. The deck is yours, Mister Duncan." He turned away, and Billy Caster, just coming from the companionway, grinned at Charley Duncan. Usually it was the boy who received the brunt or benefits of the captain's occasional penchant for teaching. It seemed to him that it should be Duncan's turn.

"Aye, sir." Duncan shrugged. He tested the wind, by thumb and gauge. "Helm, bring us four points into the wind, please. Mister Tidy, hands aloft to furl sail! Hands a'deck, stand by to come aback and trim down. Anchormen to the fore, stand by to drop the port bower.''

Dalton stood at the rail, looking away, not participating. Billy Caster looked from one to the other of them, cocking his brow at Duncan.

"I choose the port bower because it will put us closer to the wind come morning,'' Duncan snapped. "Besides, it's a better anchor than the one on starboard.''

"I didn't ask, Mister Duncan,'' Billy shrugged.

"No, but you were wonderin'.''

The ketch came left, nosing toward the gentle wind. Duncan watched its nose swing, its long snout of jib and bowsprit a distant dark finger tracing a line along the shore beyond.

"An' a half, three!''

"Flags, call in the scout boat, please. We shall need the launch again soon. Sheet off, please, Mister Tidy, and pipe furl aloft.''

"Aye, sir.''

"Foredeck, let go the port bower.''

Chain rattled as the big anchor hit the water and sank away, and they felt the tug of it as *Mystery* backed away and took up the slack.

"By the mark, three! Shoaling aft.''

Duncan counted to five, then *Mystery* came dead in the water, held by its bower anchor. "Down sails!''

"Aye, sir.'' The pipe wailed and lifts were eased aloft.

"Will you lower your spanker and staysails, Mister Duncan?'' Dalton asked conversationally.

Duncan wiped away sweat from his brow, his shoulders strained by tension. "No, sir.'' He glanced eastward. Clouds were forming there.

"Will they serve a purpose, then?''

"Not that I know of, but taking them down just

means we'd have to put them back up again come light, and God only knows what else we might be doing then, with people stalking us and all."

"Very good, Mister Duncan. You see, command is not so difficult. An ordeal, yes, but rather ordinary as ordeals go."

"Aye, sir." He looked forward, off the starboard quarter, where in the distance the launch was putting about to return to the ship. "We are anchored, sir. Do you wish me to keep command any further?"

"Of course, Mister Duncan. You are doing splendidly. Do please continue."

"Aye, sir. Mister Tidy! Please have someone set lanterns fore and aft. Mister Hoop, have our Hessians had their rest? I shall be needing them, very shortly. Mister Tidy, I'd like volunteers to man the launch when it returns, and issue arms please . . ."

"Wan' a bi' o' a loo' about?" one of the Indians swung down from the mizzen shrouds. "Coun' us in, 'en, swagger."

"I'll go along," Michael Romart shrugged. "You'll need somebody to keep you out of trouble."

"Mister Tidy, when the launch comes I intend a reconnoiter. You'll have charge until I return . . . unless the captain wants it back, of course."

"Mister Duncan," Dalton peered at him, "what are you doing?"

"Commanding the ship, sir. You said . . ."

"I know what I said. What do you intend to do with our launch?"

"Well, sir, it strikes me that during the night there's just no telling what those people in that snow might do, so I intend to lead a shore party to sort of keep an eye on them, sir."

"Mister Duncan!"

Duncan's proud stance collapsed. "Aye, sir. Well, the truth is, I'm thinkin' it's them that might want to have a look at us through the night, y'see, and I don't believe they ever saw our launch, so they may not even know we have one, and I just think it might be kind of jolly if—sayin' they was to put somebody ashore on that spit over there—if we could be there to wish the blighters well, as you might say."

"To what purpose, Mister Duncan?"

Duncan squared his shoulders again, and his mimicry of what he considered officer language. "Reconnaissance and intelligence, sir. Also morale."

"Morale? Whose morale?"

"Everybody's, sir. Trim theirs to size, and perk ours up a bit, y'see."

"In other words, you are simply spoiling for a fight."

"Aye, sir."

"A man in command of a deck does not go frolicking off to lead shore parties or war parties, Mister Duncan."

Billy Caster sucked in his breath. "But, sir, you yourself have . . ."

"That's enough, Mister Caster. Well, Mister Duncan, can you resolve this dilemma?"

"I don't know, sir. If you had command back, would you send us off to see what we could find over there?"

"Not without a good reason."

"Well, then, sir, let me ask you this: do you plan to go below for your supper soon?"

"Probably."

"Maybe about the time the launch gets here?"

"Possibly."

"Well, then!" Duncan grinned and turned. "Mister Tidy, when I give you temporary charge of this vessel, please keep in mind that the captain is belowdeck having his supper. As soon as he reappears, you will offer him the deck."

"Aye, sir."

"Now what have you resolved, Mister Duncan?

What if I do not choose to accept command from Mister Tidy?"

"Oh, I don't think there's a problem of that, sir. You're not a man who'd leave a ship uncommanded when there's an officer aboard . . . and when you come up from your supper, sir, you'll be the only officer here."

When Duncan had gone forward to meet *Something* at the taffrail, Billy Caster rubbed his chin and asked Dalton, "Sir, would you really not have sent a night party to the island?"

"I didn't say that, Mister Caster."

"But you said . . ."

"I said, 'not without a good reason.' There are, of course, several good reasons for putting a party over there, including the one Mister Duncan mentioned. A second reason is that those people may not know that we have a launch—chances are they have never seen it—and if so, I would like them to go on not knowing it. It might be handy. A third reason is that there is the possibility of taking a prisoner or two from whom we might learn something of value. For a fourth, *should* there be pirates on the island they will have come there by boat, and we could use a second boat."

"But it would be on the other side of the island, sir. And that might be a mile across."

"Mister Duncan is a resourceful forager, Mister Caster."

"Yes, sir." Billy thought about it, wondering just what sort of plans the captain had. "Then you knew what Mister Duncan would do when you gave him deck command?"

"A fair notion, yes. Also, I wanted him to have a taste of it. That might prove useful in the near future."

The captain had said all he had to say, but there was a look in his eyes that Billy had seen before, the

239

same sort of look that had been there the day Patrick Dalton had found himself in command of the Crown brig *Herrett*, and the day they had set out to seek and destroy the huge frigate *Courtesan*. Billy saw it now again, and knew it for what it was. Dalton had had his fill of being pursued, of dodging about and hiding from the predators. It was the cold, calm expression of a man who is ready to turn and fight.

XVIII

In deepening dusk, *Something* grounded at a sandy cove on the west shore of Hatteras. Eleven young men waded ashore to beach the launch, lower its mast, and snug it down, hidden in brush and debris. Two Englishmen, two American colonials, five Hessians, and two Accomac warriors, all freshly fed and armed to the teeth, set off then through the palmetto-strewn forest, the Indians in the lead, gliding like ghosts through shadowed glade and thicket. Duncan had thought the pair's bows and arrows were secured in the hold of the ketch, but when the shore party was assembled they had them, and refused muskets or rifles.

"Ta bloo'y slow," one of them had said. "Ge' orf nine a' 'ese t' one ball."

Now as they led the shore party through the deepening gloom of the long, thin island's forested crest, one said, "W' y' step 'ere mytes. Blinkin' snykes, y'know."

Directly behind them, Duncan turned to hiss, "Mister Locke, for heaven's sake, don't wander off that way. You get lost here and we'll never find you."

"Wo gehen wir hin, Korporal?" came from somewhere behind, abruptly hushed by Heinrich Weselmann's retort.

241

Ten minutes of fast, furtive march brought them to the seaward face of the forest, and they crouched there, looking out at breakers beyond a sand beach, the swell of open sea in the distance. Pitacoke pointed. *"Insini Sacco'ost sut!"*

"Le's cob plyne Henglish, swagger!" Squahamac reminded him. "'Ere's syle, 'swo' 'e's syin'."

"Sail," Michael Romart nodded. "You were right about that, Charley. She's hove to and waitin'."

The snow lay close in, at anchor barely beyond the breakers, and not more than a half mile down the coast. A wicked grin formed itself on Duncan's blunt face. "If the bugger is that interested in us, then likely he's got somebody ashore to look us over. Let's go see."

Staying to the verge of trees, they headed southward, hidden in evening shadow. They had gone a quarter mile when Duncan halted them. Ahead was flickering firelight on the beach.

"Cocky beggars, aren't they?" Romart grunted.

"What's to concern them, though? They don't know there's anybody else here." Duncan turned. "Quiet's the word now, lads. We don't know how many are . . . where have those Indians got off to?"

The rest looked around, suddenly aware that the Indians were gone. One of the Hessians raised a hesitant hand and pointed into the dark woods. *"Das Indianern . . . da drüben."*

"Blast!" Duncan shook his head. "Well, come along, we can't wait around for them."

The anchored snow loomed tall now on their left, and the firelight ahead was dancing light in the darkness, whipped by a busy offshore wind. In single file, the nine advanced, keeping to the shadows. As they neared, a shadow darted from the forest to join them, then another.

"Ich sehe zwei Indianern," someone whispered.

As though they had never been gone, Squahamac

and Pitacoke silently rejoined the party, and Squahamoc tugged at Duncan's coat sleeve. "We ha' a bi' o' loo', swagger," he murmured. "'Ere's nobbut th' bryce o' 'em 'ere. Wa' ha'dozen t'boot, but na' now."

"'Em lot's awa' t'yonder," Pitacoke added, pointing west.

"What in blazes are they talkin' about?" Michael Romart growled.

"They say there are only two Spaniards at the fire. The rest have gone west. Six of them, they think."

"Well, why can't they just say that straight out, then?"

"'Old th' lip, swagger," Pitacoke glared at the colonial. "Learn Henglish. Th' two o' us di'."

"They go' a boat?" Duncan asked.

"Haye, 'ere's a boat. Pas' th' dune . . . y'see?"

Duncan squinted. In the feeble firelight he made out the prow of a small boat, less than half the size of *Something*. "All right, then, let's go pay the two gentlemen a call. But quietly, lads . . ."

"No call f'at," Squahamac told him. "'Em two's dea'."

"Dead? They're dead?"

"Ri' 'nough." The Indian shrugged. "'Em's th' flymin' Henemy, righ'?"

"*You* killed them?"

"We foun' 'em, di'n we?"

"Jesus."

The two Spaniards lay where they had fallen, within yards of their merry little fire. One had an arrow through his neck, the other an arrow in his heart. The boat pulled up on the beach was a small shuttle, barely big enough to qualify as a jolly boat, but well constructed. Duncan inspected it, then stood over the bodies of the fallen pirates. "I'd had in mind to take some of these gentlemen back to *Mystery*," he said. "Captain might have wanted a word with 'em."

"Maybe we can salvage some of the rest," Romart

suggested. "That is, if you can control your savages, *Mister* Duncan."

"I think we should stand away from this fire," Victory Locke suggested. "Happen somebody on that ship there turns a glass this way, they could volley the lot of us with grapeshot from there."

It was a splendid suggestion, and they wasted no time fading back into the shadows.

"We'll want that little boat," Duncan said. "Can't ever have too many ship's boats."

"But how are we going to get it across the island?" Romart objected.

"Drag it, I suppose."

"Those other Spaniards are over there somewhere. They'd hear us coming halfway across."

"Then let's go find them and let them drag it for us."

Michael Romart heard the hesitation in his voice, noticed how Duncan kept looking out to sea, where clouds were rising beyond the near-anchored snow, rolling shoreward with the east wind. "That isn't really what you want to do, though, is it, Charley?"

"Does seem a shame . . . a boat at hand and all . . . not to make use of it."

"Be right dark, soon."

"Aye, I expect it will. Now, if we were to douse that fire . . ."

Within the hour, Victory Lock found himself in command of a diminished shore party, himself and five Hessians following a pair of Indians through inky forest in search of Spaniards. And with specific orders from Mister Duncan to take prisoners if possible.

Behind them on the east shore the fire had been extinguished and its remains buried in sand, and the two dead pirates had been hidden in the brush. Beyond the luminous caps of the dark breakers, a little boat with muddled oars crept close under the

244

chainplate of the silent snow, to be held there by Sam Sidney as Charley Duncan and Michael Romart swung themselves up to the shroud channel and raised cautious eyes above the gunwale. Sidney saw their silhouettes blend with the rigging shadows aloft, then disappear as they went over to the deck. Moments later there was a hiss from above and something inert rolled over the wales, hung suspended for a second, then was lowered slowly toward him. He caught the burden and eased it into the scupper of the boat. An unconscious man, smelling strongly of garlic and accumulated filth. Sidney untied the rope from him, laid him out full-length in the boat, then sat beside him. When the man stirred and groaned, Sidney delivered a judicious thump to his skull with the hilt of his cutlass.

On deck, Duncan and Romart retrieved their rope, crouching alongside a cannon, and peered carefully into the darkness around them. "I thought there was another one," Romart whispered.

"There was. He went below. There's still that helmsman aft, though. See him?"

"I hear him, too. He's snoring."

"Let him sleep," Duncan decided. "Poor soul probably needs his rest. The one that went below was an officer or something. Dressed like a dandy, and carryin' a long sword. Maybe the captain."

"More likely a passenger. An officer wouldn't have left that helmsman asleep."

"There is that. Well, then, let's look around. Meet back here in a bit, right?"

"Right."

In hammocks and tarped holds dozens of men— maybe tens of dozens—slept. Duncan prowled, pausing sometimes to loose a belayed line or remove the elevating quoin from a cannon . . . anything that occurred to him that could cause mischief and be done silently. At the quarterrail he crouched in shadow, sliced the securing lines on a pair of water kegs, then slipped across to the companion hatch, edging it open to look down into the companionway below. There was muted light there, as a lantern behind sailcloth, and the murmur of voices. He closed the hatch carefully, wishing he could have a look down there. Somewhere aboard, if they still lived, were the daughters of that dead Frenchman. Duncan had no love for Frenchmen, but his ingrained hostility had never extended to daughters—French or any other kind.

But the responsibility of command weighed heavily upon him. Dalton had trusted him with command of his deck. From that authority he had taken it upon himself to lead a shore party, and from the shore party a boarding party . . . a stretching string of decisions that still went back to the responsibility his captain had vested in him. He could afford no further gambles, at least not now.

Reluctantly he turned away from the companion hatch. In the distant fore a shadow moved, and moved again . . . Romart working his way around the deck in methodical fashion. He seemed to be carrying things as he went, but Duncan could not make them out. He started another prowl, looking for silent mischief to do, returning eventually to the main shrouds where Sam Sidney and his guest waited below in the little boat. It was time to go, and he crouched nervously, waiting for Michael Romart, as long minutes passed. Finally a shadow came from aft, along the rail, and Romart set down a pair of buckets and said, "I guess that will do it. Ready to go?"

"Ready," Duncan agreed. "What are those?"

"Buckets. Leave 'em."

"Let's go, then."

They lowered themselves to the boat, placed themselves fore and aft of Sidney and his sleeping passenger, and pushed off, letting the boat drift for a time before they manned their oars. When they had distance behind them, Duncan asked, "What were you doing back there, Mister Romart? I became impatient waiting for you."

"I found buckets of sand and water, so I made the rounds of their guns—as many as I could get to. Those people will have a surprise the next time they try to fire cannons at someone. I cleaned the powder out of their vents and reprimed them with wet sand."

It was past midnight when the boarding party rejoined the shore party on the beach. Locke and his little army had five more prisoners, surly Spaniards sitting in a circle surrounded by stolid Hessians with loaded muskets.

"There were six," Locke told Duncan. "But one of them tried to put up a fight."

"He's dead, then, I suppose."

One of the Indians appeared beside him. "As e'er was," he said. "'Ere. Brough' 'long a 'membrance.'"

Duncan had to look close at what the Indian put into his hand before he recognized it, then he gave it back, feeling slightly sick. It was a pair of ears. The Indian shrugged and put them away. "Dry 'ese, migh' sta' a necklace." With that idea in mind, he went off to find the other dead Spaniards, to add their ears to his anticipated ornamentation.

Sidney and Romart rolled the boat prisoner over the side into shallow water, and he sputtered and came around. A quarter hour's work with stout ropes and they had six unhappy Spaniards in harness, a pair of tow ropes extending back to the beached boat. Duncan pointed at the woods. "All right, pull. Let's be on our way."

The Spanish looked at one another in confusion. *"Que dice?"*

"Gi' a bi' o' tote, buggers," Pitacoke clarified.

"Los!" Wesselmann barked. *"Mak schnell!"*

247

"Estan Alemán?" a pirate wondered. *"Deutsch-landeren?"*

"Deutscher? Nein!" Heinrich growled. *"Hesse Kasselern. Sprecken sie Deutsch, Spanischer?"*

"Un poco. Ustedes no estan Ingles?"

"W'a t' blee'in 'ell 'ey goin' on abou'?"

Duncan put his face in his hands. "Mary, mother of God," he muttered. He took a slow breath, then roared, "Get that flamin' boat movin'! Now!"

Understood or not, it got them started. Indians in the lead, Spanish towing the boat at the urging of armed Hessians, Britons and Americans following with poles to boost the boat over obstacles, they disappeared into dark forest.

"Wo gehen wir hin, Korporal?" Wolfgang Mitter wondered.

"Das weiss ich micht!" Wesselmann snapped. *"Mir erzählt niemand etwas."* How do I know where we're going? Nobody tells me anything.

Three hundred and fifty miles southwest, hours before sunset, three sleek craft had put out from a fortified cove on Folly Island, using the Indies Passage to clear the reefs and shoals that dotted the treacherous sea off South Carolina. In last light of day they had stood at sea, clear of hazards, and had turned northeast in line abreast. Two were cutter-rigged, the third a Xebec of French design, but all carried multiple guns and all had a single mission. Intelligence from the north, combined with the advisories of one Felix Croney, an officer of His Majesty's Colonial Guard, had come together like a puzzle fitting, and certain royalist gentlemen in enclaves about Charleston had ordered an interception.

Someone was transporting battery pieces to Charleston, and three swift vessels were assigned to intercept and take or destroy. The cutters *Rover* and *Shark* and the Xebec *Belmont* were those vessels, and their target was an unescorted ketch lately south-bound from Chesapeake Bay. It was not in the interest of their sponsors that battery guns arrive at Charleston. It was not in the interest of His Majesty that they arrive, and His Majesty could be gracious to those who maintained his interests.

Captain Sir Henry Bartlett himself, HMRN retired, had consented to lead the hunt, and now he stood beside the trim tiller of his *Rover*, feeling the wind in his face, hearing the drum of taut sails, and relishing the sport ahead. It was likely, he estimated, that they would spot their quarry within two days. The three would fan out abreast at first light, just within topmast view of one another. In that manner they could sweep a seventy-mile path along the coast, working at their leisure. Somewhere between here and Point Lookout on the North Carolina coast, they would find the ketch. Certainly it would be armed, and probably it would put up a fight. Barlett relished the thought. It had been many a year since he had heard his own cannons thunder.

A ketch. Pity, he thought, that it couldn't be someting more worthy than a ketch. A ketch, no matter how well armed, could hardly be an adversary. Still, his sponsors would be pleased when he brought it home . . . or reported it sunk. Either would be satisfactory, although the taking of it would be preferred. Then they themselves would have the guns to present to His Majesty's officers. And if they had prisoners, they could undoubtedly learn who the scoundrel was who had sent the guns in the first place.

XIX

"On deck!"

Stretched out in his shingle chair, wrapped cozily in quilts, Dalton stirred himself and peered into the dark tops. Through the hours of darkness, the crew had maintained watch by threes—one man doing four hours on deck, two doing two each in the tops. Dalton had managed an hour's sleep below, then had dozed at the helm for a bit. It took him an instant or two to remember who was presently aloft, then he recalled. "Report, Mister Bean!"

"Lamp signal, sir. Shore party requests permission to return."

"Thank you, tops. Mister Fanshaw?"

"Aye, sir?" the deck watchman was just a shadow amidships.

"Go to the fore lantern, please. Lift the hood and show three and three."

"Aye, sir."

"What is the time, Mister Fanshaw?"

"Just past three bells of the morning watch, sir."

"Leave the lantern unhooded, Mister Fanshaw. It will show them their way home."

"Aye, sir."

Unwrapping himself, Dalton stood, folded his quilt, then stretched himself, feeling cramps and kinks in a dozen places. A man who falls asleep in a chair, he thought, deserves no better.

Here and there men stirred, aroused by the voices, and from the companion hatch came the muted clatter of dropped ironware, followed by a steady stream of cursing. Another clatter, then dim light showed up through the hatch and the cursing abated. Gerald O'Riley was starting breakfast down there.

Clouds had moved in from the east to obscure the stars, and the wee hours of morning were dark, only a hint of light from a moon somewhere above the clouds, its glow muted and its placement obscured. In the distance eastward, a mile or more away, a tiny speck of yellow light moved against a line of darkness.

Billy Caster came yawning from his bed and peered at Dalton, then said, "Good morning, sir. Have the gentlemen returned?"

"They are on their way, Mister Caster. It will be a bit. Mister Fanshaw?"

"Aye, sir?"

"Did they return the signal properly?"

"Aye, sir. They did. That's them over there, all right."

"Very well. Mister Caster, please bring me a pan and pitcher, and my razor. I would like to shave before breakfast." As the boy turned away, he raised the hood on the stern lantern, let its glow light the afterdeck, and stretched himself again, yawning.

Billy returned with pan, pitcher, shaving apparatus and a fresh shirt for his captain. "I thought you might want to spruce up a bit this morning, sir, so I had this out and hung for you."

"Thank you, Mister Caster. Have you been reading my mind?"

"No, sir. I was reading your charts again, though, after we went over them last evening, and I just thought you might require a fresh shirt this morning."

"You did."

"Yes, sir. And maybe fresh blacking for your boots as well. I've already honed your sword, sir."

"You *are* reading my mind."

"No, sir. Just the charts, and it seems to me that this is the day you'd choose to confront that snow over there."

"Well, we should reach the Ocracoke Inlet today, right enough. And it's likely the snow is making for there as well."

"Aye, sir." Billy grinned. "But to get there he has to pass that other break in the island . . . the little one. And you commented yourself, sir, that would be a handy spot to lie in wait for a strike offshore."

"You heard my muttering, then."

"Aye, sir."

"Well, we might know more in a bit. The launch is making across nicely."

"On deck!"

"Aye, tops!"

"Sir, I make it two boats, not one. The launch has brought along a jolly boat or something."

"Imagine that," Dalton breathed. "One wonders what else they may have found."

By the time the launch arrived with its captive boat, rowed by sweating pirates urged on by a lantern-lit Charley Duncan eight feet aft, training a punt gun on them, Dalton was freshly shaven and clean-shirted, and was buckling on his sword.

"Permission to come aboard, sir?"

"What have you brought us, Mister Duncan?"

"A boat, sir. Also six prisoners and a ship's bell . . . and probably quite a lot of information about the snow, sir."

In the dim predawn light, the two boats hove close alongside, and Michael Romart's hiss could be heard aboard the ketch, "What ship's bell? I didn't know we brought back a ship's bell."

"Well, I wasn't about to come away empty-handed, was I?"

"What do you mean, *probably* information about the snow?"

"Well, sir, none of us speaks Spanish, and none of these gentlemen speaks English, but one of them seems to speak a bit of German, and he and Corporal Wesselmann had quite a nice chat while we were crossing that island with this boat."

"Permission to come aboard," Dalton said. "Mister Caster, please go and find Mister Tidy. I shall need him to translate Corporal Wesselmann's translation."

They sorted most of it out over breakfast—Dalton, Duncan, Romart, and Sidney first, for a report on the boarding party, then Victory Locke joining them for details of the entire expedition ashore, while Billy Caster took notes. And finally, while Duncan and Joseph Tower installed *Fury*'s ship's bell proudly afore the helm on *Mystery*, Korporal Heinrich Wesselmann interrogated Emilio Flores in German, and John Tidy translated to English. The result was an uncertain mishmash of what Dalton assumed was largely misinformation, but three points came through clearly. There was dissension between *Capitan* and *Patron* aboard the captured ship, there were two young women captives aboard the ship, and there were approximately a hundred Spanish freebooters aboard the ship. Flores was not certain of the number, but there were certainly more than eighty, so maybe there were a hundred.

The gray light to the east grew steadily as the interrogation rambled on—interrupted once or twice by the Indians who came to squat alongside and join in while they ate their breakfast. At first Dalton was about to order them away, but then he noticed that one of them was sporting what seemed to be a necklace of fresh ears, and their presence seemed to encourage Emilio Flores to enthusiastic participation.

When it was done, and Flores had been returned to the covey of captives hovering by the mainmast, Dalton thought for a bit and said, "Suggestions, gentlemen?"

"Blow 'ell ou'em 'fore 'ey fine ou' 'eir belchers is pissed," and Indian offered.

"Hate to think of two young ladies in such company," Duncan said.

"We're going to have to face them sooner or later, sir," John Tidy suggested. "If they lay for us at Ocracoke, there'll be no way around them."

Billy Caster kept his peace, making notes and thinking about the captain's interest in that little cut at Hatteras Shoals, which the snow must pass to seaward to reach Ocracoke.

Dalton prowled the rail, looking at the sky, the windgauge, the chop of the bay. *Mystery* would do well to sustain six or seven knots in these treacherous, close waters. With the wind they had, the snow, offshore, could easily make fourteen knots—possibly sixteen beyond the dogleg where Hatteras swept southwestward and they could take the wind at its best—aft of their port beam. Still, the morning was new—just now giving light enough to see clearly—and the evidence indicated little discipline and less fine sail-handling aboard the snow. "Tell me again what sabotages you managed, Mister Duncan."

"Ah . . . well, I pretty well fouled six or seven sheet lines. It will take a while for them to get them sorted out and repinned, and with a bit of luck they might even haul a yard askew and foul their shrouds. And I filched a few quoins—hid them in a keg of salt meat—and, of course, I brought us a ship's bell."

"So, after they weigh anchor, it may take an hour or so for them to get properly under way."

"Yes, sir, I'd say so. Of course, that's after they weigh anchor. They've put out two bowers, and before they can lift them they'll have to find some bars for their captstan.''

"Oh? Where *are* their capstan bars, Mister Duncan?''

"Last I saw of them, the tide was carrying them ashore.''

John Tidy was trying, in a whisper, to keep Korporal Wesselmann advised of the discussion. Now the Hessian raised a tentative hand. *"Ist unsere gesangenen, Oberst . . . und die . . . uh, das luencher."*

"He thinks they might dally a bit looking for their missing mates,'' Tidy explained. "And more likely, looking for their boat.''

"In all,'' Dalton allowed, "we might gain a nice head start if we look lively about it.''

"Aye, sir.''

"Tops ahoy!''

"Aye, sir?''

"Have you light enough to spot channel?''

"Just a bit, sir, but it's gettin' better by the minute.''

"Mister Tidy, have those lads come down for their breakfast and put fresh spotters aloft, please. Hands afore to weigh anchor, hands to make sail . . .''

Donald O'Riley came scurrying aft to turn the glass. Duncan stepped to the coaming and ceremoniously rang the new bell six times. It was six bells of the morning watch, and *Mystery* was trimming for action.

"Pass the word among the men,'' Dalton told those around him. "The pirate has fired on us, has pursued us, and now stalks us. If he still pursues when we reach Hatteras Cut today, then he has left us no choice. I will attack him.''

".You know he'll be there, Captain,'' Duncan said. "He has invested too much now to turn away.''

"Take deck command, please, Mister Duncan. Bring us to all reasonable speed, southward with sounder at the fore and channel watchers aloft. I shall not require that command be transferred back to me, I think, so you have approximately three hours to get the feel of this ship before you take her into battle."

Duncan gawked at him. "*Me*, sir? *I'm* to fight this ship?"

"You, Mister Duncan. I have other things to do." Without a backward glance, Dalton strolled forward, leaving Charley Duncan in sole charge of the operation of the ketch.

With rising wind, and gray skies lowering in the distance, *Mystery* stepped off the miles of the bay at six knots for an hour, then found deeper water and put on sail to bring her speed to eight. At first bell of the forenoon watch there was land ahead, the barrier island curving westward to follow the turning of the coast. Here they veered to port for a few minutes while hands removed the timber cover from the forehold, lashed kegs and rail stock to it, and put it over the side. The Hessians herded their six Spanish prisoners over the rail and onto the makeshift raft, then set them adrift . . . miles south of where they had been taken, but still more miles from any point at which they might make a signal to the snow. Pitacoke and Squahamac huffed and complained at this—they had other, simpler ideas about disposing of enemy—but they brightened when it was made clear to them that there were plenty more Spaniards where those had come from.

Two miles from the turn of land, Duncan brought *Mystery* over, broad to the starboard, and the balky ketch gained another knot of speed as she took the fresh wind on her after quarter.

Titus Wilton came from the forehold carrying a rifle and shot pouch, growling over his shoulder at Victory Locke, "Just stay out of my way while I load this piece. I've no need of instruction, I was using these when you were running barefoot in the streets of London! If you want to be useful, go make those

257

aborigines leave my kit alone. They keep taking things."

With the prospect of a fight to cheer them, and lowering skies to concern them—both of them knew what wet weather could do to the sinew string on a bow—Pitacoke and Squahamac were practicing some American ingenuity. They had the sailmaker's spindles set out on deck and were turning new strings from stout linen twine. Victory Locke took one look at their determined, set faces and decided the sailmaker could jolly well do his own complaining. Those faces were smeared with warpaint, and shadowed by gaudy clusters of feathers in their hair. He went to distribute the rest of the rifles.

Enrico Pinto's sullen temper turned rapidly to a blistering rage as disaster after disaster presented itself to him on this gray morning. He strode along his deck, roaring, abusing, lashing about him with a knotted rope . . . and getting no answers. A party had gone ashore in a small boat, as *El Capitan* commanded, to cross the island and spy upon the cargo ketch. But they had not returned. The men were gone, the boat was gone—it was as though a hole had opened and they had disappeared into it . . . or, perhaps, as though they had run away in the darkness. The bell was gone, as was Emilio Flores, who had stood deck watch in the first watch hours.

Then they could not weigh their anchors because the capstan bars had disappeared, and most of an hour was lost rummaging in stores for replacements. Nothing aboard had been inventoried or catalogued, and no one knew where to look.

Finally, with the anchors raised and catted, there was the business with the sails. Some of the sheet lines were misplaced, others fouled, and *Fury* nearly ran aground before they could trim for direction.

258

They were so close that they could hear the pounding of the surf. Pinto raved and bellowed and laid his rope and the flat of his blade across many a back in that process.

And even after they were on course, there was still something else. Elevating quoins were missing from several of the cannons, and though all hands not otherwise occupied searched through the morning, they could not be found.

It was so obviously sabotage that Pinto went below, hauled back the curtain in the companionway, and strode past Lostrato and the glowering Vasco to haul open the barred door of the second cabin. The stench that hit him there, mingled odors of excrement and vomit, thick in the shuttered darkness, stopped him, and he slammed the portal closed. He whirled on the two men. "Those two! Have they so much as set foot out of that cabin? Have they been unguarded?"

"*No, Capitan,*" Vasco's eyes went wide. "We have been here all along, guarding this cabin as you commanded. The prisoners have not been out."

"*Both* of you have been here? Always?"

"I have been here. Señor Lostrato as well, except for an hour or so in the evening."

Hard eyes flashed at Lostrato. "And what did you do in that hour, Don Geraldo? A bit of sabotage, maybe?" His hand went to his sword, and abruptly the needle tip of Lostrato's blade was at his throat.

"You told me when I draw this sword that I must be ready to use it, *Capitan,*" the aristocrat smiled thinly. "Are *you* ready for me to use it now? Or do you wish to apologize?"

Pinto backed off a step, steeling himself not to draw just now against this man. Later, he told himself, later. "Account for yourself, then, if you want an apology."

Lostrato's smile loosened slightly. "I did no

sabotage to *our* ship. Why would I? It carries us toward fortune, if you can manage to get us there without wrecking us. I was on deck, yes. Once, strolling and taking the air. I was seen there."

"And those females," Pinto pointed at the closed door. "They have not been out of there, at all?"

"Not at all. I doubt if they could. I think they are both sick." Lostrato lowered his sword. "I will be glad to give you the honor of dying by this blade, Pinto. Now or another time. But do you really want to die here and now?"

"Then who has sabotaged my ship?"

"You are a stupid man, Pinto. Think about it. There has been mischief done, and some of your scum are missing. Who do you think did the mischief, then? Someone still aboard?"

Pinto regarded him with a glare of pure hatred, then turned abruptly and stalked away, toward the maindeck ladder.

Vasco turned thoughtful eyes on the aristocrat. "That was very fast, *señor*, the thing you did with your sword. I have not seen a thing like that."

Lostrato put it away. "I have told you, good Vasco, put your trust in me and don't worry about the captain. When the time is right, I will show him how a sword is to be used. Maybe I will make him like you before I kill him. Would you enjoy that?"

The pirate smiled. "*Si, señor.* I would like that very much."

"Then count on it, good Vasco. It is a promise I make you, and you know you can trust me."

Si, Don Geraldo. I know I can trust you."

Despite the delayed departure, *Fury* under sail began making up the lost time, and even Pinto was impressed. With a quartering fresh wind aft, and clear water under her keel, the snow almost danced as she sang across the swells, southward. Once the sails were finally trimmed, the vessel took spray in its teeth and held a steady fourteen knots. Ahead now, in sight, the shoreline swung away to the right, and Pinto knew that there, with the best of winds to push her, she would make sixteen.

At eight bells of the afternoon watch, *Mystery* lay close hauled in two-plus fathoms, three hundred yards in from the rim of Hatteras Cut. Her top lifts were down, no ensigns flew above the main yards, and she was as nearly invisible as tall masts could be, snugged in a'lee of the north bank of the tidal inlet. A hiding ship, waiting and strangely silent except for the lapping of waves at her hull, the small creaks and chitterings of wale and stay, the muffled snapping of luffed sails held loose by hands at pinrails and fifes. Oddly silent, Charley Duncan thought, partly because she lay to in fine sailing weather, waiting, and partly because eleven of her crew were not aboard. Of the seventeen remaining, only young Billy Caster was aloft. The boy had volunteered for lookout, and Duncan could not refuse. The lad had good eyes . . . and was least occupied of any.

All the rest were on deck now, Duncan himself at the helm and John Tidy amidships, Mister Hoop and the Hessians forward, the gunners Crosby and Pugh working along the rails readying prime and linstock at each gun, Cadman Wise standing by with an ax at the kedge-anchor's hawser, the remaining six seamen stationed and standing by to make sail.

It had crossed Duncan's mind several times how ludicrous the situation might seem—a slow, under-gunned and overloaded ketch waiting to spring upon an armed snow. Sad and ridiculous, had that been all there was to it. But there was more, and Duncan chewed his lip, hoping Patrick Dalton's strategy would work.

"On deck!"

"Aye, Mister Caster?"

"Signal from the launch, sir. The snow is in gun range and coming on . . . aye, there she is, sir. I see her now, just offshore . . . wait, sir, there's a new signal . . . Captain says attack, sir. Now!"

Duncan braced himself for the stubborn bucking of the ketch's rudder. "Make sail, Mister Tidy! As we drilled! Gunners stand by the bow pieces, fire when you have range!" Sails hauled high aloft and snapped taut hard about for a beam wind as hands on the deck trimmed their sheets. Staysails rattled, climbed, and boomed, and the spanker thundered as its gaff was hauled to take the wind. The rudder hove and bucked, bruising him with its buffeting. "Cut the kedge, Mister Wise! Mister Quinn to the maintop to read us out! Mister Romart, you may run up colors to your liking."

For hours they had drilled and practiced each maneuver, a choreography of swift, coordinated action to bring *Mystery* to speed and through the inlet on the heels of the dashing snow, a surprise attack from astern that could succeed only if everything went right. But drilling at rest and putting it into practice were different matters. Duncan drew a hissing breath and prayed that nothing had been forgotten.

Mystery lurched as Cadman Wise cut away her stern kedge, and for a moment scudded sideways while Duncan fought the cruel helm, balancing against the sudden press of sail aloft. For a moment, even the island aport fought him, breaking the low winds so that the ship's spanker sail could not assist the rudder. Then *Mystery* heeled and found way, and slid clear of the obstruction into the open wind of the little inlet. Duncan steered for best crossing angle, hoping that they had correctly sounded the depth from the little boat now in tow astern. There was no time now for correction.

"There she is, Mister Duncan!"

He looked to his left. A quarter mile abeam, the sleek snow ran into full view, great sails bright silver beneath a high, gray sky, swells spilling in wide curls beneath her slicing stem, a racing juggernaut already passing the east spit and bound downshore with the wind at its back.

See us now, he prayed. See us and come about, falter, lose way . . . "Here we are!" he shouted. "Here, you scuts! See us here!" At its speed, the snow would be beyond any firing range before the crawling ketch could clear the channel. The entire strategy depended upon *Mystery* getting in a first round or two before the snow could respond. But if he could not spring out upon its heels, if it got too far ahead before he could strike, then the plan was lost before it began.

Where were their eyes? "Here we are! Right here!" In the fore, the gunners also saw the problem and glanced back. Duncan raised an arm and sliced it downward. One of the gunners stooped to his notch and brought down his fuse. A twelve-pounder thundered, and smoke billowed ahead of *Mystery*, rolling away with the crossing wind. Almost instantly a hole appeared in the snow's fore staysail. 'Now do you see us?" Duncan hissed.

Dozens of faces aboard the snow and in its rigging turned toward him as Crosby and Pugh worked furiously to reload the discharged cannon. Its mate sat beside it, waiting its turn. There was a turmoil aboard the passing warship, and two of its beam guns belched smoke as its yards began to come about, slowly and raggedly it seemed to Duncan. The ship slowed as though confused, and he saw the brilliant colors of its captain's coat on the quarterdeck, saw his arms waving as he shouted orders.

A pair of balls gouted water ahead, far short of their mark, and Duncan's lips twisted in a wry grin.

"Hard to elevate without quoins, isn't it?" he shouted. The two guns were starboard mounts flanking the taffrail. He wondered how many more had tried to fire and failed, their vents fouled by Romart's wet sand. The two that worried him most were the snow's stern chasers, a pair of nasty eighteens that neither he nor the colonial had been able to tamper because of the helmsman dozing there. Few guns aboard the snow would fire this hour . . . but those most certainly would.

Mystery picked up way, angling across and out of the little cut, and Duncan brought her about smoothly, aided only by John Tidy's pipe calling the drill. All hands were responding as though this maneuver had been practiced for a month, not just for an hour.

The snow was still slowing, making to come about, sluggish from the moment's confusion of finding its prey behind it . . . and attacking. *Mystery's* new-trimmed canvas found the wind, and the ketch lifted its nose and took the spray on its bow, closing slowly but relentlessly. Duncan watched the serrated shoreline now off to his right, trying to count seconds and gauge distances the way he had seen Dalton do more than once. Just there, ahead, was the tidal lap where the launch waited. It was there—just there— that he must make *Fury* turn and engage. He knew— could almost feel—the stunned surprise aboard the pirate vessel. The ketch was not half the vessel that the snow was, and no warship at all. Yet the ketch had launched an outright attack, and now the snow must respond.

But surprise was a fleeting asset. Already the snow was making to come around to face him. I have two advantages left, he thought. I've spent my first and best. Now I have the weather gauge on him, the wind working for me and against him, and one other little surprise when he finds most of his guns fouled. But he already knows that some are.

Make your turn, he prayed. Come about and turn your tail away from me. I know that's where your teeth are. But the timing was too close. The snow would not have time to begin its turn before his guns were in range, and they knew that by now. He saw gunners at the warship's aftermounts and knew *Mystery* would not escape unscathed . . . if she escaped at all.

At least for the moment the snow was near dead in the water. It was the primary thing he had hoped for, the one thing that was essential. Just beyond, where the shoreline butted outward, he saw the nose of *Something* poking outward, sliding from its hole.

He held the wind and *Mystery* closed on the warship. Seconds passed and she was in range of the twin eighteens at her stern. Then, within range and still closing, then at limit range of her own forward twelves . . . and closing.

Eighty feet ahead of him, he saw Pugh and Crosby at their guns, linstocks with smoking fuse poised over their vents. What were they waiting for? Sting him, Dalton had ordered. Get in behind him, bring him to halt, and sting him if you can.

"Sting him!" Duncan shouted.

As though they had heard and responded, Pugh and Crosby found their marks and lowered their fuses. And even as the twin gouts of smoke erupted at *Mystery*'s nose, two larger clouds formed at the afterrail of the snow.

XX

Every oar on *Something* was in its loop, and a man at each oar. As smokes billowed upwind, rolling down toward them like dense fogs thunder-driven, ten strong backs lay to with a will and the launch leapt from cover into the driving surf while Dalton played its tiller and counted stroke. Before the smokes reached them they were past the pounding waves and coming hard into the wind. Again double thunder shook the murk, and Claude Mallory grunted, "Our lads that time. They've loosed the second pair afore."

"More the better," Victory Locke puffed, hauling in time. "Breathin' this stench is better'n bein' shot out of the water."

Amidships Pitacoke missed a stroke as he turned to peer ahead in the blind, rolling cloud. "Blee'in belchers! Sa' a bit f'us!"

"Lay to!" Dalton snapped. "Stroke! Stroke!" With her stub mast shipped, the launch rode low in the water, skimming across swells and spreading a wake astern as oar blades bit and hauled, bit and hauled, tholepins protesting along both rails. Rifles, muskets, and various items of personal mayhem were ranked along the benches from bow to stern, waiting to be used. Both punt guns were trained forward and tilted high.

The first reeking cloud rolled past and they were in clear air with a second, smaller cloud bearing down. Beyond it, Dalton could see the sails of the snow, though the deck was obscured. The ship was coming about, trying to bring her beams to bear on the charging ketch just beyond, and Dalton gritted his teeth, willing Charley Duncan to stay with the plan despite what his judgment might tell him. Every ounce of the tar's training, he knew, would be telling him to veer off, to try to stay upwind, to pass and broadside and come about and try for another pass with the wind on his side. But they had drilled on this. "Forget all you ever knew about tactic, Mister Duncan," Dalton breathed. "This is the test now. Hold your helm." He eased the tiller over, urging the launch a bit to starboard, tracking the seaward veer of the snow. "This will be close work at best," he said for anyone nearby to hear. "Lay to and haul like you've never hauled before, lads." In moments the second smokes would pass. By then there had to be more on the way, and now it would be up to *Mystery* to supply the cover. Hard-helmed and unresponsive as she was, the ketch must outdance the snow at least for a few more minutes. "Stroke! Stroke! Stroke!"

Aboard *Mystery*, Duncan saw splinters fly at the snow's fantail, while at the same instant a spreader stay on the ketch's nose sang and snapped, and a long gouge opened in decking alongside the forehold. The ball that opened it caromed past his ear, traveling the length of the ship with a single bounce. A second 18-pound ball tore through main and mizzen topsails, throwing bright feathers like colored snow as it rent the latter. *Mystery* was closing fast now, bearing down on the tail of the warship, and Pugh and Crosby hauled their two fired pieces aside and ran a second pair to rail, training them as they snugged lines, some of the Hessians helping. The snow was beginning to move now, veering to port to come about, gunners at its massed beam cannons.

Every instinct Duncan possessed now said hard a'port, sweep and fire. Fire and come about upwind for another pass. But he clenched his teeth and held the helm. The reserve chasers fired as a pair, billowing smoke hiding their effects ahead, although the range now was point blank. Involuntarily, Duncan braced himself. If the snow did not get out of the way within a few seconds, *Mystery* was going to put her sprit right up its sternpost. Dalton had said this would be close work. Could he have guessed how close? Smoke rolled ahead, and above it the high yards of the snow crept aside, angling seaward.

Now, he thought, gunners a'port as we discussed. And as he thought it he saw Crosby and Pugh and some of the Hessians dashing aft to take positions at the port rail where charged guns waited.

Close work, aye. Close it had to be now. If ever once the snow broke away, if it gained distance by any chance, it had only to stand off and pound them to death. He saw no sign now of the launch, but he knew where it was . . . at least he knew where it had *better* be. Dead ahead and coming on, making for the snow.

The smoke rolled down the wind, clearing ahead of *Mystery*, and Duncan sucked in his breath. Not a dozen yards beyond the ketch's jutting bowsprit, the snow's spanker loomed, just being hauled over to take the wind. Beneath it, on the deck, startled dark-bearded faces gawked at the spreaders driving toward them, the stays sweeping toward their deck, and a scramble ensued, men scurrying forward, ducking and dodging, pushing others aside in their haste.

The bowsprit touched the trailing luff of the snow's spanker, lingered lovingly there for an instant, then tore through fabric and line, splitting the sail open like a cloven bedsheet. The port spreader yard grazed the large vessel's gaffline, tugged at it, and slipped past with a twang of tormented cable, and *Mystery*'s wide beam bore in on the snow's sternpost. Duncan held his breath, refusing to edge away though every fiber of him demanded it.

"Elevate!" someone shouted. "Quoin high, go for her stern rail!"

"Mind the cabindeck! There's prisoners there!"

"Elevate! Take the rail aloft!"

From the helm, it seemed that *Mystery*'s shroud beams would chew off the snow's rudder post, but they slid by and nothing happened, though the warship's quarterdeck overhung the lower vessel just yards away. Through the crack between them, Duncan saw dark movement beyond—the launch, barely a hundred yards out and in clear view . . . if anyone looked that way.

Then one of the gunners touched his fuse, and debris flew from the stern of the snow to rain down on the ketch's deck, and again smokes rolled off ahead to hide the boat beyond. A second round fired, barely scraping shattered timbers where the first had gone, though aloft the trailing end of the snow's gaff shattered and fell away, swinging and dangling from its lines. More debris rained. Duncan held his helm secure and craned his neck to look up at the broken railing now passing over his head. A man looked back at him, a huge-shouldered, bearded man in a coat of brilliant colors. He raised a pistol, then dodged aside as splinters flew a foot from his elbow. The crack of the rifle ahead was minute against the echoes of cannonfire. Beside the mainmast Titus Wilton lowered his rifle and shook an angry fist, peering over his glasses. "What a mess you've made of my fine sails," his voice trailed back, ". . . bedamned bla'guard . . . see you in irons, low pirate. . . ."

270

A musket ball from somewhere above slapped into the mast, and the sailmaker scurried for cover, still ranting.

Ethan Crosby had a third port gun aligned, bearing astern, and he set it off as they cleared, putting a hole in the snow's hull amidships. Above and now just aft, guns trained on them from *Fury*'s starboard rails, and fuses went to vents. Nothing happened. Bless Mister Romart's sand and water, Duncan thought. It would take at least a few minutes to clean and reprime those pieces before they would fire.

And now came the final test of strategy and drill, and again a test of the will of captain and commander. Duncan steeled himself, breathed a good Church of England prayer, and crossed himself for good measure, then shouted. "Hands to sheets, Mister Tidy. Hard about to port!" God help us all, he thought, I have just put a ship under the leeward guns of a man-of-war.

"Stroke!" Dalton plied the tiller with hands knotted like iron grapples. In the trailing smoke now were great shadows looming ahead, the nearer one charging down on the little launch's path, yet just veering to come about to port, the greater one just beyond, yet still looming over the slogging ketch. "Stroke!" He eased to starboard with the stroke, then a hair more with the next, barely aware of the sweating faces, labored breaths, and straining muscles of the men ahead of him, their backs to all that he saw beyond. "Stroke!"

Mystery had been just left of dead ahead, barely on a passing course, but now her sails boomed and her nose swung directly into the path of the launch, gradual but implacable. He eased the tiller a point more, making for the close water just ahead of the ketch. He must cross her path ahead of her, yet the drill that had gone into her sail-handling worked against him. More sprightly than it seemed a ketch could be, she swung into her turn. "Stroke!" You know the drill, Mister Duncan, he thought. Bless your thieving heart, you have done what was needed. Now it is up to us, with your cover . . . if we can manage to get past without ramming you. "Stroke!" The high, thrusting sprit of the ketch was dead ahead and climbing, then directly over the nose of *Something*, and the boom of waters against the vessel's hull was like the drums of doom approaching. The dolphin striker below *Mystery*'s jib was a blade slashing toward them, head-high. "Stroke!" He ducked as the dolphin striker passed him just behind. "Stroke!" With inches to spare, *Something* shot directly under the stem of the turning ship and skimmed toward the snow just beyond.

"The guns, now, gentlemen," he snapped. At an aft oar beside him and a forward oar opposite, Purdy Fisk and Talmadge Fanshaw shipped oars and whirled to man the punt guns, gaping at the tall silhouette of the snow now looming over them.

"Midships rails," Dalton said. "Bear and fire." Two more guns for cover, Mister Duncan, he thought. Now.

Almost in unison the punt guns thumped, their barrels tilted high, two pounds apiece of quarter-inch shot tearing upward, through, and about the midships gunwales of the snow, opening holes among the men gathered there, crouching to restore priming in the deck guns.

Now, Mister Duncan. As we drilled. New thunder rolled over him from just aft, a pair of ready nine-pounders discharging a bucketful of grapeshot to follow where the punt guns' charges had gone. "Stroke!" Dalton called, then hove the tiller hard over. "Ship oars a'port! Lines and grapples! Ship

272

oars a'starboard! Stand by to snug and board!"

Grapples flew and lines were hauled. *Something* swerved in to snug herself under the bulge of the snow's keel. Dalton got his feet under him, caught a shroudstay, and drew his sword. "Board!" he shouted. He swung himself upward, got a foot onto a jutting wale, and dodged a cutlass swing from overhead, thrusting upward with his blade. It came away red. To his right Victory Locke gained the battered gunwale, paused for an instant to level his rifle and fire point-blank at a charging Spaniard, then reversed the rifle and swung it like a club. Dalton swung over the rail to face a mass of cutlass-wielding pirates pressing toward him, hampered by the fallen men underfoot, the slicks of spilled blood on the decks. He braced himself, scooped up a fallen vent-apron beside a fouled cannon, and used it as a shield while his blade danced and sang.

There were others around him, then—the brothers Fanshaw to his left, a double fury of blades and flashing clubs, Purdy Fisk at his right flank, a cradled musket on his arm, its bayonet like a lance while his cutlass beat a tattoo of defense, Claude Mallory and Ishmael Bean with keg-lid shields outthrust, their blades striking out from behind them, an O'Riley with a deck pistol in each hand and a dagger in his teeth.

The pirates were poor sailors, but they were fierce fighters, and they pressed in upon the little ring of boarders as a howling mob. The press was too much for fine swordsmanship. It was cut and slash, parry and thrust, makeshift shields doubling as second weapons at each opportunity. Dalton and those around him were spattered with blood, some of it likely their own, though they had no time to determine it. Fisk took a cut along his chest, dodged aside, and thrust with his musket, running its bayonet through the chest of his attacker. The wide blade lodged, and when the man fell away, the musket went with him.

Distantly, they could hear rifles popping in the tops of the ketch, now barely a hundred yards away, and here and there a pirate fell before a rifle ball. For minutes that seemed endless, the little group held the deck just at the rail, a tight crescent of defense, the pirates impeded by their very numbers.

A one-eyed man sliced viciously at Dalton, barely missing his head, then crumpled with an arrow standing upright in his neck. A second arrow from the other side sank deep below the armpit of an ax-swinging brawler, and over the din rose a pair of voices in high-pitched, chilling war cry. More arrows followed, and a rifle ball from somewhere gave a third eye to a brawny Spaniard trying to gut one of the Fanshaws. Dalton parried a cutlass, thrust, and parried again, and abruptly found a different foe before him—a huge man in the gaudy cuffed coat of Spanish command. The man roared, raised a long blade to strike, and slipped on the bloody deck. He went to his knees, and Dalton beat his sword aside, glancing over his shoulder as he did. The smaller boat had put out from *Mystery* and was skimming across toward them, crowded to the wales with armed men. For an instant he wondered if anyone remained on the ketch, then he had no time to wonder about it. The pirate captain was on his feet again, attacking like a wild bull. Dalton beat off an overhand slash and felt the shock of it all the way to his shoulder. The man was bulky and strong—terribly strong.

"Give me way!" he shouted at those around him, and heard his shout echoed from the shrouds above, "Th' swagger's go' 'is 'ands fu'! Ge'im a bi' o' room, 'ere!" An arrow whisked down from aloft, and another from one side, and suddenly there was space for those around Dalton to push ahead a few steps, pressing pirates ahead of them. The colorful captain roared again, and aimed a sword-blow at the back of Purdy Fisk's neck, and Dalton stepped in close to block it with his own blade. Again he felt the hard shock of the big man's strength jarring him. For an instant they strained at each other, then Dalton swore and drove a fist directly into the Spaniard's face. Blood splattered, and the big man roared again, shaking his head like an annoyed bull. Abruptly his knee came up, slammed into Dalton's hip, and spun him half-around, off balance. He went with the momentum, letting it carry him into a crouching feint, and the Spaniard's blade sang past his ear to sever a pair of sheet lines. Somewhere aloft a spar groaned and fouled itself in the shrouds. Dalton's sword licked out toward the man's midsection and was beaten away with a force that almost took it from his hand. He rolled his blade over the other's and thrust again, feeling his point find flesh. The man hissed, backstepped, and lunged again, his blade missing its mark, though a huge fist caught Dalton above his right ear, almost blinding him for a moment. He tried to rally and was hit again, knocked back against the splintered rail; he felt his feet go out from under him as he sprawled there.

The big man's beard split in a leer of pleasure. He raised his long sword as one would raise an ax . . . and stiffened, his eyes going wide. A point of red steel protruded suddenly from his chest, then withdrew as abruptly, to reappear a few inches to the side. The big man's beginning roar of victory climbed to a thin, angry scream, *"Lostrato! Hijo de puta! Pusilanime cobarde!"* Sword still raised, he tried to turn, then shuddered violently as the red tongue of steel retracted and appeared again from his belly. He gurgled, wavered, and toppled to one side. The man behind him stood over him for a moment, looking down at him in unfeigned disgust. Then he sniffed, looked at Dalton, and said, *"Capitan, yo soy el*

Conte Don Geraldo Lostrato y Baldar de Vas. A sus ordenes." With a stiff bow he turned away. Beyond him the fighting had ebbed, bloody combatants facing off or standing off at a dozen separate points on the deck. There were far more *Mysterys* now than he had brought, and he realized that the small boat had arrived to complete the boarding of *Fury*. Had Duncan left anyone aboard the ketch? Where was Duncan, then? And Billy Caster, was he here too? Everywhere he looked, he saw Hessians.

Still dazed, Dalton got his feet under him and shook his head to clear it. Across the deck two Spaniards were stalking someone around a boat tie, trying to close on him. An arrow whisked from the shrouds, and then there was only one Spaniard there. Dead and wounded lay everywhere in a chaos that seemed to have wound itself down from sheer exhaustion.

The hatchet-faced Spaniard . . . what was he? A count? Dalton couldn't remember it all . . . he raised his arms and called, *"Hombres! Esta terminado! Su capitán es muerto! Rendes ustedes, ahora!"* All about the deck, some quickly, others reluctantly, pirates laid down their arms and backed away, and Duncan realized that they still outnumbered his own men two-to-one. Yet within moments the surrender of *Fury* was complete, and Victory Locke and Claude Mallory hauled down the black flag, then brought to Dalton a folded flag, which they presented.

"Mister Duncan had the second wave bring this over," Locke said. "He allowed if you had no use for it here, then none of us was likely to need it for anything."

It was the colors *Mystery* had worn to begin the battle—the red-and-white stripes of a privateer.

"Run it up, then," Dalton told them. "How many have we lost, Mister Locke?"

"None permanently, sir, more's th' wonder. Some

of us are stove up a bit, and some cuts and bashes here an' there. One of the O'Rileys will need tendin', and Misters Quinn and Tower, a bit, but far's we can tell, we're all still living."

Michael Romart, bleeding from a cut above his eye, hurried up to them, panting and scowling. "Beg the captain's pardon, sir, but if you can find somebody to speak their kind of English, I wish you'd make those Indians quit doing that."

"Doing what, Mister Romart?"

"They're going around the deck, kicking Spaniards to see which ones wiggle. And the dead ones . . . well, sir, they're cutting off their ears."

It was an hour before any semblance of order was achieved aboard the captured snow, and by then Dalton had gone below with the Spaniard Lostrato to see about the prisoners.

"They are in there," the Spaniard said in his heavy English. "They are not harmed. I myself saw to that, though there was little more I could do for them. I am an honest privateer, sir, but when I learned that the devil Pinto was no more than a common pirate, I became a prisoner, too." He pointed at the dead man lying across the companionway, his throat slashed. "I freed myself only by killing that one, then found my sword and—as you yourself know—went on deck to assist you in your fight."

Dalton opened the cabin door, appalled by the stench that came from it, and as he looked inside, Lostrato glanced again at the body on the companionway deck. Ah, good Vasco, he thought. How good of you to trust me. You have been of greater assistance to me than ever you could have known.

XXI

It was customary and accepted, upon the taking of prisoners known to have committed piracy, to knock the injured ones in the head and put them over the side. Though Dalton had not ordered this—in fact had not had time to think about it yet—the matter was taken out of his hands. By the time he came on deck again, shepherding the most unsightly and evil-smelling pair of young women he had ever encountered, Mister Hoop and his Hessian marines had attended to that detail. Pitacoke and Squahamac now wore great necklaces of festooned ears and were taking great delight in wandering among the remaining prisoners, selecting choice ears for later harvest. With their painted faces and tall crowns of brilliant feathers, the two looked for all the world like a pair of happy gamecocks anxious for further use of their spurs.

"Fact of the matter is, sir," Victory Locke apologized to Dalton, "some of those as went overside wasn't much more than scratched up a bit. But the aborigines, they got so enthusiastic about it all that Mister Hoop and his Hessians was a bit carried away."

Dalton shook his aching head, sighing. What was done was done.

"I'd be happy to arrange for hangin' the rest, sir," Locke offered. "Mister Fisk and me, we counted heads, and figurin' in the tops and gallants, sir, this vessel has enough yardarms that if we sort of pair them up and maybe dangle three or four from the spanker gaff, we can hang the whole lot of 'em in one jolly bash."

Such also was accepted practice for dealing with pirates, but Dalton was taken by the erratic tar's grasp of means and methods. The snow did, in fact, mount yardarms enough for two dozen simultaneous hangings. Looking around at the littered deck, though, he hesitated. "We are short-handed, Mister Locke. I think it would be better to see if we can't make some productive use of them before we pass sentence."

"Well, sir, we have plenty of chain below for leg-irons for the lot."

"Very good, Mister Locke. See to it, then. And when they are secured, set them to cleaning up this mess."

He walked the length of the ship, then, taking its measure and learning its sets. Abaft the mainmast, several of his crew had formed a circle around the two French girls—a wide circle—and were gawking at them. Dalton paused to break that up. "These young ladies have had a terrible experience," he told all present. "Now let us treat them with a bit of respect. They need to be bathed and . . ."

"I volunteer, sir."

"Aye, me too, sir."

"I wouldn't mind helpin' out, sir."

"And me, sir, I . . ."

"Gentlemen!"

"Sir?"

"Mister Romart, see to the rigging of a shelter on the quarterdeck, please. Canvas curtains, head-high. Put tubs there with water and some soap. I think the ladies can bathe themselves without your help."

"I volunteer for maintop watch, sir," Ishmael Bean offered.

Claude Mallory glared at him. "It's my shift at maintop. You wait your turn."

"Gentlemen!"

"Aye, sir."

"There will be no maintop watch while the ladies are bathing. Mister Mallory and Mister Bean, you can go below and see about cleaning and airing the cabins. Scrub them down, if you have to."

"Aye, sir."

"And see if there is any clean clothing for the young ladies."

"Aye, sir."

"And have Mister O'Riley prepare some sort of meal for them."

"Which Mister O'Riley, sir?"

"Whichever one is available."

"Aye, sir."

When the Spanish were shackled and set to sprucing up *Fury*, Dalton sent the launch across to *Mystery* to put a crew aboard her and bring Charley Duncan back to the snow. Through most of the day, well into the evening, the two vessels had simply drifted on a longshore wind, rarely more than three hundred yards apart. Duncan had almost depopulated the ketch to send the second boarding party across. Only he, Billy Caster, and the sailmaker Titus Wilton had remained behind. But now a bruised and battered short crew of eight reboarded the ketch and set about scrubbing her down and battening for the night, under the direction of John Tidy, while Charley Duncan and Billy Caster were rowed across to *Fury*.

"Commodore's conference," Duncan muttered as they approached. "Imagine that."

"Sir?"

"We've been invited to the flagship of the fleet."

The launch hove alongside, and Duncan stood and saluted. "Permission to come aboard, sir?"

Above him one of the Indians let down a scaling web. "Wa' y' step, swagger," he suggested.

Aft on the quarterdeck, Dalton leaned against the helm housing, gazing at two fresh-scrubbed young women wrapped in bulky quilts. Beyond him, staying apart but watching with quick, secretive eyes, was a hatchet-faced Spaniard with a flaring mustache and fine clothing. The man wore a fencing sword at his hip, and Duncan eyed him restlessly, wondering why he wasn't down on the main deck with the other Spaniards, in irons.

Dalton glanced around. "Welcome aboard *Fury*, Mister Duncan. You certainly were right about this vessel. She is as sweet a cruiser as I've seen, and we've decisions to make now. But first, we have a problem. Do you speak any French?"

"Me, sir?" Duncan was surprised. "No, sir. Not but a phrase or two, and I'm not sure what they mean. Things like, *le derrière de ma tante*, y'know, and *j'boeuf sois avec moi* . . . just some things any man might hear in port. Why?"

The older of the two girls had turned red, and the younger giggled. Duncan wondered what, if anything, he had said.

"These ladies speak no English, Mister Duncan, nor any other language we have means to produce here. We have tried German as well, and a bit of Spanish, and your aborigines even attempted to communicate with them in whatever they speak, but we haven't had much luck beyond learning that this is Eugenie and her sister is Lucette . . . beg pardon, ladies. . . ." he gestured, "This is Mister Duncan . . . Duncan, yes. And Mister Caster." They removed their hats and bowed courteously, and the girls nodded, wide-eyed. Duncan found it difficult to look away from the big, frightened eyes of the older one. She seemed so . . . like a trembling doe ready to leap and flee, yet there was in the set of her fine, small chin a hint of something that might be courage, or defiance, or both. He felt himself blushing clear to his tousle of sandy hair, and covered it with a friendly grin. "Charmed, miss. Truly. Ah . . . *le derrière de ma tante* to you this evenin'."

That set them both to giggling, and he blushed even more.

The Spanish dandy smiled an ingratiating smile and stepped over beside Dalton. "My apologies, *Capitan*," he said. "Had I known of your problem, I would of course have offered my services. You see, I do speak a little French. I will be gald to assist."

Dalton glanced down at him, surprised. He had almost forgotten the man in the press of duties. Now he wondered how he could have forgotten the man who saved his life . . . and why he instantly and instinctively disliked him. "Don . . . ah . . ."

"*Don Geraldo, mi capitan. A sus ordenes.*"

"Yes. Don Heraldo. Why, of course I will appreciate your assistance. I would like to know what we might do for these ladies' comfort, and whether they have relatives whom we might contact, when there is opportunity, and anything else they might want to say to us. Also, I would like them to know they are safe with us . . ." he glanced to his right, making judgments of those in view. ". . . at least most of us, and certainly none of us wishes them any harm."

"*Si, Señor Capitan.* I shall discuss all this with them." The man bowed smoothly and stepped to the girls, urging them ahead of him as he went. Duncan raised a brow at Dalton, feeling that something here was not as it should be.

"I quite agree, Mister Duncan," Dalton said quietly. "The Don says he was a prisoner aboard this ship, just as the young ladies were. I keep wondering

283

about that."

"Do you intend to trust him, sir?"

"Not for an instant. You seem to have quite charmed one of the ladies, though. I would appreciate your keeping a weather eye out for their comfort, please."

"Aye, sir." They strode forward a dozen steps to stand side by side, hands behind their backs, looking along the trim, deadly gundeck of the snow. "Sir, do you suppose we could spare another man or two to help Mister Tidy with the ketch? She's a stubborn craft at times, and should we meet any seas he'll need . . ."

"Mister Tidy won't command *Mystery*, Mister Duncan. You will. I believe I told you that before."

"Sir? Ah, I thought that was just for the recent engagement."

"Not at all. I told you that no matter what happened, I would not resume command aboard *Mystery*. That was because if we had failed, there would have been no command to resume, obviously. Of course, we didn't fail, did we?"

"No, sir. We didn't fail."

"That was a fine bit of ship-handling you did with the ketch, Mister Duncan. Precise and direct. I compliment you."

Duncan flushed with pleasure. "Thank you, sir."

"You shall have the men I sent aboard, including Mister Tidy, with whom you work quite well, as I have seen. Also, once we have divested ourselves of Spaniards and whatnot, I might spare one or two more lads if we have seas. You may keep Mister Wilton aboard. It would probably upset the gentleman all over again to have to change ships at this juncture. And, of course, the Indians." He cocked a mischievous brow at Duncan. "They are your recruits, you'll recall. Not mine."

"Aye, sir."

284

Dalton glanced around. Except for Billy Caster, a step back, they were alone. "Another thing, Mister Duncan. I intend to transfer the young ladies to *Mystery*. They will be in your care, of course." He saw the instant's pleasure on the sailor's pug face, and the concern that followed it.

"Sir," Duncan said, "I don't like the looks of that Spanish gentleman. I'd worry about turning my back on him."

And with good reason, Dalton thought. "Don't worry, Mister Duncan. Don Heraldo will remain aboard *Fury* as my guest. I should like him where I can keep an eye on him."

"But with the young ladies, sir . . . and no one to translate . . ."

"You will manage, Mister Duncan. You are a resourceful man."

"But, sir . . ."

"Consider it this way, Mister Duncan. Do you think I would enjoy explaining to Constance Ramsey . . . which I am sure there will be occasion to do, eventually . . . how I happened to go voyaging with two attractive—in fact, quite attractive—young French ladies?"

Duncan thought about it. "No, sir, you surely wouldn't enjoy doing that."

"Then it is settled. But nothing is to be said of this to Don Heraldo. He will learn of it only when we transfer passengers in the morning. Do you hear me, as well, Mister Caster?"

"Aye, sir."

"One of the O'Rileys is in the galley below, and should have our supper ready soon. You will dine with me, Mister Duncan, then you can take your Indians and the small boat and return to your ship. Congratulations, Commander Duncan."

"Aye, sir." Duncan beamed.

"Ah, one slight suggestion, Mister Duncan. You

might want to avoid references to your aunt's posterior in the presence of ladies. It isn't in the best of taste, you know. Mister Caster, please find Mister Wise and ask him for the inventory of stores the lads found below. I'd like an accounting of what was available on this vessel when it was seized, and what remains of it. Also, a roster of guns and armament. And have Mister O'Riley address ship's provisions, please."

"Which Mister O'Riley, sir?"

"The one in the galley, preparing our supper."

"Aye, sir."

"Mister Duncan, I'll have to ask for the return of the ship's bell. She's ours for the moment, and it wouldn't do to steal from our own ships, would it?"

Don Geraldo Lostrato came from astern. "*Capitan,* I have spoken with the young ladies as you requested. They say they would like food, please, and a clean place to sleep, where the air is fresh."

"They shall have that. What about relatives or friends?"

"They and their parents were bound for Charleston, *Capitan.* They have relatives there. They ask whether the *capitan* might take them there."

"And?"

Lostrato smiled, a patronizing expression to convey both understanding and sincerity. Somehow Dalton found the message unconvincing. "They are very frightened, *Señor.* They have had a bad time, and are timid. They . . . they look to me as a known friend, *Señor,* because I have been a prisoner of the pirates also. Therefore I have told them that if the *capitan* decides to take them to Charleston, I will go ashore first and find their relatives and arrange for them to be met by their loved ones. I am sure the *capitan* understands how that would comfort them, and it is not so much to ask, is it, my friend?"

Dalton barely noticed Duncan's caught breath, but

286

he held himself in check and nodded amiably. "I assure you, Don Heraldo. I will seriously consider the wisdom of doing as you suggest. Mister Duncan, please see that the ladies' cabin has been cleaned and aired, and escort them there. Have Mister Hoop place a pair of his marines below to see that they are not disturbed."

Duncan hid his grin by turning away. "Aye, sir."

"*Señor*, I would be glad to . . ."

"Of course you would, *Señor*. But we must see to your comfort as well, mustn't we? We shall have some splendid hammocks here shortly, and I believe you will be quite comfortable on deck, where we can all look after your welfare. Thank you."

With twenty-four pirates in chains to help, they worked until full dark putting *Fury* shipshape once more. Then, over the protests of several tars who favored hanging and two Indians who coveted ears for their collections, Dalton had the prisoners unchained a few at a time and put ashore on the island. It was fair exchange he felt, for the information Billy Caster had gained from a pair of them who spoke a bit of English. Don Heraldo may or may not ever have been a prisoner aboard *Fury*, but he had never been without his sword.

As Charley Duncan was rowed back to *Mystery*, to prepare for sailing at first light, he was full of mixed emotions—pride at having command of a vessel, and uncertainty as to whether he could live up to Dalton's trust.

He looked back across dark waters at the stern lanterns of the tall, fighting snow. At the very least, he told himself, I shall have one very devil of an escort.

287

XXII

With daylight the overcast had eased, swept inshore by consistent easterly winds, and pink dawn set *Fury*'s sails aglow as Dalton held her outbound, straining her limits, putting her so close to the wind that even the finest-trimmed of her canvases fluttered in the luff. The freedom of the sea washed through him, heady and glorious, a tonic that allayed the long months of fighting and running, of hiding and lurking, of furtive thoughts and furtive actions necessary to a fugitive on alien shores. He felt more wholly alive now, at command of this laughing, dancing warrior of a ship than he had in . . . how long? Certainly since the *Faith* was lost.

Fury was no schooner. *Fury* did not slice deep waters as a hot knife through butter, or waggle a slim, flirtatious stern at the merest touch of a tiller. *Fury* was not *Faith*. But for every thing that *Faith* had been, *Fury* was something equal and in some respects far more. The Yankee craftsmen who had designed her had known what they were doing. In setting a jackmast just aft her main, they had given her powers that her cousins the brigs had never had. In deepening her keel a bit, they had bought her the advantage of weight of sail, and in adding studding yards and ringtail rigging they had given her the means to use her advantage.

Even at forty degrees from the wind, she made four knots, and at sixty degrees—as close to the wind as any square-rigger could make way at all—*Fury* hummed along at six. She was no schooner, but she was a lady, a Valkyrie formidable in her armament and beautiful to behold. A warship, designed to go anywhere that enemies or prizes might be found, and built to the scale of dashing assault or the strength of toe-to-toe battle, whichever was required.

"On deck!"

Dalton handed the helm to Claude Mallory and stepped back to peer into high, sun-bright tops aloft the great mainmast. The morning's wind washed across his face and smelled of salt and clean distances. "Aye, Mister Locke?"

"*Mystery* is hull-down, sir, dead astern."

"Thank you, Mister Locke." He had instructed a watch be kept on the ketch, not to lose sight of it while he worked the kinks out of *Fury* and trained his crew to her moods. "Time to come about, then, Mister Mallory. I'll take the helm again. Please stand by the spanker sheets."

"Aye, sir."

"We'll test her knees and her footings now."

Mallory grinned. "Aye, sir."

At more than twenty knots and steady by the gauge, it was a perfect wind for learning the responses of a vessel of small cruiser class, as well as for another test of what advantages this Yankee snow might have over a brig of similar size. He had found several advantages already.

"Hands a'deck, stand by sheets! Stand by to come full about and trim!" Ahead, Cadman Wise, acting as bosum, relayed the orders. Dalton watched critically as all hands, even including his gunnery chief Ethan Crosby and those Hessians not otherwise occupied, scurried to station for coming about. A bit more practice would be needed, but he knew that already their handling of sails and lines was superior to the skills of the pirates who had so recently had her. Most of these had trained and drilled on warships, and most on ships of the king. Whatever their condition or their politics now, those skills remained with them. Even as fugitives, and a few outright renegades, they were products of the greatest navy in the world.

At a respectable distance to one side, Don Geraldo stood watching the performance, his dark eyes glittering. The man had been sullen since the transfer of the French girls to *Mystery*, and Dalton had not bothered to give him any explanation whatever. Still he had eyes, and Dalton knew he saw what use could be made of a vessel such as this if the men handling her knew what they were about. And not far from the Spaniard, Corporal Heinrich Wesselmann—late of His Majesty's Grenadiers and now chief of marines for whatever vessel Patrick Dalton assigned him to—stood by the rail, pretending not to be on guard despite the readiness of his musket. If Lostrato had noticed his ever-present guard, he made no sign of it.

Now Lostrato read the wind as Dalton had, and there was an edginess to his voice. *"Señor Capitan,* you take great risk for nothing. Full about with such sail . . . you could damage the ship."

"One doesn't learn a lady without testing her moods," Dalton said absently, his eyes still on the men making ready to reset. Then they were ready. "Hands to sheets! Full about and trim! Look lively!" He spun the helm and *Fury* heeled sharply, four strakes of her starboard beam leaning into the swell as canvas boomed aloft and spars shrieked with the strain. Deep in the snow's belly there were rumblings as masts fought their stays and footings adjusted. *Fury* leaned with the wind, leaned further, and her starboard bow breasted rolling seas to throw curtains of bright water high in the sunlight. She throbbed and thundered, and her rising bow cast curls of spray. He held the helm and felt her respond as eagerly as a warhorse, as high spars turned on their sleeves and lines were hauled and cleated at each quarter to take all the wind her sails could hold. Mallory hove the spanker full out on the port, and Dalton felt the response in the helm as sail assisted rudder to bring her stern about smartly.

Sixty degrees from the wind, and she was gaining speed. Ninety degrees, and she rode like a slanted tower of high sails, Victory Locke clinging in the maintop with nothing but water under him. A hundred and twenty degrees off the wind, her sails recleated and booming like the roll of thunder, she began to lift her nose as high staysails curled taut above her forepeak. It was her best wind, and she climbed the swells and showed her legs. No one was on log and line now. They had too few men. But Dalton could read the speed himself. Moments into her turn, *Fury* was nudging sixteen knots and gaining. The heady beauty of her made Dalton want to throw back his head and laugh aloud. But he had not finished with her yet. Full about, he had said, and the handling of sails in the fore was following the drill. At a hundred and eighty degrees from the wind, she had it directly on her tail and dipped her nose just slightly. Her staysails were suited for angles of wind, and did not help her as much on a straight run. Still, though she slacked a bit, she held a good fourteen knots, and Dalton knew she was straining her hull speed even now.

He held hard over, and *Fury*'s finger of bowsprit continued to trace the horizon. Now the wind was off her starboard beam . . . twenty degrees and sails were trimmed again . . . thirty . . . forty!

"Trim for course!" he shouted. "Full and by! Full and by!" He trimmed her a point, and spun the helm until the rudder was amidships. Now she had her best wind again, this time off her starboard beam, and this time without a rudder to fight. She lifted her nose, took spray in her teeth, and ran.

"God love you," Dalton muttered, "you are a jaunty lady." At full sixteen they headed due west, and he turned to feel the wind of morning on his face. Afore, Cadman Wise piped the stand down, and sailors returned to other tasks, the drill completed.

"On deck!"

"Aye, Mister Locke?"

"I didn't know a warship would do that, sir!"

"A ship that's made to sail will sail," he called, "if those who sail her know how!"

"*Mystery* still in sight, sir! Broad a'port!"

"Very good, Mister Locke!"

"Impressive, *Señor Capitan*," Lostrato admitted. "The pirate Pinto could not have done so well. Even I could not do better."

Dalton had no doubt of it. But there was an odd tone to Lostrato's voice now, something insinuating. He gave the helm to Mallory and turned. "You have commanded vessels, then?"

"*Si, Señor*. I told you, I have a privateer's commission. I had intended to make use of it, but of course when I learned that Enrico Pinto was no more than a pirate . . ." he spread his hands. "Of course I could never condone piracy, so I was made a prisoner."

"And you were a prisoner even at the time this ship was taken."

"Of course, *Señor*. I had nothing to do with that. That was an act of piracy."

"Of course."

"But you, *Señor* . . . and most of your men . . . I think you have sailed men-of-war. For the English king. No, I don't ask, I only tell you what I see."

"You will see whatever you think you see, Don Heraldo."

"Oh, I think I see a way that you and I can be of service to each other, *Señor* Dalton."

"And what way is that?"

"We are men who understand necessity, are we not? I, as a warranted privateer who found myself in waters where I should not have been . . . and you, as a man who sailed for the English king, and obviously do not sail for him now, though you are in contested waters just the same as I . . . it would be well for us to trust each other, *Señor*. I think we both need to avoid notice if we can."

"You are my passenger, Don Heraldo. I see nothing more than that in common between us."

"Ah, my friend," Lostrato's voice became silky. "Your little ketch . . . that the fool Pinto wanted so much to see . . . if what it carries were not contraband, it would have had an escort all along. And if it were not a fugitive, it would never have attempted an attack on a ship such as this."

"I attacked this ship for one reason. I was jolly well fed up with being annoyed by your Captain Pinto."

"Certainly." Lostrato's smile was of a point made. "Any fugitive captain would have been."

"What is your point?" Dalton gazed off into the distance, estimating times and courses, tired of playing games with the Spaniard.

"I believe your destination is Charleston, *Capitan*. But I think you will have difficulties going into so busy a port and making contacts to discharge your cargo. I am a noncombatant, though. I can easily go ashore on your behalf, and make your arrangements for you . . . as well as my own for me."

"Your own?"

"The young ladies, *Capitan*. I expect their family to show a certain . . . ah . . . gratitude to me for returning them. We will share, of course . . ."

Dalton nodded. "I thought it was something like that. Please stand aside now, Don Heraldo, or go below. I am busy at the moment. I'll take the helm again for a bit, Mister Mallory. Please assist with the spanker. We are coming about to go and find our ketch."

"Aye, sir."

"Hands a'deck, stand by to change course, coming to port!"

There was a thing Dalton had noticed during his conversation with the Spanish count. The man's hand tended always to linger near his belt, sometimes a thumb thrust behind it just aside from the buckle, sometimes casually atilt, but always near the front of his belt. It was a thing some learned, so thoroughly that it became second nature to them. It was a habit taught by fencing masters. He would keep the observation in mind.

Bag and baggage, servants and silverware, John Singleton Ramsey arrived in Baltimore by private coach and wagons, his own retinue part of a greater caravan of migrants coming in along the Joppa Road. Delaware Bay had fallen, its defenses battered aside by Howe's fleet, and even the most stubborn of noncombatants now fled for their safety as king's patrols subdued the upper peninsula, establishing a line of supply for the redcoat armies.

Ramsey had held on at Eagle Head long enough to see his battery guns on their way, and to close down his warehouses, dispersing their goods among a dozen bay merchants. Now he wheeled into the streets of Baltimore and sent his wagons off to the hills above Frederick Town. Accompanied only by Colly and a driver and footman, then, he proceeded to the estate of Ian McCall to join his daughter.

High sun glinted on the polished brass and apple-green side panels of the squire's phaeton as it rolled along the tree-lined drive, awash in brilliant foliage, and pulled up before the portico. Liveried servants met him there and escorted him into the great hall, where a butler took charge to show him to the parlor.

"Ramsey!" McCall greeted him, real pleasure in his handshake. "I wondered how long you would play hide-and-seek with the Georgies up there before you backed away."

"Not hide-and-seek," Ramsey corrected him. "Just a bloody nuisance when a man is trying to keep his business affairs in order. Things have been quiet here, I trust."

"Hardly quiet, but the war hasn't come our way just yet. And the gentlemen of the Continental Congress are still quartering hereabout, so one can assume this is as safe a place as any for the moment. Do come and sit by the fire, and we can talk. I'll have a toddy fetched for us . . . or do you still prefer that awful concoction the sailors' taverns serve?"

"Grog," Ramsey said, making himself comfortable. "Merely rum and water, but it's called grog—at least the story goes so—because the ship's captain who ired his crew by watering their rum wore a coat of groggin. But I do favor it, yes. Two-water, please."

McCall rang for a servant, then settled by the fire. "Having had the pleasure of your beautiful daughter's company these recent times, John, I hope now we shall have the pleasure of yours."

"If it isn't a bother, of course. Just until something is resolved upwater. How is Constance? I've looked forward to seeing her."

McCall cocked a brow at his guest, slightly confused. "Very well the last we saw of her, John. But there's been no word since she left."

"Left? She isn't here?"

"Why, no. She made her departure several days ago. Didn't you . . . ah, I mean, since she was going to visit her aunt, I took it you had arranged . . . uh . . . you didn't know?"

"What aunt?" Ramsey's cheeks had gone ruddy, his jaws tight and his eyes shone with premonition. "Where?"

"The one in Charleston. John, what is it? I . . ."

"She has done it again," Ramsey gritted. "Lord help me, the vixen has done it again. But how did she know?"

"How did she know what? Do you mean . . ." McCall had a premonition now of his own. "The Irishman? The one she found with your schooner? Is *that* . . ."

Ramsey closed his eyes and nodded. "Constance has no aunt at Charleston, Ian. But Charleston is where I sent her Irishman."

McCall's servant entered, bearing a rum jug, a water pitcher, and two pewter mugs. McCall gazed across the hearth at his guest, feeling deep sympathy for the man. It was seldom that one saw Squire John Singleton Ramsey so distraught as to cover his face and mutter curses into his hands.

"Leave the rum," McCall told the servant. "But you can take the water away. This is not a time for niceties."

At morning of the second day Captain Sir Henry Bartlett rounded off Cape Fear with his little flotilla of destroyers, beating against a stubborn wind that yet held from the east, his tops using glasses to scan for sign of the reefs that had been the fate of more than one ship in these waters. With his flag at its pinnacle, *Rover* led the pack, *Shark* following tack for reach, while the graceful xebec *Belmont* stood out a bit, its angled sails requiring a different pattern of progression.

Despite their small size, each of the three interceptors had at least a dozen crew, men seasoned with sail and great gun, and each had a commander who would do Sir Henry's bidding without question. Sir Henry could have had volunteers for many of the berths—men like himself who feared the insurgency in the colonies, who would stop at nothing to quell it, men whose fortunes and ambitions depended upon the good will of the Court of St. James or of Whitehall, or of the British East India Company, or of Lloyd's, or even of the Admiralty. He knew many such, but he preferred his own pick of men for his ships, and his arrangements with them were simple. Such men were mercenaries without political leaning or philosophical bent. He paid them well, and therefore he could count on them.

For himself, he saw two prizes for this venture beyond the fugitive ketch itself and the value of its cargo. He saw increased favor for himself in circles close to the king, and he saw a chance to gain the one thing that his knighthood had not given him—landed nobility with an estate in the home islands. There was the conscripted land in Ireland, land just waiting to be ceded to the right man, and he intended to be that man. What the Fitzgerald and his clan no longer held, Sir Henry Bartlett coveted.

Rounding off Cape Fear he ran up signals. From here the three would spread and sweep, like hounds in the fields. *Shark*, the smaller of the cutters, would range alongshore within sight of land. *Belmont*, with the best bottom, would stand out to sea. His own *Rover* would search the middle path. Somewhere ahead—and not far ahead now, he was sure, a lonely ketch sailed southward with the wind off its beam. And aboard that ketch was the future for Sir Henry Bartlett.

It was past noon when *Shark* reported a sighting—a speck of sail, hard down and dead ahead.

XXIII

Once her name had been *Chanteuse*, but after her capture off Normandy, officers of the British Registry Service had renamed her *Belmont* and put her on the auction block. Three-masted and delicate-seeming, with her sleek lugsails and trim lines, she semed more pleasure craft than warship, but that appearance was deceiving. By whatever name, the xebec was a swift and deadly raider, and she had made her mark more than once on colonial privateers. At the hand and command of Alva Hazelton, exercising her for the profit of Sir Henry Barlett, *Belmont* was one of the most feared raiders among the loyalist warrant force.

Sailing outward flank for Bartlett's flotilla, *Belmont* had beat more than thirty miles to sea on a long running tack when her spotter reported Barlett's *Rover* changing course to landward. They glassed the distant cutter, now hull-down on the northwest horizon, but could read no signals, so Hazelton decided to complete his outward sweep before turning. He guessed that the smaller cutter, *Shark*, holding close in, might have seen a sail, and that Bartlett was responding with *Rover*. But the distances were great, and another hour, more or less, would make little enough difference. If the sighting was indeed the cargo ketch they had put out to intercept, the action would all be over long before *Belmont* could reach the scene. No slogging ketch could last more than a few minutes against either *Rover* or *Shark*, much less the two of them in concert. But there might be other prizes as well. This far asea, he was near the trade lanes. And sometimes of late Dale's privateers or one of McCall's vessels had been reported lurking out here to prey upon British transports.

Hazelton held his course at fifty degrees from the wind, heading almost straight east, as *Rover*'s tops— only a speck of color so many miles away—sank from sight. For a bell he held, and was at the point of turning back when his spotter glassed another sail bearing almost due north, and westbound.

"Can you read her, Mister Blake?" he shouted.

There was a long pause, then a response. "I read her now, sir. A brig, I think . . . no, sir, a snow. She's jack-masted. Can't make her colors, though, sir."

"Then we'll have a better look," Hazelton decided. "Come about, Mister Kent. Trim for starboard tack, to intercept."

Patrick Dalton trained his glass on the sail closing on him from the south, and a smile of appreciation touched his cheek even as his eyes went hard. He had not seen a xebec since the days of the *Athene*, and then only a few. But he agreed with many a seafarer of his time: no more graceful cruiser had ever sailed the seas, and to view a xebec—even a hostile one—was to feel a moment's pleasure at the simple artistry of its design.

Yet now the raider's colors were in sight, and he knew her for an enemy. *Fury* still flew the colors Charley Duncan had transferred from *Mystery*—the red-and-white stripes of a colonial free-lancer—and any vessel so designated was fair game for the privately financed warships of the empire's petty nobles. They were not Royal Navy, but they allied themselves with the Admiralty for profit and sport, and this was one of them. The xebec's flag was a red hart rampant on blue field. He searched his memory. House of Harcourt . . . a power in the southern colonies, established during the Seven Years' War . . . what was the man's name? Bartlett, that was it. Sir Henry Bartlett. This was not likely Sir Henry himself, though. He had several ships, usually employing them as wolf packs. He himself would not likely engage anyone alone. But this was one of his ships, and there was no questeion about its course. It had *Fury* in sight and its colors up. It intended to fight.

Dalton sighed, kicking himself mentally. He had given in to the desire for one more maneuver upwind—just perfecting his knowledge of the snow, he told himself, though he knew there had been another reason as well—his own devils nagging at him, urging him to have one last feel of the freedom of the sea, one last moment of fancy . . . the feel of a deck beneath his feet, a swift, fine ship that could take him anywhere he wanted to go and nothing between him and the English coast and a chance to demand a hearing and regain the honor of a clear name . . . before returning to the task at hand. The latest commitment came first. He must escort *Mystery* down to Charleston and complete his pact with Squire Ramsey.

Reluctantly, he had come about once more. In the meantime, *Mystery* was out of sight, somewhere near the now-invisible shoreline many miles away. And now this . . . a warrant xebec closing on him, demanding an engagement.

"On deck!"

"Aye, tops!"

301

"She's signaling, sir. She demands we strike our colors or stand and fight."

Dalton shook his head slowly. The man on the xebec—whoever he was—had no lack of courage. Few single raiders would relish an attack on an armed snow, and there were no other sails in sight. Still, though a bit smaller, the xebec might be a fair match. She would be quick and agile, certainly—maybe enough to gain the weather gauge on him and dictate the terms of battle. Part of him—a large part—he realized—would relish the chance of a no-holds-barred, head-on fight at sea. As though he were bred to it, the notion excited him, made his blood surge.

But just as with the fantasy of setting an eastward course and making his own way to England to clear his name in the proper court, it was a thing best postponed for now. He had other duties first.

"Signals," he said. "Send our respects, but we have no time now to amuse ourselves with him. Tell him we will neither strike nor fight. Tell him possibly another day."

"Aye, sir."

"Come a bit to starboard, helm. Let's have a course for broad reach. Hands a'deck, make all sail for starboard reach, full and by."

"Aye, sir."

"Mister Crosby to the stern, please, and a gun crew here. Ready both stern chasers."

Billy Caster came from the ladder. "Will he let us run away without a fight, sir?"

"He won't have much to say about it, Mister Caster. We can outrun him, I think. But if he wants to force the issue, he'll have opportunity for a shot or two before we gain distance. I suppose we'll have to honor him with an exchange, at least."

The xebec was fast in a crossing wind. Even though *Fury* bore off on a new direction, still the range continued to close, as Dalton had known it would. Within minues the xebec lay at hard range off the snow's port beam, still closing as its course slid aft from the prancing *Fury*. And as it closed, it began to come to port, trying for gun range.

"Stubborn soul, there," Purdy Fisk noted. "He does want a game, sir."

"If we had the time, he'd have his game, Mister Fisk."

"Will he pursue, do you think, Captain?" Billy wondered.

"He might, Mister Caster. We'll show him our heels presently, but if he has nothing better to do he might make a chase of it. I would, if I were him."

"How so, sir?"

"We're only a few hours from shore. He'd have reason to expect that if we don't engage him here he might force a fight when we arrive there. We can outdistance the xebec, right enough, but it would take more than the hours remaining this day to lose him."

Implacably, the xebec bore in on *Fury*'s wake, angling to give direct chase, gaining speed with a broad reach on the wind just as the snow did, and Dalton gazed across at the sleek vessel, still feeling the pleasure of watching a truly efficient craft exercising its legs. Not as fast a vessel as the snow with its mighty press of sail, but the xebec would not be left frothing in their wake, either. Again, Dalton wished there were time for a duel. He would have relished the action, had there been time for it.

"He's come astern of us, sir. Chasers at the ready. Shall we volley him?"

"Give him honor of the first salute, Mister Crosby. But we won't hesitate to respond. You may return fire at your pleasure."

"Thank you, sir." The gunner had both his chasers trained, and stepped to the breech of the port-

303

side gun to crouch at his notch, linstock with its slow match ready at hand.

Two bow chasers aboard the xebec blossomed in unison, and Dalton revised his estimate of the vessel. She might have fewer guns than *Fury*—maybe only half as many—but she had ample crew aboard to load and fire. She would be formidable in a head-to-head or beam-to-beam contest.

Ehtan Crosby had taken him at his word. Even before the balls from the xebec arrived, *Fury*'s port stern chaser roared, and a moment later the starboard gun echoed its challenge, Crosby firing the second while others began reloading the first.

The first of the xebec's shots cut a long trough in the rising swell just under *Fury*'s starboard rail. Spray like a sudden rain squall fell on the wind afore, dancing to the thunders arriving from astern, and Dalton felt a shudder beneath his feet as the second ball crunched into the snow's little stern gallery.

A hole had appeared in the xebec's forecourse, and splinters flew as Crosby's second round smashed the rail above a gunsnout. Even at this distance they could see men scurrying back, away from the hit.

"That stung them a bit," Dalton said. "Stern chasers reloaded, Mister Crosby?"

"Aye, sir. But we're losing our range."

"Try your hand just once more, if you please, Mister Crosby. Same elevation, hold true on his stem."

"Aye, sir." The gunner knelt, sighted, and touched fuse. Smokes rolled off ahead, and a gout of water erupted dead ahead of the xebec, the ball emerging at a skip to slam into the heavy keel timber of her bow, arc out ahead and hit the water a second time. The thump of its collision—iron ball against hardwood timber—drifted back on the wind. "Pity, sir," Crosby said. "Dead on the keel member. Had it been off six inches, it would have holed him sure."

"A true aim, Mister Crosby. No apology necessary."

"Thank you, sir."

Geraldo Lostrato came boiling from the companion hatch, wild-eyed, with a marine right behind him. Three steps back a swearing O'Riley emerged in their wake. All three were heavily splattered with gray paste, and O'Riley carried a cannonball in his hands. Billy Caster met them at the quarter ladder, listened to O'Riley's harangue for a moment, then came back to report.

"Damage below, sir," he said. "That ball there took out a deck support and the port cabin's hatch frame, then it carried on into the galley. Mister O'Riley's stowage bulkhead is a shambles, he says, and supper will be late."

"No injuries?"

"No, sir, but there's a mess down there. The ball lost its momentum and bounced off a stanchion, and it fell into the oatmeal pot."

Lostrato and his marine guard were at the stern rail now, looking back at the slowly receding xebec. O'Riley had stopped at the quarterrail, still carrying his cannonball. Dalton beckoned at him and he came, patches of oatmeal dripping from him. As he approached Dalton he snapped a salute, cradling the cannonball in one large hand. "Captain, pardon, sir, but would it be all right with you if we put this in a gun and sent it back where it came from, sir?"

Dalton turned. "Range, Mister Crosby?"

"Out of range, sir. Sorry."

To the fuming O'Riley Dalton said, "We don't have the time now, Mister O'Riley. But hold the thought. That gentleman back there seems to have decided to give chase to us. We may yet have the opportunity."

"Yes, sir. Thank you, sir. I'd like the chance to put a little something in that bugger's oatmeal, sir, if there's ever opportunity."

305

"On deck!"

"Report, tops!"

"Sails ahead, sir. One of them's *Mystery*!"

"How many sails, tops?"

"Two others, sir. Pair of cutters, I think. One's closin' on *Mystery*, the other coming in from south."

The stern deck of *Mystery* now bore more resemblance to a circus than to the command station of a cargo vessel. Between the huge, enshrouded gun with its camouflaging heaps of kegs, tarps, and coils occupying the length of the deck from deckhouse to afterrail on his right, and the ornate little pavilion erected for the comfort of the ladies on his left, Ishmael Bean at the helm of the ketch felt like a man wrestling a large wheel in a narrow aisle. There was barely room for a man to negotiate fore and aft along the port side of the helm housing, and no room at all to starboard.

The deck pavilion was a far more lavish affair than any one of them might have imagined—the combining of separate efforts by Joseph Tower, John Tidy, and Titus Wilton, the result of Mister Duncan's announcement that two attractive young women were to be deck passengers, and his request that accommodation be made for their comfort. Tidy had selected the location—aft where fresh breezes would carry no hint of the heady odors of the working decks forward, a'port because the battery gun on its mounts and with its heaps of camouflage left no space a'starboard—and paced off the minimum area that he deemed suitable for the comforts of two young women. Mister Tower then had studded in footings there, set waist-high stanchions and a top rail enclosing the space, and built benches within it, slings for a pair of hammocks, and a centerpost with cable stays for an awning.

Titus Wilton had created the awning, working with sailcloth and twine, and had added drop curtains which could be closed when the ladies wanted privacy.

Coming on deck after a night of puzzling over charts below, Duncan had—so it seemed at least to Ishmael Bean and Tobias Quinn, exchanging duty at the helm—been somewhat stunned at the magnitude of what had grown on his deck overnight. And truly the pavilion did seem to dominate the deck, when the light of morning finally revealed it in its full glory. But Duncan had taken it calmly as befitted the commander of a vessel inspecting works he himself had ordered, and had even commented that since Misters Tidy, Tower, and Wilton were the oldest men aboard and probably the only ones with any real experience of ladies, it was bound to be just what was needed.

If the commander remained slightly dazed for a time at what the morning sun revealed, Bean felt it probably was because of the lavish decoration that had been bestowed upon the awning and curtains by the two aborigines, Pitacoke and Squahamac. Acting on their own initiative, those two had taken it upon themselves to decorate every seam and joint of the new pavilion with lavish arrangements of garish colored feathers. The pavilion quite put to shame the startling emblazonage of the topsail above it.

But then the ladies had been lightered across, and few aboard gave further thought to the peculiarities of deck ornamentation. Bathed, rested, and freshly fed, Eugenie and Lucette Toussaint—with their great lustrous eyes, piquant lips, and brushed hair like two shades of sunlight—would have caught the eye of any man anywhere, even fully dressed. And clad in little more than shifts and quilts, the two thoroughly disrupted ship's discipline for several minutes simply by coming aboard.

Even Squahamac and Pitacoke, who had made various comments comparing white female skin to fish bellies, had startled all present by favoring the young ladies with a pair of courtly, befeathered bows.

Bean himself was entertaining thoughts of proposing marriage to one or the other, should the opportunity arise. "It isn't as though I hadn't proposed marriage before," he confided to Quinn. "I've probably proposed fifty or a hundred times, to as many women. Nothing to be lost by it, you know. It never hurts to ask."

At first the girls had seemed very frightened, but after Titus Wilton addressed them in passable French they seemed more comfortable, addressing him as "Monsieur le Docteur Franklin," and refusing to believe his denials of being that person.

Mystery held due southwest through the morning with the steady wind at her tail. The course took her slowly farther and farther from shore, but that was in the arc of the coastline. "Like a string on a bow," Commander Duncan said. "We hold the straight line and the coast recedes off our beam. Yet by the charts, by evening, the same coast will have come back to see us again." It was a thing he had said, hoping that Mister Wilton would translate it for the ladies and that the very wisdom of it might impress them. It had impressed Ishmael Bean fairly enough. He had not seen the charts.

Nor had he seen very much of Mister Duncan, though the newly named commander was only four paces away. Duncan was behind the pavilion's curtain, with Mister Wilton, discussing things with the young ladies. Bean turned the helm a spoke or two, trimming by the wind, and leaned back to look out to sea past the bright trim of the pavilion's intruding corner. *Fury* had been in sight from time to time, running in close, then making eastward again as Captain Dalton learned her tempers. But now she was not in sight, had not been for some time, and Bean wondered if he should mention that to Commander Duncan . . . *Commander* Duncan—so fine it sounded, and Bean was proud for the sandy-haired young man, yet it would take some practice to get it firmly in mind. It wasn't that long since the two of them—aye, and some others as well—had been stockade mates at Long Island.

Lashing the helm for a moment, Bean stepped to the stern rail and leaned out for a clear look a'port. There was no sign of *Fury* anywhere. He squinted and scratched his chin, then shrugged. Such things were up to Commander Duncan. As for Bean, as helmsman at present his duty was to keep the ketch on course and try not to run into anything.

"Oh deck!"

He tilted back his head, squinting. "Aye, Mister Sidney?"

"Sail ahead, helm!"

"Whereaway?"

"Dead ahead and coming on!"

There was a quick scuff of shoes, and Duncan came from the pavilion, looking bright-eyed and ruddy as any man might who has been in the presence of young ladies. "I heard, Mister Bean. Hold course, please." He fetched his glass and scanned ahead, finally holding steady. "Aye, there she is." He looked aloft. "Can you read her, Mister Sidney?"

"Might be a cutter, sir. That's all I can tell, bow-on, but I think there's just one mast, and she heels like a fore-and-after."

Duncan muttered to himself as he tried to reckon distances the way Captain Dalton had told him. A cutter's mast might be sixty or seventy feet high, not much more, usually, and the captain had said that on a clear day the topmast lookout aboard a ship of the line could see the tops of another ship of the line . . . how many miles away had he said? Twenty-two miles? Twenty-one? Some odd number. Eight-sevenths times the square root of the height of the observer, he had said, is the distance to the horizon in miles. Duncan remembered that but wasn't quite sure what to make of it. Cyphering had never come easily. He shrugged and made a guess. "He's about ten miles ahead, then. What is our speed, Mister Bean?"

"Seven or eight knots, sir. About like that."

"Then if he just stands dead there, we should reach him in about an hour, doesn't that seem right?"

"Sounds all right to me, Commander."

"But he's coming this way so it won't take that long. I wonder who he is."

"On deck!"

"Aye, tops?"

"There's another one, sir. Farther away, a bit east of south. Three points on our port beam, sir."

Duncan put the glass to his eye and muttered a curse. All he could see was a blur of sailcloth and colored feathers. He strode forward past the pavilion and tried again. After a time he saw it, a second cutter tacking shoreward, on a course to intercept their own. He returned to the helm. "Any sign of *Fury* just lately, Mister Bean?"

"No, sir, I haven't seen her lately."

"Ahoy the tops! Mister Sidney!"

"Aye, sir?"

"Have you seen Captain Dalton lately?"

"I believe he's aboard the snow, sir!"

"I know he's aboard the snow, Mister Sidney. Have you seen the snow?"

"Not lately, sir!"

"Mister Duncan . . ."

Duncan turned. Titus Wilton stood before him, scowling over his spectacles. "Mister Duncan, I have just heard the most despicable thing!"

"You have? What?"

"Miss Eugenie . . . Mister Duncan, did you know that there is a Spanish pirate aboard your captain's ship?"

"Yes, sir. I know that. I saw him. Captain Dalton knows he is there, too."

"Well, sir, let me tell you, that gentleman is not to be trusted. Not even so much as condoned, is my opinion. Do you know what he proposed to do with the young ladies, Mister Duncan?"

"Ah . . . no, I don't think so. I mean, he might have . . . but I'm sure he didn't, sir. They wouldn't have allowed . . ."

"Oh, stop blithering, young man! That person proposed to hold those young ladies for ransom! Absolutely despicable! He as much as intended to *sell* them . . . do you understand?"

"Ah . . . yes, sir. I believe that. I didn't know it, I mean, but I understand what you're saying . . ."

"Li' t' go a fair bob, 'ey?"

Duncan turned. Pitacoke was squatting atop the cannon heap, taking it all in. Duncan ignored him and turned his attention again to the sailmaker. "I understand, sir. But why are you telling me about that? Right now, I mean? There's other concerns at the . . ."

"I want to know what you are going to do about it."

"About what, sir?"

"About the Spanish gentleman proposing to sell the young ladies!"

"Oh." Duncan hesitated, noticing that the cutter ahead was becoming more discernible by the moment. "Well, sir, I believe I'll give him a piece of my mind the very next time I see him."

"On deck!"

"Aye, tops?"

"I read her colors, sir. She's a tory raider . . . what you English might call a 'casual friendly,' though we

311

sure as hell don't call them that over here, the friggin' . . . !"

"Mind your mouth, tops! There's ladies present!"

"Sorry, sir. I forgot! But she's no friendly, sir, and neither is the other one! And she's signaling for us to stand and strike our colors!"

XXIV

As delicately as the situation allowed, Charley Duncan hustled Eugenie and Lucette down the companion hatch and into the portside cabin, then placed the complaining Titus Wilton in there with them. It was a safer place, at least, than the deck pavilion, and he left the sailmaker to try to explain that to the girls.

On deck once more, he studied the situation as he imagined Dalton might have done. Two cutters bearing in on *Mystery*. Each smaller than the ketch, but far swifter to maneuver, faster on the wind and probably better armed. The one dead ahead would be in position to engage first, but the other wouldn't be far behind. Either of the interceptors, generally speaking, was more than a match for a sluggish ketch. Both of them together . . . the outlook seemed gloomy indeed. What would Patrick Dalton do in a situation like this?

"Mister Romart!" he called. "Come aft, please!"

When Romart arrived beside him, Duncan pointed. "You see the situation here?"

"I certainly do," the colonial nodded. "Those people don't wish us well, by any means."

"Do you have any idea of what one does in a case like this?"

"Sure. One loses."

"I'm serious, Michael . . . Mister Romart. Those people in the nearest cutter are demanding that we strike our colors. Any advice would be appreciated."

"You're the commander."

"I know that, but I don't have very much experience at being a commander. I've been trying to think what Captain Dalton might do now."

"He'd think of some way to amuse the enemy, as he puts it."

"So what would you think might amuse them?"

"I don't know . . ." Romart screwed his face into contortions of thought.

"Gi' 'm blee'in 'ell," Pitacoke suggested.

Romart turned and looked up at the flag streaming from its mast aft the mizzen—a smaller version of the red and white stripes that *Fury* now flew. "Are you partial to our colors, Charley?"

"Not especially . . . not personally, anyway."

"Then why not strike them? That's what those people want us to do."

"I'm not going to strike . . . !"

"I wish you'd quit being so damned English. I didn't say to surrender, I just said all they're asking is that we take down our flag. So why not take it down, just to amuse them?"

"But that's a sign of surrender! If we do that, they'll come right on up to us and . . . ah?"

"Exactly. Of course, they might not trust us enough to come abeam right at first, but they'll stand off our bow for a close look."

"And if we could put as many guns as possible in the forecastle . . ."

"And obscure them just a bit with sailcloth . . ."

"And feathers?"

"Feathers are amusing, I'd say."

"And a man at each gun . . . we could almost make

314

it seem a broadside if we worked it right, couldn't we?"

"Of course, there's still another cutter out there."

"One thing at a time. How many guns can we get into the bow in rather a hurry?"

"Four easily. Maybe six. It will be awkward, but . . ."

"Then get to it, Mister Romart! Don't just stand there talking, there is work to do."

"Aye, sir."

"On deck!"

"Aye, tops!"

"Mister . . . ah, Commander Duncan, I see the snow, sir. Hard down and east by north. With another vessel following."

"What sort of other vessel, Mister Sidney?"

"Damned if I know, sir. I never saw the like of it."

Hard down, east by north. It would be a while before *Fury* could close and give the ketch a hand. Duncan hoped he and the rest would still be around to welcome the support.

"Mister Tidy, all hands to the guns, please!" He had said it before he realized that, with all hands at the guns on the forecastle deck, he would be in a spot, should he need to reset any sails. And with his colors down, the oncoming cutter would expect him to furl his squares at the very least so that it could stand afore to inspect him. "If this works at all, Mister Bean, that gentleman off there may be far more amused than he has ever expected to be."

"Aye, Commander," Bean scowled. "So might we if it comes to steerin' this bucket on rudder alone. Last time I tried a hard come-over I wound up asquat atop th' bleedin' wheel, it's that stubborn."

Duncan turned and beckoned to the nearest Indian. "'Ere, Pi'acoke! Tag in yer myte, swagger, an' th' lot o' ye gi' a lean as eed is. Ri'?"

315

"Ri'," the Indian agreed, and scurried off to find Squahamac.

With everyone else now occupied, Duncan lowered *Mystery*'s colors himself, furling the flag as it came down though he did not release its grommets from the lanyard. "Mister Tidy, please ask Mister Pugh to act as gunnery officer and direct fire once we have engaged, but hold for my command."

"Aye, sir."

Peering along the length of the ketch's deck, Duncan saw a massing of guns being snugged in the fore . . . six guns in all, two of them actually braced at the catheads. He frowned, hoping that in his enthusiasm Mister Pugh would not shoot off their own jibstays. Flagless but still under sail, *Mystery* plowed along at her steady six knots or so, directly toward the veering cutter as it completed a short tack and came through the wind for its approach.

They were near enough now that he could see the men on the cutter's deck—even her commander at the stern, training a glass on him. The men on *Mystery*'s foredeck had strung a ragged curtain of sailcloth across the jib's butt, and Duncan could only guess what it might look like from ahead. It might pass for cargo tarping, he thought. He hoped so. If the cutter saw it for what it was—a screen with guns behind it—there would be little chance to use those guns or any others. With every hand a'fore, *Mystery*'s firepower was concentrated there. Should the cutter swing wide and come in abeam, its guns trained broadside, there would be no one to return its fire.

"At this moment I surely don't know why it seemed an honor to be given command," Duncan muttered to himself.

"On deck!"

"Aye, tops?"

"His topman is signaling, sir. He says to stand

for boarding."

"Can you respond, Mister Sidney?"

"Aye, I know the hand codes."

"Tell him we can't stand because our pins are afoul."

At the helm, Ishmael Bean glanced around. "What the devil does that mean?"

"It doesn't mean anything that I know of. I just don't know what else to tell him, short of explaining that I've got every hand aboard tied up, waitin' to blast him out of the water. And I don't want to tell him about that just yet."

"I wouldn't think so, no."

"No, *sir*."

"Oh, aye. No, *sir*. Commander. I'll get the hang of that after a bit, Charley."

"Forward guns ready, Commander," John Tidy called.

"Tell them to keep down, out of sight! He's looking us over!"

"Aye, sir."

On impulse, Duncan strode forward, well past the pavilion, stood aside from the masts, and raised a hand in formal salute, directing it at the closing cuter. The man over there had decided to be cautious, and not come abeam. Instead he was loosing the tall sails on his single mast, losing way to stand beam-to-bow to the ketch, letting wind drift carry him as the distance between the vessels closed to a double cable-length, then to less than that. Starboard guns lining the cutter's beam were squat, dark hell-muzzles trained on *Mystery*.

"Mister Tidy," Duncan tried to make his voice sound calm, "Tell our lads to train on his rail."

"Aye, sir."

"On deck!"

"Aye, Mister Sidney?"

"His tops wants to know what is in the tent, sir."

"Tell him you didn't understand the signal, Mister Sidney."

"Aye, sir."

The distance closed to a cable-length, and Duncan could see the faces of the men on the other vessel. Deliberately he turned, strode back to his stern rail, and gripped the ensign halyard. He took a deep breath, hauled the rope, and called back over his shoulder, "Fore guns bear and fire!"

On the foredeck the screening cloth was whipped away, hands adjusted gun tackles, gunners knelt to their notches, and Floyd Pugh's voice roared, "Volley!" A half-dozen smoking fuses touched vents, and *Mystery* shuddered in her timbers as the belches of hell roared and echoed at her nose. The cloud of smoke that grew there obscured everything beyond her own jib.

Duncan cleated the halyard rope and turned. "Hard a'starboard, Mister Bean! Now! Help him, swaggers! Lay on that wheel!" There were more roars somewhere, and splinters flew as something just to his left crashed and shattered. He heard the *whump* of a cannonball cutting wind almost at his ear, and heard tackle sing aloft. A yard away Ishmael Bean fought the stubborn rudder, turning the helm with the help of two Indians, one crouched at his left, feeding spokes upward, the other pulling from the right. Amidships Floyd Pugh and several others had rallied at the port beam to train guns there as they came about. Somewhere forward heavy wood screamed and splintered, and there was a deep, ringing tone as though someone had set a cathedral bell to sounding.

Without help from sails, *Mystery*'s rudder fought viciously, but slowly the three there brought her over . . . a point, three points, broad to course . . . abeam to course, and now the high sails whipped and chattered, doing nothing but serving as vanes, while spanker and staysails heeled the ketch to port, taking the wind. The helm eased and Indians scattered aside as Bean spun it violently.

"Volley!" Pugh shouted. Guns a'port thundered, again blanking the heeling cutter that had just become visible. Sounds from the smokes—the cacophony of splintering timbers, tortured stays, and a scream—said they had scored. But there was return fire again, this time coming across the port beam. Duncan felt as much as heard another strike on *Mystery*'s hull. The mizzenmast just ahead of him sprouted a bright flower of gouge, a splintered gnaw twice the size of a fist. A pair of sheetlines just beyond parted and snapped away like long whips. Distantly in the smokes there was a rending, crashing sound that seemed to go on and on, and above it he heard Sam Sidney's shout from aloft, "On deck! We've holed her mast, sir. It's leaning! She's losing trim . . . it's down, sir, hanging from its gaff tackle!"

Duncan fairly danced in his excitement. "Rudder amid, Mister Bean! Hands a'deck, to sheets. Trim for beam a'starboard! Look lively!"

John Tidy's whistle wailed, and *Mystery* began righting itself, picking its way as its sails took the side wind and thrust its nose forward, at right angles now to its earlier course. The same wind cleared away the smokes, and the cutter was out there, angled away from them, its topmast and five feet of its main dangling upside down alongside its jutting stump. He realized that he was seeing it clearly, without interference, and blinked in surprise. The proud deck pavilion just left of his helm was a mass of wrecked struts and beragged canvas, a steady shower of bright feathers floating off on the wind to enliven the waters beyond. Somewhere close behind him a bow twanged and a dark arrow streaked out across the waters, arcing upward to fall amid the wreckage and turmoil of the cutter's deck. A second followed close behind it, and when it landed he heard the thin, keening sound of a man in pain somewhere downwind.

"'Stook'n on," a savage announced. "Gi' 'm blee'in 'ell, righ'?"

"Sir, we've lost Mister Quinn," John Tidy told Duncan. "Ball took him full on. Carried him right away overside."

"Quinn," Duncan repeated, trying to get his thoughts in order. "Anyone else, Mister Tidy?"

"Two or three bleedin' from splinters. That's all on deck, sir. We've taken at least two shots below, though . . ."

Below . . . "Hold course, Mister Bean." Duncan raced to the companion hatch and dropped into the cabinway without touching the ladder. He crouched, turning blind in the darkness, bumped into a bulkhead, and scurried around it to the port cabin. Its portal hung open, and beyond was pale smoke, daylit from the stern galleries. There were people there, in the shadows, and voices. Titus Wilton was cursing, a continuing monologue of sound, and Duncan vaulted through into the little space. "Eugenie?"

For a moment there was no response, then two shadows moved in the smokes. "Oui, M'sieur?"

Without ever giving it a thought, Duncan swept her up in his arms and hugged her to him, seeing her sister just beyond her, Wilton getting to his feet in the opposite corner. "Eugenie," he whispered, trembling with the release of dread. "Eugenie . . ."

Titus Wilton put a hard hand on his shoulder. "Young man, unless you intend to marry this lady, I demand that you release her this instant and turn away while she puts her quilt on again. You've practically disrobed the poor thing! Turn loose, I say! This is . . . this is unseemly!"

In the distance, through the sailmaker's babble

and the surprised, breathy murmurs of Eugenie, Duncan made out another, more strident voice: "On deck!"

From a diminishing mile away, Sir Henry Bartlett watched the encounter, his eyes narrowing in hard anger. He saw the exchange of signals, saw the brightly festooned ketch strike its colors, saw the care with which *Shark* eased in a'fore to look over the prize, and for a moment he was pleased. *Shark* moved meticulously, avoiding the beams of the ketch where guns might lurk, simply easing to a halt to drift on the wind, letting the ketch come to her while her guns dominated the situation. Professional, he thought . . . very neat. Then the unthinkable occurred. Suddenly the ketch's colors climbed at its stern, and the smoke of massed guns bloomed at its bow, and the two—predator and prey—were at each other's throats. Sir Henry stood stunned, watching the smokes grow . . . the unthinkable smokes of battle joined by a slogging, laden cargo vessel against a trim and toothy cutter.

Smokes obscured the scene, then wind revealed it again and the two were beam to beam . . . but something was wrong with the cutter! He braced his elbows, squinting through his glass. The cutter's mast had buckled—high up, just below the trees, yet buckled it had, and he saw it topple and hang from its tackle, the sails fore and aft going slack, crumpling upon their booms, their sagging stays.

Unthinkable . . . yet there it was—the armed cutter drifting away, helpless to take the wind, while the ketch crept shoreward beyond it. Fugitives, the report had said. Fugitives with contraband. Not unthinkable, then, that they might put up a fight. But so useless. Certainly they knew they had just sealed their death warrants to the last man of them. Through subterfuge and luck, they had crippled *Shark*. But no subterfuge was left to them now, and no more luck, either. The ketch was no match for even *Shark*, in a standup fight. And certainly not for *Rover*. Not even a moment's work for *Rover* and *Belmont* combined.

He sighted again on the distant ketch, saw it making about to continue its downcoast course, and pursed his lips. "Tiller, quarter a'port," he said. "Trim to course to intercept." Alva Hazelton would be along directly with the xebec, he knew. They would not long stay out of sight. In the meantime, the ketch was only a ketch. It could sail its plodding course, but it would not get away. It had nowhere to go and nowhere to hide. In an hour it would all be over.

Bartlett tilted his head to squint aloft. "Lookout, have you found *Belmont* yet?"

"No, sir, not . . . wait. Yes, sir, I make a sail just coming up east-northeast. Twelve miles if it's *Belmont*, sir."

It might not even take an hour, he thought. Certainly not more.

"Run in on that ketch yonder, tiller. We'll see if we can't play him back toward the xebec as it comes."

"Aye, sir."

"'Hoy the deck!"

"Report, lookout."

"It's two sails, sir. Commander Hazelton in pursuit of another craft, bringing it this way. I make that a brig, sir."

"Colors, lookout?"

"Same as the ketch flies, sir. The stripes."

Bartlett revised his plan, but only a little. Hazelton had found another rebel . . . or another fugitive. Two, then, for the price of one. "Intercept the ketch, tiller, but belay the rest of that. We shall proceed to attack and destroy when we have the range. Then we can go and help Commander Hazelton deal with his prize."

A brig, eh? The thought pleased him. The ketch would be worth little on any wartime block he could access as a civilian. A brig, though . . .

"'Hoy the deck!"

"Report, lookout!"

"It's not a brig, sir." There was a pause, then, "I believe that's a full snow Commander Hazelton is herding to us."

Bartlett's thin lips tightened in an unaccustomed smile. A snow! He knew people who would give a fancy price for a snow. Half again, at least, what an ordinary brig might bring. More than enough to cover the costs of this venture and take him to England where, he could lay claim to a nice piece of the Fitzgerald leavings.

"Ready those ranging guns a'fore," Bartlett ordered. "We'll turn the ketch into the wind and hole her astern. I shan't waste time with a scow when there is a real ship to be claimed."

Like a wind-heeled nemesis, its teeth bristling and its high cloth singing, *Rover* headed for the kill.

XXV

Now with smokes rising ahead, Dalton bent on all of the sail that *Fury* had rig to carry and the trim warship breasted rolling seas at better than eighteen knots. Deep keel and high sail in precarious balance, the snow sheeted bright veils of spray as she drove southwestward. Cadman Wise as bosun and Purdy Fisk at the helm were wide-eyed and intent, Fisk sweating in the cool wind as white-knuckled hands held a fine trim. It was a test of the American snow that it could amass more sail than any ship of its size, and run beyond its own hull speed. It was a test of a helmsman in such a run to hold full and by with never a waver. More than one swift ship had capsized at such speeds and gone down with all hands.

By the turning of a glass, the xebec lay a mile astern, still pursuing but without the speed to catch a snow under critical sail.

Dalton climbed high on the starboard shrouds and clung there, glass in hand, peering ahead. Just a few miles away now, on climbing seas, *Mystery*, with its emblazoned topsail, made downshore, while a crippled cutter drifted helpless in her wake. But from the east and closing, another, larger cutter bore in on the ketch, and Dalton knew he could not be there in time to intercept.

Their colors said the cutters were companions of the ranging xebec. Someone had laid a trap, then, and *Mystery* had plodded into it. Somehow Duncan had broken the wing of the first attacker, but there would be little chance against the second. He reckoned courses and saw a strategy there, the cutter's course telling him what its master had in mind. The man was aiming ahead of *Mystery*, to cross afore and swing about. He would have his guns trained at approach, and would waste no time in dealing with the ketch. He would force Duncan to come about, into the wind. Then he would take his choice of shots, and it would all be over.

I could have been there, Dalton cursed himself. Mister Duncan counted on me to give him safe escort. But I dawdled. While the trap was closing about him, I was off on my own courses, looking at the open sea to England.

"Inattention to duty," he muttered. "Laxity aboard ship."

"Sir?" Claude Mallory's face peered at him from a few feet above, where the tar crouched at the masthead.

"Nothing, Mister Mallory. I was reprimanding myself."

"About that yonder, sir? Seems to me like Mister Duncan is givin' a fair accountin' of himself. One down, one to go, I make it."

"It's that 'one to go' that's the problem, Mister Mallory. A cargo ketch is not made for doing battle with warships. Not even cutters."

"I wonder if that busted cutter yonder knows that, sir."

Dalton turned to look back. The xebec was still there, a mile back now but following implacably—a formidable opponent for a time outdistanced, but confident of a chance at battle soon. The ranges were wrong. The cutter was too near *Mystery* for the

326

snow to help, the xebec too close to the snow not to intercept if the cutter dealt with *Mystery*, then swept in to head him off—as it would. Looking again a'fore he saw the inevitable begin to happen. The cutter swept in ahead of the ketch, and its ranging guns blossomed their smokes. Return fire from *Mystery*, but at extreme range. Then as the cutter banked to bring her snout to bear, the ketch began to turn away. Dalton looked down at his racing deck. A fine, beautiful snow, equipped to do battle—but without enough men aboard to handle both sail and guns in a slash-and-dance fight against two armed vessels. Against the xebec they would have a chance . . . but only until the cutter came.

Moisture gathered in his eyes as he looked a last time at the turning ketch, too far away to be helped. "God help you, Mister Duncan," he muttered. "God help you all, for I no longer can."

Ignoring the astonished gaze of Claude Mallory, Dalton put away his glass and lowered himself down the shrouds and ratlines. On deck he paused for a moment to feel the keening song of the fine ship beneath his boots—a ship running free with the wind, doing what its designers had meant to do. Then he beckoned the bosun. "Hands to the fifes, Mister Wise. Take in the studs'ls, stand by the sheets. All hands stand by to come about and trim, all hands then to battle station."

At the quarterrail Don Geraldo Lostrato met him, hand on his sword. "It is a shame, *Capitan*. In a moment you will have lost your ketch, and I will have lost my ransom prizes. Had you done as I asked, I might have been of service to you now. But you would not trust me. Now I must act for myself. Please either hand me your sword, or draw it and die."

Dalton noticed then, just beyond the Spaniard, a pair of boots in the shadow of the quarterdeck— boots of a Hessian field soldier, toes up, still in the shadows. He turned expressionless eyes back to the Spaniard. "How did you get behind him, Don Heraldo? I know you were behind him, because facing a man is not your style."

Lostrato's dark eyes blazed, and his sword whipped from his buckler. "Draw your blade, Irishman. I will show you what a swordsman of the school of Las Palmas de Toledo can do."

Dalton drew his sword, touched its point to the deck. "You've chosen a poor time to show your true colors, Don Heraldo. And a worse time to test your swordsmanship. I have no time for you now."

"You have no time at all, *Capitan*." The Spaniard crouched, spread-legged in classical position, and raised his blade.

Dalton heard the luffing of high sails, the intake of breaths as men at the fiferail realized what was happening, and he turned a bit to call, "You men! Tend your stations!" The blade that darted forward in that instant was a quick, searing pain below his left shoulder. In his moment's inattention, Lostrato had thrust, withdrawn, and lunged to thrust again. But his second thrust met the steel of Dalton's blade and slid harmlessly aside. Before he could recover, the Irishman's boot caught him in midsection and threw him back against the rail.

Dalton did not press in, but simply gazed at the man with contempt. "I knew you were of the Toledo schools, Don Heraldo. Your stance has told me. A pity you were there, and not learning the art in Dublin." He raised his blade casually. "I told you, I have no time for you now."

With a hiss of rage, Lostrato crouched and edged in, a ringing succession of thrusts and parries, the snake-tongue dance of foil and rapier seeking an opening. But he found none. The Irishman's curved sword seemed to be everywhere, blocking him effortlessly at each thrust. He tightened his arcs and

328

bored in, the needle point of his rapier a glinting six-inch pattern of dazzling steel. He sensed his opening and thrust, and suddenly his sword was a fury against his hand, lashing to the side, twisting, swinging against his wrist . . .

Dalton completed the disarm with a flourish that jerked the Spaniard's blade from him and sent it arcing out to sea. Then, while Lostrato still stood watching where it had gone, Dalton put away his own sword, stepped to the Spaniard, and hit him full in the face with a rocklike fist. Lostrato flipped backward, skidding into the quarterdeck shadow to thump against the body of the Hessian there.

Dalton crouched, looking into the shadows. Klaus Doste would not farm in America. His heart had been pierced by a single sword-thrust, from behind. Lostrato groaned and rolled over, half conscious. Dalton stepped to the mainmast fife, aware of anxious faces watching him. He released a signal hoist from its pin, lowered its tackle, and carried it to where the Spaniard lay, moaning and beginning to stir. With quick, sure movements, Dalton secured a line to the man's ankles, attached it to the signal block, then retrieved the hoist line and began hauling it in. The Spaniard was dragged from the quarter hatch, along the deck, then upward, suspended by his ankles. When he was turning and dangling twenty feet above the deck, Dalton secured the line, then turned to his bosun. "When time allows, Mister Wise, you may turn the *Conte* over to Corporal Wesselmann and his lads with my compliments. I am sure they will know what to do with him. Now, hands a'deck, let's come about to port, please. Smartly, then gun stations."

"Aye, sir."

At the helm, Purdy Fisk gawked at him. "What did the man think he could accomplish, Captain? I mean, had he killed you?"

"I think he expected to take command of this vessel, Mister Fisk."

"But, sir . . . how? I mean, nobody here'd take orders from him, even if he is a mariner."

"He's dealt too long with pirates, Mister Fisk. He doesn't know the makings of honorable men." He watched the sheets playing, the sails reorienting. "Ease a'port, helm. There . . . she's trim. Hard over now, to come quarter about. The xebec wants a game. We'll play his game now, by our terms."

"Aye, sir. Ah, sir . . . the *Mystery*?"

Dalton took a deep breath and squared his shoulders, looking back at the pursuing xebec. "*Mystery* is in Mister Duncan's hands . . . and God's. Both have proven their resourcefulness from time to time."

First fire from the cutter told Charley Duncan the worst of it. Whatever was at its rails, the big cutter had a pair of long twelves at its nose, and it knew how to use them. The first volley, beyond range of anything *Mystery* could bring to bear, sheeted water at her bow and tore an escutcheon from its mount. The man out there was giving him little choice— stand and be battered to pieces from a distance of six cables, or turn and try to run. He wants us to turn, Duncan thought. We'll come aback and he can bore in from astern and deal with us quickly. He knows we can't outrun him, but he wants us to try.

At Duncan's signal, Floyd Pugh returned fire from the bow guns, elevating high. Gouts of water appeared, one short of the cutter, the other off to one side. "Too far," Pugh shook his head. "If he closes to bring us under his waist guns, though, I can score him at bit then."

But the cutter did not close. Instead, it made about on the wind, circled to stand off at six cables again, and once more the big ranging guns spoke. A ball came under the spreader stays, collapsed a yard of decking amidships, and sheered a stanchion out of the portside stern rail. Its companion gouged the starboard hull wales.

"He's making us turn," Michael Romart noted. "He's trying to drive us about."

"I know," Duncan said. "He is in a hurry. He wants to finish us off and not waste time." Abruptly he understood. "If I were him, that's what I would want. With those twelves . . . all he needs is our tail for a target. He can break down our sternpost, take out our rudder, leave us dead in the water, then pick us off as he pleases. That's what he's after. He wants to tuck us safely away, then go after *Fury*."

"Then what can we . . . ?"

"Go and fetch Misters Pugh and Tower, please, Mister Romart."

Romart's eyes widened. Just in that moment, the sandy-haired tar had sounded just like Patrick Dalton. "Aye, sir," he said.

When the carpenter and the gunner came aft, Duncan was pacing the deck, watching the cutter out ahead making another circle. "Mister Tower, when Captain Dalton had you make mounts for that battery gun on our deck, what did you do?"

"Made mounts, sir. Like he said."

"But how are they secured below?"

"Well, the muzzle is lashed and pinned, but mainly there is a timber down through the deck—through the starboard cabin and the galley—that abuts the keelson at the mast footing. That was as much as I could do to really brace a thing that size."

"And would it hold . . . if we were to fire this gun?"

Tower shook his head. "Lord only knows. The timber itself would hold, I guess. The problem is, sir, there isn't a ship built that's designed to take the recoil of a shore battery piece. Not even a ship of the line, and this ketch surely isn't!"

"What would happen?"

"Either the gun would break its lashings and flip itself over and sink us, or the timber would hold it and drive the keelson out from under our mast and sink us."

"Not very pleasant either way."

"No, sir."

Duncan stepped to the top of the hooded great cannon and looked forward along his deck . . . an eighty-foot corridor of planking, bounded by masts on one side, rails and shrouds on the other, rising away past the forehold to a sweep of bow with spreader stays climbing away beyond.

"Remove the restraining timber, please, Mister Tower."

"Sir?"

"I said, remove the . . ."

"Sir, Captain Dalton had me put it there."

"And Commander Duncan will have you take it out. Do it now, please, Mister Tower. Immediately."

"Aye, sir."

"Mister Pugh, can you load this forty-eight-pounder?"

"It's already loaded, sir. Mister Crosby and me, we did that a long time back when we thought that was what the captain wanted."

"It is ready to be fired?"

"A bit of fresh prime in the vent and this beast will bellow like the very fires of hell . . . sir."

"Prepare it for firing, Mister Pugh." All around Duncan, faces were going pale.

"Aye, sir."

Out ahead, the cutter was completing its turn. Soon another pair of balls would come their way.

"Mister Tidy, prepare to come about."

"Aye, sir."

"That's just what that man wants us to do," Romart reminded him.

"Aye. He wants a stern shot. I think I shall show him one."

Hands at sheets, they prepared to turn into the wind, the sound of Joseph Tower's sledge below the deck beating like a death knell. Then the beating stopped and Tower emerged. "It's out, sir. Nothing holding that beast now but its muzzle lashing."

"Thank you, Mister Tower. Hands to sheets, Mister Tidy, and bring us full about."

Slowly, stubbornly, *Mystery*'s bowsprit swung to the left, sails coming over as Ishmael Bean and a pair of painted Indians wrestled with the wheel of the helm. The cutter in the distance had taken station again, but it held its fire. Things were going as it wanted.

Mystery came about and stood aback, her nose to the longshore wind. Far out at sea, off her starboard bow, smokes arose where other ships did battle, and Duncan gazed at them. It was *Fury*, he knew. *Fury* and another foe. For a moment he thought of the proud, beautiful snow as he had first seen it, and his eyes misted a bit. There was every chance now that he would not see it again . . . not see Patrick Dalton again or any of the other brave lads who had come so far together and shared so much—a very good chance that not he nor anyone else aboard the ketch *Mystery* would ever seen anyone again. Eugenie, he thought . . . Eugenie, how I wish I'd had the time to come to know you.

"Mister Tidy!" He shook himself like a tormented hound, fighting off the fancies. "Mister Tidy, clear tops! Clear the deck! All hands below! Help him, Mister Romart. Mister Pugh will remain here with me. I want everyone else below, in the cabin where Mister Wilton and the ladies are. Everyone, Mister Romart."

"Aye, s . . . aye, Commander Duncan, sir."

"No' me!" an Indian barked. "No blee'in way!"

"Stow 'em," the other agreed. "I'll 'ave no blinkin' 'ole, swagger!"

"Very well," Duncan shrugged. "Leave the Indians, Mister Romart. Their necklaces would probably offend the ladies, anyway. But all the rest, below! Now!"

"Aye, sir."

"You pair!" Duncan told the savages. "Pu' yer blee'in arses jus' 'ere an' don't move!"

"Haye, swagger, sor!"

With the Indians crouched a'port the helmbox, Duncan stood at his helm, looking out over the stern rail. The cutter was moving, tacking short, coming in for its kill. "Come right on in, ye bugger," Duncan breathed. "Come and have a good, close look at what you're fixing to shoot." To Pugh, crouched in front of the helm housing out of sight of the cutter and a long arm's reach from the vent of the great battery gun, he said, "Steady, Mister Pugh, and stay out of sight. I'll tell you when."

Seemingly alone now, Charley Duncan stood at his helm and watched the approaching cutter. He took off his hat and held it at his side, seeing the snouts of guns at the kill-ship's stem, the faces of men behind them, ready to pour iron into the unmoving stern of the ketch. Three cables . . . two . . . then the cutter lay dead astern, bringing its nose around into firing position. Duncan put on his hat.

"Now, Mister Pugh," he said quietly, then turned and dived for cover behind the helmbox.

The roar of the forty-eight-pounder was like the thunders of a hundred storms, its flash was hellfire studded with lightnings, and the cloud of white smoke that grew before it was a stupendous blossom erupting upon the sea. And all hell broke loose aboard *Mystery*. Lashings sang and parted, the deck lurched as though rammed from a'port, shrouds aloft shrieked, and tackle rattled. Rending crashes sounded fore and aft, the din of timbers parting, stays cracking, planks being rent and sundered. In the rolling echoes of the discharge, the sounds seemed to go on and on, blind raging sounds hidden by thick, sulfurous smoke rolling back. Somewhere forward was another crash, and the howl of snapped rigging. Aft, like an echo, a chorus of wails and thuddings, and somewhere a prodigious splash. *Mystery* rolled this way and that, bucking like a tormented steed, and everywhere was smoke and noise and confusion. Then, as abruptly, it died away to ominous gurglings, creaks, and the rumbling of loosed joints deep in the keel.

Duncan lay stunned, feeling a weight upon him; then the weight shifted and he recognized the voice of it. "Lord, have mercy . . . ." It was Floyd Pugh. A foot that was not his or Pugh's scuffed his ear, and there was another voice, strident, "Blinkin' bloo'y belcher 'at wa', by gor!"

Duncan raised himself to sore elbows and shook his head, trying to clear the roarings that still drummed in his ears. He blinked, coughed powder smoke, and looked around. The helmbox stood, and the mizzen beyond, and beyond that the mainmast, shrouds and stays shivering like great fiddle strings in the aftershocks. The horizon was where it should be, though tilted a bit, and the sky was where it should be, above it. He got to his knees, then to his feet, staggering as he braced himself on the helmbox. Its far side was black—scorched and smoking. And beyond it was the splintered, smoking wreckage of what had once been a carrying cradle for a battery gun.

He stepped around the helm and peered forward, blinking and shaking his head. At first there seemed to be no deck on the starboard side, then he realized it was still a deck, though disjointed and sundered, planks bowed this way and that, ends sticking up a weird angles, and beyond was a deep, splintered trough that ran forward to where there had once been a bow rail. There was no bow rail now. The depressed, indented deck simply ran out and stopped.

Eight thousand pounds of cannon had traveled the length of the deck, between fifes and gunwales, then had plunged off the bow of the ketch and into the sea. Nearly three kegs of gunpowder had sent a forty-eight-pound ball one way and a four-ton cannon the other. Slowly, almost dreading to look, Dalton turned.

Where once had stood a proud cutter, homing to the kill, now flotsam spread across the water around a towering jib and a bowsprit that pointed nearly straight up . . . a broken stem with no bow under it, just a gaping hole in a confusion of shattered timbers. And as he stared at it, it slid slowly downward, into the waiting sea.

At his elbow, Pitacoke, half his face daubed with war paint, the other half black with soot, said, "Ga' 'at'n blee'in 'ell, wot?"

"Mister Pugh," Duncan coughed and started again, "Mister Pugh, please have Mister Tidy bring all hands to deck . . ." he glanced aloft, where the ketch's colors—the red-and-white striped banner— stood just overhead, rippling from its halyard. "And let's get those colors off that stick and run 'em to the masthead, by God! This damned scow is a fighting ship. At least what's left of it is."

The xebec had not expected *Fury* to turn, and had closed to less than half a mile before reacting. But when it did, the reaction was simple and direct. As though he knew the snow carried only a partial crew—and thus was hampered in the handling of sail and gun both at once—the xebec's commander veered a bit to port, circled on the wind to a crosswind vantage, then drove at *Fury* from abeam and opened fire with his bow chasers. So quick were the little three-master's movements, so dainty-seeming under her press of soaring lugsails and reefed squares, that she seemed almost to skate across the swelling sea.

. Dalton saw the maneuver and knew its intent. The commander over there was a canny fighting man, using all the range and angle he could achieve. He would close and fire again for effect, then come suddenly to a new course—more suddenly with the xebec than the snow could follow. He had guns, and a lot of men to use them, and he intended to get in as many shots as he could to each that came his way. He probably would veer upwind when he turned, to seek the weather gauge for another pass . . . or would he? The two ships had exchanged fire earlier, and each commander would have the measure of the other. Dalton knew the man across there was an able fighter, and so would he know now of Dalton. And so he would expect . . . "He'll come downwind," he decided. "Catch us off our guard and try for a broadside on a fast pass."

In the fore, Ethan Crosby and someone else had fired, almost simultaneously, and the xebec answered with a second round from its paired chasers. "Now he'll deceive me if he can," Dalton muttered. He called, "Mister Wise, reverse our trim, please! Come to starboard, smartly! Mister Fisk, hold your rudder amidships . . . hold . . . now put her over to starboard. Come to beam reach." He cupped his hands. "All guns a'port, fire as she bears."

As surely as though guided by his own decision, the xebec had heeled sharply downwind, expecting a vulnerable beam for its target. Instead it found a jutting bow closing on its course, gathering speed, on course to ram. Again the tall lugsails—like great lateen traingles with only the lower corner snipped away—turned and it continued its arc, trying to recover, trying to get away from the approaching broadside of the snow. But it was too late. Dalton had gambled and won the pass. Along *Fury*'s port gunwales thunders rolled, and their iron lightnings struck again and again at the tall, sweeping stern of the graceful foe. Then they were past, and Dalton had *Fury* brought over to port, a wider arc outside the xebec's short turn, giving his gunners time to reload and fire again. Smokes blossomed on the xebec, and Dalton knew that *Fury* was being hit again and again, being battered even as she pressed the attack. A gunwale exploded beyond the foremast, and a spray of bright blood washed the deck. Then *Fury*'s guns were speaking again, and the xebec's stern quarter shuddered with impacts. At forty degrees to the wind the xebec came sharply aback, wearing across the wind while its sails were hauled around, and Dalton broke off the chase to turn again southwestward. He would distance himself, then stand around and wait. The xebec would have to come to him again as it had before, and now he had its measure.

A pity, he thought, watching the swift, beautiful little enemy behind him now, wearing over to find the wind. A pity that such jaunty vessels should be pitted one against the other. A pity that the lithe power of a snow and the swift grace of a xebec must be tested by destroying each other. He remembered a thing Old Hawser had said, back in the training days: "A man's a fool who has a love of ships, young sir. A ship of war is a floating gunstage, nothing more. Its purpose is to kill and be killed. If you must have a love of something, let it be of music or of magic or the colors of evening sky. Or of a woman. A woman might break your heart, but there's always a chance she won't. A warship will.''

I wasn't dry behind the ears, Dalton thought, and he knew me for the fool I'd be, even then.

The xebec had its wind now, and had come about, and Dalton eyed the windvane, deciding which way best to turn to put a finish to this business. Odd, though . . . the xebec faltered, seemed to tarry.

"On deck!"

"Aye, Mister Mallory?"

"Look ahead, Captain! Look at the colors flying there!"

Dalton raised his glass. The smokes southwest had blown away, and one vessel stood there alone. A ketch, and at its mainmast flew the red-and-white stripes.

He looked back at the xebec. It stood a'quarter, not attacking now, and he knew the man there had seen what he had seen. He raised his glass. On the high stern of the little three-master, just where its sterncastle peaked, a man stood alone, using a glass to look back at him. The man lowered his glass, stood for a moment, then raised his arm in salute. And the xebec set its sails a'beam, turned its nose to sea, and dwindled in distance as he watched.

Maybe I'm not the only fool who'd feel the pains of a pretty ship, Dalton thought. Then he turned his attention to the somber task of inventory—of damage and of crew.

He glanced upward, then glanced again, remembering. "Mister Wise, where is our Spaniard?"

The bosun looked around at him. "You said to give him to the Hessians when we had the time, sir. We had time when the lads were reloading, so I did."

"Well, where is he? What did they do with him?"

"Nothing much, sir. You'd left him adangle from the signal yard, so they just hove him outboard and cut the line. I guess they didn't have any use for him, sir."

The brothers Fanshaw had manned a cannon in the fore. Now they lay side by side next to the wrecked gunwale there, and others came to carry the body of Klaus Doste forward to join them.

XXVI

On a bright morning when the onshore breeze blew lively and touched the tops of wavecaps with white froth, two mismatched vessels rounded off Isle of Palms and stood off Sullivan's Point, while the larger of the two raised signals to people ashore.

A snow by design, trim and lithe, the guns at her ports were her authority, and the fothering on her hull and patching on her sails were her credentials. Just off the fairway she dropped her anchor and ran up pennants, and the signal was prearranged.

The craft that stood below her was a battered, tilting ketch with a strange, emblazoned mizzen topsail, its seams and grommets worked out in bright feathers. On Sullivan's Point and across the harbor entrance on James Morris Island people came out to look. Here and there boats put out, but they stood off and turned away when no invitations went up on either craft. The snow in particular had a grim and unfriendly look to it, and none cared to try its patience. Here and there other vessels stood at anchor or came and went, but no contacts were made. The snow had raised its signals, and when someone came who recognized them, it would be his business to respond.

Charleston Harbor was a busy port, but since the

battle of Sullivan's Point a year before, when troops of the king had been put to rout, the rules of the place were simple: each man went his own way, each vessel conducted its business and no colors were flown within sight of John's Point—no king's colors, no privateer flags, no Whig or Tory banners. How long Charleston could enforce such sensible politics was a question, but as long as it worked, the place could provide trade and profit for all who obeyed the rules.

Some said the British plan, to fortify Sumter at the harbor's mouth, was being pursued privately by business interests who were amassing great guns for that very purpose, and that such might prolong the calm of Charleston. Most agreed that the Admiralty would return in its good time, and that Charleston could not long evade a state of war. But as long as it lasted, this tiny motte of peace among troubled colonies was an oasis for many. Trade, for the moment, held sway.

Noontime had come and gone when the snow's signals were answered ashore, and sometime after that two boats put out—one from Sullivan's Point, bearing on the anchored vessels, another from the ketch, a sailing launch with punt guns bow and stern, making for the inner harbor and the Charleston ways.

Each boat carried passengers. In the outbound lighter sat a group of colonial businessmen and a young woman accompanied by a maidservant. The inbound armed launch was more densely populated, its company including a stocky, distinguished-looking gentleman with a tricorn hat and eyeglasses, a pair of brightly decorated young Indians, a sandy-haired young sailor with the queue of a British tar, four stern-looking young men in motley clothing, and a pair of pretty young women.

The two boats passed within fifty yards in the channel's mouth, and their passengers stared at one another. Aboard the lighter, one of the businessmen pointed. "By the almighty, Henry, there is Dr. Franklin."

"It can't be Dr. Franklin," another said. "They say he has gone to France."

"Well, then, they are mistaken," the first asserted. "I have met Dr. Franklin, and that gentleman is him, no mistaking it."

The young woman sitting behind them was not looking at Dr. Franklin, though. Dark eyes in a pixie face haloed by auburn hair were fixed on the two girls in the launch, and a dainty brow lofted just a touch in thought.

On the launch, Charley Duncan was barely aware of another boat at first. He was little aware of anything except the proximity of Eugenie Toussaint and the quick smiles she returned in answer to his own. Inwardly he was sealing a pledge to himself, to learn French at the earliest opportunity. Then he glanced aside and noticed the other boat. His eyes widened, his mouth dropped open and he rose to his feet, removing his hat. "Miss Constance?" he murmured. "Is that . . . but how could that be? . . . here? . . . Miss Constance?"

The two French girls followed his gaze. Lucette leaned close to Eugenie to whisper, *"Qui est cette jeune fille?"*

Titus Wilton peered over his glasses, then said to Duncan, "The young ladies wish to know who that young lady is. As a matter of fact, so do I."

"That is Miss Constance Ramsey, sir. She's Squire Ramsey's daughter. Though for the life of me, I can't understand why she is here."

Eugenie heard the translation, then turned large eyes on Duncan. *"Est-ce qu' elle vous est important, monsieur?"*

Duncan sat down again, nearly melting at the luster of her gaze. "What?"

343

"She wants to know whether that young lady . . . Miss Ramsey . . . is important to you."

"Finest hand with a small cannon that ever I met," Duncan said. "I've seen her take the mast right off a gunboat with a four-pounder . . . though what her pa is thinkin' to let her go off on such adventures is beyond me. But no, I don't expect Miss Constance is my problem. Most likely she's Captain Dalton's problem. Lord knows she's somebody's."

Pitacoke's befeathered face was split by a leering grin. "A loo'er, wot?"

"So's 'ese 'ere," Squahamac growled at him. "Kee' y' min' on't, swagger. Y' wan' a squaw, go home."

Wilton glanced around at the savages. "What?"

"They said . . ."

"*Indianern,*" Wolfgang Mitter opined. "*Indianern und Englandern. Sie sind sich sehr ahnlich, mit das frauleinen.*"

Duncan turned. "What?"

"*Monsieur le commandeur vous adore, Eugenie,*" Lucette giggled.

Titus Wilton turned away to stare fixedly at the approaching quay. "Lord help us," he muttered. "It's the bubbling boat of Babel."

They tied the launch at a fishing dock and paid a boy there to guard it, though with the armed snow sitting just offshore in plain sight, it was unlikely that anyone would bother it there. The two Indians went bounding away to look at ships and things, and Duncan helped the girls from the boat. "We'll ask around a bit," he told Wilton. "We'll find a proper quarter for these ladies."

"It's best I attend to the young ladies," Wilton said. "Were you to set foot in proper quarters hereabouts, there'd be trouble. You look like a British tar."

"I *am* a British tar," Duncan bristled. "And I can jolly well . . ."

"Far better," Wilton insisted, "that you take these

344

four German gentlemen and set them on their way inland before anyone suspicions who they might be."

"I . . ."

"Lead them by the back ways. There's a west road beyond the town. You can put them on a wagon there, give them their coin, and they'll be all right. There are German folk in the hills who'll guide them from there."

"But, I . . ."

"Mister Duncan, are you prepared to take on the responsibility for these young women?"

Duncan hesitated, the enormity of it striking him. These were ladies of peerage . . . of French nobility. He was only a sailor, and a fugitive at that. "What will you do with them, then?"

"Their home is in France, young man. I believe I can arrange safe passage for them. At least that is what I shall try to do."

"But then . . ."

"This is a very small world, Mister Duncan. The young lady knows your feelings for her, and I shouldn't be at all surprised if you should find a way to express those feelings properly . . . at the proper place and time. Captain Dalton says you are a resourceful man."

Duncan conceded with a sigh, knowing the sailmaker was right. With an aching heart and tight dignity, then, he bowed to them, took Eugenie's hand in his, and kissed it. "There will come a time," he said. "I swear there will. Please tell her what I said, Mister Wilton."

Duncan watched them away, then, and turned finally to the waiting Hessians. "Achtung, you rutters. Follow me and keep your bloody mouths shut."

*   *   *

Wilton left the French girls at a seamstress's shop, to be properly gowned while he himself sought out a tailor, then a barber, a clothier, and a cobbler. After that he returned to the tailor's shop. Adequately groomed then, he exectued drafts against the credit of John Singleton Ramsey, then returned for his waifs and found two splendid young ladies waiting there. With one on each elbow and strutting a bit in his bandy-legged fashion, he escorted them to the Lion's Head, Charleston's finest, and sent a messenger to the Honorable Clayborn Long, Executor of Affairs for the Great Atlantic Merchant Company. Not once did he state his name, leaving the messenger to make his own deductions.

Within the hour, the honorable Long was deposited by coach at the Lion's Head, and his greeting was effusive. "Ah, Doctor! What a great and unexpected pleasure, that you should visit our city."

Wilton gazed over his glasses at the man. "My name is Wilton, sir. Titus Wilton."

Long cocked a knowing brow. "Ah, of course, sir. Troubled times, yes. Ah . . . Mister Wilton, is it, then? Yes. Mister Wilton. How may I be of service to you, sir? You have only to ask."

"It is these young ladies, Squire Long. I wish to see them safely to their home in France. To Versailles. But of course, you will understand, it is difficult for me to attend to that personally. You do understand that, don't you?"

"Of course I do." Long winked and nodded. "Since you are already in France, sir . . . even at this moment, as I understand . . . ah, yes. I do understand the problem."

"I knew you would. And you understand that this must be attended to with every attention to the comfort and safety of the young ladies . . . and with great discretion, as well."

"Of course, sir. Think no more about it. They shall

346

be treated as though they were my own daughters. And as to the discretion, sir, you will find I am the very soul of . . ."

"I know that," Wilton said. "It's why I wanted to deal with you personally."

"With our contacts in France, sir, I believe I can have these young ladies delivered to you personally there, if you would like . . . since you already are there and doubtless awaiting them anxiously."

Wilton hesitated, then smiled, his eyes twinkling behind his glasses. "The very thing. Have them escorted safely to me, to me personally. And be so good as to have their guardian at Versailles—an uncle whose name I will give you—meet them . . . and me, of course . . . there. Thank you, Squire Long. I knew I could count on you."

"Any time at all, Doctor . . . ah, Mister Wilton. And about the expenses, sir? How should I handle that?"

"Address your voucher to the Continental Congress, Squire Long. I haven't known them to be tardy in repaying my expenses."

"An honor, ah . . . Mister Wilton."

"Indeed it is, sir. Indeed it is."

The hour was late when Charley Duncan returned to the fish dock, to find a coach with footman and escort there, and Titus Wilton awaiting him.

"You seem to have disposed of your Germans," the sailmaker said.

"They'll be all right. I found a family to take care of them. Wolfgang Dressler. Wife and about a dozen daughters. They all speak German. I thought those Hessians were going to break their faces, grinning like that. They wanted to farm . . . well, I expect they will have plenty of opportunity. Ah . . . Eugenie and Lucette?"

"They couldn't be in better hands, young man. They will be home in France by the end of the season, and making the acquaintance of some very distinguished people." He handed a folded paper to Duncan. "Names and addresses. All here. Now if I were a young man—a very resourceful young man—I think I might find a way one day to smuggle myself into France and . . ."

"Aye, sir. Thank you." He looked at the waiting coach, wondering why it was there. "By the way, have you seen my Indians?"

"As a matter of fact, I have. They went aboard the merchantman *Cooksey's Pride* a few hours ago. I expect by now they've signed on for the Indies."

"Oh. Well, then I suppose we'd best be getting back."

"I won't be going either, Mister Duncan." He indicated the coach. "I'm too old for any more of that sort of thing. I have other arrangements to get home."

"Oh. Well, then I guess it's just me. Good journey to you, sir. Ah, sir?"

"Yes?"

"Why do these Colonials keep calling you Dr. Franklin?"

"I haven't the slightest idea," Wilton said.

"The gentlemen didn't seem too taken aback," Constance Ramsey noted, wrapping a quilt around her shoulders against the evening chill. Across the harbor a crimson sky haloed the town of Charleston.

Dalton stood stiffly at the starboard rail, looking out across the darkling waters. He didn't turn, nor, for a moment, did he respond. When he did, his voice was as distant as the faraway places his gaze seemed to seek. "Why would they have been taken aback? I expect they were delighted."

"Oh, I mean receiving only four battery guns when they had expected five. I'm sure battery guns are not easily found these days. But I think they were satisfied."

"I'm sure they were . . . when you gave them the ketch to make up the difference."

"It was the best thing I knew to do. Otherwise my father would have lost a great deal of his investment, you know."

"The ketch was not yours to give, Miss Ramsey."

"Oh, poo! It was so. My father outfitted the blasted thing for you, didn't he? On the understanding that you would deliver five battery guns for him. So, acting as my father's agent, it seems to me that I squared things rather nicely."

"The ketch was mine. My men found it. We repaired it. And your father, blast his black heart, never once indicated to me that the cargo I was to carry would bring half the Tories in the Carolinas down on us."

She placed determined hands on her hips, the quilt falling loose at her shoulders. "Patrick Dalton, you are a thoroughly irritating man! Here I journey all the way to Charleston, just because of my concern for you, and not a word of thanks have I heard. Not one!"

"You gave away my ketch!"

"Poo. You have another ship now. This one. And it doesn't take a sailor to know that *Fury* is a far better ship than *Mystery* ever was. I have heard Mister McCall talk about this snow, you know . . ."

"Who?"

"Ian McCall. It *is* his snow, after all."

"It is not his. It is mine. I took it from Spanish pirates."

"Of course you did. But only after they stole it from him."

"They may have stolen Mister McCall's snow. What I took was a renegade Spanish pirate vessel, and this is it. It's mine, Miss Ramsey. Not your father's, not Mister McCall's, not the king's himself! It is mine, and I intend to use it."

"To do what?"

"I don't know." He turned then, his shoulders sagging, to lean against the rail. "I've had thoughts of returning to England to face the charges against me there. It's the only way I can ever clear my name . . . what *are* you doing here, anyway?"

"I told you. I came because I was concerned about you. I noticed some time back that you have very little head for business. It's a good thing I came, too, you must admit. Those gentlemen *did* expect a full five count of cannon."

"They're lucky to have any at all. Do you know what we went through, just getting here? It's a lord's wonder . . ."

"Those were charming young ladies you had aboard, Patrick."

"We rescued them. They were prisoners."

"Mister Romart told me all about the pavilion on the deck, and . . ."

"That was on the ketch, not on the snow! That was Mister Duncan's doing, not mine. And as for Mister Romart . . ."

"Don't pluck at straws, Patrick. It really isn't necessary. I understand."

He shook his head, looking away. In the distance he saw Charley Duncan approaching, alone and dejected-seeming aboard *Something*. "My launch is returning, Miss Constance. And it's getting dark. I'll see you safely ashore . . ."

"You'll do no such thing. I am not going ashore."

"But I plan to set sail with the tide."

"Then by all means, do so. Only I don't intend to go ashore."

"Miss Ramsey . . ."

"Set sail for where? England? Patrick, don't be

350

foolish. There is a war going on, you know."

"Miss Constance, will you . . ."

"Besides, while you were wangling with those Charleston gentlemen, I had Dora bring my belongings aboard. Mister Caster helped us stow everything in the portside cabin. I'm sure I shall be very comfortable there. It is, after all, much more commodious than a schooner."

"Constance . . ."

"And anyway, there are other things to do first. If you plan to keep poor Mister McCall's ship, the least you might do is to serve escort on his flotilla from Savannah. And most of the merchandise he is shipping belongs to my father . . ."

"Constance!"

"Yes?"

"Will you please shut up? If you're going to sail on my ship, I shall insist upon certain protocols. To begin with, I specifically will not abide laxity on board my . . ."

"Patrick?"

"What?"

"When you finish your tirade, there is a cozy stove below. And a bit of rum for toddies, as well. There will be plenty of time to discuss protocols. It is, I understand, some distance from here to Savannah."

BLOCKBUSTER FICTION FROM PINNACLE BOOKS!

THE FINAL VOYAGE OF THE S.S.N. SKATE   (17-157, $3.95)
by Stephen Cassell
The "leper" of the U.S. Pacific Fleet, SSN 578 nuclear attack sub
SKATE, has one final mission to perform—an impossible act of
piracy that will pit the underwater deathtrap and its inexperienced
crew against the combined might of the Soviet Navy's finest!

QUEENS GATE RECKONING   (17-164, $3.95)
by Lewis Purdue
Only a wounded CIA operative and a defecting Soviet ballerina
stand in the way of a vast consortium of treason that speeds toward the hour of mankind's ultimate reckoning! From the best-
selling author of THE LINZ TESTAMENT.

FAREWELL TO RUSSIA   (17-165, $4.50)
by Richard Hugo
A KGB agent must race against time to infiltrate the confines of
U.S. nuclear technology after a terrifying accident threatens to
unleash unmitigated devastation!

THE NICODEMUS CODE   (17-133, $3.95)
by Graham N. Smith and Donna Smith
A two-thousand-year-old parchment has been unearthed, un-
leashing a terrifying conspiracy unlike any the world has previously known, one that threatens the life of the Pope himself, and
the ultimate destruction of Christianity!

*Available wherever paperbacks are sold, or order direct from the
Publisher. Send cover price plus 50¢ per copy for mailing and
handling to Pinnacle Books, Dept.17-291, 475 Park Avenue
South, New York, N.Y. 10016. Residents of New York, New Jer-
sey and Pennsylvania must include sales tax. DO NOT SEND
CASH.*